October Suite

This Large Print Book carries the
Seal of Approval of N.A.V.H.

OCTOBER SUITE

Maxine Clair

Thorndike Press • Waterville, Maine

Copyright © 2001 by Maxine Clair

This is a work of fiction. The characters and events in it are inventions of the author and do not depict any real persons or events.

Published in 2002 by arrangement with Random House, Inc.

Thorndike Press Large Print African-American Series.

The tree indicium is a trademark of Thorndike Press.

The text of this Large Print edition is unabridged.
Other aspects of the book may vary from the original edition.

Set in 16 pt. Plantin by Rick Gundberg.

Printed in the United States on permanent paper.

Library of Congress Cataloging-in-Publication Data

Clair, Maxine, 1939–
    October suite : a novel / Maxine Clair.
        p. cm.
    ISBN 0-7862-4094-6 (lg. print : hc : alk. paper)
    1. African American families — Fiction. 2. Parent and child
— Fiction. 3. Young women — Fiction. 4. Sisters — Fiction.
5. Large type books. I. Title.
PS3553.L2225 O29 2002
813′.54—dc21   2001058424

For Lucy
and always for Stephen, Michael, Joey, and
Adrienne

And God gave Solomon wisdom and understanding exceeding much, and largeness of heart, even as the sand that is on the sea shore.

Then came there two women, that were harlots, unto the king, and stood before him.

Then said the king, The one saith, This is my son that liveth, and thy son is the dead: and the other saith, Nay; but thy son is the dead, and my son is the living.

And the king said, Bring me a sword. And they brought a sword before the king.

And the king said, Divide the living child in two, and give half to the one, and half to the other.

Then spake the woman whose the living child was unto the king . . . and she said, O my lord, give her the living child, and in no wise slay it. But the other said, Let it be neither mine nor thine, but divide it.

Then the king answered and said, Give her the living child, and in no wise slay it: she is the mother thereof.

I KINGS: 4:29; 3:16, 23–27

Part One

CHAPTER 1

In the Midwest, October comes in when the pale coverlet of sky lifts away, exposing an eternity of deep and certain blue. The sun no longer stares, merely glances and makes long shadows much like the uneven fading of green from trees just before the lesser pigments fire-light the whole outdoors. The air cools to crisp, carries sound farther. Last pears ripen and fall, ferment on the ground; the aroma of their wine mixes with the pungency of leaf smoke from nowhere and everywhere. At nightfall, the wing-song shrill of crickets announces that this season has a natural pathos to it, the brief and flaming brilliance of everything at the climax of life moving toward death.

October Brown had named herself for all of that. Unwittingly at first. When she began occasionally calling herself October, she was only ten years old. Others said it was ridiculous, said she was nobody trying to be somebody. But she made convincing noises about given names, how you could give one to yourself, how it could be more like you than your real name. She never dared say she hated the name that her father had saddled on her, never said the new name had anything to do with the memory of her mother, who had lost her life. Instead she had mentioned all the strange names of people they knew, like Daybreak Honor, and a classmate's aunt, Fourteen. The pastor of their church had named his daughter Dainty. Usually that fact had made people stop and consider.

Then when she was girl-turned-grown-seventeen, struck by her own strangeness and by the whole idea of seasons, she had put it on like a coat and fastened it around her. October was her name.

Midmorning, on a flaming day in that season — a Saturday — October sat in the upstairs kitchenette at Pemberton House, sewing on her black iron Singer. It was 1950. She was twenty-three, and thanking her lucky stars for a room in the best house for Negro women teachers in Wyandotte County. Situated in the middle of the block on Oceola Avenue, the two-story white clapboard set the standard for decent, with its deep front yard and arborlike pear trees, its clipped hedges and the painted wicker chairs on the porch.

From her window she could look down on the backyard and see Mrs. Pemberton's precious marigolds bunched along the back fence, and in front of them, a few wilting tomato plants and short rows of collards that waited to be tenderized by the first frost in Mr. Pemberton's garden.

A few months before, on the very same June day that Cora had pushed her to take advantage of the vacancy coming up at Pemberton House, October Brown had knocked on the door, hoping. Word was that you had to know somebody. For her cadet-teacher year at Stowe School, she had lived with the Reverend Jackson and his wife. Not so bad, but farther away and further down the scale of nice. Mr. Pemberton, in undershirt and suspenders, had opened the door, but his wife, Lydia Pemberton — gold hoops sparkling, crown of silvery braids — had invited her in.

"We don't take nothin but schoolteachers," Mrs. Pemberton had said. When October explained that indeed, she was a teacher, Mrs. Pemberton had looked her up and down.

"Whereabouts?"

And October had told her about her cadet year at Stowe, her room at the Jacksons' place, mentioned Chillicothe, Ohio, where she had grown up, and — because Mrs. Pemberton had seemed unmoved and uninterested so far — spoken of her two aunts who had raised her and her sister Vergie with good home training.

"Y'all are getting younger every year. You

know any of the other girls here?" Mrs. Pemberton had asked.

October explained that Cora Joycelyn Jones had been her lead teacher at Stowe, that they had become good friends. The mention of an established connection to a recognized good citizen had finally satisfied Mrs. Pemberton.

"Follow me," she said, and led October on a two-story tour of hardwood floors and high ceilings, French Provincial sitting room (smoke blue), damask drapes and lace sheers, mahogany dining table that could comfortably seat twelve, at least, two buffets, china closets, curio cabinets full of whatnots. Upstairs, all the women's rooms — Mrs. Pemberton did tap lightly before she charged in — had highly polished mahogany or oak beds, tables, desks, quilts or chenille bedspreads, no-nails-allowed papered walls. Photographs, though, on desks, and floor lamps and wing chairs, stuffed chairs, venetian blinds and valances. Then she showed her the kitchenette, a larger bedroom with a two-burner and a tiny icebox and "you see the sun goes down right outside that window right there."

And as they went back down the stairs, Mrs. Pemberton told her in no uncertain terms that she and Mr. Pemberton operated a *decent* house, that nobody under their roof smoked or drank, and that no men were allowed upstairs, but that the women could "have company" in the sitting room downstairs. Yes, October understood.

Yes, she was lucky to have her kitchenette.

Since daybreak of that October Saturday, she had been up sewing, fiddling with the buttons on the lightweight wool suit that she planned to wear to the first Du Bois Club meeting that afternoon. She had nearly finished reinforcing the zipper when she felt the loud thump of something entirely too heavy against the back of the house.

She wrapped herself more tightly in her housecoat and went to the window. Without raising the shade higher, she could see a man — muscular, youngish — in the yard below, struggling to shift a ladder closer to her window.

She had seen him before. One morning, weeks earlier, she had been waiting on the porch for her ride to school with Cora, and she had been nervous about the ride. Cora was her friend, had been her mentor. Still, these were October's first days on her own in the classroom, and Cora was sure to ask about the supplies that October had forgotten to order. In the presence of Cora's boyfriend — he was driving them to school that day — she would feel even dumber. Too bad she had already said yes to the ride, or she would have skipped it.

And too, at the dinner table the night before, Albertine Scott — one of the other teachers — had offered to turn October's hair under with a straightening comb, a sure put-down, since it was obvious that October had taken pride in what a little Hair Rep and water could do. Seasoned teachers were like that, though — ready to tap cadets on the shoulder and point out the least little misstep in or out of the classroom. In the name of caution, they could brew terror with stories of cadets who dared dream that they would swim through their first stand-alone year but couldn't even float, and went on to become elevator operators. Seasoned teachers would do that. Except for Cora. October had suffered nothing like that from Cora. Woman-after-my-own-heart. Sisterfriend.

And so, thus preoccupied on the porch that morning as she waited for her ride, October had let her eyes wander in the shadows of the arborly front yard. And saw, suddenly, a man out there, dappled by sunplay through the leaves, a hidden picture in a trees-and-grass puzzle, dark arms in a pale undershirt, bib overalls faded blue, his thumbs hooked into the straps. A man turning to go, a mystery vanishing, just somebody taking a break from his work on the Pembertons' half-finished retaining wall out near the street.

She wondered if he'd been there in the yard all along, watching her. She didn't look directly at him, but observed that he had perched himself on top of a mound of fieldstones and begun eating something that the wind carried as hickory smoke. He had flung his hand as if to say hi, being friendly, she thought, and she flung her hand, too. But then she saw the swarm of gnats and realized her mistake. He was swatting flies.

Later, when she walked with Cora and Ed to Ed's car, Ed had stopped to admire the man's handiwork, but the man's faded-blue back was turned, busy, and he didn't even look up. He had a fresh haircut. Neat around the edges. His undershirt had seen a lot of washings.

This was the same man. Looking down from her window, she saw that at the moment he was focused on the bottom rungs. Impulsively, just as his head tilted up, she stepped back out of sight and pulled her window shade all the way down.

A few minutes went by, and she could hear the ladder scraping the house, approaching her window. Then a knock on the window. She got up from the sewing machine again and let up the shade. Head and shoulders right there on the other side of the glass and screen, there he was. Edges of very white teeth showed in a round face the color of pecans and just as shiny. A face not particularly piqued, either. And so it was a little surprising when he did a quick twirl with a screwdriver and yelled through the glass, "You didn't have to pull down the shade — I don't go around peeping in windows."

Though she understood and felt a little guilty, she palmed the air and hunched her shoulders as if to say, *I don't know what you're talking about.* He did a little up-up motion with his thumb, she hurried to raise the window.

His mouth looked like it wanted to smile. "You don't have to worry, I'm just putting up storm windows," he said. "Can you give me a hand and unhook your screen?"

"Sure," she said, and undid the four metal hook-and-eyes that held in the screen.

He pulled the screen out, tossed it like a saucer to the ground. "Stay right there for a minute, do you mind?"

Back down the ladder he went, then climbed slowly up again, lugging a heavy storm window in one hand. This time he stood higher on the ladder so that they were nearly face to face.

"Mr. Pemberton's got too many windows," he said and chuckled a little, held on to the wood-frame window, looked right at her too long. She didn't know whether to smile or frown. What was he looking at? But anyway there was his easy, fleshy mouth to focus on, maybe.

Automatically her hands went to smooth her hair and at the same time cover the white splash of vitiligo on her cheek. But then her thoughts caught up. This was her room. He really had no business up here, and she didn't have to look like she was dressed for school.

He wore a rag of a shirt with rolled sleeves and no buttons, no collar, so that he might as well have been bare from the waist up. Repositioning the large storm window, he was — for two seconds — a three-dimensional man in a window. Focused on his task now, he bit his bottom lip with those white teeth and hoisted the window into position. Her eyes caught on the patch of fine hairs that parted just below his navel where his dark pants rode loosely on his hips. He was short, muscular in a smooth, curvy way.

"When I slide this into the frame, you hook the top and bottom, okay?" he said.

He slid in the storm window and tapped it solidly with his hands. She hooked all four of the hooks.

"Thanks," he said through the glass. "You're handy to have around." And he disappeared down the ladder, whistling something he probably made up.

October finished the zipper, pressed the suit, took a bath in the hall bathroom, dripped her way back, fighting the impulse to whistle. *Whistling woman, cackling hen, always come to no good end.* She laid the suit on the bed and congratulated herself. The Vogue Pattern Company wouldn't know hers from the one in the picture: nutmeg with a straight skirt, kick pleats, a cropped jacket; double-breasted, with covered buttons and self-belt with the special pewter buckle she had retrieved from one of her aunt Maude's throwaways.

Noon came and she put it on, set off the collar with a white rayon blouse. She saw herself on her way to the Du Bois Club meeting, coming down to the front room and encountering tall skinny Albertine. Or, better yet, walking across the lawn of the YWCA, right past proper Mary Esther and the others dressed in their serious-and-dedicated blouses and reasonable-navy or practical-beige skirts, their correct nylons and low pumps. And she smiled at the mirror, glad not to see a schoolmarm standing there.

The whistling started somewhere downstairs, then made its way up the steps and stopped; then footsteps continued softly to her door. He knocked. She wondered what excuse he would have for being up here.

18

As soon as she opened the door, he leaned in. "You interested in helping me do the other windows?" he asked, face full of eyes. Now that they stood on the same ground, he looked like he could be the tiniest inch shorter than she was.

She began stuttering out the explanation that she had something else to do that afternoon, and his face broke into a big grin.

"Boy, by the look on your face, it's a good thing I wasn't counting on you."

Teasing. Her face felt hot.

"I just came up to show you how to get some air if you want to." He brushed right past her and went to the window.

"See this little lever here?"

She followed him.

"Just unhook the bottom, slide the lever, and it props the window open just enough to let in a little air."

"Okay," she said. "Thanks. I never want to feel like I'm sealed in for the winter. Not yet, anyway."

Wide strides and he was back at the door. "Thank *you*," he said. "It can be a job. Lydia Pemberton's got too many windows." Was he nervous?

"My name's James Wilson," he said. "I help out around here sometimes. You must be a new teacher."

"Yes, I am. October Brown," she said and neither of them put out a hand. She found the hem of the nutmeg jacket to straighten. It wasn't all right to say nothing, and she didn't see how she could just tell him to leave. It was good that he didn't try to make some smart remark about her name, and they stood there too long not talking.

"It's probably going to be too hot for storm windows today, so thanks for showing me . . ." she said.

"Where're you from?"

"I'm from Ohio," she said.

"Columbus?"

"No, Chillicothe. You've probably never heard of it."

"I've got a buddy from Akron," he said. "Nice place."

"I never went to Akron, but I hear it's nice."

He stepped into the hallway. She took the doorknob into her hand and pushed the door a little. Across the hall, Cora opened her door and saw them. Saw them, October thought, because Cora's brow furrowed just a little.

Cora threw "Hi, James" in his direction and threw "Ed's on the way, you about ready?" into October's wide-open kitchenette.

With Cora watching, James turned to October and took in her outfit. "You look like something out of a magazine," he said, easy with his loose jive, now that he had an audience.

"Thanks," October said, trying to smile. She all but closed the door. James finally smiled his way down the hall, whistled his way down the stairs.

Cora called, "Let me get my purse and I'm ready," and disappeared.

October left her door ajar and rubbed her sweaty palms together.

Downstairs in the front room, sure enough, Albertine and Mary Esther sat all prim on the French Provincial loveseat. October thought to wait on the porch, but Cora swept into the sitting room, and October followed.

Albertine remarked, "You all look very nice."

"I'm already excited just by this weather," Mary Esther said.

Albertine wore a shirtwaist — flannel, it looked like — of a new color, cranberry, with pearls, and her hair was finger-waved to her shoulders. Mary Esther in forest green and little gold earrings, too. No navy. No beige.

"Thanks," October said. "You do, too."

"Looks like everybody had the same idea," Cora said. "Break into fall."

October observed that Cora could wear a gunny sack and look good. Their principal at

Stowe had once asked October if they were related. Cora was a head shorter, slimmer, too, with Ethiopian features, but she and October had the same dark complexions, only October had the mark of vitiligo. Same thick hair, too, only Cora wouldn't be caught dead with hers nappy.

Mrs. Pemberton came in from the kitchen, untying her apron. "My, my, my — don't we look like a parade," she said.

And then Ed's horn blared twice. "Here's Ed," Cora said.

"Don't be too late tonight," Mrs. Pemberton said. "Church in the morning."

October stooped to look through the front window. Ed had pulled his old Buick up to the curb and was getting out, saying something to James, who stood in the yard with his foot up casually on the low stone wall that he had built with his own hands.

"Coming, coming," Cora said mostly to herself, and snapped her purse closed. "Ready?" to the others.

They all went out to the porch as Ed approached, calling "Hey bob-a-ree-bop" to them, laughing. "I don't know if I can stand all this fineness riding in my backseat."

"Don't hurt his feelings, y'all," Cora said loudly. "Smile like you're flattered."

They laughed.

"Sorry, but Norman is coming by to get me and Mary Esther," Albertine said. News to everybody. And she asked, "Who's that with you?"

Out at the curb, a young man had gotten out of Ed's car and was leaning against it, hugging a black case, some kind of musical instrument. October scanned the arbor. James had disappeared.

"That's Lonny," Cora said.

"Leon, my brother," Ed finished. "I'm dropping him off overtown."

Mrs. Pemberton and retired Miss Dumas came out to the porch, too. "Hello there, mister," Mrs. Pemberton said. Ed stepped up onto the porch and took Mrs. Pemberton's hand.

"When are you going to make one of your pineapple upside-down cakes again?" he asked.

"Chile, hush up." She brushed him away.

But Miss Dumas, ninety going on forty, spoke up. "If Cora ain't bakin your cakes, somethin's rotten in Denmark," and they all knew that she wasn't talking dessert.

Ed took a breath. "Wup, time to go." October followed him and Cora down the porch steps, out the bricked path through the yard's shade of pear trees, where no James could possibly have disappeared without her noticing what direction, past the very decent stone wall to the curb.

"Hi," Ed's brother said to October, and, "Hey, Cora."

Ed introduced them. Leon shifted his black case. "Your name's October? You must have a birthday coming up soon."

Rather than try to come back, October smiled. Ed held the back door for her and she climbed into the backseat.

Cora waved Leon into the car. "Her birthday's in April. Just get in the backseat and be quiet, little brother," she said. They chuckled; doors slammed and the Buick pulled into the flaming noon traffic of Oceola Avenue.

According to long tradition the Du Bois Club — Negro teachers in primary grades — kicked off the school year at the Yates Branch of the YWCA. Tudor house, immaculate lawn, impressive verandah, it buzzed that afternoon when the Douglass School group outdid itself with a buffet under the yellow canopy on the lawn: everything from shrimp salad to chocolate cream pies.

The teachers met and mingled, auditioned their clothes and sampled the spread. Then they got serious. What *real* issues had been covered by the powers-that-be during the state meeting in Topeka last month? The word was that the white schools were getting funds for experimenting with a new way to improve reading skills. Reading modules, they were called. The women broke into groups, put brains to work on theme and project, and came back with solid plans for their own reading modules.

They would need wood: crates, perhaps. And they all knew somebody who could saw beveled angles and nail two pieces of wood together to make benches and tables. They could come up with cushions themselves. But they would need money to pull it off at all the schools.

October thought that her group — teachers from Stowe — came up with the best idea for fund-raising. A fashion show. "And," she tried to tell sixty serious teachers, "all the fashions can be auctioned off. That way . . . ," and she went on to explain in detail how to make double the money.

Eyes rolled. Nobody liked the idea. Instead they all went for the same old have-a-cabaret plan: sell tickets, sell food and drinks, raffle off a door prize. *Next time,* she thought.

As the meeting wound down and they went their ways, October admired this group of women. They were dedicated, willing to take money from their own pockets to fill in the slight to their schools when the Board of Education turned its ever-deaf ear. Willing to sacrifice in unspoken ways, too.

She went inside to call a cab. As she passed through the hallway one of the Douglass teachers called from the kitchen, "Want to take home some cake?"

"No, thanks," October called back. It was good to be a part of something. She found the little office with the phone and got in line, three women ahead of her. Mary Esther came up and asked why she wasn't riding with Cora.

October didn't feel like explaining all the reasons why Cora and Ed didn't need a third thumb. It brought up the married-woman-teacher stipulation in their contracts — that item that the superintendent had pointed to when he hired her. She had seen the dubious advantage that day and filed it away as one more thing to live with, one of the unspoken sacrifices. And here was Cora waiting six years for Ed, who had never gotten around to the ring and the question because — theoretically at least — if she got married, Cora could lose her job.

It didn't matter that the rule had been struck down in the thirties and was no longer practiced in most places; in Wyandotte County, it was the law. Superintendent

Arledge's law. Only single women for the Negro schools. Dime a dozen. If you marry, you must resign. Maybe you'll be hired back as a permanent substitute. Maybe not.

Rather than go into all of that with Mary Esther, October told her, "They aren't going that way — you want to split a cab?," and Mary Esther said sure.

Mary Esther should have understood. As the women had begun packing up, October had watched Albertine parade herself across the Yates lawn and climb into the front seat of Norman's cab. Norman had looked far too pleased for a cabdriver merely picking up a fare. And Mary Esther couldn't help herself. She had caught October's eye and tapped her ring finger. Norman was a married man, and Albertine was settling.

No wonder Mrs. Pemberton was such a housemother, keeping tabs, keeping the chicks in line, not so different from the way October's own aunts had been. Aunt Frances, the take-no-prisoners general; Aunt Maude, the reasonable lieutenant. Frances and Maude Cooper, her big-boned, ginger-colored saviors, had always drawn clear lines that she and Vergie crossed at their peril. And hadn't she and Vergie been a handful, tall like their aunts, but blackberries like their father. Not that black skin was a curse, per se, but who could imagine a blessing in anything from him?

They had survived. She was twenty-three, making a life of her own. Vergie was married and happy in Ohio. October dialed zero for the operator, who would give her the number for a cab.

Monday evening, not a week later, October had another little brush with James Wilson. She and Cora went upstairs together from school to find an RCA record in its brown sleeve propped against October's door. "O.B. — J.W." had been scribbled in pencil on the sleeve. October did her best to pretend *Who-on-earth? What-is-this?*, but she knew and knew that Cora knew, too. When it came to a man and a woman, Cora would never resort to tact.

"What's his problem?" Cora said. October had barely had time to see that the record was Billy Eckstine's Orchestra, Eckstine featuring Sarah Vaughan.

She said to Cora, "Wait a minute, let me see what it is. . . . We don't even know . . ."

"Why can't he just give it to you instead of leaving it out here for everybody to see?" Cora said. "I know Mrs. Pemberton didn't let him up here for this."

"It's just a record, Cora," October said. "I don't know — maybe he thinks I like Billy

Eckstine. Maybe he had two of them." Lame, she knew.

"I've been meaning to ask you why he keeps showing up here without calling you?"

Keeps showing up?

"Cora, I just met him last week. He wasn't 'showing up' — he was installing storm windows. He left me a record to listen to. What's wrong with that?"

Lately Cora had been dropping hints to October that Ed had been dropping hints about a job he might take in St. Louis, teaching industrial arts and coaching the basketball team. Better money. Good opportunity. In Cora's spillovers about Ed, October had heard her attempts to sound cheery — a sure sign of worry. Probably Cora worried that she had turned into a convenience. Ed might just walk away. So no wonder Cora would be irritated if any man was doing anything halfway hidden with any woman.

October quickly stuck the record under her arm and slipped through her door, leaving Cora and her skepticism in the hallway. Once she was in her room, she put the record on the bed, weighing when might be the best time to play it.

She slipped her feet out of her pumps, rolled down her stockings, and inspected her legs. Fine. No vitiligo. Once she had finally understood that it wouldn't kill her, she had discovered that vitiligo was an ancient disease, benign for the most part. People said that even the Bible mentioned it. Yet no one knew why a patch of skin cells would suddenly stop making brown pigment, or how to trigger them to function again. At the moment, though, she had one visible spot on her left cheek. Perhaps there was something to the wives'-tale theories about nervous strain.

Barefoot, she padded across the cold wood floor and lit the two-burner, then filled her teakettle with water. When she turned to face the room again, she saw it anew, the way a stranger might see it. Her bed in neat blue chenille. Her worn-out record player near the window. The tapestry upholstery on the stuffed chair in the corner looked more steadfast than easy. A softening wouldn't hurt. She dropped a few drops of Evening in Paris on the lightbulb, then draped her floral print silk scarf over the lampshade. When the tea was sufficiently steeped, she sat down with the teacup her aunt Maude had given her — real china — and wondered where she might get another such cup in case she ever had company in her room.

Finally, when Cora did knock, October opened the door but didn't get a word out before Cora said, "If you like him, make him take you out."

October stepped out and closed her door. "He seems nice," she said.

"You don't know him," Cora reminded her. They were going down the stairs. Cora hushed her voice a little. "Men can be very nice when they're getting what they want, especially if you're the chick on the side."

October touched Cora's shoulder. "Are you trying to tell me that he's married?"

"No, October, I'm just saying that you don't know him. Ed has worked with him at Tobin's Construction off and on. Seems to me Ed said something that made me think Shorty's got somebody already."

"Oh," October said. "You're right, I don't even know him. Why would I care if he's got somebody?" And she flounced on down the stairs ahead of Cora. *So, they call him Shorty.*

At the table that evening they had hardly passed the potatoes when Mrs. Pemberton got started again about how much electricity "you girls" were using, and went right from that into how they might think about getting their souls saved by avoiding "these honky-tonks I hear tell about" and doing more "in the church." October had to listen to Mrs. Pemberton low-rate dancing and listening to

31

lowlife music, knowing that she had a record upstairs waiting to be played and that James-called-Shorty had left it there. She tuned in again to hear Albertine say to Mary Esther, "Oh, hush, Mary Esther, you don't even know what a honky-tonk is."

Since forever, October's Aunt Frances had worked out in the world as a licensed practical nurse, but church was *her* passion, too, just as it was Mrs. Pemberton's. And Aunt Maude was no different. She had worked at the Meade Paper Mill, but all she knew was church.

October believed in God, liked gospel music — but, listening to Mrs. Pemberton, she considered that that give-all kind of dedication to religion must have something to do with age. In the name of advising, threatening, and comforting her and Vergie, her aunts had always spouted religion. Even when she or Vergie was inconsolable, their aunts had offered the only solace they could: they would cook enough food to feed a city, set her and Vergie down to it, and feed them *sowing and reaping,* and *Unto every thing there is a season —* holy words about all things coming to pass, nothing coming to stay.

Though she had never come right out and challenged her aunts, October had understood since she was five that some things do come to stay. Their mother's unspeakable death, for instance, had come to stay.

Wednesday, two nights later, at around eight, *my goodness surely not,* October heard a soft rapping on her door. He had never telephoned, and definitely had no business upstairs — handyman or not — at that hour. She was in her robe with her midweek hair shouting.

In one move it was robe into closet, skirt zipped with no slip, scratchy sweater but it matches, bare legs are all right in house shoes but nylons are better in high heels, hair — *Where is my brush?* — hair back in a rubber band, no, ribbon, no, combs. Combs, *Where are Auntie Maude's combs?* Lipstick, *I need to buy some earrings,* splash of Evening in Paris, and *I wonder how I look?*

"Hi," he said. Work clothes. White shirt speckled with paint, dark pants, work boots. Clean, though.

"Mrs. Pemberton is going to have a fit," October said, stepping back to let him in. She could see the strand of light under Cora's door.

"Mrs. P. is at church, but I came up on the elevator," he said, motioning toward the fire escape door at the back end of the hall.

He looked around the room. She saw the

softness of the silk scarf that he might see.

"You want to sit down?" she asked.

"Um-ummm," he said, shaking his head. "I just wondered if you got a chance to listen to the record I left for you."

She could smell castile soap and something sweeter. She smiled. "I did," she said. "Billy Eckstine can really sing. Sarah Vaughan, too."

"Know what?" he said, eyes a little brighter. "You remind me of her."

It wasn't the first time that anyone had mentioned Sarah Vaughan as a look-alike compliment, and she had long since figured out the only possible resemblance was in the shape of their mouths and the dark of their skin.

"Really?" she said, wondering how flattered she should be.

"Well, I mean, you-all do favor. You might be a little bit bigger . . ."

She smiled brighter. "Bigger?"

"You know, taller . . ." He hesitated, then threw his arm straight up and bent his wrist in an upside-down *L*. Did this mean that he would be self-conscious about her height over his?

". . . And pretty," he said. "Prettier."

October brushed the air between them. *Pretty* she didn't recognize too well. *Attractive,* maybe. She was wearing Aunt Maude's combs. It was nice to be called pretty. He was holding an LP. Her record player played only 78s.

"I wanted to bring you this," he said. "It's one of the new long-playing records, Nat King Cole."

She motioned toward the window where her record player stood. "I can't play it on that," she said, sure that she sounded like a dunce who had bought the wrong record player.

"Well, in that case," James said, "you'll have to come listen to it with me sometime."

He grinned and his ripe lips went flat across the top of his teeth, turning his mouth into a shallow bowl of pearls. He had almost asked her out. Almost. This was something she could give to Cora.

"Until then," he said, "I brought some of my old stuff over." He opened the door and picked up the stack of records he had stashed there. "I've got a whole collection, more than I know what to do with. I collect LPs now."

He handed them over, each in its own sleeve. His collection. Something he cherished. She knew it would be foolish, but she felt like giving him her silk scarf.

She said to him, "You sure you want to part with these?"

"Well, yeah," he said. "For a while, anyway. I never hear music up here. Thought I'd do something new and different for the teachers" — smiling. "One of them, anyway."

They were quiet.

"Besides," he ducked his head, "it'll give me an excuse to be up here."

"Mrs. Pemberton will call the police," she said, smiley-voiced, then braver. "Besides, who says you need an excuse?" And she slipped one of the Sarah Vaughan records out of its sleeve and took it over to her turntable. She pulled the changer arm over and watched the needle land gently in the groove. Sarah Vaughan's voice cried, *"In my solitude . . ."*

James was suddenly standing close behind her. "I'd ask you to dance but I don't have on my dancin shoes," he said.

The yearning of Sarah Vaughan filled in the space. "That's all right," October said, meaning *It's okay that we don't dance*. But James reached around her, made her deal with the warmth of his body. Ungracefully she wiggled away, stood aside to watch something she couldn't name in the way his thumb and forefinger lifted the needle arm, something about the gentle placement of the needle in the groove. That and clumsy brogans.

The arc of his arm caught her at the waist. "I promise I won't break your toes."

It was all right. She breathed and breathed in again. He was a wave — castile and whatever sweet else, coarse stubble, hard chest — that made her hands want to fly all over him. His hand caught hers and inch-for-inch they stepped into the music. One turn and she found herself giving up her breath to the sudden softness of his mouth.

But another wave broke like a trapdoor giving way under her feet. She wanted to say something, but one of those same flitting hands with its own intelligence went wild, slapped his face, and flitted to the shelter of her armpit.

"No," she said, pushing him away, and he was saying, ". . . Sorry, I just wanted to dance. Don't think I meant to do that . . ."

"It's all right," she said. And in a way it was. "You just surprised me, is all."

He stuck his hands into his pockets, watching her. Pulled something — lint — out of his pocket and rolled it between his fingers, examining it.

Probably she shouldn't have let him in. She started to say as much, but he cut in.

"Guess I'd better get out of here." But he didn't move. Instead, October moved, pulled the record off the metal stem of the turntable, traced the circle of hard shellac with her fingers, then slid it back into the paper sleeve.

"Maybe you ought to keep these," she said, and she held it out to him.

He ignored the record. "Let's start all over again," he said. "What do you say we just go out sometime, get to know each other?"

Why hadn't he said this at first? She didn't meet his eyes.

"We could take in a set at Shady Maurice's sometime. Like maybe Friday night — what do you say?"

Chez de Maurice's, but who was grading papers? "I don't know. . . ." she said.

"You can bring anybody, bring your friend Cora. We can listen to the guys play awhile."

"Maurice's is a honky-tonk, right?" she said.

He laughed, making the label seem ridiculous even to her.

"It's an after-hours place. Don't worry, won't be no hoodlums. Truth be told, I've seen Ed and your friend Cora out there a time or two when his brother was playing. It's private, you know? I mean, nobody knows nobody."

October let it percolate, good news and bad. A date, finally. She had never been out to Chez de Maurice's. She was sure Cora would be up for the idea, because Ed was taking the weekend to look-see in St. Louis. Cora would figure a night out as her best revenge. Still, the chaperone in Cora might spoil everything.

"Cora and I have a meeting Friday night until nine," she said. "I guess we could go for a while."

"Just tell me where to pick y'all up," James said, "and we're in business."

CHAPTER 2

October would remember the blur of coming and going that Friday night, and snatches of club life in between. First the three of them in James's borrowed car out on Highway 24 where dark waves of prairie grass turned land liquid until the cut-off at the fading red-and-white of checkered Purina. Then a hump on the horizon, a flat bunker with painted-over windows, and *Chez de Maurice* in green on the Coca-Cola sign.

Inside, the club had a bar at one end, bandstand at the other, and — as if it were the club's whole reason for being — a dance floor stretching in between. The throb of a bass being played over the whirr of soft talk suggested that they whisper, but once Cora spotted Ed's brother, she ignored the atmosphere.

"There's Leon!" she yelled right out. "Lonny!" Set October off. Suppose she had not wanted to be seen?

"Let's sit here," James said, choosing the first empty table he saw — to get Cora seated and settled, she thought.

"Yes, this is perfect," Cora said. Since they were in clear sight of the bandstand, October figured that Cora would let well enough alone. But no.

"Order me a Singapore sling," Cora said, and ran off like Leon was a long-lost brother who didn't know he was about to be found.

"I don't know why Cora's so excited to see Ed's brother playing," October said. As far as she knew, Leon was a fledgling.

"He's out here all the time," James said. "Keeps things going till the biggies show up. What would you like to drink?"

Her experience with drinks went from soda water with a splash of Mogen David wine, to beer with salt to take away the bitterness. Live a little. She ordered herself a sweet red Singapore sling. James asked for scotch and water.

"Nice," he said, looking long at her. "If I'da known you were going all out, I would have put on a tie."

She *had* gone all out and worn her just-in-case navy crepe with exaggerated shoulders, fitted waist and hips, flounce lined with polka-dot rayon, and high, open-toed blue pumps. Too audacious for church, and, therefore, sharp. She hoped.

In his outfit, James looked more like somebody down-to-earth. He wore a white shirt, creased right out of the package. His blue suit coat did sag a little, and it didn't even try to go with his brown trousers.

41

Cora returned to the table just as drinks arrived. "Let's toast," she said. "To fun for a change." She lifted her glass. October and James sipped and smiled. Cora took a long swallow of her drink. "Leon said Joe Williams is coming tonight and I, for one, want to meet him. . . ."

The combo had begun another number — fast, with what sounded to October like some version of musical scales.

"You have to pay attention," James told them, "or you miss half of what these cats are trying to do. Listen."

October listened, knowing that she was missing half. "I don't think I've ever heard this song," she said.

"It's bebop, baby," he said. "If you've ever heard the tune like this before, they aren't doing what they're supposed to be doing. What's hip is in the spur of the moment."

She watched James more than she listened. By the time the piano player got to his solo, James was spellbound. He yelled, "That's it, that's it!" And, when Leon soloed on his saxophone, "Now you sayin somethin."

After about an hour, the musicians took a break and James left the table. October watched him move among the tables, laughing, talking, knowing everybody.

"James is on home ground," Cora said. "I

wonder how he knows all these people."

"He probably comes out here all the time," October said.

"He's after you," Cora said. "He seems okay, but he knows his way around. Be sure you don't get caught up in something you can't handle."

Cora couldn't see that knowing his way around made him all the more interesting. "I don't think I'd have to *handle* him," October said.

"Yeah," Cora said, "but I'll bet he knows more about you than you do about him."

October shook her head. "He doesn't know anything about me."

"He knows where you live. Where does *he* live? Who does he live with?"

Cora probably wouldn't know either. "He lives over on Rowland," she said, guessing.

"With . . . ?"

"Alone."

"He told you that, or are you just guessing?"

"What difference does it make? We're not doing anything."

"I can't believe you believe that, but okay, if you say so. Remember Connie what's-her-name, when she brought Sherman to Darby's and his other girlfriend showed up raising Cain?"

Cora's whole face changed and October looked to see Leon coming their way, trying on suave, she thought. He asked them what they were drinking, and what they wanted to hear. Flirting maybe, but that was okay. This was Chez de Maurice's.

"In My Solitude" popped into October's head.

"Ladies like the ballads," he said, and was he possibly disappointed about that choice? He ordered them two more slings and got up to leave. "Listen for your song," he said.

When he was out of earshot, Cora told her, "Leon is a mess. He asked me if you were with James, and I told him yes, for now."

October ignored Cora's remark but reminded her, "You know, don't you, that Ed's going to hear about you and your night out without him."

"He'd better hear, or Leon's name is mud," Cora said.

The bebop started up again, and when James came back to the table he brought a friend he called School Boy who had gone to A & T and who kept calling Cora "Doll Baby." He made himself at home and kept their glasses filled.

October watched Cora's ease with men, watched how she sparred as well as they did, without taking them seriously, nothing personally. October admired that.

As the music got more intense, and James got more involved, School Boy remarked that "the cats sound canned to me, but they're tryin — I'll give 'em that — they're tryin."

Cora jumped right on his case. "I'll have you know that Lonny has people from New York interested in him. I'm talking about record contracts and things."

"Whoops," School Boy said. "Didn't mean to step on any toes."

October thought that loyalty might have Cora making up stories, but James was on Cora's side — he liked the group, and so October did, too.

As if on cue, the combo played a version of "In My Solitude." Right away James caught on and said to October, "I saw him over here — did you ask him to play it?" Big grin.

And with her best Cora-like attitude, October shrugged: "Um-hmm." James closed his hand over hers on the table. Cora looked away.

A little after midnight a commotion signaled that one of the biggies had arrived. Mr. Maurice went to the microphone and announced, "Ladies and gentlemen, give Mr. Joe Williams a minute to compose himself. Lonny Haskins and the Tones will take a break and come back to play for Mr. Williams." Singapore slings moved up to rum-and-Cokes.

In person Joe Williams was much better-looking than the pictures October had seen; flesh and blood tells. Plus, he sang songs she knew — "Going to Chicago," "Every Day I Have the Blues." She was more excited by the idea of being there than by hearing him sing. When he crooned "My Foolish Heart," jazz club became dance place and James and October swam with all the others around a dance floor under low lights.

And then they were in the car, October and James, and had Cora really left with School Boy?

"She's a big girl," James said. He kissed her. No trapdoors now, just his heat and his words, "Come go with me," in her ear.

"Go where?"

"Don't worry, just say you'll go," he said, kissing her neck.

Wherever he wanted to take her, she wanted to go. "Yes, okay."

And down the silver strip of promise they rode, him driving, her hanging, head-heavy, on his shoulder, arms encircling him as much for balance as anything. The road tilted from side to side, rose, widened, narrowed, fell, slipping away, slipping.

The next morning — Sunday — Cora stood over October's bed with a glass of cold water. "No big deal. Everybody gets a little drunk at least once in her life. Be glad I was here. But," she said, "Mrs. Pemberton was none too pleased. We made a ruckus and she came out of her room while I was getting you upstairs." And Cora went back to bed.

Where was the ice bag? October was head sick and heart sick. Remembered none of it. Wondered. On the basis of her limited experience, she thought surely she would feel sore or something if . . .

Sunday morning in a quiet house makes a phone ring very loudly. Very long.

"I'll get it," Cora called. Stairs creaked loudly, Cora creeping down. Everyone else must have gone to church.

"It's for you!" Cora yelled.

October scrambled as well as she could, got out of bed and made it down to the telephone. She could feel her own footsteps inside her head.

"How are you doing?" James asked. From the sincerity in his voice she figured she must have been pitiful the night before.

"Fine," she said.

"No headache?"

"A little."

"Look," he said. "I hope you're not mad about last night. You don't drink, and probably we should have gone light on the rum."

Nice man. "I'm the one who should be apologizing," she said. "I was probably a mess." She hoped there wasn't anything more that they should be discussing, but she wasn't sure.

"Just a little tipsy," he said. He seemed to be stalling.

"The next time, I'll be sure to order water with Coca-Cola on the side," she said. Was there more?

"Can we talk — I mean, can I come by today? I mean, if you've got some time . . ."

There was more. "Yes, I guess so," she said. "I try to take Sunday afternoon to get ready for the week, but I can work it out."

"It doesn't have to be the whole afternoon," he said. "What are you doing now?"

"Well . . . nothing."

"What if I pick you up in half an hour?"

"That'll be all right." Just let her off the phone now. Cora would have an answer. She raced back upstairs and into Cora's room.

Cora turned over in her bed. "What's the matter? Was that James?"

"Yes, and he sounded strange. Guilty. He apologized for getting me drunk and now I'm really wondering . . ."

"Hold it, hold it . . ." Cora said. She unwrapped the covers further and sat up, rubbing her face.

"You passed out, girl. You probably scared him. Nothing happened. You got home a minute before I did, and I came straight home. You probably scared him."

Thirty minutes later, when October opened the door, it was clear to her that James had not slept. Same shirt and pants, and now a peacoat against the gray and bluster outside.

"Come on in," she told him. "I'll get my coat."

"We can talk here, can't we?" he said. "I take it everybody is at church."

Not the slightest play in him — he was definitely on purpose. This had to be about more than James being worried about her headache.

"Okay," she said. They went into the front room, and he turned to face her. *Haggard,* she thought. *He's nervous.*

"Is something wrong?" she asked. How little she knew him.

He looked at her. "Nothing that you or me can do anything about," he said. Not good.

She sat down on Mrs. Pemberton's love seat. He didn't sit, just dug his hands too deeply in his pockets and scraped the pile of the rug with the toe of his shoe. Was he concocting a story?

"I just came over to talk, but there really isn't anything to say. Nothing happened. I mean between you and me, and so nobody has anything to be sorry for, right?" Toeing the rug. Man with news?

"I guess I'm wondering why you thought we needed to talk," she said.

"*I* needed to talk," he said. He perched on Mrs. Pemberton's French Provincial chair.

"You gotta know I wasn't trying to be slick. I didn't have any particular plans or anything. I had to at least talk to you, I mean period, you know, talk to you."

He was backing off, but she couldn't see why. "What are you saying?"

"I'm saying that I probably did want to get next to you. I was wrong. I should have let well enough alone with saying hi and 'bye."

She was getting it now. "Are you saying that you're involved with somebody else?"

"I'm married, October. Things are real bad, but I've got a wife. I shouldn't have . . . you know . . ."

She looked at her hands. She should have put on cream, but it doesn't matter now. She shouldn't have hoped. She should have said no from the first.

She stood up. "Well, thanks for telling me,"

she said. "We never should have gone out."

Without even clearing his throat, all in one breath he said, "You may as well know I've got a daughter, too. Irene is my daughter. Irene Wilson."

October's mind struggled to pick it up, but the fact that she was his child's teacher, his daughter was in her room every day — it was too much. She stayed with the moment, his ugly shoes, her ashy hands, until the little round face began to insinuate itself between them.

"You would have figured it out anyway," James said. "I sign her grade cards."

October didn't know him in the least — not in the least. A wife, and a daughter in *her* classroom. What had he thought, that she wouldn't find out? Good thing Cora had come with them.

"Irene Wilson is your daughter," she declared, letting it sink in.

"Yep," James said, as if he had performed the miracle of birth himself. This was the wrong time, wrong situation, to beat his chest about being a daddy, and he must have realized it. "Yes, Irene is my daughter," he said.

October added it all up. It embarrassed her. In the scheme of things, she couldn't have meant anything more to him than an interesting stone he fit into a wall that he was building. Once it was in place, you couldn't tell it from all the other stones. How could she have thought that he liked her?

She remembered Cora's warnings, but better, Cora's acumen. A finesse, a way to give them both the benefit of the doubt.

"Well," she said. "You did insist on bringing Cora with us, and now I understand why."

He looked relieved. "Like I said, you're really some kind of woman . . . lady . . . and I want, wanted . . ."

"Church will be out soon. I guess you should go on home."

"Yeah, yeah," he said. "I just came over to apologize."

"Good-bye," she said. She wished she could have shown him something else, but anger didn't come up. Nothing had happened.

CHAPTER 3

The blur of events that night in the car with James called up other, darker memories, elusive details of a distant October 26 when she was still a girl. In her grown years, October had never adopted any particular ritual to mark the anniversary. Her intention was always to honor the fact that she and Vergie had started out in a normal way, in a normal family, mother and father. She never wanted to let the day go by without saying to Carrie Cooper Brown, wherever in heaven she was, "I remember you." But from the beginning, their aunts had had conniptions if October or Vergie even looked like they wanted to remember the anniversary. Long since, October had thought she recognized rue in her aunts' impatience, and kept her memorials to herself.

This October 26 was a school day. As it always was, some way would just be there, and she would know that this was the moment to stop and remember. The solar eclipse one year, or, another year, when someone had left a brand-new silk scarf on the bus. The chance sighting, once, of Joe Louis passing through

Columbus, the first snow two years straight — something would show up.

"All right, boys and girls," she said to her third-graders. "You may sit down. Who remembered to bring in leaves?"

They had finished Bible verses and the Pledge of Allegiance and were already fumbling in brown sacks or pressing newspaper preciously over layers of treasure. Hands shot up and pumped the air for emphasis.

"Good," she said. "Everyone will choose two of their best leaves for art this afternoon and share the rest with those who didn't bring any."

Forty pairs of hands got busy — "quietly, now" — choosing. She took up the extras, instructed them to put the leaves into their activity boxes, and went on with the morning lessons. At afternoon art time she encouraged them to try matching nature's improbable tones: trace the leaves, tempera-paint the paper look-alikes, cut out and string them — haphazardly — to simulate leaves falling all over the room like the snowflake cutouts that would soon replace them.

Irene Wilson. Crackerjack smart. As October moved among the children, wiping up spilled paint, sprinkling compliments, she watched Irene working. It had been two weeks since James Wilson had broken the seal on his real life and left October to pick apart the details.

When she got to Irene's desk she said, "This looks very nice, Irene. You may make another one, since this one came out so well." The round face. The mouth. Why had James Wilson done that? What had made him start up with her in the first place? If he had seen her as easy pickings, he never would have confessed when he did. She wasn't easy pickings.

She hadn't had all that much to do with men. Probably she and Vergie were the only two women she knew who had gotten to age eighteen with their hymens intact, thanks to the fact that they were raised in Chillicothe by two women who were death on men. October had been reckless one time, vowing not to graduate college wearing a chastity belt. But she wasn't easy.

James Wilson did actually resort to honesty. Give him that.

"Miss Brown," Irene was asking, "can we paint them on both sides?"

"Yes, of course," October Brown said. "Class, let's let your leaves dry and after recess, we'll paint the other side."

After school, as she cleaned up the classroom, October came upon an assortment of extra leaves. What stood out was the softest buckeye leaf, yellow center, radiating to tangerine at the edges. She sat at her desk twirling the leaf by its stem.

Remembering. Her mother giving her a bath. She cannot see Momma's face because water pours over her head, and she can hear Momma laugh. Her eyes catch fire. Momma snatches her out of the big oval tub and douses the sting with more water. Another memory: She remembers being at the Free Show, sitting on large boulders in a field, watching people dance on the outdoor screen. Momma gives her and Vergie handfuls of peanuts to eat.

When a person remembers an event, what she recalls is not the actual event but her most recent memory of it. Over time, details shift and change. To October this explanation made sense of why, after nearly twenty years, terror had no place in her memory of her mother's murder. Sometimes she reasoned that she had been young when it happened — too young, perhaps, to take it all in. Other times she thought that her mind had merely found a clever way to cope. At any rate, the scene remained improbable:

They sit at the dinner table at their house in Cleveland — Poppa, Momma, Vergie, and she. Their kitchen chairs are painted blue, with a creamy stenciled-leaf design on the chair backs. Outside, autumn light fades.

Poppa is erect in his Sunday-white shirt, and he wears a stocking cap to slick down his hair. He says something. Momma — silent; angry? — does not answer him. Creamed potatoes overrun candied carrots on pale green plates. She can see Momma in the dim hallway, walking away, hair in an upsweep with a pompadour in front, skirt swirling around her ankles. When Momma catches hold of the banister and turns to go upstairs, she can't see her face, but she knows it is set, stone, and Momma does not look back through the hallway at them in the kitchen. The swirling skirt disappears up the stairs. Poppa's chair is pushed back, empty. Somehow he has disappeared, too. Alone at the table, she and Vergie make potato sandwiches. They take turns on the step stool, washing and drying dishes. They sing, "Look who's here, Punchinella, Punchinella, Look who's here, Punchinella, little girl" — twirling until they are dizzy. A stark, black cricket springs from under the icebox and goes berserk over the kitchen. Vergie smashes it with the broom. *Who do you choose, Punchinella, Punchinella? Who do you choose . . .*"

Then, for some reason, she and Vergie rush up the stairs. Suddenly Vergie's whole face opens in a bawl. Their mother seems to be kneeling at the side of the bed, then laying her head down gently, both hands over her heart, as if she were falling asleep praying. Poppa is gone. Vergie won't let her lie on the bed with Momma.

Then there is the blur of the woman next door — Miss Cordelia Butler is her name, and she cradles the girls, sets them down in a strange house with an overstuffed chair. They cannot go home. The woman's dimples and gold tooth say that their mother is dead. Their father has killed her. That someone is taking Poppa away and that they cannot go back home. This is where they will stay until their aunties get things straightened out. The woman talks about heaven, golden streets, life everlasting.

On what seems like the same day, Vergie is going up the stairs again, and she follows. When Vergie opens the door, October can see that the room is very big. The bed is gone. Their mother is gone. Poppa is gone. No one is there. They can never come back again.

Aunt Frances and Aunt Maude are coming all the way to Cleveland to collect them, take them back to Chillicothe, where they will live. They go for a long ride in the hearse to Chillicothe and the cemetery, where she is too young to get out of the car. The house in Chillicothe has a great stone porch and a varnished swing. With fallen leaves and snow flurries, the yard is like cornflakes with a fine sprinkling of sugar. Inside the front door sits a great chair with hooks for umbrellas and hats. In the mirror to the side of it, she glimpses herself wearing her blue snowsuit. It is then, in the mirror of that dim entranceway, that she sees the first white freckle appear on her cheek, the new-birth mark of vitiligo, odd and mysterious. Her name is Lillian Brown. She is five.

At Pemberton house on the evening of the twenty-sixth, October convinced Mrs. Pemberton to give her a small block of paraffin, the kind her aunts used for sealing their home-made jelly in jars. Up in her kitchenette, October melted the wax in a saucepan. For the briefest second, she dipped the leaf and held it in midair by the stem to dry. Obscured by the wax, some of the vibrancy was gone, but the veins and perfect shape remained.

I will not spell out the details of my death here; they will come soon enough. But I will say that on that October day I did what was mine to do. I stood by and held for both my daughters. Vergie was married and settled, but this one — my younger — was on her own in the world, waiting for her life to blossom. As I watched her with her precious leaf, I marveled that for my sake, she had named herself October.

CHAPTER 4

Early in November, Ed Haskins accepted the job in St. Louis — he would be replacing a teacher who had been unable to finish out the semester. Whether Cora had been clever enough to play her cards right, or Ed was simply wise enough to hold on to his best chance, they decided to get married. Secretly.

And so, early in November, since Cora's sister couldn't come, the four of them — October, Cora, Ed, and Ed's brother, Leon — drove to St. Louis for the ceremony. October worried that they might all look back on this little trip as reckless. Once again, she got out her contract. It would behoove Cora to be well-informed.

Mr. Arledge, the superintendent, was a small, gray man who mistook his position for genuine superiority. A force to reckon with if anything went wrong. October remembered his expression when he told her to be sure to read such-and-such points. Now she looked at the contract again.

4. You agree to reside in the school dis-

trict of Wyandotte County, Kansas, during the term of this contract unless excused in writing by the Superintendent of Schools.

5. Contracts for the employ of women teachers are subject to cancellation at the discretion of the Superintendent on the marriage of such teachers. In case a woman teacher marries, she agrees to give immediate notification in writing to the Superintendent of Schools.

6. It is understood and agreed upon that no teacher will play society to the detriment of the school or engage or indulge in activities of questionable morality. The Superintendent shall be judge in these matters and violations shall be deemed sufficient cause for dismissal.

In the best of the possible circumstances, Cora and Ed would marry and live in some clandestine arrangement until they decided to have children or until enough of the women teachers reached the end of what they could stand and decided to change the game. At some point those who made these unspoken sacrifices — the women who owned houses with one "roomer," the husband, upstairs; women who lived next door, across the street, around the corner from their dear and legal mates — at some point they had to say no.

But Cora and Ed's was not the best possible circumstance. They would live two hundred miles apart, spend Fridays and Sundays on the road, steal holidays, develop a telephone relationship, and sneak around like they were pulling a creep.

Short of car rides and greetings here and there, October had spent little time with them as a couple. What she knew of Ed came from Cora's gushing stories or bitter complaints — Ed was five years older, had held jobs since he was fourteen, pinched a penny until Lincoln winked. But anyone watching knew that Cora was important to Ed. October saw how attentive he could be. Riding with them to St. Louis, she wondered if she would ever be that important to anyone.

Ed drove and Leon rode in the front seat while Cora and October settled in the back. Leon talked about music. Ed listened. For all his style as a jazz musician, October thought Leon would be a better down-home bluesman: he was tall and slight, like he had missed a few meals. He sported a mustache and goatee and what was supposed to be part of the hipster uniform — a black beret.

She didn't like his clothes. So far they all looked too flashy, and he chewed on an eternal toothpick. She wondered if he just didn't believe in haircuts or if this, too, was part of the look. Around his neck he wore a sling affair for his horn, though he wore it like anyone else would wear a tie.

He went on to Ed about "the scene," and how famous he would be, once he got his break. Judging from what October had heard at Maurice's, he might do all right, but she couldn't imagine him being the star he seemed so convinced he would be.

At one point on the trip, when Cora half joked that the night before her wedding was not the time to plan out Leon's career, he told her, "Don't worry, sis-in-law, I got you covered. Tell me what you want to hear." And he patted the case on the floor. "I'm your musician–best man rolled up in one."

"We'll stick to the Mendelssohn," Cora said, and Ed put in that it was the only song the minister's wife could play, the Wedding March, and he went into "Dum, dum, da-dum." "You can do the trumpet part on your sax, huh?"

"It's y'all's party," Leon said. Then he looked back over the seat at October and asked, "What do you think, Miss October Brown?"

"I think the Wedding March is fine," she said.

"Would you have it at your wedding?" he asked.

She said, "Oh, I don't know."

Cora gave him the eye.

"Just making conversation," he said.

"Man, you'll learn," Ed said. "Women don't play around when it comes to wedding stuff. It's as serious as a mother-in-law at the door. Oops." He laughed.

Leon said, "I can dig it. Hooking up for life is serious business, all right. You two are the only people in the world who I think are ready for it."

"Well, thank you," Cora said.

"Six years," Ed said, and he flung his arm across the back of the seat and gave Cora's hand a squeeze. He slowed the car and pulled over to the shoulder.

"This is the night before the wedding," he said. "I want my sweetie to ride up front with me."

For the rest of the trip October sat in the back with Leon and observed the possibility of two becoming one.

The wedding took place in a small chapel of a Lutheran church in St. Louis with the minister, his wife, October, and Leon making it a ceremony. How easily an atmosphere can be created when a woman drapes herself in white lace. October observed the difference between *looking at* and *beholding* somebody you love. She observed the worlds words can convey when they are vowed.

After the wedding, the four of them had a spectacular dinner including trout amandine and baked Alaska, all at the Vincent Downtown Hotel, where Leon knew the manager. Later that night Leon invited her to come to his jam session in the hotel lounge, but she went to bed instead. She had had enough for one day.

They had agreed to leave at one o'clock on Sunday, but instead of the luggage-laden newlyweds October expected, Cora and Ed trotted down the stairs into the lobby and announced that they were staying. Because Leon had been so generously entertaining in the lounge, the manager had given them a second night's stay on the house. Ed had already quit his construction company job. Cora could call in sick at school. Leon could take the car and pick them up at Union Station the next night.

On the drive home, October tolerated Leon's nonstop catalogue of his career again — the story of his perfect pitch, how he had gotten started, who had heard him play, his story of meeting Charlie Parker in the middle of the street one day, his plan to make it in New York, who had said what about his playing, and on and on. Mostly he talked to hear himself think, and October mostly kept her thoughts to herself. All in all, James Wilson had been an honest man. At least that.

On Monday, October knew things had gone well: a substitute teacher appeared in Cora's place. On Monday evening, Cora phoned from St. Louis to say that they were staying one more night. And again on Tuesday evening, Cora telephoned to say that they were staying yet another night. October worried.

"Spare me the details," Miss Olfield, the principal, told Miss October Brown. "If you talk to her, remind her that there is no such thing as a private life if you're teaching in Wyandotte County."

When Cora called again, October relayed the message. "Maybe you-all ought to come on back now," she said.

Cora laughed. "I know, I know. But we've never had so much fun doing nothing," she said.

They came back late Wednesday night. All day Thursday October watched Cora mope through her lessons and stand in the doorway as if the classroom were the snake pit that separated her from Ed. On Friday Mr. Connors, the black Assistant Superintendent for Negro Schools, visited the classes. At the end of the day Cora told October that he had told her there were questions downtown about her absence, where she had been, why she hadn't made three-day plans ahead of time.

"What did you tell him?" October asked.

"I told him I had a sick friend in St. Louis," she said. "Miss Olfield was happy not to know the difference."

But Mr. Assistant Superintendent said that Cora could expect that this wouldn't be the end of it.

October would have been fit to be tied over such a threat. But not Cora. Over the weekend October watched her phone an old friend in East St. Louis to concoct a possible cover story. And on Monday the Board of Education called to give her a Wednesday afternoon appointment with the superintendent himself, Mr. Arledge. Obviously he had smelled something more titillating than the sickfriend story.

As Cora described it to October, Mr. Arledge asked for the "sick friend's" telephone number and right then he picked up his phone, dialed zero, and asked for the long-distance operator.

It just so happened that this woman, Cora's friend Betty Rae Keith, had been fighting the fight for a long time in East St. Louis. When it came to administrators, she had a kiss-my-butt attitude. According to Cora, the small, gray Mr. Arledge turned purple as Betty Rae reamed him about the arrogance he must possess to so freely disturb her, about prying into her personal business just because a friend — who had held her hand through a difficult time — was one of his employees, about creating friction between friends, about intimidating and interrogating women at his slightest whim because nobody in the Wyandotte School District would confront him. And she advised him that he was fortunate that she worked in St. Louis, that days for overseers like him were numbered.

"Well," Cora said, "when I left his office I'm sure he had a seizure."

If ever October were to find herself in a mess, she would choose Cora to bail her out.

CHAPTER 5

When forces of nature are involved, Fate gets all the blame.

A hundred million years ago, when Earth had one solid landmass, the land began breaking into pieces — continents — which drifted north, south, east, and west. Forces were released, creating gaps, ridges, bucklings — mountain-building forces that, in North America, created the uplift known as the Rockies. That drastic tilt drained the ancient sea that had once occupied the land to the east, leaving the whole interior of a continent a monotonous swamp. Another million years and the swamp became the vast indomitable sweep of prairie grasses, the Great Plains. Now that the sea was gone, every living thing on these plains understood what it was to be landlocked.

No large bodies of water to hold coolness to temper summer, or warmth to forestall winter. Seasons arrive unrefined, delivering harsh edges. The sun crosses the plane of the equator, and somewhere way north a coalescence of frost gathers, spreads itself in a heavy mantle of air that drops southward. Somewhere far south a balm blows northward. Mid-continent, with no mountains and scarce hills, their tempestuous union spreads havoc.

A silver morning turns leaden, wind comes to be terror-song. Snow — in the span of an hour — goes from dust mote to whiteout.

It was mid-November. At ten o'clock in the morning, when October looked out the classroom window, she could still see the fence where the playground ended and the street began. Miss Olfield had announced the school's noon closing, and parents had already begun to arrive. Cars crept by, chains jingling. Fifteen or twenty of October's forty-odd pupils had already gone.

By ten-thirty, she could see only the top of the fence. There was still a tire path in the middle of the street, and she could still see headlights as cars stole eerily by, muted in the atmosphere of heavy snow.

By eleven o'clock the howling had started. As the remaining children did arithmetic at the blackboard, October glanced out to see whorls of white and an occasional headlight peering like a candle in dense fog. She could make out wrapped figures — ghouls — coming out of nowhere, stealing toward the school building, then stealing away, hand in looping hand, with their little ghouls. The fence had disappeared.

She needed to stop this nervous storm-watching because the children were watching her, looking — eyes scary bright — at the white blank window. By no means was it her first blizzard, but it was the first storm where she had so many children looking to her to get them home safely.

A few minutes after eleven, Cora appeared, waving in the window of the door to October's classroom, signaling for October to come into the hallway.

"I called Mr. Pemberton," Cora said, "and he's going to borrow a truck and come get us around one. We'll have to sit on top of each other, but he'll take all four of us home."

"Good thing," October said. "If the wind picks up, we could get lost just walking around the playground. What about the children?"

"Well, we'll see," Cora said. "Most times they're all picked up by the time we close. If not — well, you know. Nobody leaves until the school is empty. How many do you have left?"

"At least half of them," October said. She reminded herself that all the children lived within a few miles of school. All of them could be walked home if necessary. But who wanted to brave a blizzard with a brood? She had worn only overshoes, not boots.

Within the next half hour, parents — bless their reliable souls — had come to collect all except five or six of the children in October's third-grade class. Several of the parents who were walking more than one child home brought ropes to tie around waists, extra socks for mittens, and huge swatches of cloth for headgear. And they brought peanut-butter-and-jelly sandwiches to fortify little stomachs for the trek.

October passed around chunks of peppermint cane to the children who remained. Although she had her doubts, she reassured them: "Everyone will be taken home today. If your parents don't come, I will personally walk you to your door, so don't worry."

When James Wilson arrived, because his arms were full and the classroom door was closed, he had to kick it. October went immediately to see who and what on earth. And because sensible gear for blizzards can obliterate features on faces, she did not recognize him. The man wore hip boots and a mackinaw, a hunting cap with the flaps down, and a kerchief tied masklike around his face. He hugged a wooden crate with an army blanket covering what looked to be a large pot.

The minute he said "Hey," she saw his eyes.

Before she could ask "What?" he handed

over the crate — she took it — and he yanked off his mask.

White teeth. "Hi," he said. "I brought chili enough for everybody."

She had not laid eyes on him for more than a month. Apparently, his messin-around status had not been news to anyone at the house except her, and October had decided that this was why he had disappeared. Mary Esther and Albertine, even retired Miss Dumas, had each come to see her privately — to recruit her for a Bible-study group, in Mary Esther's case, and to invite her to the Beau Brummells' December ball, in Albertine's case. The first two had found the time to mention in passing that women have to be careful where they are seen and with whom — a warning from Mary Esther, a word to the wise from the experienced Albertine. Miss Dumas, however, got right to the point. "I hear you've been out with Shorty from around here, daughter," she said. "Everybody knows he's married. Don't let him in your pants."

"I didn't know . . . ," October had said, and had gone on trying to explain, but Miss Dumas waved her silent. "I'm just telling you like any mother would tell any daughter," she said. "Watch out."

And over the weeks October had weighed things. Three friends — Cora, James, and she

73

— had gone out to listen to music one night. Nothing had happened. Nobody had done anything wrong.

"Come in," she said to James, who was still standing in front of her in the schoolroom door. "Children, say good morning to Mr. Wilson. He's Irene's father."

"Good morning, Mr. Wilson" rang out. James nodded hello to the class, grinned at his daughter.

Irene made a self-conscious little wave in bald-faced joy.

October announced, "Mr. Wilson has brought hot lunch for everyone." She set the crate on her desk and discovered paper cups and crackers inside.

James Wilson began shaking and brushing snow everywhere. Unzipping his coat and untying his flaps, he went down the aisle, patted Irene on the head, continued to the back of the room, sat on top of the last desk in the row, and watched.

October's first wish was that she had worn her form-fitting sweater dress today. Then that she had tied back her hair. Then that she wouldn't wish these things. She unpacked the crate and let the children crowd in with their cups for hot chili and crackers. Once all the cups were filled and the children were settled and relishing their lunch, she joined James at the back of the room, sat on a desk right across from him.

"Mr. Pemberton sent me after you-all," he said. "Said Cora called."

"Oh," October said. "You mean you're taking us home?"

"I was coming anyway," he said. "To get Irene, I mean. He called and I told him I'd bring you-all, too."

"Can we all fit into your truck?" October asked him. He said sure, and as he pointed out the versatility of trucks, she watched his mouth, his hands, the nervous way he scoured his thighs with his hands. Rough hands. Lotion. She looked at her smooth hands.

He cleared his throat. "How about this weather?" he said. "Took a storm to get us talking again."

What did he mean "talking"? He was the one who'd disappeared.

"No hard feelings?" he asked.

She shook her head, no. They were quiet. She got up nerve enough to say, "If you had just said everything up front . . ."

"You aren't telling me anything I don't know," he said. "I just couldn't get it out — we never got to the time when I could tell you. God's truth, I wanted to."

"Well, now the air is clear," October said.

She looked at him and a smile spread right out of her face.

"What I said was true, too," he said. "Things just weren't — aren't — doing nothing between Pearl and me."

"Pearl."

"Yeah, my wife. I was wrong to press you. What can I say — I went over the line."

October nodded, sat on her hands. She remembered her orange and the boiled egg in her desk. Should she go get it, share it?

"Don't you want some chili?" she asked him.

"Nah," he said, shaking his head. "I ate before I came."

"I think I'll get my lunch," she said. "Never can tell what will happen in a storm, and I didn't eat breakfast."

"Sure," he said.

She put one foot in front of the other and walked up the aisle to her desk, backside burning where she was sure James's eyes were glued. Once she saw the crumpled sack lunch, she had second thoughts. And then remembered the nice plate — real china — she had used for Cora's birthday cake. She unwrapped it in the bottom drawer and assembled her orange, her boiled egg, and her paper napkin. Done. And then she glimpsed her grade book and was doubly pleased.

Fortified with a topic of conversation, she went back to her perch across from James.

She began peeling her orange and steered casually. "Irene has done so well this grade period," she said. "You-all must be so proud. She's a little crackerjack."

"Um-hmm," James said. "But before we talk about Reenie, just for the record I want to say there wasn't nothing 'bout to be happening between you and me anyway." He was grinning, his face full of play, and he shook his head, laughing softly.

"What's funny?" October asked. She offered him half her orange. He shook his head, still chuckling.

"If the truth be told, a man would have to be born with a caul to get next to you," he said.

She smiled understanding-like, but she didn't quite get it. There hadn't been any time for him to know this. "I guess I'm just careful," she said.

" 'Careful' wasn't the half of it," he said, still full of play. "First time I tried to get a kiss, you almost gave me a black eye. Roped me in so nice." And he went into a silly falsetto voice: " 'Nice music, James, sure we can dance,' and then *wham!*" He faked a blow to his cheek.

October laughed. "No, I didn't. You surprised me is all. I wasn't ready. . . ."

"Almost gave me a black eye," James said, laughing.

"You deserved it then," October said, laughing.

"Mean head-tripper," he said, laughing.

"Casanova," she said, laughing.

He reached over and tore a section of her orange right off, squished it into his mouth, laughing. She tossed a whole section into her mouth, laughing. He took the rest from her hand, ate it whole, juice playing around the corners and across his lips. He wiped his mouth with the back of his hand.

Now she was in the spirit of it. "It was you who changed the drinks to rum at Maurice's," she charged, making light.

" 'Scuse me, ma'am, but I didn't think a woman like you could get loose in her boots," he said.

"That's when I should have called the police," she said.

"Not true," he said. "I wasn't whippin no game on you. But you didn't lose no points. There is nothing worse than a woman snoring just when you're trying to talk serious trash," he said. Funny.

She sat smiling to herself, quietly nodding, remembering, knowing that he remembered, too. Glad to be laughing. Glad he had been honest.

"Guess we'd better load up," he said, and he picked up his hunting cap off the desk. Stuffed inside it, something red.

"I bought these for Reenie," he said. A pair of red earmuffs. "Could we talk sometime?" he said. "Me and you?"

October hunched her shoulders, shook her head. "I don't know," she said. "It might not be a good idea."

"Friends, I mean. Just friends. It'll be on the up-and-up, not on the sly."

"I have to give you your records," she said. "You could come by to get them. That's talking," she added. Proud.

"Those are yours," he said. "I don't really want them back. Let's just say I owe you, so keep the records."

She smiled, but she didn't answer, because she couldn't think of the right thing to say. Things felt right. Fate had brought them back together in a good way. She didn't want to risk spoiling or sparking whatever was between them.

At that wrong moment, Cora peered through the window of the classroom door.

October fairly leaped off the desk and straightened her dress. "Time to get started, I guess," she said. And louder, "Children, finish up your lunch and line up for the water fountain and the lavatory. Whoever needs a ride will go with Irene's father in his truck. Miss Olfield will call your parents to let them know."

She went to the door. "What's up?" she asked Cora.

"What is James Wilson doing here?" Cora asked.

"Mr. Pemberton sent him," October said. "He said you called and he was coming anyway to get his daughter. He's taking everybody."

Once October had blurted out the sad facts of James's life that ugly Sunday morning, Cora had boiled over with her didn't-I-tell-you-men-are-dogs speech. But then a month later, Ed had come through in the best of all possible ways and Cora had forgiven all men. By then, October had shed her own shame and convinced Cora that James had always been careful not to go too far. He had invited Cora to chaperone them, hadn't he? He had told the truth, albeit late.

"Okay," Cora said, "but how is he going to get all of us into that truck?"

October didn't know that, either, but if anyone could, James Wilson could.

Later, out in the knee-deep snow with needles of sleet stinging their faces, four women and four children stood waiting for James Wilson to explain how they must shrivel up to fit into the cab of a panel truck.

Over the wind's whistle, James yelled, "I thought you two ladies" — and he pointed to Albertine and Mary Esther — "could ride back here." He jumped up onto the bed of the truck, stripped back a large tarpaulin and dumped off mounds of snow. Underneath, October could see he had rigged a huge chest as a seat.

"You can sit on the tool chest," James yelled. "And cover like this."

He had somehow hooked the tarp to the back of the truck's cab so that it created a little covered shed where they could ride.

Albertine shook her head and clutched her coat closed, snow and sleet flying into her mouth. "We'll freeze to death back here," she yelled.

Mary Esther, face scrunched against pelting ice, yelled to Albertine, "Where is Norman? Can't he come and get us?"

James yelled, motioning to his daughter, "Reenie, you and the kids get in." Then, "What are y'all gonna do?" to Albertine and Mary Esther.

The wind screamed. Cora grabbed October's arm. "Me and October can ride back here. Let's just go."

It wasn't what October wanted, but she went along. Albertine and Mary Esther climbed into the cab, each taking a child onto her lap. Irene got behind the wheel with a classmate at her side. No room yet for the driver. James helped Cora and October up onto the bed of his truck, and as he sat them down, he said to October, "Don't worry, I'll get you home safe," like he was taking special care of her. He covered her and Cora over with a blanket, told them that if anything went wrong they were to knock on the window of the cab. And then he pulled the tent-like tarp over them and hooked it. Instantly, October could see herself and Cora at an outpost, transported back to the foreign land of childhood where, at any given moment, everything can be make-believe.

James climbed into the driver's side and through the tiny window, October watched him — gentle as ever — take his daughter onto his lap, whisper into the red earmuffs, probably telling her not to worry, he would get her home. And he did.

After that, she saw him all the time, mostly when she was going to school. Blue skies could glare with burning cold, and clouds could deliver payloads of anything frozen, but James Wilson came by and got her to school. Magical slices of time to October, even with Cora ho-humming and complaining that next trip up, Ed should leave her the car. Slices too thin for mischief, too thick to be casual. Minutes between home and school. And since he seldom plied his trade in bad weather, James came to school on Parents' Day. Flipped through Irene's tablets. Ate peanuts and mints with the other parents. Watched her. Smiled.

He volunteered to make another crate-bench for the reading modules. Just a parent helping out. On delivery day, he stayed late and drove October home. He volunteered to go with the class on the next field trip, whenever and wherever it was.

For a change, Miss Olfield had suggested Armour's Packing House as a possible field trip. Up until then, the children visited the Nelson Art Gallery and the Manor Bakery each year with little enthusiasm, and October could see why. When she was their age, her aunts had made a tradition of taking her and Vergie to see Chillicothe's claim to archeological fame: the Mounds. According to her aunts, children needed to develop an appreciation for preserving the buried past. But to an eight-year-old there was nothing exciting about looking at prehistoric burial grounds.

For field trips that involved places not yet on the Board-approved list, it was customary for the teachers to make a preliminary, check-out jaunt, then submit a written proposal to the Board for putting the site on the list. October volunteered to make the Saturday visit and write the proposal, mostly because Cora had reminded her of her newest-teacher status. But October agreed with Miss Olfield that the visit was a good idea. The children would probably be excited to see how bacon got sliced, how lunchmeat was made.

Cora, too, was going, along with another teacher, Lottie Palmer. After the fiasco of Cora riding through a blizzard on a truck bed, Ed had left her the car. She would drive them.

Their guide — a man Mr. Pemberton's age, with Mr. Pemberton's shuffle — met them at the front door of the plant and assured them that the slaughter would be humane, efficient. Said the cattle were first rested, then watered, inspected, confined, then stunned and sacrificed. The whole process took place in one wing, and if they decided that it would be too much for the children, they could omit that part of the tour. Fine.

Once inside the plant, where hickory smoke took over, the cattle stench that fouled the air throughout the city turned into only the faintest whiff of dung. "Distribution" had men and women in dark blue jumpers on both sides of a wide assembly belt, and bins choked with slabs of bacon ready for machine-slicing and moving on a conveyor to be wrapped and packed at a station beyond.

At "Processing," streak-o'-lean, gristle, strange-looking "trimmings" were tossed into grinders to be seasoned. Wheelbarrows full of gruel the colorless beige of animal skin stood waiting to be shoveled into a funnel-shaped contraption that resembled a small cement mixer. Their guide showed them the tub of red food-coloring pills. Then, with a thump, pink gruel shot out of one side of the mixer into a long tube of cellophane. The mixer whined, forcing the stuff to the very end of the cellophane; then, *whump, whump, whump,* it was stapled into loaves of baloney, ready for slicing. Anybody want a sample of sandwich meat? Everybody said no.

At "Cutting," headless carcasses hung by the front hooves. Red flesh, trimmed in pink fat and with deep cavities, swayed. Quarter-carcasses lay stacked on tables. This was meat now, so many roasts to be cut, T-bone steaks coming into view, filets, short ribs, chops.

And then on to "Slaughtering," a long room with open passageways for entering and leaving. High windows, high ceiling. Men dressed in yellow slickers, yellow thigh boots — firemen, they could be — stationed along the floor, joking, smoking, handling their tools. The guide led the women to a roped-off section to watch.

From somewhere beyond, October could hear thunder, and saw the conveyor belt start up — like an oversize bicycle chain — moving near one wall, high up over the floor. The sight of one brown cow — eyes huge, body hung upside down and coming toward her through the passageway — and she figured out the thunder. A stationary stampede of panicked cattle. And the hum under the thunder? Broken ululations of pinned cows cut off from the herd. Cows being hosed down, Mr. Guide said, though she didn't need him to tell them that. This mewling brown animal being pulleyed along low over the floor was at just the right angle to receive the full blow of the stunner's sledgehammer. A bolt of blood parted the hair on its head, blood trickled from its nose, its mouth drooled red. And still it whined. Stunned now, it surrendered to the conveyor's smooth and steady grind, surrendered to the will of the bleeder, who wielded a bloody knife. One hack at the throat and blood splashed over the floor and over the rubber suit of the bleeder, over his arms, spattering his goggles. Then a wash from a large hose, and another gash, and the crinkle of hide being torn away and the smell . . . Jagged pieces of guts being thrown like rags into a barrel, and the smell . . . the "Look who's here, Punchinella" smell.

"Look who's here, Punchinella little girl," twirling until they are dizzy, and upstairs somebody is mad. Poppa is cussing. Momma is cussing back. "What can you do, Punchinella, Punchinella, What can you do, Punchinella, little girl?" Something falling down is making the ceiling shake. She and Vergie washing dishes, the cricket Vergie smashes with the broom. "We can do it too, Punchinella, Punchinella." Momma is crying, they can hear her. She and Vergie run up the steps and Poppa is standing at the head of the bed and he's got his fish knife in his hand, blood on it. Vergie yells crying, and Poppa runs right over them down the steps. Momma is kneeling beside the bed pulling on her dress, her eyes are closed and she can't hear, can't see the blood all over the bed, on the floor, blood soaking through her filmy dress. It smells like something ripe. She bends more, holding her chest, lays her head down on the bed like she is falling asleep praying —

In the ladies' room Cora splashed cold water on October's face, wet a paper towel and mopped the vomit from her chin. Her clothes were probably ruined, Cora told her.

October leaned against the cold tile of the wall, quaking, crying. For all these years, how could she not have remembered the smell of blood?

That evening she wasn't able to sit still. *Killed* now took on real meaning. She cut a wrong seam, paced until Mrs. Pemberton tapped on the ceiling with the broom. Who could possibly fathom what it was like? A *killing*. No wonder Aunt Frances had always come down on her and Vergie if they so much as mentioned Cleveland, or their father's name, or even their most tender memories of Carrie Cooper Brown.

She needed to talk to someone. Unless she wanted to blab it to the whole world, she would have to use some telephone other than the one in the downstairs hallway. Cora, of course, had some inkling. October had made no secret of the fact that both her parents were dead, and once, when Cora had asked how they died, October had said that her mother had died suddenly and her father had died in jail. That had been close enough. After the episode at the packing house, Cora might fill in the blanks. But she wanted to talk first to someone even closer.

That night October stole out of Pemberton House to Manny's Drug Store, four blocks away. With a handful of dimes she dialed long distance on his pay phone. She hadn't known what she would say — only that she wanted Vergie to answer.

"Hello." It was her Aunt Frances.

"Hi, Auntie," October said.

"It's Saturday — what's wrong, honey?"

"I don't know," she said. "I just wanted to hear you-all's voice, I guess." And she ventured, "Is Vergie home?"

"Sure, she's here, what's the matter?"

"Nothing, Auntie. I wanted to say hi to everybody. Where's Aunt Maude?"

"Well, hi yourself. We just got back from the progressive dinner at church. You talk about good cooking — we had the best. Went to five places — Miss Hargraves, you remember her? Miss Foster . . ."

October had to listen first, and finally her aunt Frances put her aunt Maude on the phone, and then finally Vergie.

"Hi," Vergie said. "What are you doing calling us on a Saturday night — gettin lonesome?"

"Hi, Verge," October said. "Something happened today."

"What?"

"Is Auntie listening?"

"Chile, *Amos 'N Andy* is on the radio. Auntie can't hear a thing."

October began spelling out the details of the packing-house tour. When she got to the part where blood spilled, she started to cry.

"Oh," Vergie breathed. She waited until October got quiet again. "I'll bet I know what happened," she said softly. "You remembered Momma."

"Yeah," October whispered. "I remembered all of it."

"It happened a long time ago," Vergie said. "There wasn't anything you and I could do about it. We were little girls. That's what Auntie was always trying to tell us."

"He just *killed* her," October said. "I don't think I really understood that until today."

"Oh," Vergie said. "Yeah, he did. But he got what he deserved. He went to hell."

"I don't see how I could have not known that," October said.

"That he died in jail?"

"No, just how awful it was — the knife and all."

"Um-umm, girl. Don't think about it. Let it go. Remember what Auntie always said — things come to pass and then they're over. It's been over."

"Okay," October said. "I guess I just wanted to know if you remembered, too."

"I don't think about that part, but it doesn't mean that I can forget it. I was there. Me and you. As long as I live, I'll never forget that."

Word got around. A few people thought it

was funny, the sickening-at-the-sight-of-blood episode. At any rate, October would not be recommending a field trip to the packing house, and James Wilson would have to wait. A day or so later he came by school, and offered October a ride home.

Once she was inside the truck, he told her he had something to show her, that it would only take a few minutes. He turned away from the usual route and drove out to the highway. Patches of snow glistened in the last sunlight, water ran in the gullies. A few miles outside the city limits he turned into a new housing development where work had been halted because of the weather and pulled over to one of the houses that was nearly finished.

"I put in all this," he said. Foundation, gate stones, ornate retaining wall — he had done it all. "Over there, too," he said, pointing across the street. "That's mine. It's my real work, what I really like doing." He showed her where he had worked slate into shingles around a small fountain at the center of a little park, showed her the flagstone he'd made into a garden walkway to be.

Parked and watching the sun sink, James remembered what he'd heard.

"Hey," he said, "I heard you fainted the other day at the packing house. What happened?"

"I didn't faint," she told him. "I got sick. I hate the smell of blood." The cab of the truck was cooler, now, and she buttoned her coat again.

"I saw a lot of blood and guts in the war; I don't know whether it bothered me or not. I do know something changed."

He told her about flying in planes and sailing on ships to jungles, places he hadn't even known existed.

"There was something about being cut off from everything. . . . Anyway, when I got back stateside, I knew I needed to get my bearings some kind of way. It was like I couldn't feel right, couldn't be my old self. The day I got out of the Army, we were in Norfolk, Virginia. They sent us to Oklahoma, then to Fort Riley. Eighty miles from here. Almost home. But what did I do? I got on a bus in Fort Riley and went to Sacramento, California — as far as the bus would carry me. Sacramento. I guess I couldn't come home, like it was this little-bitty corner where I was supposed to fit. I went to San Francisco and to Los Angeles. San Diego. I would stand down right next to the water and look at that ocean, that Pacific Ocean, and try to feel the way I had felt in the jungle. The same ocean was all around me in the jungle, but I wasn't the same. It wasn't the war so much as finding out that you can be one way and never know the other ways you are."

October kept quiet, pressed her gloves in her lap until he asked, "You know what I mean?"

She nodded, understanding that something had happened to him, something that words couldn't capture. Some things just couldn't be explained.

"Anyway, I stayed away from home a whole month," he told her. "Pearl never knew what was wrong. I couldn't tell her. Hell, I couldn't understand it myself. Still don't."

He breathed deeply and took her hand.

"I'd better get out of here — it's probably six by now," she said.

He drove her home and squeezed her hand as they drove up to the front of Pemberton House. "Thanks," he said.

And so this was to be their haunt. The Estates, out of building season. Every so often James would appear and drive her to school or home, and they would park and talk. He told October once that he and his wife never got used to each other after he came back.

But he didn't low-rate his wife. October was glad of that. He didn't talk bad about her. Just said they fussed and fought about every little thing. That they couldn't hold a conversation without getting angry. Things like that.

For October, it was simple. All that she knew about marriage was that people should love each other or leave each other alone. For right now, James needed someone to talk to. Nothing more. They had a lot in common, or at least they could talk to each other forever and not get tired. She told him about growing up with her aunts, that her parents were dead, but not how they died. Talked about slaving away at Emporia State, having to live with five different Negro families. About The Boy her senior year, and getting her first job.

October had gotten to know James. She liked him. He needed someone to talk to. He never touched her or talked about touching her. If she thought about the two times he had kissed her, they were only memories that meant nothing. And wasn't it natural to wonder what he really thought of her?

Natural until the day he turned to her and said, "Look, I know I'm wrong for thinking this, let alone saying it. All these days we've been together . . . I can't help it. You've got to know how it makes me feel."

Her heart jumped. He felt like she felt. Her heart stopped. Nothing had happened, nothing could happen. Just knowing he felt for her was enough. Had to be. There was the line they couldn't cross.

"Don't say any more, James," she said.

"Damn," he said. "You make it hard."

She took his rough hand in her smooth one. "There's nothing we can do," she said.

All through the Christmas holidays she thought about him, though she didn't dare think *dilemma*. He was married. *Infatuation* came nowhere close. And she tried to let it go, only to come back to the two kisses, the look on his face when he said thanks, his profile, his bowl of pearly teeth, the way his pants might ride his hips in the summertime.

Back at school toward the end of January, he telephoned her. A first. A serious first. And he got quickly to the point.

"Tomorrow after school I want you to go someplace with me. Don't worry. You can trust me. I won't let you down."

What could she say, but okay?

CHAPTER 6

A new blue shirt, the spring sun in February, ice floes on the river they were crossing, the rows of nice duplexes in Missouri where nobody knew or cared what she was doing, a touching, child-built snowman in the vacant lot next to the apartment house where James stopped the truck — October noticed signs.

"Don't say anything," he said. "Just follow me."

She was out of the truck and climbing three flights of stairs before she thought of James's friend School Boy, who had said he lived in Missouri. James was using a key that fit the first time, pushing open the door before she got a little shaky thinking this could be a mistake.

"Go ahead in," he said. And she did, to an altogether different style of pretty: studio-couch geometry in blue and green, triangular tables with spread-angle legs, papyrus lampshades, oval ashtrays.

"Who lives here?" October asked.

"You like it?"

"Um-hmm," she said, "but whose is it?"

"Mine," he said. "Mostly mine, anyway," he admitted.

She would get details later, but for now she had trouble believing what he was saying. "When did all this happen?"

"Last weekend," James said. He closed the door and peeled her out of her coat. "Pearl and me split up," he said casually, folding her coat and straightening the rug under the coffee table.

This had to be no joke, no kidding, no by-the-way maybe. She took her coat back.

"What are you talking about?" Looking directly into his eyes.

"Well," he said, walking around in a little circle, scratching the back of his neck. "I guess it was really same-ol'-same-ol'. We can't make it — we've been knowing that. One of us had to do something and she sure couldn't, so I did." He took in a resigned breath.

"You mean . . ." She was catching on.

"Yep," he said. He was in front of her again, shrugging. "It's been coming for so long it was just a matter of me moving my clothes."

"What about Irene?" she said — why was she saying this? "I wouldn't want to hurt anybody. . . ."

"Whoa," James said. He took her coat

again. "Nobody is crying, nobody is having a fit. This doesn't have anything to do with you — I told you, it's been coming for a long time."

"It's just a big surprise," she said. A real surprise.

"You thought I didn't have the guts. It's *been* over — it was time, that's all."

October looked around. Back in the kitchen she could see a little dinette, no curtains, but a teakettle on the stove.

"Put down your purse and stay awhile," he said. "I've got soda pop and Bacardi, what do you say?"

Before she could turn her frown brighter, he said, "Okay — pop, then," and went to the kitchen.

What was that he had said once, about being one way and not knowing the other you? How quickly things change.

She called after him, "What did you mean, almost yours?"

He yelled back, "It's School Boy's place, but now I'm paying half the rent. The couch is mine, too. Wait till I show you the rest."

October sat on the studio couch and put her purse on the triangle. His place. She added up details to see if they pointed in the right direction. James had left his wife. He had gotten himself half a nice place. Finally decided to move on. People don't buy furniture unless they plan to keep it. He had left not because of her. No. But because his marriage didn't work out. He was decent, he had never said anything ugly about his wife. He was honest, he had never lied about what was going on.

It counted that she had never pressed him. Instead, she had been a patient friend, and cautious at the same time. They had gotten to know each other. Very well.

"Okay, a drop of Bacardi!" she yelled to him.

James came back clinking two glasses. "Don't worry, School's working swing shift. He won't be here until tomorrow morning, if he comes then. He stays over to his woman's house most of the time."

October wasn't worried. If all this was true, she didn't care who knew what. How soon things change. One day a person is afraid to dream, and the next day she is folding dreams neatly in a hope chest.

He sat down beside her. "October, you know how long I've been waiting for this day to come?" he said. "Here's to you and me."

She sipped.

"Well, what do you think?" he asked.

She felt like laughing. "I can't believe it," she said. Her face felt hot. He pushed back her crinkled hair, put down his glass, and kissed her cheek. "This spot is mine," he said, then seemed to remember something and picked up his drink again.

"I've got steaks, I've got stuff for spaghetti, fruit cocktail — what do you want?"

She wanted to touch him. "Nothing," she said. She had a clear sense that there was a deep place she wanted to get to, and that she didn't know the way. Maybe true love. Because she was convinced that his leaving his wife meant that he wanted to go there with her, she was sure that together, they would find the way. She took his drink from his hand, set them both on the table, placed his hands on her waist, took his stubbled face in her hands, and bussed his mouth lightly, hoping that it would be enough for him to take the lead.

In his bedroom she sensed him slowing his hands as he undressed her, and it excited her. Once he touched her nakedness, he went wild, couldn't slow down. That excited her, too. He kissed her closed eyes, slipped inside her with sweet pain, and filled her up.

Now that they were lovers, October saw no need to be discreet. James and I, James and I, she told the world. She set aside Wednesday nights and weekends — Saturday and Sunday

— as theirs, overtown, where they seldom saw people they knew. But why hide? October wanted to show off her newfound love to people who could appreciate it.

Cora could not appreciate it. "A man who leaves his wife for another woman will leave the other woman, too," she told October.

Cora was a wife. A wife with a husband two hundred miles away. October gave up on convincing her that the other woman was not always to blame. Enough that Cora wished her well. Enough that Cora said, "We'll see."

And when Mrs. Pemberton, too, put in a word about what kind of women lived in her house, making it clear that loose women didn't, October decided that discretion had some merit. What went on between her and James wasn't anybody's business.

She got busy introducing herself anew to James, discovered the unflawed look of Pan-Cake makeup. Straightened her hair even though, in the sweat of lovemaking, it went back. Spent all her free time sewing dresses to delight him whenever his eyes wandered in her direction. She was Toomer's cotton flower: *Brown eyes that loved without a trace of fear/Beauty so sudden for that time of year.*

And she saw that James, too, had gotten busy being new: new shirts (one with cuff links), new pants without pleats (she cuffed them for him), show-off meals he could cook, of chicken livers and tuna surprise, no work clothes, new haircut.

Saturday nights, October ran the bath and bathed him. They did it in the bathtub. He hid little presents in her shoes, pockets, cereal bowls. She learned to keep quiet when he complained about the money that he didn't have, or worried aloud about his daughter. Patience is a virtue. October did her part, favoring Irene in little ways at school.

One morning, a couple of months into their special Sundays, October noticed that although James was chattering about a football game that he wished he could listen to, he had the daydreaming look on his face again, and hadn't bothered to finish his pancakes.

Because she was learning to love him, she poked around the edges. "Want to see what's playing at the Lincoln? We could go to the three o'clock show."

"Nah," he said. "There's something I need to do."

And because her love was fearless, she tuned in to every nuance and understood that the "something" involved his old life. She could figure out where he was going and didn't mind. She just wanted to know why.

"I need to spend some time with Irene," he said.

What better thing? She thought how comfortable she herself would be with James and Irene on a Sunday afternoon. Someday.

"I need to do some things around the house while I'm there," he said.

Made sense. It was what he did. Build things, fix them.

She told him, "Guess I'll just listen to your football game. When do you think you'll be back?"

He didn't know. "You can stay here if you want, but it'll take a few hours." He hesitated. "Or I could drop you by the house."

She couldn't fathom saying good-bye to Sunday with him when it wasn't even noon yet. She told him she would wait, and he said okay. No, she changed her mind. Late Sunday afternoon was the usual time School Boy came to exchange dirty laundry for clean, check his mail and check on the state of James's relationship with her. She didn't want to be there alone when he came.

"I didn't bring any schoolwork with me," she said. "I think I'll go on back to the house."

And when he dropped her off she said, "I'm missing you already," surprised by the tears at the back of her throat.

"Me, too," he told her.

The fact that James wasn't constantly talking about divorce didn't trouble her. Obviously they were in love. It would take time to finalize things — time and money. If she were James, she would give her mate time to get used to the idea — after all, they had Irene to think about. Divorce was inevitable, and from what she could tell, James was making plans. He had dropped hints — this and that about what his buddies said. But she knew James to be honorable. It would take time.

Cora didn't give October too much trouble, because she had been putting all her extra energy into moving to Ed's old apartment (she didn't care what the Board said — they needed more privacy). But whenever October shared woman-to-woman with her, Cora pushed caution.

"You're a mess, girl," she told her. "I would tell you to be careful, but who am I to talk? Everybody deserves to be happy. Maybe you needed this. Maybe he did, too."

When the first wave of nausea hit, October remembered the onions in the potato salad she had eaten the night before, and maybe the fish had been a little tainted. Another wave another time, and she thought the milk had been a little sour. Over the next days she thought, *I need to drink more water in the morning,* and *I need to trade the Colgate for Pepsodent. Eat later. Eat less.* She never thought *blue booties, umbilical, trimester.* On the second week that she had gotten up earlier than anyone else to hog the bathroom with her nervous stomach, it came like a blow. She was pregnant.

Her next thought was not about her condition but what James would say. She worried that he was already too worried over how to get the divorce right, how to handle his daughter. The timing wasn't so good. But on the other hand, they had each other, and that counted for a lot. She remembered him whispering into those red earmuffs. He liked children. And who knew? Maybe a baby coming would speed things up.

When should she tell him? This wasn't a *good* thing, but not a bad thing either. She would tell him on the weekend. She would tell him, he would be upset, or he could just as easily laugh and swing her around.

This was the end of March. How long before she would be showing? She and James would have to do some serious planning. It wasn't written that she had to tell anybody anything yet. Surely she wouldn't be showing before the end of school. Maybe they could marry quietly before the baby came. Probably not. Once she was showing, though, they could at least get a place together. He'd have to get the divorce really soon.

What about her job? Better not to muddy

the teaching waters just yet. Sufficient unto the day is the evil thereof. Something like that.

On a cold Saturday night, they decided to stay in rather than play cards with Ed and Cora — James didn't play bridge anyway. October sat on the couch with his head in her lap, tweezed ingrown hairs from his chin — a once-lovey ritual that, now that she was pregnant, turned her stomach.

"There is something we need to talk about," she said to him.

"Um-hmm," he answered, eyes closed, drowsily allowing himself to be groomed.

"Wake up, honey," she sang. "You have to hear this."

"I'm awake," he said, drowsily, allowing himself to be cajoled.

Her voice couldn't hold the lilt of music and just spat out, "I'm pregnant." She hadn't meant it to sound so bad-news flat.

But James, drowsily allowing himself to be teased, smiled and said, "I don't play with that, baby."

She would have to say it again. She stopped the tweezing, and he moved her hands altogether from his face.

His eyes opened in a startling, dead stare at her. "What?"

"I am," she said.

He sat up and stuck his feet into his house slippers, turned his back. "When did you find out?"

"I haven't talked to a doctor yet, but I know the signs," she told him.

"Then it's not a sure thing, right?" Over his shoulder.

"Well, I'm pretty sure. . . ." she said, and decided that he was telling her he needed concrete facts to know the lay of the land. She couldn't yet give him that.

"I thought I'd see a doctor next week," she said.

James got up and went to the kitchen. She heard him pouring himself a drink. Shaking ice around in the glass, he came back and stood at the end of the couch.

"You haven't had a test, right?"

"No." She felt like he was scolding her. "I wanted to tell you first," she said.

"Nothing to tell, then, is it?"

She wanted to say that she didn't need a test to know this. In a hundred ways her body had convinced her. But he was acting like he didn't believe her.

"Maybe this is just you wishing," he said.

He had never said anything like that to her before. What had she done that he would so suddenly distrust her?

"What are you talking about, James?" she

said. "I'm not wishing for anything."

"You're a smart lady — you figure it out." He went to the closet and took out his peacoat and boots.

When she asked him where he was going, he gave her the proverbial "Cigarettes" with the proverbial sneer, pulled on his boots, and dusted the dust of being bothered off his hands.

She was too dumbfounded to remember what he had said once about how he could be one way at one time and not feel connected to other ways he could be. All she knew was that he was mad at her and it wasn't her fault.

She waited until midnight, and when he didn't return, she went to bed, not to sleep. At first light she heard him come in and let out the studio couch. When she got up later, she made a point of banging around the kitchen until he sat up. She was mad, too.

He sat like a zombie with his elbows on his knees, propping up a heavy head.

She threw out a threat. "I'm going home," she said. When he didn't register anything she said, "Whenever you're ready."

Before she went back to the bedroom to pack her overnight bag, she thought she'd give him time to respond in a kinder way.

He merely hopped awake, sprang into action with pants and shoes and shirt, and in less time than it took her to say, "I don't understand, James," he was jangling his keys.

No one had anything more to say, but now she was really mad. This was no way to treat her. She stuffed her things into her bag and followed him out to the cold cab of his truck.

On the Sunday-morning streets, people were bundled against the wind but had on their glorious hats and heels anyway — churchgoing families, oblivious of the fact that not everybody lived the same kind of life.

If he wouldn't talk in the truck, she wouldn't either. She wouldn't look at him. She felt him glancing sideways at her.

Finally he said, "I can't handle this, October. You know my situation. I can't handle it."

She was relieved. Last night had been a shock to him, and he was coming around. His face already had a shadow.

"James, I know it's a shock," she said. "We've got plenty of time to work things out." And she gave him a bone. "*If* I am pregnant, I'm not too far along. It'll be months before I'm showing."

"Go to the doctor, okay?" he said.

"I will," she promised, though she knew already what the news would be. "I'll go right away."

They saw each other only once in the next week. She went to the doctor and waited five days for the predictable results.

All over again, James was impossible to talk to.

"I can't handle this" was all he could think to say. Couldn't think of anything reassuring. Didn't seem to remember that they were in this together.

In the truck going home one more Sunday morning (Sunday afternoons he had to spend time with his daughter), she asked him, "What about me?," meaning that he should consider her feelings, too. "What do you want me to do?" she asked him.

He was several steps ahead of her. "Whatever you have to do," he said, " 'cause I can't handle it."

They didn't speak for another week, during which time October charted a course. James would have to get a divorce and it would have to be the first thing. It could be friendly, but she would insist. She would teach until the end of the year; meanwhile they could be looking for an apartment together in Missouri. The baby would come before January, which meant that she wouldn't have to miss but one semester.

James seemed to be paralyzed, and she could fix that. On Saturday she took a bus to his place. She stopped to pick up cut flowers, two steaks, and hand-packed ice cream. She knew he'd be at home, and she hoped he'd smile when he saw her.

She nearly cried when he did open the door and smile. "Come on in," he said. "I hoped it would be you."

The ways he could be. He took her coat and the bag of groceries. "You should let me cook tonight," he said.

He put on a stack of LPs and in the kitchen set burners blazing and dishes and skillets rattling. She sipped ginger ale and danced with herself. He brought her a batter-fried mushroom on waxed paper to try. Ways he could be. When the food was ready, they stuffed their faces and each other's, laughed themselves silly. That night, when he held her, anyone would have thought he was afraid, so careful was his touch.

During that week apart, she had not been the only one to use her head. James unfolded his plan the next morning while they took turns in the bathroom. For a few weeks, he would take on extra jobs, make extra money. He would never deny support to a child of his, but he was in no position to handle another responsibility, and wouldn't be for a while. Maybe someday, but not now.

"Think of the mess," he said, standing in the bathroom door with his towel. "I'm married. You're trying to teach school. It'll never work. In a couple of weeks, I'll have some money I can give you."

He seemed convinced that this was the perfect answer, that saying it made it so.

What had last night been about? She was still sitting in the bed, waiting for her turn in the bathroom. "Are you saying that I shouldn't have the baby?"

He came and sat beside her, covered her hands with his.

"October, baby, think about what's happening. I don't know what Pearl and me are gonna do. You've got a good job, a good reputation . . ."

Now, all of a sudden, he was confused about him and Pearl?

"What about us?" she asked.

Too automatically, he squeezed her hands, and it made her snatch away from him.

"You know how I feel about you," he said. "I always will. But this is a mess that doesn't have to happen unless you want it to. I'm making a big leap now, thinking that you didn't set out to make a mess, right? Is this what you want?"

It felt like an actual blow, nearly took her breath away. What she wanted was the life she had thought they were building. What she wanted was to be together, working out things together, helping him with his daughter —

that was what she wanted.

She didn't see that that day would turn out to be their last Sunday together. On Wednesday he phoned to say that he would come by, and although she packed her overnight bag, they merely rode four blocks to Manny's for a magazine. He gave her bills folded to a wad. She accepted the money without protest because she could tell that he was relieved. On the other hand, assuming she had six or seven months, things could change.

"This is the best way," he said, and by the way, he needed to be alone some.

On the weekend he said that he would be working every night, and the following week he delivered more cash. A ride to Manny's, a bottle of Vess Cola in the truck.

"Let me know if it's not enough," he said. She told him it was all she needed.

By then she saw that he couldn't meet her eyes, and some part of her recognized that she just might possibly be on her way down a slope more stony than she wanted to think about, and that she might hurt a lot before she got to level ground again. Next week he phoned again. He wouldn't be by. No face-to-face. He'd just as well tell her on the telephone that his wife needed him, that he couldn't leave his family stranded like that. That was it.

CHAPTER 7

Talk about a fall from grace.

No one would ever accuse her of being a lackadaisical woman, though she did consider that James may have thought she was and that if he did, he had another thought coming. To her way of thinking, this new set of circumstances gave them more reason to be one, more reason for two minds to dream one dream. She loved him, and the one thing she knew for sure about love she had carried around in a fold of memory since high school and all through college: *Love is not love / Which alters when it alteration finds, / Or bends with the remover to remove.* She loved him.

It would take a long, long time to grow a baby, and that would give her a long, long time to make things right. James's first impulse had been to run, but she could live with that. Hadn't he bought a roomful of permanent furniture? Didn't he say he loved her that last night, before she refused to get rid of the baby? His love for her hadn't vanished, just ducked underground when things started moving too fast.

No, she was pretty sure that he would never

go back to fussing and fighting with a woman he didn't love. He was just giving himself squirming room.

She went once to see him. Before she got to the door of the apartment, she could hear the hi-fi, and she had to knock four times to get School to stick his head out and put a stop to somebody messing up his love life. "Look, baby," he said. "Me and my lady don't want to be disturbed. You've got to get a grip. The man is married. That wasn't no big surprise. So he took a little recess from his wife, okay? He was only out here a couple of months. Go ahead and get yourself somebody and forget him. He's gone. Next time call before you come."

James didn't call. Another week of her patience and her crackers-until-noon diet, and she began to wish Cora still lived across the hall. She needed some advice. James was wearing a hole in her confidence. Sharp rocks in the stony slope. What if?

Cora's advice was simple. "You just have to pretend that he died."

But wasn't Cora, herself, planning to move to St. Louis? Could *Cora* ever pretend that Ed had died? October didn't think so.

"Listen, girl, you're in trouble," Cora told her. "He isn't worth it. Your job now is to figure out what you want to do about the baby."

After a while, Cora admitted that breaking up was hard, and in the same breath offered that she knew a certain "doctor." But if October needed a way to be sure James would return, the baby was it. She told Cora she'd think about it, but deep down she didn't budge. What if a child — probably a son — turned out to mean everything to James? For the time being, she hid herself upstairs in Pemberton House and waited.

And then on down the slope. Mrs. Pemberton may not have known every jot and tittle, but she let it be known that she had heard gossip and that October's name had been at the root of it. Outrageous scandal numbered October's days at Pemberton House.

And Irene Wilson's attitude just might number her teaching days. Irene Wilson, her little crackerjack, turned belligerent. *Conniving* wouldn't have been too strong a word. One of the pupils claimed that October had lost her temper as she escorted him down the hall to the office and had struck him in the face. A pure lie. But when the principal asked the class, Irene had sworn that she had seen it happen. Said that she had gotten out of her seat and watched from the doorway. How could Irene know anything about her and James? October couldn't answer that question, but anyone could recognize revenge.

The code against corporal punishment automatically put her in trouble.

And on down. Mrs. Pemberton served notice: October would have to move out at the end of April, one month before the end of school. No James. The Jacksons said they'd take her in. Her clothes were getting tight. James didn't call. A wait-and-see paralysis set in.

October's room at the Jacksons' place amounted to what had once been a pantry off the kitchen, with a door, a cot, and a tiny window high up. For the last six weeks of the term, just like mentor-and-cadet, Cora stayed at October's elbow throughout the school day, brought her chipped ice at recess, sat with her through the final maddening minutes of closing down a year.

October waited, would wait, but dignity was now out of the question. She made no plans beyond the final day of school and then to sleep until James came to end the nightmare. He had to come. It was her only way out.

Because October couldn't stand the smell of blood in the meat Mrs. Jackson cooked, couldn't stomach the consistency of mashed potatoes or any cereal, and because green vegetables left a coating on her tongue, she picked at anything set before her. Cora nagged her about eating. "Call James and tell him," October said to Cora's worry.

October couldn't stand bindings, either — waistbands, buttoned sleeves, elastic in her panties, hooked bras, scarves that tied up her hair — couldn't stand the feeling of being smothered. Her bathrobe felt right. "Do you think James knows I'm showing?" she asked Cora.

One dismal afternoon as a fly buzzed and dived around October's head on the pillow, she tried to distract herself with a book. Someone rang the doorbell and she held her breath. Women's voices. No James. Mrs. Jackson was having company — someone, people, were moving through the house. She heard them nearing her door and sat up.

In less than a shuffle, without warning, the door flew open and the shock of her aunt Frances's large frame in the doorway made her lightheaded. Hand on hip, her aunt declared, "October, girl, now you know *better* than this."

Then she saw her aunt Maude behind Aunt Frances, already wiping tears. Her aunt Maude pushed into the little room.

"Chile, look at you," she said. "You know we don't live like this."

And then Vergie, looking grand as Marian Anderson, slipped past her aunts and stood over October. She touched her sister's shoulder and told her, "We're taking you home. Thank the Lord your friend Cora called us. You've got *people*, October. Come on, now, get up."

In Chillicothe, when Vergie had married Gene and taken over two of the upstairs rooms, the house had shrunk. To spare, now, there was only the made-over side porch that Gene had enclosed with four windows and a carpeted floor. Un-cheery. October's aunts gave it to her, and she revived the antiquated idea of confinement, stayed out of their way. Better not to have everybody condemning her for what they didn't understand.

Not that anybody in the house made a peep about the how and the why of the man who had brought her to this. No one asked or ventured to guess if she had plans or what her dreams might be. Whenever she sat with October or washed and braided her hair, Vergie talked mostly about their small world — Mrs. Hopp next door and the rotten nephew who was stealing all Mrs. Hopp's money. Or she explained her frustration about Gene having a backbreaking loading-dock job at Meade's paper mill — "They know he's too old to be lifting all that stuff" — when Aunt Frances had a place in Mrs. Meade's will for her six years of private duty. "It just doesn't make sense," Vergie said. "They know we're all related. Seems like they'd let Gene work somewhere else." Never anything about what might have happened in Kansas. Nothing about what was coming.

To give herself something to do until James came back to himself and got around to asking Cora about her, October thought that she might sew. She had catalogues of patterns, pictures that Aunt Frances and Vergie were happy to match at the fabric store. It seemed natural to sew what she knew — dresses, suits, skirts for herself.

"I don't know who you're sewing for," Aunt Frances said one day after work. "It isn't going to fit anybody around here."

October hunched her shoulders. "It keeps me busy," she said. But it didn't matter that she couldn't wear them now; sewing satisfied something. She could finish a piece every three or four days and not remember whole afternoons. And the times when she wasn't bent over a pattern or guiding a seam under the thundering Singer needle, she wrote letters in her head. To James.

She broke down and called him long distance one night. Just to hear his voice. And who knows, she thought; depending on how he sounded, she might venture to tell him that she still had all of his money. That she hadn't seen the "doctor" after all. That she could come back anytime he wanted. She rehearsed her first few lines and dialed.

"Hello, James," she said when he answered. "It's October. I just called to say hi and see how you're doing."

"Okay," he said, sounding to her like he had turned a somersault and surprised himself by landing on his feet.

"How are you?" he asked. Now here was the question. What would she tell him? What did he think, and what did he know for sure? She fished.

"I'm fine, really. A little tired is all."

"Are you working?" he asked. And she said no, but sewing a lot. Would he think, *Maternity clothes?*

"Where are you?" he asked, as she hoped he would.

"I'm in Ohio with my aunts," she said.

"You aren't . . . you know . . . sick or anything, are you?"

"No," she said. "I'm fine."

"You sound fine," he said. "Like your old self."

So he had been counting on her being her *old self.* "Yes," she said.

"Look," he said. "I don't mind saying hi, I mean, I'm glad to know everything came out all right, but do you think it's a good idea to call me?"

Too much. She had called him at his house. Suddenly she was nerves and stammers just remembering that she had flirted with the idea of telling him the truth.

"I just wanted to say hi," she said.

"I know," he said, "but I can't be talking . . . you know . . . to you on the phone. It wouldn't be right, you know?"

"Okay," she said.

"You were always decent," he said. "I never met your aunts, but tell them I said they raised a decent woman."

She hung up and went straight to her room. A full moon, heavy and golden, climbed half the sky, getting smaller and smaller as it climbed. When it was a dime-size eye way up, it threw its argentine light over her bed and found her staring back, stunned that there was the chance that James didn't know what she knew about love.

As if it had been a bad idea, she stopped sewing and put away the fabrics. She let tears spill out of her now, all the time, with aunties and Vergie and Gene sitting right there at the dinner table or right out there on the front porch. Having a baby was one thing. But there were worse things. It could be that James had talked so guardedly about his wife not because of decency but because his wife was the woman that he loved.

She wrote two letters, one to the Board of Education, one to Cora. To the Board she explained that she had had a change of address and that she would not be available for the fall term. Family matters, she said. If they saw fit to hire her for January, they could send her contract to her address in Ohio. If not, she would reapply in the winter for the following year, adding that she had loved her job at Stowe, and worrying that either her pregnancy or the children's lie about the hitting incident would destroy her chances. Yet she hoped that no one had said anything to anyone about anything.

To Cora, October sent a sad longing for the classroom days that the two of them had once spent, scraping gum off the floor. She had a single question: What were people saying? She had complaints, too, about being nauseated all the time and craving onions in vinegar. Of James, she said only that she hadn't heard from him.

The first time the baby kicked, October jerked back from the table and held her stomach still against the live something in there. The months were passing. James had been the immediate future she understood. She could not yet fathom it, but she knew that another future was shaping itself.

The baby grew, seemed to influence her whole body to go along with the program. Her hair grew longer, fuller, wilder. Her aunts' eyes were on her as the bittersweet chocolate of her skin turned milkier.

"You're looking mighty spiffy these days," Aunt Frances said. And Aunt Maude backed it up with, "You see, you turned out to be some kind of pretty, didn't you?"

"It's like a religious thing," Vergie said. "This is what happens to a woman — you shine from the inside." Vergie was four years older than October, married to Gene for eight years, with no baby in sight.

When October looked into the mirror, she saw the shine, all right, but it looked more like oil than illumination on her skin. Her nose spread wider above her swollen lips. Once, when Aunt Frances caught her looking at herself in the hallway mirror, she said, "You know you always were so touchy about how you look. Don't worry, you'll get your size back." How could she? She looked like a horse.

She was the vessel; the baby possessed her. It grew by itself, slept, kicked, flaunted its unlimited rights to her blood and bones and left her tired. It didn't need her consent; it willed itself into existence within its own world, pound for pound, inches at a time.

At the end of the summer, Cora finally responded to October's letter. Sure, people gossip, and then they move on to the next piece of news. It was good that October had left. Word was that a few people had been too curious about October's health and her sudden desire to spend the summer in Ohio. And Cora swore that she never breathed a hint. And yes, there had been a report about the corporal punishment incident at the end of the year. Cora couldn't say whether or not it had gone into October's permanent file.

There was no stopping the progress of a determined birth.

Early in November, with winter already turning the sky to ashes, October gave up nighttime altogether and kept the lamps burning in her room all the time. She couldn't rest; the baby kicked and turned and scraped against her insides. And when she lay down to try to sleep, her breath wouldn't come or she felt like she was smothering. Vergie moved Gene's easy chair into October's room so that she could nap some. But it got so bad that somebody needed to promise they would sit watch to be sure she kept breathing or October would refuse to sit in the chair.

She was in the bathroom sitting on the toilet to relieve the gas pains when it began. Her water broke. The doctor, young and new at Ross County General, had told them that her labor would be slow. Aunt Frances had said to ignore him — nobody can ever tell about the first one. And so they rushed. In the Negro ward at the hospital, while her aunts and Vergie and Gene were out of her reach, October lay in the labor room counting the tiles of the walls and the minutes between the vises of contractions. A nurse the color of honey with a record for a voice checked periodically for dilation and smiled and patted but went away every time. "You'll know when it's time," she said.

The clench-and-loosen rhythm went on for another short while. Then a wave crashed pain across her back, and October knew it was time. The nurse had just measured and patted and left, and she thought she might have to call out. The next wave crashing made her forget decorum, and she hollered, "Somebody!"

The nurse came running. Without a trace of condescension, she told her, "I'm here, Miss Brown. It's time for you to sit up. Now put your feet on the floor and stand up."

Trying to hold her back in one piece, October did as she was told.

"Now turn around and sit on the gurney —

I'm going to wheel you in."

She shook out a sheet to cover October, but then said, "Oh, oh," and "Keep breathing real deep, honey."

The head and shoulders split her in two, and then the hard body slid out. As the nurse worked at wiping and swabbing and smacking, October heard the wail. In a minute the young doctor pushed the gurney with her and the baby to the delivery room. Too late. By then a baby boy had already torn his way into her life.

And what did I do? I stood by and held for her and her new baby son.

Delicacy dictated that she carefully consider declaring the name of the father. *Unknown* was the choice she most favored, and since it was strictly up to her, she scribbled *Unknown* on the form. She knew that the actual naming of the Baby would be more than she could manage — a complicated matter — and she had no interest in figuring it all out. She thought maybe if she had had the normal options — a father for him, a grandfather's blessing to pass on, a favorite uncle or movie star, or staunch faith in one of the biblical heroes — a name might come to mind. She decided to wait until she took him home. Maybe then.

She never really got a good look at him, either, until they were at home, and at eight days old he didn't look to her like anyone in particular. Just a baby, brown with a smooth cap of hair, in a bassinet that Vergie had draped with white scalloped eyelet. The first few nights, October slept with the bassinet right up against her bed. But then she began to listen to his breathing, and her vigilance kept her awake. She moved him a few feet away from her bed.

When he cried, she had trouble holding his head and body so that they didn't wobble. He was too small to fit comfortably in the crook of her arm. No worry. If he so much as sneezed or whimpered, Auntie or Vergie would rush in — "Is he all right?" — and pick him up.

And then her milk came down and engorged the glands so that they felt like stones lodged in her breasts and under her arms. They would harden until the Baby was ready to be suckled and she could trade one kind of pain for another. All the lanolin in the world could not toughen her tender nipples for the strong jaws of the Baby.

October was nursing one morning, sitting in Gene's easy chair in the living room, when Vergie came in with two cups of tea. She sat one on the table beside Gene's chair and sat cradling the other in her lap.

"When Auntie gets off today," Vergie said, "I thought we could go out to Sears and look at some baby clothes. He needs a couple more things, don't you think?"

October looked down at the Baby at her breast. His eyes were closed and he was making the slurping noises he always made when he nursed. What was it about a baby that made everybody go soft? And why didn't she go soft holding him? She tried hugging him closer, wanting to feel like his mother but feeling only the clumsy cramp of forcing her arms to work on their own.

He was tensed and his fists were clenched, all of his focus on her nipple. She had dressed him in an undershirt and diaper and wrapped him in a small blanket. At night she or someone else always put him in a nightgown and pulled the drawstring to protect his feet. Those things were simple and conveniently changed whenever he wet his diaper. It had never occurred to her to buy all those other things made for a boy.

But the snow outside was gray, and October couldn't think of being seen at Sears in any of the oversize clothes she had to wear still. She told Vergie, "I'll order him some things from the catalogue. You all can pick them up."

"Good," Vergie said, reaching down under the coffee table for the Sears catalogue. She turned to the baby section and scooted her chair up to October's side.

"Look at these," she said.

October glanced at the pages of baby clothes all looking alike. If the Baby needed coveralls now, and jumpers, she guessed that she should be the one to buy them.

"Sure," she told Vergie. "Let's order him some today on the phone. Why don't we get three or four of each?"

"I think you could start out with just two," Vergie said. "They cost, you know."

October wanted to say that she had enough money, but in fact after paying her own hospital bill she had very little at the bank. "Okay," she said to Vergie, "two."

"Have you been thinking about what to name him?" Vergie asked all of a sudden.

October looked down at the Baby and shook her head. Days before she had been reading *Ebony* and saw the name *Nathaniel* and thought she would just give him that name, or the next name that she came upon. And then the moment passed.

"Me and Aunt Maude were wondering what you thought of David."

"I guess it's all right," October said. The Baby had relaxed his suck and was dozing now. She slipped her nipple back into her nursing bra, slung a diaper over her shoulder, and began burping him. This wasn't the time to worry about a name again, or clothes for that matter. He was only six weeks old.

The Baby let out a big burp, and as October tucked him away in his bassinet, he began to fret. "Let me hold him," Vergie said. "David means 'beloved,' you know." Vergie began rocking him.

October glanced out the window. Outside, the gray of old snow didn't seem to bother neighborhood children, snow-crusted and laughing, sliding down their short terraces on sleds.

"Um-umm, I didn't know that," October said. A name, nothing special. She would get to it soon enough.

Vergie rocked and cooed, "Him don't want us callin' him Baby till him is grown, do you, pumpkins?" She pressed her lips to his forehead. He dozed.

"I know," October said. "I just can't worry about that yet."

"Things happen to people," Vergie said. "I gather from the birth certificate that you won't be getting any help from the father."

October had forgotten the very public fact of that document. She shook her head.

"You know that me and Gene and Aunt

Frances and Aunt Maude will see to it that you never go without — you or the baby."

"I know," October said.

"Like I said, things happen to people, and you just have to keep on going."

"I know," October said.

It was easy for Vergie to say. Vergie hadn't fallen in love with someone who didn't want her. Gene had plucked her from the vine when Vergie was lucky nineteen. Married her. Neither Aunt Frances nor Aunt Maude had ever married, and she couldn't imagine either of them ever falling for a man. What could any of them possibly know about how she felt? Her mother, Carrie, would probably have known something about being down in the dumps, and she probably carried it to her grave. Carrie would know.

After a few weeks of salves and compresses, a manual pump and sugar water, it became clear to October that she could not produce sufficient milk. She was secretly relieved to move on to bottle feeding, where everyone could participate. The Baby did fine on his own, eating, sleeping, pooping.

Next it was Aunt Frances's turn. October had begun pulling out fabric again and sewing in her room. Often she kept the bassinet nearby, but since Vergie was at home all day, October sometimes let the Baby enjoy sunlight in the living room with Vergie.

Aunt Frances had worked a private-duty swing shift the evening before and wouldn't be going back to the hospital until the afternoon that day. Bent over the Singer in her room, October sensed Auntie's approach and hoped that she wasn't coming in to have a serious sit-down about the Baby. The subject of what she would do with the Baby seemed to preoccupy the whole house.

Aunt Frances tapped lightly on the open door and came into October's room.

"Girl, you need some light in here — you'll ruin your eyes," she said, and she let up all the shades.

"I can see by the light on the machine," October told her.

"I came in to talk about your child," Aunt Frances said. She sat down on October's bed. "If you don't want to hear what I've got to say, just tell me. I know how to keep my mouth shut."

October folded the panel of fabric she had been working on, then pulled her hair back and twisted it into a bushy ball with the rubber band.

"No, it's okay, Auntie," she said. "I know you're worried about his name."

"His name isn't what's got me worried, honey — it's you. You don't seem too bothered about him."

How had she come to such a conclusion? She fed him on time, kept his diaper changed, bathed him every morning.

"I'm with him all day," October said. "Ask Vergie."

"I think you're still stuck on that man," her auntie said.

"No," October said. "I'm not." She wanted to believe her own words. She would just as soon eat crushed glass as run into James Wilson again.

"Then what is it? You act like you don't know the Baby is here, you never pick him up, never even look at him unless you have to. And you haven't had on a decent dress, haven't let Verge do your hair, haven't been out of this house since you came back from the hospital."

So Auntie had been watching her every move, passing judgment.

"I told Vergie that I would think about naming him David," she said.

"That isn't what a mother does, honey. David is fine if that's what you want, but you don't let somebody else name your child."

Tears cramped her throat. She was doing the best she could. What did they want her to do?

"You've got to make some changes. He's

two months old. I know you're down, but start thinking about *him* for a change."

After her auntie left, October went out to the living room. Vergie sat near the window, rocking the Baby.

"Tomorrow," she said to Vergie, "I have to go down and get the Baby's birth certificate finished. I know Auntie will think I'm wrong, but I like David."

Vergie's face showed relief. "That's so good, October," she said. "We can't take him out in this weather, but I'll bet Aunt Maude will be glad to stay here with him while you and me go." She looked at the bundle in her arms. "David is a fine name. He'll love it."

She named him David, but it was clear to her that her aunt Frances had seen the dead place in her. Over the weeks Vergie could coo and lullaby all day, and October had never figured out how she thought up such things. And so October made a point of trying to sing and entertain whenever she bathed him, only to discover that while Vergie or her aunties had sudden ideas for cute expressions, she didn't. When his eyes found her, they looked strange and powerful all at the same time. If he was kicking or cooing when she approached, she noticed that he would get still, as if to brace himself, or observe her. And she noticed that he seldom made noises unless someone else was present.

"I don't think he likes me," October halfway joked once with Vergie. "Look," she said. She had laid him on a pad on the sofa and made silly faces at him, wriggling her fingers. He watched her, but remained very still.

"Girl, hush," Vergie said. Vergie got up and came over to where October sat making faces.

In baby-talk Vergie said, "Hi, Baby," and tickled his belly with her fingertips. October saw the joy on his face as he began frantically kicking.

"See?" October said.

"You have to talk to him," Vergie said. And she went on goo-gooing and ga-gaaing. "Play with him," she said. "He's a baby. They don't come here knowing you, you have to *make* him know you."

Just like October had a knack for sewing, Vergie seemed to have a knack for baby-knowing. And just as Vergie could be thoroughly absorbed in David's care and entertainment for hours, October could get herself lost in pleats and bodices and zippers.

Ever since she was knee-high to a duck, October could cut out a pattern and baste seams. But the very first thing she had ever made she had sewn without a pattern, and had done it for Vergie in a single day. October had been nine at the time, and Vergie had been thirteen or fourteen, with a first crush on a boy who had made her the butt of a mean joke. The end of the world, as Vergie saw it.

It had been October who came up with the idea of a new skirt to cheer her up — turned three yards of orange and purple print into a gathered skirt with two buttons on the waistband and a close-over placket on the side. Right out of her own head.

And she had sewn anything she wanted to sew ever since. As soon as David was out of the womb, her hands had needed to do something that made her feel like herself, and her mind had nudged her toward sewing. What started out as busywork soon became a mission. First just for something to put on, then for something decent to put on, then for something new and different.

In her room with the door closed, she could finish the skirt or blouse and try it on. Even though her breasts and hips were not hers anymore, she sewed as if they were. If she continued to eat small, she would come back to her size, and back to clothes that made her look like her old self, and then, who knew? She traded woolens and knits for cotton and rayon because one day soon she would wake up and it would be summer. Her daydreams left off right there: summertime, and she's wearing a shirtwaist dress with a cinch waist, aqua color, and white sling pumps. Walking along the sidewalk, maybe in front of the building overtown in Missouri where James Wilson used to live. Maybe School Boy seeing her and saying wow.

In march, when David was three months old, October, Vergie, and their aunt Maude took him for his checkup at the clinic in Ross County General. He had outgrown the bassinet, graduated to three other cereals and all kinds of little Gerber's jars. And constantly squealed and grunted. The doctor declared that he was a healthy baby, and happy. Up until that visit, October had worried that her shortcomings as his mother would somehow mark him. Now it was clear that he thrived because he was in the house on Monroe Street with four women and a man who saw to his every need.

Around that same time, October had sent a letter to Cora as part of her contact with her old self, her old life. What was Cora doing, how was Ed, when was she moving to St. Louis, and, too, if you were me, would you try to get a job again in Wyandotte County? No mention of David. Not yet.

Not that October wanted to return to the scene of her crime. Not that she wanted anything to do with James Wilson — at least that was what she told herself. Just that it was the only job she had known, something begun that she never finished, or never finished sufficiently. The sense of maybe climbing back onto the horse that had thrown her. Undoing the bad impression she had left. These were only fantasies, and a baby son didn't have to fit in.

When she came home from the clinic that afternoon in March, she helped Vergie get David fed and down for his nap in his new crib, in his new corner of the dining room, where there was steady traffic and he could always be the center of attention. October closed the door of her room and took off her clothes. In the closet, she slipped the aqua shirtwaist off its hanger and unbuttoned all the buttons, slipped it over her head and snapped the snaps, buttoned it again. Without looking in the mirror yet, she belted it with the self-belt she had made — the cinch fitting would be too much to hope for — and pushed the shoulder pads into place. Then she looked.

Didn't she look nice! Spring. School Boy would say to James, *I saw October, she sure was looking good.* She got herself out of the dress and put it back into the closet. Tomorrow she would get Aunt Maude to stop on her way home and buy more material from the Sears catalogue.

There was no scheme, no plan to up and leave Chillicothe. If she didn't want to work ever again, nobody in the household would force her into it — she knew that. But she had had that taste of life outside the scrutiny of aunts who could read her thoughts. She had made a career. At least that.

What Cora said in her letter made sense. No, don't even think of going back to Wyandotte. But she could come to Missouri, where Cora now lived. Jackson County covered most of Kansas City, and its school district was known for hiring women who had worked in Wyandotte, where rigor was the byword. Think about Jackson. And besides, now that Cora had moved into Ed's old place, and with him in St. Louis most of the time, she could use the company. There was only one bedroom, though.

And speaking of company, what about the baby? Did you find a name for him yet? I know why you couldn't right at first, but I hope you have now. Last I heard you were switching him to the bottle and he was sleeping all night. I'm dying to see him.

There was no scheme, no plan.

Late one afternoon, October finished up a collar and opened the door to her room, something she tried to do before her aunts got off from work and worried that she stayed to herself too much without you-know-who.

Vergie had already put meatloaf in the oven and was holding a serious conversation with baby David about the cost of hamburger. "That you?" she called.

October answered yes, thinking, Let me just get my shoes and stockings on, please, before it starts. What would happen if Aunt Frances came home and found her lollygagging in the bathtub with the radio on and baby David needing to be changed?

In the kitchen, Vergie sat balancing baby David and a basin for snap beans on her lap. He had a pacifier in his mouth; when he saw October, he stopped sucking for a minute, then went on sucking and playing with his hands.

"Wave to him," Vergie said. "He's waving at you!"

October waved her fingers but not because she thought the baby and she had something going. Although he did stop sucking again and let the pacifier fall.

"Guess what," Vergie said. "He had a soft egg yolk today. I was just about to give him a dinner treat. Sit down."

Vergie got up and put the beans on the table, and motioned for October to sit down.

Then plopped David into her lap.

"Tell him what you've been doin all day," she said. She began warming a jar of applesauce in a pan of water.

October cradled David and looked down at him. Maybe when he could talk, she would know what to say to him.

Maybe when he could talk and walk and play, she would start feeling like a mother. Because right now, to her, after all this time, he was still just the Baby that lived with them. She wouldn't let herself dig down too far, for fear that the dead place in her had turned to stone.

Then instinctively, for the first time, baby David reached his hand out to touch the spot of vitiligo on her face. October wondered if maybe that was what he had always seen, why he always sobered when he looked at her. Maybe she scared him. She brought him close enough to touch it.

His hand, soft on her face, felt sad, made her want to cry, like maybe he had something awful wrong with him and he didn't know it. She felt so sorry for him so suddenly that she could hardly stand it.

"Here, take him," she blurted out to Vergie.

But Vergie had her back turned. "Don't tell me he's wet again."

CHAPTER 8

Digging up the past was not something to be tolerated in their Monroe Street house in Chillicothe. Vergie knew that. But mind-reading was another story. She figured that she knew what went on in October's mind because her talent for reading minds went way back.

For instance, when she was nine she had known that if her mother, Carrie, didn't stop being how she was being, her father, Franklin, would do something. She could have told her mother, reminded her that when Franklin Brown was mad, he was mad. Hadn't they seen him drunk and cursing-mad before? But she hadn't said a word to Carrie.

A thousand regrets ago, Vergie could have told her mother that her father had been watching. She had stood right there with him in the screen door and read his mind, just like she had read her mother's mind every time Mr. Bailey had come across the alley to talk, every time she had seen Carrie leaning up against the fence like she was in love with the wood. But Vergie hadn't said a word.

A nine-year-old thinks wrong is wrong.

And even if it wasn't, she had supposed that Carrie had decided to go off with Mr. Bailey one day and take her and her sister with her. Vergie would never hear her father whistling again, never sit with him on the piano stool and play two-handed boogie-woogie. Or worse, Carrie might leave her and her sister behind.

And that day in Cleveland, at the table, Vergie had felt the storm gathering, felt lightning in the ping of a fork against a plate, thunder in Carrie's shoes on the stairs. In the kitchen, when she heard Carrie and Franklin fussing and carrying on upstairs, she knew that if she went upstairs and stood in the doorway as she had so many times before, Carrie or Franklin, one or the other, would have noticed her, would have thrown shoes at *her* instead of continuing their fight, fussed at her for sticking her nose into grown-folks business. Franklin never would have gotten pushed to a thought about knives. But what had she done?

Who do you choose, Punchinella, Punchinella? She had twirled her little sister faster and sung louder until they had twirled and sung too long.

And October's troubles? If Vergie hadn't always read it in her sister, she had heard enough from Auntie Frances and Aunt

Maude to know that October was more like Carrie than Vergie was. That fact certainly had never hurt Vergie's feelings.

From the day October got it into her head that she was too big for Chillicothe, and went straight from the college at Emporia, Kansas, to a job in Wyandotte County — where she didn't know a soul and had no place to live — Vergie had known there would be trouble. No surprise. The minute Cora called and said that October was in trouble, Vergie knew what kind of trouble, and knew that the man was trifling. She knew that October wouldn't have the gumption to save herself, not to mention a baby.

There was no scheme, no plan for Vergie, either. She couldn't help herself, couldn't help loving baby David. Gene didn't play with him much and she knew why. In his quiet way Gene saw her getting too attached, and then what would happen if October left? The baby would be gone, and she would be hurting. Having a baby around could be worse than hoping for one someday.

But Vergie knew things. Could see things. October wasn't a bit interested in raising a baby. October hadn't even gotten to where she could see herself as a grown woman yet. Vergie could see how October wouldn't, either, for years — years enough for David to grow up under their Monroe Street roof, never knowing the difference between auntie and mother.

And so, that day in March, as she watched the bubbles form in the water around the jar of Gerber's applesauce, she could feel October's indifference and confusion. When October cried, "Take him," Vergie knew what October had not figured out: what was true in that moment could be true forever.

On the evening when October called everyone together in the living room, Vergie sensed a strong wind blowing, but not furious enough to blow down the house. October had insisted on carrying David around all evening, and when they gathered, October sat him up in her lap, his head a little wobbly. *Watch his head*, Vergie thought. In Aunt Maude's face, Vergie could see the excitement. October was finally shaping up. Behind Aunt Frances's eyes, Vergie could hear the gears churning. *What next?*

Vergie sat with Gene on the sofa in front of the window, Aunt Frances and Aunt Maude sat in their stuffed chairs on either side of the console, and October perched on the edge of the rocking chair, holding baby David against her in her lap. Trying to make him sit up too soon, Vergie thought.

To Vergie, her sister looked the same as she did when she was seventeen. Face wide open, pretty but marked, which made her look gullible. Hair in that wild-looking way October always mistook for beautiful. Eyes batting in terror or excitement — didn't matter which, the expression was the same. Ever-new skirt and blouse, wearing good stockings around the house, trying to be more, always trying to be more.

As Vergie watched her sister, she remembered the day, years before, when October had changed her name. That had been a surprise. Vergie hadn't believed that October had it in her. It could be, now, that October would leave and take the baby with her. And the thought took Vergie's breath away. She reached for Gene's hand.

"I have to do something about my situation," October began. She looked off in the distance. Nobody said anything.

"I mean, I knew I had to get a job or something," she said. "I can't just go on living here like I don't eat and sleep on you-all's money."

"Now, honey," Aunt Maude said softly, "you know nobody's keeping account of what you eat. We're your people. If we've got, you've got."

"I know that, Auntie," October said. "But I'm grown now."

147

"Don't make no difference to us," Aunt Maude said, and Aunt Frances cut in with "Let her finish, Maudie."

Vergie didn't like the sound of this. October thinking about some other food and some other shelter.

"I've been talking to Cora Haskins — you know, my friend Cora."

"Yes . . ." Aunt Frances took over, for the moment.

October looked at Aunt Frances now, and Vergie had seen that look before. Like she might as well come clean.

"I've got a job if I want it. It's in Missouri — Kansas City. Substitute teaching." Vergie squeezed Gene's hand. He would know what she was feeling.

"Why can't you teach here?" Vergie asked. "Isn't that the place you left? Why would you go back there?"

October fidgeted in the chair and shifted David to her cradling arm, held him closer to her. Claiming him, Vergie thought.

"This is in Missouri. Wyandotte County was in Kansas. I can make more money there, and besides, there's only one Negro school here. I'll never get a job at Bryant."

It was probably true, but how could she know that? Vergie had never seen her sister lift the phone or lick a stamp to find out about

148

teaching in Chillicothe.

"And so you want to move there, is that it?" Aunt Frances asked, taking charge again.

"Well, yes," October answered, but Vergie could see that there was more.

"What about the baby?" Thank God Aunt Frances had gotten to the point.

"That's . . . He's . . . I don't know yet. That's what I'm trying to figure out."

She fidgeted with baby David again, and Vergie could see she just didn't know how to hold him. October looked again at Aunt Frances.

"It'll take me all summer to get situated out there. I can stay with Cora at first but not for the whole time. I'll need to work and find myself a place. Save money until the fall, when I start teaching."

"Who'll keep the baby?" Aunt Maude asked.

Vergie relaxed her hold on Gene's hand. She could see where it was going.

"I was wondering . . . I was thinking maybe you-all . . . Well, mostly you, Vergie — you and Gene — what would you-all think about me leaving him here for a while?"

Gene, the quintessential quiet man, spoke up immediately. "How long?"

Vergie couldn't believe that he would make a to-do without discussing it with her privately.

"I'm not sure, but maybe until the end of the summer."

Vergie counted. Five or six months. A long time in a baby's life. And she knew that Gene was counting, and that he wasn't likely to be inclined to let it happen. Thinking he was protecting her.

Aunt Frances spoke. "This house is home to all of us. Me and Maude got jobs to attend, and we're not spring chickens anymore."

October began, "That's why I'm asking you, Vergie. . . ."

Aunt Frances continued. "Vergie, you and Gene — this isn't the time to say what you will or what you won't do. You have to think about it together."

Vergie nodded and looked into Gene's face full of doubt. "We will," she said. "We'll talk."

There was no question. Vergie would take baby David on any terms for any length of time. It was just a matter of convincing Gene. She had prayed for a baby, and maybe this was the answer.

Over the next few days, what disturbed Vergie most was the rock-and-hard-place in what had seemed like heaven. In a single conversation, Gene made her see the precipice where they stood, and the pit with no bottom where they — especially Vergie — could fall.

After six months, when October came back for baby David, Vergie would die dead. He didn't think they should take that chance.

But in six more months wouldn't baby David be able to at least hold his own head up and crawl? Wouldn't he be able to eat solid food by then? Six months would be a gift for his aunt Vergie, and when he left she would just have to get over it. How could they say no? They couldn't.

In another conversation, Vergie asked Gene what if October let them keep the baby for a whole year? Okay, then — two years. Three?

And when Gene first wondered aloud if Vergie thought October might give the baby to them, her comeback had been sheer disbelief. "Just *give* him to us? Why would she do that?"

"Just askin," Gene said.

Plant a seed, grow an idea that roots and riots like wildflowers on a generous hill. Hadn't she prayed for a baby? Her own? Was this to be the answer — baby David for a few months here and there? What is *right?* Surely God is able.

Vergie couldn't sleep for dreaming mother-dreams. But shook herself awake with the reality that it was October's decision. And hadn't they ought to sound out Aunt Frances about the temporary and permanent possibilities?

In another few days, when levelheaded Aunt Frances called them all together again, Vergie felt calm: the time had come.

Vergie couldn't imagine what made her sister want to put on her best clothes around the house. October had dressed up like she was going somewhere, like she didn't know babies can spit up. Aunt Frances had to ask October to put David to sleep in his crib this time. Serious business.

Vergie herself hadn't been able to eat anything all day, not to mention give a thought to clothes and fingernail polish. One thing was for sure — with Aunt Frances handling things, there would be no more tipping around. Something would be decided.

Vergie sat with Gene on the sofa; Aunt Maude sat in her easy chair; Aunt Frances took the rocking chair and left her chair for October.

Without warning, as Aunt Frances rocked herself slowly in the rocking chair, she said, "Vergie and Gene have something they want to say," and she looked at Vergie.

She hadn't expected that. She didn't know how to begin. She looked at Gene. He looked right back.

"Well, I guess what we came to," she said,

"was that we really do understand you can't take baby David out to Missouri. I mean . . ." and she looked to Aunt Frances for help.

Aunt Frances said, "Just tell her what you want to say."

Vergie began again. "Me and Gene thought it might not be such a good idea if we got used to having him, and then you come back and take him."

She looked to see how it had registered but couldn't read good or bad in the clench of fingers in her sister's lap.

"There's something me and Gene want you to think about," Vergie told her. "You don't have to answer right away — just think about it."

Vergie looked at Gene. He took her hand. "We want to make baby David ours," Vergie said.

The surprise in October's eyes made Vergie hurry to repeat, "You don't have to answer. Just think about it, is all."

Aunt Frances leaped over the suggestion that October should take her time and went right to her own point. "It's not what we hoped would happen," she said to October. "But the baby needs more than you seem to be able to give him. So think about it hard."

To Vergie, October looked stunned. Her eyes welled up. Aunt Maude must have seen the tears forming, too, because she said, "You don't have to do this at all if you don't want to, honey. Nobody is saying you have to. Think hard."

It never ceased to amaze Vergie that Gene could be stubborn. "He would be our son," he said. "We would keep him, raise him. Wouldn't be no giving him back."

October was looking down at her hands by then. "I don't know . . ." she said.

Gene pushed. "Wouldn't be no giving him back. Wouldn't be no telling him, either. He never can know the difference. Period, or it's no go."

"I think she understands, Gene," Aunt Frances said.

Then Aunt Frances said, "You take your time. Think about it a few days. We'll talk again. Now I think I'll make me a cup of tea." She got up to go.

Later, October would try to tell Vergie what she had felt at the time. Later she would say that she had thought she couldn't love him because she hadn't felt connected to him those sad times when she held him. That she had shied away from holding him *because* of those damning feelings.

Later she would say that she hadn't understood all of what happened, the opening she had seen — one of those times that come only once. Later Vergie would hear the story of how, in that moment, October had been afraid to wait, afraid that she would drift forever. And that this plan had seemed like a good thing for everybody.

Later Vergie would try her best to understand how being a mother could have made October feel lost for a whole year of her life, and Vergie *would* understand that October had thought baby David deserved a better chance. A mother and a father. Them.

In that moment, however, when October said to them all, "Wait," and Vergie saw the answer in her sister's eyes, and Aunt Maude murmured that she hoped none of them would live to regret that day, and Vergie took October's hands in hers — what disturbed Vergie most was the ease of it. Like a cat finding a bird's nest on the ground.

As much as I might have wished otherwise, my girls' lives were not mine to change. Their lives belonged to them alone to do what they would do and to live out what they chose. And so I held for them.

CHAPTER 9

Easy and *simple* were two different things. For October, letting Vergie adopt the baby had seemed scary but not devastating. After all, everybody must be right — she didn't have what it took to be a mother. Vergie and Gene had been desperate for him. The baby would be better off with a normal life. That was all true.

And there was more truth to be told. October had looked at herself twice in the mirror, seen her old shape coming back, seen her new look, seen the woman James Wilson had fallen in love with. Weighed that. Maybe she had been fooling herself thinking she didn't still care about him. Added to it, she had saved in her head the picture of their last night together, when he had flung open the apartment door, hoping it would be her, had cooked for her, made love to her like she was the next best thing to divine. He had thought they wouldn't be having a baby.

Until the day she left Chillicothe to take the subbing job, October had gone to Missouri with one thing making her heart pump with purpose: getting back the life she had lost, getting back together with James. She hadn't let herself realize it until she was in Cora's apartment, sitting on the sofa bed dreaming up ways. Get herself into the classroom teaching again. Get her own place. Let him see her all over again — let him know that bygones could be bygones after all — that all along he had been right about loving her.

Nobody had ever told her to be wary of missions when it comes to men. October arrived at Cora's in March. It took only a month of sniffing around the edges of James's life for her to discover the scalding truth. James Wilson had got back the life he had almost lost, too. He had had another child with his wife — a baby boy born in January, one month after baby David had made his way out of October's body and into the world. To her, the arithmetic was simple. Two women and one man. October figured that she had been the spare. She felt sure now that, baby or not, he had never loved her.

When she found out, she went — halfheartedly — to Cora's medicine chest and swallowed what was left of the tin of Bayer that she found there. Halfheartedly, because the other half of her was busy asking, *Damn fool woman — what did you think?*

For two days, she went to sleep and woke up with indigestion and diarrhea. A mess.

Cora was straight with her. *You should have. You could have. I would have.* Couldn't believe October had still been after that man. Couldn't believe October had actually *given* the baby to her sister. Was sure nobody in Ohio meant for it to be *permanent.* Said *Just wait.* Said *You'll be sorry.* Said *You don't need to be moping around here — you need a full-time job, so take all the subbing you can get. Make them hire you. Go ahead, girl, show them your stuff.*

She showed them, all right: she needed no lesson plans, had no authority, no responsibility, really, outside of showing up and keeping the children busy, no one praised or condemned her. What was there to show?

Five days a week she woke up with a stiff neck on Cora's sofa bed, not knowing where she would be working that day. Morning and night, she and Cora tripped over each other, tipped over each other's things, stretched politeness until it snapped and stung. October couldn't stand the lovey-dovey silliness that Ed seemed to bring with him whenever he came home for the weekend.

After the roof caved in on a life with James Wilson, October had planned to just grit her teeth and get through the summer, make a go of subbing again in the fall. Even though subs merely kept order, no one could quibble with her college degree. She was qualified and available. Once she got her foot firmly in the door, they would have to give her a permanent job.

To get through the summer, she took herself down to Macy's department store and applied for a job in the alterations department. Though she hoped that "pickup girl" meant that she would step in and do the odds-and-ends sewing jobs that cropped up, she found that the description was literal. She would be picking up remnants of cloth that could be salvaged; bolts of fabric left on the tables; flowers, bows, belt buckles, and all other extraneous ornaments that mysteriously fell to the floor. They all had to go back to the stockroom, into proper bins and shelves. Inventory had to be kept straight. That was easy.

Sweeping up straight pins, fabric dust, and snippets of thread, wiping up the forbidden soda pop the "girls" spilled, fetching lunch for the head seamstress from Watkins Drug Store, where she had to stand back two feet from the whites-only counter to wait, that was harder.

But to be surrounded by exquisite fabrics, quality bindings, one-of-a-kind buttons, and clever designs in the barn of a room with its yellow walls, bare wood floor, and fluorescent ceiling lights — that was hardest. But so what if for the entire summer she never touched a single garment with a sewing hand? She was getting back on her feet.

Come fall, Macy's offered her part-time, Thursday evenings and Saturdays. They even hinted that they might allow her to let down a hem or a cuff or put in a zipper when they needed extra help. The extra money from Macy's meant that she could get on with her life that much sooner. Though they graduated her only to altering an occasional hemline, she resigned herself to the fact that money was money. She could buy herself decent fabric for one or two new winter things, or decent stockings every now and then. Once a month she could splurge and buy steaks for her and Cora. On weekday evenings when she wasn't working at Macy's or trying to decipher handwriting in some other teacher's lesson plans, she pulled her sewing machine out of Cora's closet and got busy. Christmas was coming.

Subbing was steady. By November her rounds at the schools had become so familiar that she felt more like an itinerant teacher than a substitute. For Thanksgiving Cora invited her to come with her to St. Louis. Instead of going with Cora, October used the time to make headway with the new suit she was sewing for Christmas. She did send a

Thanksgiving card home to Ohio, and a few weeks later she sent a pop-up card for David's birthday. She jotted a note telling them that Cora had invited her for Thanksgiving, but she didn't mention that she'd spent the day sewing. She didn't mention work, either. The subject of work would come up when they saw her again, but she wouldn't say much to her aunties about it until she could tell them that she had a permanent teaching job. She wanted to pump up Aunt Frances's chest, make her proud again. Hadn't she already fixed things for the baby, cleaned up part of the mess she had made? It had been almost nine months since she had seen him. Baby David was probably well and happy with Vergie and Gene. And that would have to be that.

Then she went home for Christmas.

The train arrived in Columbus on the snowy afternoon of Christmas Eve. As she climbed down the steps of the coach onto the concrete platform, Gene stood snow-laden, as if he'd been there all day.

"Good to see you," he said, with what passed for a hug. And then, taking her suitcases, he told her, "Everybody's waitin."

When Gene spoke, he usually pronounced the bottom line. She knew that, and wondered if they'd all be standing on the porch to see what they could see of this person she was supposed to be by now. She hadn't really kept in touch. Aunt Frances had been the one to call all the time, and Aunt Frances had sent notes and one little snapshot of "the gang." As Gene drove the thirty miles to Chillicothe, she tried to forget the last image she had of the family: three women crowded in the open doorway, arms folded to hold in any capricious word or wave, watching her leave like a flimsy page torn out of the sacred family Bible.

How would she look to them? She hoped, for one thing, that the girlish look was gone, and that she finally looked like the woman she thought she had become, wiser for her failures. She had been careful to pack her suits, and she had started wearing her hair in a more dignified style. At least now she could tell them about the permanent job she was in line for, and about the apartment search so far. At least she had brought them decent presents — perfume and a manicure set for Vergie, for example.

When they drove up she expected to see an auntie or somebody looking out the big oval window of the front door, but the curtain was drawn. Then she saw Vergie at the upstairs window and waved. Vergie waved back. She went ahead of Gene, and when she got to the porch she heard Aunt Frances's voice. Just as she started to knock, Aunt Frances snatched open the door and yelled, "Let me look at you, girl," and she could hear Aunt Maude squawking from somewhere deep in the house, "Is that her?"

Aunt Frances pulled her inside. Those first few seconds, October took in the little changes — Aunt Frances's hair more white than gray, frame more slight than stout, more balm than boom in her voice.

Then, as Aunt Maude shuffled her way to the front of the house, Vergie came down the stairs holding a brown little boy on her hip. He wore a tiny undershirt with snaps and a diaper. One glimpse and October told herself, *It's just the Baby. You just haven't seen him for a long time.* Her insides started to tilt. Things were going too fast.

She couldn't help but see his pudgy little legs, little feet. Then he twisted around and his eyes flashed on her, gave her chill bumps. She had to look away. But then she had to look back to see his little cheeks, the little pearly teeth in his liquid mouth. Silk-perfect skin. Precious. *It's just the baby.*

He ducked and clung to Vergie with his head on her breasts.

"Hi, October," Vergie said, swaying him,

not really looking at her. Vergie had a diaper slung over her shoulder. "Say hi to your auntie," she said, bouncing him.

October couldn't say hi. Couldn't say anything that would cover the shock and confusion that were rushing her blood.

"He's a big boy now," Aunt Maude said.

All of a sudden he spread all five fingers and pointed his little hand, said something like "Ut?"

"No, baby, no hurt," Vergie said, caressing away his hand. "He thinks your vitiligo hurts."

October's bones were fast turning into rubber, and she needed to lean somewhere.

"He'll get used to you after a bit," Aunt Frances said. "Looks like you're pretty tired."

October nodded, yes, she was. *This is him. This is my son.*

And Aunt Maude threw up her cane. "You see I'm walking with a cane nowadays, don't you?"

October knew that they saw the shock on her, saw that she couldn't even look at him, for falling apart. *Aunt Maude.*

"What happened?" she asked Aunt Maude.

Aunt Maude said something about falling down and her hip being out of joint. "I'm fine — just can't take the steps like I used to," she said.

Then everybody seemed to be waiting for everybody else to say something, and Aunt Frances took up the challenge. "Come on, honey, and sit down. I'll make us some tea. We moved Maudie's bedroom down here, and you'll be in with her. That's a nice suitcase you've got there."

Aunt Frances, Aunt Maude, Gene, Vergie — they were taking her coat, showing her the Christmas tree, going on about the train ride and all the food they'd cooked, and then ushering her into the dining room, sitting her down in the armchair at the head of the table.

October saw a look pass between Aunt Frances and Vergie, and without warning, Vergie stepped over to October and plopped David down in her lap.

"Here," she said. "Say hi to him before I put him to bed." And she stepped back to watch her do it.

Something told her she'd be sorry if she held him. But it was too late. She could smell him. Vergie had perched him on her knees, and October held on to the trunk of his warm little body with both hands. A baby boy too precious for words.

He stuck his finger in his mouth and stared at her. For the first time in her life, she really looked at her son. Right into him. In that little minute that they sat like that, time turned around and ran the other way, erasing its tracks. October felt him in her blood, in her bones, felt him being her son. Like a reflex, as automatic as blinking, she hugged him and pressed her face to his. And she knew immediately that everything she had believed about her life up until then was about to unravel.

Here was her beautiful, precious child, and she had given him away.

Vergie then snatched him up off her lap like the treasure that he was, and for the first time, October felt him being taken away. She caressed his foot as it passed through her eager hand. She wanted right then to put on her coat and go on back where she came from, because she sure couldn't stay in that house, or come there again.

How could she have given him away?

CHAPTER 10

For Vergie, up until October came that Christmas, it had been easy. She had got herself and everyone else ready. And good thing Christmas came only once a year, or everybody would have had to go on bed rest.

Not only did Gene steam loose the wallpaper in every single room, scrape the walls smooth, and repaper them with a better grade and pattern, but he also sanded and varnished the floors. He couldn't figure for what — just did it because Vergie was having a fit about Christmas.

This time Vergie didn't care that October had a knack for picking fabrics; when she put her mind to it, she, too, could mix and match like no tomorrow. New café curtains in the kitchen made it brighter, new drapes upstairs converted her and Gene's plain room to poshy.

Starting on the day October had left for Kansas City, Vergie had announced her wishes for her baby. Simply turn the house upside down — David's room upstairs with her and Gene, Aunt Maude's room downstairs, on the closed-in side porch that had been October's. Aunt Frances could stay up-stairs if she wanted to, but it had quickly be-come clear that her room there was only for sleeping. If she could have, Vergie would have built a kitchen upstairs, too.

No, she told Gene, she didn't want to move — just wanted her family to have its privacy. And yes, she guessed it would be all right to put a playpen downstairs so that David could remain at the center of life on Monroe Street.

Morning of Christmas Eve, the house smelled right. Turpentine fumes and the sour odor of flour paste had been chased by the aroma of cloves studded on a baking ham and nutmeg in sweet potato pies.

For Vergie, none of that held a candle to the smell of a real live baby. She had closed the door to the dining room and opened the oven door to keep the kitchen toasty. No bathtub in the world could compare with the kitchen sink for giving David his bath.

She took off his nightgown and sat him on a towel folded on the drainboard. Inch by inch, she inspected his brown little body for the white freckles that might link him to October. There were none. *Dear God, may there never be one.*

"In you go," she said, and before she could get her naked little pickaninny baby into the dishpan-turned-bathtub, David kicked and splashed his delight all over her and the floor. No matter. That's why they made mops.

Once she had him sitting, he squealed, and splashed with his hands, making bubbles and giggling, too tickled at his smart self. Nine little white teeth — four top front, four bottom front, one stray on the bottom toward the back of his mouth — his smooth nose, those stark black eyes in his brown round face looking up at her did it.

"Hey, dumplin," she said, and smack-kissed his drooling mouth. "Momma's got a big surprise for you. You just wait." She cupped water over him with her hands and soaped the washcloth. As she began washing his back and shoulders, he reached for the floating Ivory, too slippery to catch, and he started to fret, reaching and crying "Unhhh, unhh."

"Boy, look at you," she said, laughing. "Auntie!"

Aunt Frances came running, Aunt Maude came shuffling through the kitchen door, panic in their steps, fear in their faces.

"What — is he all right?"

"Watch!" Vergie said.

David, too, had stopped to see what all the ruckus was about, but when Vergie pushed the soap toward him and he tried to grasp it, and it again slid away from him, he fluttered and jerked his little legs and went to fretting — "unhh, unhh" — and reaching, looking at Vergie.

"You little devil," Aunt Frances said, "acting up already." And she tapped the bar toward him and watched as he failed once again to catch it.

"Don't tease him," Aunt Maude said. "You'll make him mean."

"I wasn't teasing him," Aunt Frances said, and she held the bar of soap still in the water, within his reach.

Little fingers splayed, David grabbed at the big soft bar, couldn't grasp it, and settled for tasting the matter on his fingers.

"No!" they all yelled, startling him to crying, and he reached both arms out for Vergie.

In real contrition they aw-babyed him and rubbed and soothed his slick wetness in Vergie's arms, she petting and kissing him.

Gene came into the kitchen. "The boy's gonna be so rotten we won't be able to stand him." And he got in on the petting, too, smoothed David's tight curly cap. "What these women doin to you, huh?"

When his bath was over, Vergie baby-oiled and baby-powdered him, dressed him in his new corduroy jumper and soft-soled tie-ups, brushed his hair, and buried her face in the sweetness of his neck. Then she gave him the surprise of a homemade ice pop she had frozen overnight and let him slurp it until his chin and his jumper ran red.

Over the nine months there had been several crises, but the first stood out in her mind as a marker for how far they'd come.

One day — only a month or so after October had left them last spring — they had gotten worried. David wouldn't take his afternoon bottle. Cried and fretted and divided the rest of Vergie's evening into offer-and-soothe, anything to quiet him.

By that night, he had out-and-out wailed. Aunt Frances, a chief LPN at Ross County General, couldn't find anything wrong. Yes, of course his pulse was racing — he was wailing. Maybe his temperature was up, but not more than a degree. No, he wasn't wet or hungry, no diaper pins sticking him, no rash to itch. Vergie had rubbed his stomach, burped him twice. Aunt Frances had listened to his bowel sounds, worked his fingers and toes, arms and legs. No pain there that she could see. Mrs. Hopp from next door said they should give him warm lemonade with a little flaxseed, or boiled potato water, slippery elm.

By ten o'clock, weary from crying, David had finally dozed off in Vergie's arms. The rocking chair worked to keep him dozing and

Vergie's back comfortable, and she was afraid to leave it, lest she wake him.

"You get some sleep," Aunt Maude said. "Let me sit with him awhile." But Vergie said no.

And sure enough, after only half an hour, David woke up crying his little eyes out. Against Aunt Frances's wishes, from the beginning Gene had wanted to call the home nurse. Once baby David woke again in the same state, Gene didn't hesitate. No answer, but he dialed again and again until the nurse's sleepy voice said all right, she would come.

Near midnight, with her aunts and Gene standing guard, Vergie held her crying baby still on the kitchen table so that the nurse could examine him. Heart, lungs, legs, arms, eyes, ears, nose, throat.

"Oh," the grayer-than-Aunt Frances nurse said, and chuckled a little. "I see, little fella." She said to Vergie, "Take a look."

David kicked and wailed as the nurse shifted the tongue depressor in his mouth and aimed her little flashlight. "See — right there."

Vergie saw the slightest rise and redness along one ridge of David's gums, and she certainly didn't think it was funny.

"He's got a renegade tooth coming in," the nurse said. "Hurts, too. The front ones usually come in first, these come in later."

She dug around in her black bag, cautioning them to hold on to David. Vergie's finger along David's gums found the hard place, but she couldn't kiss away the pain.

Gene whispered, "What do they do for this?" to Aunt Frances, and looked disappointed when she reminded him that she had only taken care of grown people.

The nurse handed Vergie a small bottle of what smelled like juniper tar, instructing her to rub a little on David's gums every three hours until the tooth broke through, and suggested she also buy a rubber teething ring.

All of that for the first tooth.

And David had fallen once, too — rolled off the bed, no telling how, but after that, he slept in his crib or on a quilt on the floor, which he seemed to favor. Once he could sit up, he had the oddest way of navigating. Using one arm, he would lean to one side and push off against the floor, scooting his little bottom along toward wherever he thought he wanted to go. After the teething incident, Aunt Frances's baby-care wisdom was suspect. Normal, the doctor said. And crawling backward? Normal too.

By his birthday on the tenth (October had sent a pop-up card) he had started pulling up on furniture. Vergie wondered what it would be like for October to see him take his first step.

Around noon on Christmas Eve, when flurries started, Gene told her he thought he ought to leave early, one or one-thirty. If October's train got to Columbus on time, he didn't want to make her wait, didn't want to be trying to get back to Chillicothe in the dark and snow. Columbus might be a stone's throw away, but thirty miles could stretch to three hours if the weather turned bad. And off he went.

It was difficult to put herself in October's place, but she sensed that once October had flown the coop and gotten out from under, she hadn't bothered to look back. Vergie believed that October had been ducking Aunt Frances's telephone calls; her sister's face at the Thanksgiving table would have been nice. No show, though. October had called the Sunday before to say that four days was not enough to see family and travel, too. She wasn't coming. And Vergie had heard Aunt Frances's ultimatum.

"You're coming here for Christmas," Aunt Frances had told October. "Whatever you have to do to get here, we're your family. You may not want to see us, but we need to see you." And Aunt Frances had hung up. Vergie knew then that October would come for a week, show off her newfound whatever-it-was: job, clothes, friends. And then be gone. And that was fine.

Or there was the off chance that October had put David in some other part of her memory where he was just a fact, and seeing him might send her back to feeling sorry for herself. Or, October might go back to wishing: David was a boy now — she might see in him the man she had fallen for. Or she might wish other things, things that sat way too heavily in Vergie's stomach. David was hers now. She needed to stop scaring herself.

Just after sundown, as Vergie looked out of the upstairs window at the light snow cover, Gene's old station wagon pulled up. Both car doors opened at the same time, and Vergie watched October get out, stand on the sidewalk, and look up at the house. Remembering, Vergie thought, and she waved. October grinned and ran up the steps to the front porch.

"She's here!" Aunt Frances called, and Vergie heard her snatch open the door and yell to October, "Let me look at you, girl!," and heard Aunt Maude, too, shuffling her way to the front of the house, calling, "Is that her?"

It was time. She hoisted David — in his

nightshirt and diaper — on her hip and started down the stairs. Halfway down she hesitated. October glanced up and right then it felt like everybody hushed and waited for Vergie to come on down to the bottom of the stairs.

"Hi, October," Vergie said, and tried to get David to say hi, but he just stared.

October almost smiled, and Vergie could see her sister trying to hold her mouth right.

Could see, too, that October was dressed to the nines in what had to be some kind of ten-piece outfit, with a two-piece suit and a cape number, a hat and an underblouse all the same color dark green, and brown alligator heels. Brown alligator pocketbook.

"Say hi to your auntie," Vergie said to baby David.

David stuck his finger in his mouth, but he didn't take his eyes off October.

"He'll get used to you after a bit," Aunt Frances said.

She saw October trying to look at him without looking at him, smiling at Aunt Maude and glimpsing baby David's bare feet. Vergie wished she had kept him with his clothes on.

Aunt Maude showed off her cane. "What happened?" October said, about Aunt Maude's cane.

Aunt Maude told her about her fall and her

hip and they all stood in the vestibule waiting for Vergie didn't know what, and suddenly baby David spread all five fingers and pointed to October's white spot.

She bounced David on her hip a little and said to October, "He thinks your vitiligo hurts," and was flabbergasted by sudden tears shining in October's eyes.

Vergie stood there for what seemed long minutes bouncing David, Aunt Frances peeling October out of her coat, Aunt Maude admiring the shoes and purse, October trying to look without looking until Gene pushed open the front door and hauled in the suitcases.

"What you got in these things," he asked, "— iron?" They all laughed as he struggled to drag the suitcases into the house. And they all moved to the living room like tomatoes on the same vine.

"What a beautiful tree," October said. "New lights," she said, looking around at the new wallpaper and shiny floors.

"Yes," Aunt Frances said. "We thought David would like the little bubbles."

Nothing else to say.

But David said it. He patty-caked his hands and giggled, pointing to the lit tree, and squealed out what was meant to be "tree." Then "Da-da," and Gene came to him. "Treeee," David said, with Gene pulling on his little leg. October looked startled. Vergie tried to think of something to say.

"How was the train ride?" she asked, jiggling David-with-finger-in-mouth-looking-at-October-again.

"It was nice," October said. "I had forgotten how long it can be, but it was all right."

Nothing else.

"I'm glad you came home," Aunt Maude said.

That seemed to break the spell. October looked relieved. Aunt Frances said, "We've been cooking up a storm, and I know you haven't had nothing decent to eat since yesterday, so get ready. It's Christmas Eve."

The fruits on the vine rose and moved to the dining room, where Vergie had set the table earlier, and where she had suggested they let October sit in the guest place.

"Gene should be sitting here," October said, now in green satin blouse and green wool skirt that looked like she painted it on herself, hair pulled back nice and smooth in a bun.

Vergie wore her brown shirtwaist, and it sure beat skintight. Her dress looked just fine.

Before Aunt Frances started loading down the table, Vergie needed to get David down for the night. And something else.

Gene pulled out the chair for October. October plopped down.

"Here," Vergie said, and plopped David down in October's lap. "Say good night before I put him to bed." She stepped back a little, remembering how awkward October had always been when it came to holding David. Now October perched David on her knees and, with both hands, held on to his trunk just like Vergie would have done. He stuck his finger in his mouth again and stared at her. October stared back like he was a window on a crystal ball, and she had this one chance to see inside.

Then October hugged him. From what Vergie saw on October's face, she knew it was time to take David upstairs.

"Beddie-bye," she said, and took him up in her arms. "You-all go ahead. I'll be down in a minute."

Upstairs, she sat in the rocking chair and rocked, sang softly to him. " *'Bye a baby bunting, / Daddy's gone a-hunting, / To get a little rabbit skin, / To wrap the baby bunting in, / 'Bye a baby bunting, 'bye.* "

It was a song she had always known, but she didn't know when she learned it. Probably one of those things tucked away in a memory from the years in the other life she had once had, which seemed now like a dream. Probably from Carrie. Until she got David, she couldn't remember ever singing it.

She buried her face in his sweet hair; he dozed on her chest until she could feel him dreaming.

Back downstairs, Mrs. Hopp from next door had come in. "I done got too old to eat at night," she said, but she made her way to the table and pulled up a chair.

"So are you back or just passing through?" she asked October. October began to talk about her trip and her job in Missouri, and Vergie settled down. This was going to be all right. She looked across the table at Gene burying his face in his plate, looked long enough for him to feel her, and when he looked up to see what she wanted, she smiled and he smiled back.

Christmas morning Vergie made it her business to be the first one up. David's first real Christmas couldn't get started soon enough — she could hardly wait to see his face when he discovered he could beat out music on his toy xylophone, see him watch the windmill spin. But he did have to have his breakfast. She sponged him off upstairs and told Gene to wait upstairs until everyone was up. "Nobody wants to miss anything." Then she went down to make David's oatmeal.

Whisking a sleepy baby David past the living room treasury, she thought she heard crying. Stopped. Waited for the sound from Aunt Maude's room. Crying. October was crying. Vergie crept nearer the door and listened.

"Hush now," Aunt Maude was saying, "it'll be all right."

And October muttering something about the baby.

Aunt Maude said clearly, "I prayed you would see the light before now, then prayed you wouldn't. Sometimes when we can't hear God tryin to tell us something, he turns up the volume."

Silence again, then weeping.

Aunt Maude: "Be thankful you got your health at least," and something else about God fixing things.

Trouble.

Vergie was spooning the last of the oatmeal into David's mouth when Aunt Maude came into the kitchen, humming her nervous hum.

"It's Christmas," she said. Like Vergie didn't know it. "Jesus' birthday, you know."

Vergie said yes, she knew that.

Moments later October came into the kitchen, face swollen like she'd been through the mill and cried all the way. Vergie didn't want to ignore it, didn't want to know what she already knew. Better not to let October's eyes catch hers.

October made it easy. Not once did she raise her head high enough for anyone to see her face. Talked to the floor the whole morning.

By the time Gene and Aunt Frances joined them, David was squirming and grunting to get out of his high chair. Aunt Frances must have decided against noticing October in return, because she never said a word about her swollen face. Vergie undid the tray to David's high chair and took him in to Christmas.

Later in the day, after October had quietly handed Aunt Frances and Aunt Maude their twin sets of cologne and powder, quietly laid Vergie's manicure set with five colors beside her on the chair, and pushed David's toy truck toward Vergie's feet, she said she was tired and could they just excuse her for a while. Aunt Frances said take some headache powders because they wouldn't eat without her.

Because it was a banquet of surprise after surprise, dinner passed for enjoyable. And after dinner, without the pretense of a reason, October announced that she would leave the next morning.

All night upstairs, Vergie whispered to

Gene that this was bound to happen. A person can't just up and leave home and not feel anything when they come back. October was high strung, or low strung, one or the other. She made a to-do over everything. Always did. A person can't have something bad happen to them and just forget it. Probably Chillicothe had brought it all back. But she would get over it. Next time, she would be all right.

Early the next morning at the front door, Vergie put David down and hugged October.

"I'm sorry you're feeling so bad," she whispered. She meant it.

October didn't say anything, just nodded her head.

Vergie picked up David again. "Say bye-bye to your auntie," she said. But David was too absorbed with the hammer of his xylophone to say 'bye.

CHAPTER 11

Never was a long time. As soon as the weather broke that spring, October wrote a note to Vergie. She was sorry for being so strange at Christmas. She slipped in *I am sorry for so many things. Seeing David was a shock.* Said that she hadn't expected to feel *this way,* though she didn't explain what she meant. Wrote, *There is just one thing I would ask. The next time Auntie takes pictures, I would like so much to have one of David.*

And she got busy trying to find ways to live with herself. First of all, to live meant that she had to have a bed to sleep in and a closet to hang up her clothes. She had to stop borrowing carfare and begging rides from Cora and get away from Ed and his little digs about how many people it takes to make a crowd. Cora would never put her out, though she was very good at dropping hints.

Applying for a permanent position with the school board required that October walk on sharp tacks and pretend that she didn't feel them. Aside from the written application, she sat across the desk from a woman with bluish-gray hair who studied her for a long time, then fired bald questions at her — *Who was your cadet leader? What subjects did you teach in third grade? What is your idea of lesson plans? Why did the boy say you struck him? Why did you leave Wyandotte? Where have you been? What have you been doing? Why do you want a permanent position? Why should we hire you?* — and watched October pick her way among the prickles, wrote God-knew-what about October on her confidential form. Then told October she would have to wait. For however long it took.

Once school was out and subbing dried up, a make-do summer job at Kresge's didn't seem like a bad idea. Downtown Main Street came alive around lunchtime, and in October's one outing each day she walked the five blocks from Kresge's to the public park, where she could sit on a bench and eat the sandwich she had packed for lunch. From her first day at Kresge's in June, when she had seen the blue-uniformed brigade of her fellow employees lined up along the "colored" counter at the rear of the store, eating their hot dogs and French fries, she decided she would rather get out and walk.

After the first few hours that first day, she had recognized that what they wanted her to do she could do in half a day, and she figured out how to stretch it. In the kingdom of

"Sewing Needs" she wiped mirrors and dusted lint until the cows came home. She filed patterns in numerical order and checked the catalogues to mark which ones they had in stock. She sorted bolts by price, rewound them, repinned them, and removed them from the cutting table when the two clerks finished with them. Neither seemed to know fabrics by feel, and they both had to read the bolt tabs. October saw them mismatching thread with fabric, too, ignoring texture and thinking color was all. When October restocked spools, she made a point of asking, "Do you-all want the cotton thread in with the synthetics, or not?" At least there was the pastime of looking at pattern books.

It worked out that if she hurried, and if she brought the newspaper with her, she could read it in the shade and cool off a little before she hurried back. That way she fit in, too, with the white people who sat reading on the other benches.

Pigeons flitted and begged around her feet, and the softness of grass made her want to slip off her shoes.

Times like these, when she thought she might sit idle, her stomach rose to her throat in a wave of shame. Panic. She didn't dare go near it, or all the details would make her sick.

She unfolded her newspaper to a picture of

General Eisenhower in military regalia. "If Not Truman, Who?" said the headline, and below the fold a picture of just-crowned Princess Elizabeth. "Long Live the Queen," the caption said. Queen or no, the girl's father had died. October looked closer to see if a princess could feel sadness behind those dark eyes.

That day on the noontime bench she finished her sandwich and folded her newspaper, and just as she stood up to go, she saw the possibility of trouble coming her way — a familiar-looking brown face. October sat down again and opened her newspaper.

The high-heeled shoes hesitated as they passed her bench but kept going. Once the woman was well past, October looked to see if, indeed, it had been one of the room mothers from Stowe School.

Just seeing somebody who knew-her-when nearly brought up her lunch. In Missouri she had counted on being a relative stranger, stayed behind the doors of Cora's place, where her business was her business. The minute she stepped outside of school and outside Cora's into other parts of the world, her business could turn into a piece of cloth flapping in the wind, tearing every which way.

She had to guess that the money earned and saved would be worth whatever she had to face. The wages of sin. Knowing that she deserved ashes, for the first time since James Wilson finally tore his pants and showed her his truly awful behind, she got down on her knees beside the sofa that night. Knowing that a wrathful God would not be vaguely interested in her plight, she folded her hands and tried to find the right words. She prayed *If you can, please forgive me.*

Short of a miracle, there was no way that she could see forgiveness coming to her. You just don't bring a baby into the world and give him away. And married men? If they ran around they were dogs, period. Aunt Frances had preached against lying down with dogs too many times for October not to know she had gotten up with the kind of fleas that would be around forever.

When, one July day, she got the contract for a permanent position at R. T. Coles Elementary, she clutched the paper to her breast and bowed, thanking a wrathful God for his pity.

Her first days at Coles transported her back to Stowe, even down to the inkwells fitted with metal caps. At Stowe, she had taken Cora's advice and gone in like gangbusters. Set the pace on the first day. Show them you're in charge. Dare them to cross you. At Stowe once, she had even thrown a book across the room and hit the wall. That had definitely set the tone for no foolishness. There was the possibility that that strategy had backfired, though, and laid the foundation for the charge later made against her.

At Coles, she couldn't find the energy to push the tough approach anymore. Plain old reasoning would have to do.

Way ahead of time, she reviewed her lesson plans and arranged the textbooks in each desk. So that when the bell sounded and thirty-five little busy bodies rushed in exploding in noise and punching each other to attention, she sat behind her desk, folded her hands, and waited. When they didn't get quiet, she went to the window and turned her back on them. After a few minutes, they settled down and she turned around and bade them good morning.

The Lord's Prayer, *the Pledge of Allegiance*, *O Beautiful* — good start. She read them the Twenty-third Psalm and told them to bring a Bible verse every day. And then inspection. Fingernails, polished shoes, no safety pins showing. Only one or two girls weren't wearing ribbons that first day, and October made a note to bring some in. Shoelaces too. Especially for Walter Jean Campbell, with the curious name for a girl and the tie-up shoes with no laces.

Sometime during those first few weeks, October bought black and brown laces and good satin ribbons from Kresge's and passed them out. Now everyone looked bright and shiny, except for Walter Jean's shoes. At least they were laced. For at least a while. Until one afternoon October dismissed the class for the day and found Walter Jean still in her seat.

"Come up here," October told her, pulling up a chair beside her desk for the girl. Walter Jean was a sandy little girl with coarse reddish-brown hair, lightly toasted skin, and light brown eyes. And meek. Never raised her hand, never said a word unless October called on her. And then, though she spoke in the voice of a five-year-old, she usually had a good answer.

"What's the trouble?" October asked her.

She didn't answer, just bowed her head and let the tears run.

October gave her a Kleenex.

"What is it, Walter Jean?" October asked. "I can't help you if you won't tell me."

The girl reached into her dress pocket and brought out a folded pink ribbon and a wad of worn shoelaces.

"My mother said I have to give these back," she said.

"Did she say why?"

Walter Jean shook her head.

October took the ribbon and was tempted to reserve it in her drawer, just for Walter Jean.

"It's all right," she said. "I passed them out just in case girls who don't usually wear ribbons wanted to try one. Nobody *has* to wear them."

"Yes, ma'am," Walter Jean said, wiping her face with the back of her hand.

Parents were funny about some things. Offending a parent was the last thing she wanted to do.

For a few days Walter Jean came to school with new shoelaces and unadorned hair. But children are clever. Walter Jean had figured out how to fold a pastel-colored Kleenex into fanlike folds, cinch it in the middle with a rubber band, and peel back the folds so that it looked like a flower. Every morning, with a hairpin, she attached her "flower" and stood proudly for inspection.

A little girl like that needed to know that she, too, was clever. Not only did October find it easy to praise her, she found many small ways for Walter Jean to shine. Take the time and any good student can do better. Walter Jean's reading and spelling sent her right to the first seat in the first row. To be called teacher's pet was nothing to a little girl who obviously rubbed Vaseline on her shoes and kept a small stack of pale blue Kleenex in her desk.

Five days teaching, Thursday nights and Saturdays at Kresge's, spare-time looking and finding and moving her things to a one-bedroom at the Woodlands kept October's mind full, feet moving, nose to the grindstone. Usually the rest of her floated, untethered to any future or past. Except that every other Sunday night she was on the telephone with the whole other life in Chillicothe. The one she had ruined.

Her place at the Woodlands had come furnished, which meant stick-furniture tables, hard shabby sofa and chair. Narrow bed, unfinished chest. Top lights in all the ceilings. Bare, spare. She bought a cotton tablecloth for a sofa throw, scatter rugs for the dull wood floors. She had dressed her dress form in her own old gingham dress and sewn artificial flowers on the old straw hat that sat on the dress form's wire head. Once she added a tiny Formica table and two chairs along the wall of the long front room, the dress form served as room divider.

One of her first purchases had been a new fold-down Singer with a hundred clever attachments. The old Singer, then — with its immutable black iron body, its crooked foot that could clamp any thickness of cloth, its easy wheel and wrought-iron treadle all held together with oaken planes — became a found treasure in front of the small picture window. Scarlet-tipped coleus and philodendron climbed over its body, maidenhair fern hung down its side, and succulent fingers of jade plant reached up from the treadle.

Someday she would replace the stained window shades and buy herself a full-size bed. But for the time being she was satisfied to call it home.

The photograph of David arrived that fall, too. Had Aunt Frances snapped the picture at the wrong time, or was this the way it would be? Gene and Vergie sat on the front-room sofa. David sat on Vergie's lap, head buried in Vergie's breasts, so that only his profile showed. No eyes, no little white teeth. On the back, Vergie had written, "The gang." October had found a brass frame and placed the photograph next to the cheap brass lamp on the end table. Every time she sat on the sofa, David shied away from her.

Some of the teachers at Coles had cars or rode with other teachers, though some did ride the bus to and from school. Rain or shine found October walking the three blocks to the bus stop, and the early dark descending on a November evening found her hunched against the cold.

And that evening, who was walking ahead of her? Was that Walter Jean with no scarf and coat flying open like it was eighty degrees? And why was she out here at this hour, when cars already had on their headlights?

"Walter Jean?"

The child turned around. "Aw, hi, Miss Brown," she said.

"Don't you live on Twenty-seventh Street?" October asked. "Where are you going?"

"No, ma'am," Walter Jean said, teeth chattering. No buttons on that coat. October wished for a safety pin. Those arms in the sleeves of that coat had to be shivering. Those fingertips showing had to be cold.

"We moved," she said. "I went over to my friend's house next door where we used to live. We live down on Vine now."

"Does your mother know where you are?" October asked. Too much time had passed for a mother not to know.

"No, ma'am," the little girl said. "She don't —"

"Doesn't."

"She doesn't get home till late. My brother is home. He's fourteen."

"You should go straight home from school every day. I'm sure your mother wouldn't want you out here at dark."

"I'm going," Walter Jean said.

But Vine was six or so blocks, and it was cold.

"I'll walk you," October said. "Next time, don't go over to your old neighborhood unless somebody takes you over there."

"Yes, ma'am."

On the way over the six blocks, October managed to find out that Walter Jean's mother worked for the Fairfax plant, different shifts, and from what she could tell, evenings sometimes. The brother was responsible for warming the dinner pot and locking the door.

They walked. October tried, but little Walter Jean wouldn't wear October's gloves, not even one. A shame, because every child needs somebody looking after the little things like lost gloves and buttons on coats. They got to the apartment house. Not bad. Not great, but relatively clean and no winos hanging around. For whatever reason, October felt grateful for that, glad she had come to see for herself. At the door on the second floor, Walter Jean slapped the door with her open palm and yelled, "Billy! Open the door."

Silence on the other side. Maybe the brother wasn't there.

"Billy! It's me. My teacher is here!"

The door flew open. The sandy brother looked sheepish and said, "What happened?"

"Nothing happened," October said to the boy. "I just came to make sure your sister gets in all right."

"Yes, ma'am," he said.

Walter Jean went in. " 'Bye, Miss Brown" — proudly, like having an escort had changed her station in life.

Two more such evenings October just happened to see Walter Jean up ahead near dark, and just decided why not? and walked the child home, pressing her to promise that she wouldn't go to her old neighborhood every day. Saying that she would call her mother if it happened again.

Once again, October had an opportunity to admire the ingenuity of children. Walter Jean had been timing her jaunts to meet up with October, actually waiting a couple of times, not even pretending an accidental meeting when she stepped out into the sidewalk near the bus stop. Three or four evenings a week. Just to be walked home? October supposed that the child was afraid to go alone to a strange neighborhood, or maybe she just liked having this one woman who bothered to see that she got there.

Usually the brother — unfazed that his sister's teacher was there, too — opened the door after a few knocks. Fourteen-year-olds. Inevitably there came the evening when he didn't open the door, wasn't there at all, and Walter Jean didn't know anything about a key, and looked in terror at the next door, where new neighbors might know something. October was suspicious, but Walter Jean swore, "No, ma'am, I don't have the telephone number to Fairfax."

And so October wrote a note for Walter Jean's mother, included her telephone number, pushed it under the door, and took sandy little Walter Jean home with her on the bus.

She got her out of her coat and went straight to the kitchen for the cocoa.

"Sit down and I'll make you something hot to drink," she told the girl. As she heated milk, she took peeks at the sandy one, who looked lost, sitting on the sofa, hands in lap, looking around the foreign country of Miss Brown's apartment.

"Come sit over here," she called to her, and sat two cups of cocoa on the Formica table near the kitchen.

As Walter Jean passed the dress form she looked up and smiled. "What's that?" she said. October could see a giggle wanting to bubble up.

October explained a dress form, and the clever little sandy girl asked, "What's her name?"

October had never thought of giving a

name to it. "What do you think her name should be?" she asked.

Walter Jean hunched her shoulders and sang, "Um-um-ummm." She didn't know.

"Think of one," October said. They sipped their cocoa.

"I'm going to call your mother," October said. "But first, what do you like to eat for dinner?"

"I like everything," Walter Jean told her.

"Like what?"

"I like fried chicken and stew and rice and pork and beans, and hot dogs, and corn on the cob and chili and cabbage and black-eyed peas and cornbread . . ."

The child was hungry. With a hungry child, Aunt Frances and Aunt Maude would have expected no less from her than a well-laid feast. October had to hurry. When had she last made cornbread? And there was half a pint of ice cream left in her Frigidaire.

Probably the girl's mother was working the evening shift and the brother was out playing somewhere. He would get home and wonder. October would phone the plant first. Then try calling the brother. If he was at their apartment, she would call a cab and take Walter Jean home. Right after dinner.

Walter Jean gave a baby "Yes, ma'am" when October said she could use some help, and for the smothered pork chops they let the flour fly. Mashed potatoes — let them boil first. Break the crispy bacon into little pieces for the canned green beans. Break the egg into the milk before you add it to the corn-meal. You like applesauce? Put in one spoonful of maple syrup, too.

They heaped their plates from the feast laid out on the kitchen counter. When they sat down and October blessed the table, she felt the blessing of someone to eat with. It tickled her to watch Walter Jean put away huge forkfuls in a single chew-and-swallow.

"You like it?" October said.

The girl nodded and kept right on going.

"You can have some more," October said. "Just ask for it."

"May I have some more?" Walter Jean said, plate not yet empty.

"Finish what you have; then you can help yourself."

Walter Jean polished her plate and sat for a moment with her hands in her lap.

"Who is that?" she asked, pointing to the one photograph in the apartment.

"That's my family," October said.

"Your mother?"

"No," October said, "my sister and her husband and their little boy."

Their little boy. She had never disowned

him to another person before now.

"What are their names?" Walter Jean wanted to know.

October told her.

"Where are they?"

"Ohio."

"Oh."

And October brought Walter Jean's plate over and filled it up again.

After dinner and before ice cream, October got out the phone book and found the number for the Fairfax munitions plant. It was only seven o'clock.

Sure enough, Mrs. Campbell was at work that evening and could come to the telephone.

October said who she was and that she had brought Walter Jean home with her because —

"Lord have mercy," the mother said. "We've been calling all over for her. Where is she?"

"Right here," October explained. "You see, her brother wasn't —"

"Put her on the phone," the mother said.

October handed the telephone to the girl. "Your mother wants to speak to you."

Walter Jean happily took the receiver. "Hi, Momma," she said. But as she listened to her mother on the other end, October could see the crest falling. "Yes, ma'am," a dozen times. "Yes, ma'am."

Then, "She wants to speak to you."

October took the phone again.

"Where do you live?" the mother asked. October gave her the address but said not to bother. "I was planning to leave in a few minutes. I've already called a cab," she lied. "I gave her something to eat, and I'm taking her home now unless you want to wait . . ."

"I'll be there when you get there," the mother said, and hung up.

All the way over in the cab the air was like flint. Walter Jean was afraid. October sensed that one brush of two wrong words together and a fire would break out. And so she didn't ask the questions that might give her a clue to what was coming.

The mother stood waving, flagging down the cab at the curb. Before it came to a complete halt, she snatched open the door. "Come on, girl," she said, reaching in for her child.

Walter Jean got out and surrendered to her mother.

October got out too. "I'm sorry," she said. "No one was at home."

The mother stood still long enough for October to get out whatever it was she wanted to say, but it was clear that the mother didn't want to hear it.

"I didn't want to leave her there by herself," October said. "I probably should have tried to reach you earlier."

"Um-hmm," the mother said. "Well, you didn't, did you? Come on, girl," and October watched her pull her child along.

She should have called the woman earlier.

In the normal pecking order, Aunt Frances dialed all the phone calls to October. When she had finished what she had to say, she would put Aunt Maude on, and then Vergie would say hello while Aunt Frances complained in the background about the cost of long distance.

This time, Aunt Maude called. On a Wednesday night. Thanksgiving was almost here, and she wanted to know October's holiday plans.

Where were Aunt Frances and Vergie? Gene had driven them to church. Aunt Maude had stayed home.

October, who had hoped for the miracle that would deliver her from all that was wrong in Chillicothe, considered the out-of-normal order, and the urgency in Aunt Maude's voice. But Aunt Maude said, no, nothing was wrong.

After a short how-are-things, Aunt Maude

said, "I know you're hurtin, but nobody's any worse off, now are we?"

Of course they were, October thought. She was. If the baby ever found out that she had given him to Vergie, he wouldn't be so well off. It might destroy him.

"We've been through a lot," Aunt Maude said. "We're a family. You don't want to go making it worse now, do you?"

"I can't come home," October said. "I just can't." She didn't see why they would want her there.

"Me and Frances ain't gettin no younger," Aunt Maude said. "Keep it under your hat, but she's retiring. Can't cut it anymore. You and Vergie are all we've got. You know that. We need to see you."

October wouldn't be ready to face them by Thanksgiving. She'd have a month, six weeks to get herself ready for Christmas. "Christmas," she told her aunt.

On the eve of Thanksgiving, though October could read between the lines, Cora pleaded for help. In Ed's old kitchen with Ed and two friends making a party in the front room, October and Cora chopped and braised, sautéed and boiled, whipped, baked, and iced without stepping on each other, even as they sipped too many fingers of sherry.

Weary of being a long-distance wife, Cora had made plans to move to St. Louis as soon as there was an opening, which seemed likely in the spring. October would see even less of her.

"I worry about you," Cora said. "You spend too much time alone. You need to get out some."

"You're the one we should worry about," October said. "New place, new job, new marriage . . ."

"Yes," Cora said. "But at least I'll have a decent social life."

"Who's getting a social life?" Ed asked, coming into the tiny kitchen.

Cora told him, "You and me, sweetie."

"I was just telling her," October said. "I'm really going to miss her, but I know the way to St. Louis."

He slid his arms around Cora's waist. "Didn't we have us a good ol' time? . . . Which reminds me — Lonny's supposed to be here for dinner tomorrow. He's got a gig in the Ozarks, but getting him to drive up here for the day was like pulling teeth."

October thought of the long and boring ride back from St. Louis with Leon when Cora and Ed had gotten married.

"I guess he'll be bringing his horn," she said.

Ed laughed. "Don't worry. He's climbing the ladder in New York. Us peons have to pay to see him show off now."

All evening, as they cooked, people dropped by. People October didn't know. She had begun to cover the cooled dishes and put them away for the next day's banquet. She held the roaster pan while Cora lifted out the golden-glazed goose.

"Auntie always saves the drippings for the gravy," she said.

As Cora wrapped the bird in foil, she said, "You don't talk much about David and Vergie. I'm wondering how it is for you these days. What are you going to do?"

October hadn't come prepared to dredge it all up. "It's not something I rattle on about every day," she said. "There's nothing *to* do. It's all done."

She hadn't intended that pitiful tone, either.

"You don't want to hear this," Cora said, "but I'm glad he's with family, so when you change your mind —"

"Who says I haven't changed my mind already?" October said. "But it's too late, Cora. He's Vergie's son now."

"How do you know? Did you ask her? You don't let people walk all over you, girl."

"It wasn't like she *took* him," October said.

"I gave him up. I just didn't know."

"I know, I know, but you brought him into the world, didn't you? He's *your* son. Tell her you made a mistake."

So simple. Cora didn't understand. She couldn't just walk up and take him. Not after all the mess she had made in their lives. Now make *another* mess, in his life? She couldn't.

It was Leon who actually uttered the most telling word for the Thanksgiving Day celebration. *Swell* with a lot of attitude. A good idea that never took off. No real spirit. October did meet some new people who might have been interesting some other time. Two of Ed's friends from St. Louis; a woman friend whom Leon knew from his days in Jefferson City; Alvin, a lawyer from Cora's church, who October suspected had been invited for her sake; and another teacher Cora knew — Donetta something.

They rigged a dining table from a desk and the kitchen dinette and covered them with a white tablecloth, used Cora's new china. Correct glassware and forks. Everybody polite. Bored and boring.

At the end of the so-so dinner, when Leon decided to grace them with the history of his climb in the jazz world so far, October began thinking up her good-bye speech. Bless Ed for yawning "Yeah, yeah, yeah," which bothered

Leon and the woman he had intended to impress. And so Leon took his friend's hand and said, "We'd better split. Thanks, everything was *swell.*"

It was October's cue. One holiday down, one to go.

She'd be brushing her teeth, or walking to the bus, or opening a can of tomatoes, and Cora's words would come back to her in a very sane, very reasonable voice. *Ask Vergie. Tell her you made a mistake. Then work out the details.*

And then the details would explode her into panic. *Whose baby? Where is the daddy? Raise him by myself?* And further explosions, memories of Carrie and Franklin and what happens to children without real parents, what didn't have to happen to David. What he would never have to know.

And October would be back at thinking about saying no to Christmas.

But she didn't. Just like before, Gene met her evening train at Columbus. After weeks of carrying on, she had settled down to being glad about the idea of just seeing David, and holding him, having him in a room all to herself for five minutes. She dared not think the word *love.*

When they got to the Monroe Street house, she helped Gene bring up the footlocker and suitcases. Peered into the oval glass in the heavy door, hoping to see before being seen. She could hear David wailing.

Gene came up behind her. "Knock hard," he said. "Frances and Verge are probably putting David down, and Maude can't hear nothing."

She could see Aunt Frances coming down the stairs.

"Lordy, lordy," she called and swung open the door. "Here's my girl."

My girl. From years ago. My girls. Her and Vergie. Wishes. And Aunt Frances looked older, smaller.

Aunt Maude came through the dining room — frail-looking, too, with her cane — but October had tuned in to Vergie cooing upstairs.

"Lemme see you," Aunt Maude called.

October slipped out of her coat and began helping Gene with the bags. Upstairs had gotten quiet.

"Vergie'll be down directly," Aunt Frances said. "She's trying to get David to sleep. What's all this?"

"Just a few presents and things," October said, and she couldn't hold back. "I was hoping to see David tonight." And, "Can't I just go on up?"

"Sounds like Vergie's just gotten him quiet," Aunt Frances said. "No need to wake him back up tonight."

"Oh, go on up, chile," Aunt Maude said. "Take a little peek. He's the devil in the mornings, but he's a little angel right now."

Vergie was already coming down the stairs. "Sounds like somebody's home for Christmas."

Vergie's hair fell loose in big curls around her shoulders, like she had worn it in high school. Diaper slung over one shoulder, print dress; the serious face was the face of the sister October had always known and mostly loved. When she said hello to Vergie, the distance seemed so great she could have yelled and waited for an echo. She couldn't ask Vergie or tell Vergie anything.

"Take her up to see David, why don't you?" Aunt Maude said.

"He's asleep, but you can look in if you want to," Vergie said. Willing to try.

October followed her up the stairs.

"He's in his own room up here now."

The room was dark, but October could see that it had been papered and painted. Vergie switched on a small lamp and there was David, lying asleep on his stomach in the baby bed on a braided rug in the middle of the room. His head faced them, his arms were at his sides. A study in brown in the white sheets.

Instinctively October smoothed his back.

"Don't wake him up," Vergie whispered. "It's late."

"I won't," October whispered back, and patted the bulge of his bottom. Too precious.

After a moment more, they left him and went back downstairs to food and a warm kitchen. If October had nothing more that Christmas, she would have the touch of him under her smoothing hand.

The next morning, Christmas Eve, October walked into the kitchen and another golden moment. They were all seated around the table and there was David, in his big-boy high chair with a baby dish of scrambled eggs in front of him. Aunt Maude hobbled in behind October, and when David saw her, his face lit; he threw up his hands and danced in his chair, fairly cheered "Hi!" to Aunt Maude.

And she cheered right back at him, cane in air, "Hi, baby!"

"Say hi to your auntie, David," Vergie said.

A question came over his face. October grinned at him. Should she cheer? She wiggled her fingers at him and gave a cheery "Hi, David."

He tried to wiggle his little fingers. "Hi," he

sang softly — melodiously, she noticed.

"Girl, you can do better than that," Aunt Maude said. "Tell him" — and she whooped with her cane, making all kinds of noise, then ended it with a loud "Hi!"

It tickled him so, he could hardly catch his breath. Aunt Maude was funny. October laughed, too, and in the spirit of it she cheered, "Hi!"

He threw up his little arms again — "Hi!" — and giggled at the sheer pleasure of it. She put that in her treasure bag for lean times. For now he was their entertainment at breakfast. Underneath that, he was her son.

"Jooz!" he yelled. Vergie grinned the grin of proud mothers, and poured orange juice into his special cup.

He threw back his little head and whined "Jooz, jooz," and pointed to Aunt Maude's cup of coffee.

Aunt Frances came into the kitchen. "You see, Maudie — I told you you're spoiling him. He can't take coffee."

"Ah Fans!" David called, melting her.

"A teaspoonful won't hurt him," Aunt Maude said, and let David sip from her spoon.

"Ah Mod," he said, rehearsing who was who. Aunt Maude.

"Who is that, David?" Vergie asked him, pointing to Gene.

"Paw-paw," David said. Clowning, he put his hands over his eyes, giggling.

"This is your auntie October," Vergie told him. "Can you say 'Auntie October'?"

Of course he couldn't.

"Aunt Tee," October pronounced slowly. She had yet to hear what he called Vergie.

"Ah Tee," he repeated, looking now to October for the payoff.

"Yes!" she said, undone and awed at the same time. "Aunt Tee."

She could have sat at the table forever, drinking him in.

"Bathtime," Vergie announced, and she undid the tray of his chair. "I saw all the loot you brought," she said to October. Lifting David into her arms. "I can't wait to see what it is."

October checked herself for wear. She was doing fine. "I thought you and I might wrap presents all day like we used to, remember?"

Vergie chuckled. "That's what *you* think. This little devil will be in the middle of everything — won't you, Davie-do?" She tickled his ribs. He erupted in giggles. Mother-and-son unit. Just like that.

"Come on, you gotta have a bath," Vergie said.

David squirmed and fretted to get down. "Paw-paw," he said to Gene, reaching.

"He's scared bath means bed. You'll scrub the hide off of him washing him morning and night. Why don't you just wash him up?"

Looking at David, Vergie said, "He's used to having his bath. I don't want him getting sick or anything for Christmas."

"He's having a ball," Aunt Maude said. "Let him play awhile."

"He's had enough excitement for one morning," Vergie said. "When you see him again, he'll be brand-spanking new — won't you, Davie-do?"

Aunt Maude told her, "Suit yourself, honey."

And October thought, *Don't worry. I can wait my turn to touch him.* What she already had in her sack of treasure would last for months of lean times: his round face, the flawless matte of his bittersweet skin, nose like Vergie's, maybe — family resemblance — liquid mouth with all those little teeth. And the eyes, wonder-wide, laughter-soft, frantic with feeble revolt — they danced and bored in wherever they alit.

Three times, October tried to get Vergie to come down and wrap presents. October didn't care if David tore up paper and trampled on presents — the morning of Christmas Eve could be as big as Christmas. Besides, she had spent weeks sewing and shopping for the best presents for everyone. No perfume and nail polish this time. This time for Aunt Maude she had sewn a gabardine suit with a box jacket, and for Aunt Frances a long-sleeved dress of worsted wool, charcoal with a detachable piqué collar and skirt full enough to cover, gracefully, Aunt Frances's large following.

Vergie never did care that much for handmade things. Instead, October had gotten her something so un-Vergie-like that Vergie would wonder if she had lost her mind. A nightgown and peignoir made out of sheerest voile, trimmed in mignonette lace. For Gene, October had gotten two new blue twill jumpers, the kind that he wore to the paper mill — nothing special — and a special something that he'd probably never wear: a small-print challis shirt. Red.

What is Christmas to a child if not everything he could ever want? A two-year-old wasn't old enough to want much, but he had needs, and other people had to want to see to all of his needs. October wanted that and more for him. Everything she brought should amount to *Christmas:* the smallest, cutest three-wheeler ever made — red with white wheels and black rims and the little rubber bulb thing for the horn; and once she and Vergie and Gene put it together, the horn would screw onto shiny handlebars with yellow tassels. How was that for a boy?

A smart-thing savings bond for him would go over big with Aunt Frances, and nowadays they made tiny little cars that wound up and zoomed. Two of them. So what if he couldn't read and wouldn't for some time? She had found the perfect bunch of animal picture books to get him interested. And why not the wooden triangles, rectangles, squares that all fit together? Dexterity, the thing said. Buster Brown outdid themselves when it came to little-boy clothes — the little corduroy pants that went with the little striped knit shirts: two for now, two for him to grow into. And the best — a navy blue suit with the shorty pants, knee socks, and Buster Brown high-tops. Little man on Sundays.

Didn't they always say that children spend underclothes like pennies? To make it easier on Vergie and Gene, undershirts, socks, baby pajamas with the feet in.

Except for the carton with all the tricycle parts, in the trunk of Gene's car, the loot covered the whole room, including Aunt Maude's bed. October took out the packages of wrapping paper and ribbon and began writing the note cards. The October she used to be would have been thrilled to buy and give and wrap up pretty. Right then, she felt like her old self.

Vergie tapped on the door. "Can I come in?"

"Nobody here but us chickens," October said.

Vergie came in. "David's up with Aunt Frances." She looked around. "My goodness, you've got a whole store in here. These are pretty," she said, touching the stack of boxes already wrapped and waiting for ribbon.

October had laid David's things on the bed — some wrapped, some in open boxes, the way she would like him to discover them under the tree on Christmas morning.

"And what's all this?" Vergie asked.

"For David," October said. She had done well. "Wait till you see what I got him. It's out in the car. We probably ought to bring it in and put it together."

Looking around, Vergie said, "You overdid." October heard the sour note of — what? Disappointment? Envy?

"Come on," she said, cheerleading, "you've got to see it."

"I'll have to get Gene's keys," Vergie said, resigned.

The big brown carton said "Schwinn Tricycle."

Vergie looked at the box. October waited. "That's nice," Vergie said.

October pushed. She lifted one end of the

carton. "We could put it together now, in the room, if you want to."

Vergie pushed back. "We should wait for Gene. He's got a lot to do today. We can do it later."

At lunchtime Aunt Frances brought David downstairs and fed him some of her oxtail soup. After lunch they all got him jigging to music on the radio. Early afternoon Vergie and Gene surprised October by leaving him to her aunts and her in the kitchen while they took their coffee and went upstairs. This could be the moment when she would hold David on her lap.

"Vergie says you outdid yourself this year," Aunt Frances said, "especially for you-know-who."

"I wanted to make it really nice," October said. "I hope you *all* like what I got you."

"Oh, we'll like the things, I know that — you always did have a good eye for nice things," Aunt Frances said.

"Sure did, always did," Aunt Maude said. She offered David a bite of peppermint. He crunched it with his little teeth.

Aunt Frances greased the turkey and began stuffing it. "You know, mothers and daddies don't always take too well to other folks giving the world to their children," she said.

Other folks?

217

"Vergie didn't say anything to me about doing too much," she said. Vergie hadn't been serious, she was sure.

"Come on, Sweet'nin," Aunt Maude said to David. "Let's go watch the bubbles in the lights. Want to see the tree?"

"My teee!" David squealed, hands in the air, and off he ran.

Aunt Frances continued, "Well, you know Vergie. She doesn't like to start anything."

October stopped to consider the whole picture. She had brought home a houseful of gifts. Maybe she had overspent a little. But it was Christmas. She hadn't felt this good in this house for a long, long time. And besides, truth be told, David was her child. She would give him the world if she could. And she knew, of course, that she couldn't — at least, not now. Wasn't Christmas for children? He was a child, the only child in the Monroe Street house. He should have a good Christmas, and they should all enjoy him having a good Christmas.

Aunt Frances asked her, "Are you sure you're not trying to make up for anything?"

No, she wasn't *sure* about anything anymore. But her intentions had been good. She just wanted him, *them*, to have a nice time.

"There is nothing to make up for," she said. Better not to open it up.

"Well, I'll leave it between you and your sister. Maybe she's fine with it. You don't have to listen to an old lady meddling."

October knew about this old lady and meddling. Aunt Frances read signs better than anybody she knew. When Gene and Vergie came downstairs, October understood that Aunt Frances had really intended her word to be heard by the wise.

There Vergie and Gene stood, she a little taller than he, faces like a fort on a hill — nothing would be getting in.

"Mommie!" David squealed like he hadn't seen her just minutes before.

Gene scooped him up — "Hey, little man" — and carried him out of the kitchen. "Let's go see if Santy Claus'll have any snow."

Aunt Maude called from the bedroom, "Bring the baby in here, Gene. I've got something sweet."

Aunt Frances stayed in the kitchen with October and Vergie, puttered over the stove while Vergie fiddled with the knob about to fall off the cabinet drawer.

"When these potatoes boil, turn the fire down, will you, honey?" Aunt Frances said to either of them, and she, too, made herself scarce.

October sat down for this one. She wiped make-believe crumbs off the old wooden table.

Vergie leaned on the chair across the table. "October, I know you want good things for David, just like me and Gene."

"Yes, I do, Vergie," October said. "What . . . ?" She had been about to ask what was wrong with that.

"Don't go getting all upset," Vergie said.

Who was getting upset? October had been about to ask what was wrong with wanting good things for David.

"I'm not getting upset . . ."

Vergie went on.

"Me and Gene think one present from you is enough. Just one."

"What?" And October couldn't get out the "Why?"

"I know, I know," Vergie said. "You went all-out, and we didn't tell you before you got here. We don't want to spoil our son. We want him to appreciate what he has and not take it for granted." She stopped and stared at the table, giving October a chance to say something.

What voice do you use when the wind is knocked out of you?

"Vergie," October said, willing to meet her sister's eyes. "He's only two. It's Christmas, for Pete's sake. A few presents aren't going to spoil him. He won't even know what-all he's got."

But Vergie had obviously rehearsed, and she wasn't going to ad-lib one line.

"Gene and I don't want to spoil our son. We have to do what we think is best. Now, you can give him one present. That's all." She let the silence take over.

Trying to get her mind to bend, October said, "I don't get it."

Vergie let go of her single song to spit out, "And he's *much* too young to be riding a tricycle, for goodness' sake."

Okay, so they didn't want him to have a tricycle. "Is he too young for clothes, too?"

"You can be mad if you want to," Vergie said. "But I'm not having a big fight about it, October. You can get your money back or save the outfits for another time. Me and Gene mean it."

It had nothing to do with money. October knew Vergie knew that. No need to pretend, either.

"All right, Vergie, maybe I splurged a little. I was thinking about all the things that would make him happy. Just like you and Gene. And I was thinking about all the things he probably needs . . ."

"Me and Gene are his mother and father," Vergie said. "We'll get him whatever he needs."

Now October was getting it loud and clear.

"You mean to tell me that *I* can't give him anything besides one present at Christmas? That's crazy!"

Vergie had been holding on to the chair back. She leaned so heavily against it, now, that the chair slid into the table. From the force, October knew that the whole conversation was coming down to a battle.

"*I'm* his mother," Vergie said. "I" — and she tapped her chest with her thumb — "*I* decide."

It wasn't about what toys or how many presents to give — it was about who decides.

October scooted back from the table. She stretched out her arms. "Fine. You decide. Nobody's trying to take that away from you."

There was nothing else to say without getting into the whole other layer of what happened and why and who lost and who won. If October didn't hold an ace, she did have a high card — one strong point.

"Remember," she said. "I teach little boys and girls every day. He's a smart little boy — I can see it already. I may just know something about what he needs and when he needs it."

Gasoline on a match. "Don't you *dare* try to tell me what he needs," Vergie said, jaws tight, breath loud. "You don't know what he needs. You don't *know* him — you just *think* you do."

Before October could think of all the reasons not to prick the boil between them, she said, "I brought him into this world. You don't know *what* I know." She could feel her own breath now, hot on her lips.

"And what does that make you?" Vergie said, daring her.

"I'm not trying to take anything away from you, Vergie — I'm just saying I care about him." The only place to stand.

Vergie leaned out over the table and nearly spit, "Ha."

"You think I don't care. You think I don't love him. You think I wouldn't give anything to be able to do it all over again?"

"You should've thought about that a long time ago. I watched him lay in that crib waiting for you to touch him, just touch him." Vergie's voice wavered. "You wouldn't even *look* at him." Vergie sniffed.

And went on, "Don't come telling me nothing about how you love him. You don't know nothing about loving him."

October wanted to jump up and slap Vergie for that. She wanted to throw into her face that Vergie and Gene had grabbed so fast — too fast — because they couldn't have their own baby.

But the picture of her sitting at the sewing machine, ignoring that little boy who had never asked to be born, was too vivid. It cut her down too far to come back. Her own tears cramped her throat. How was it she had thought they could have a nice Christmas with all this between them?

Through tears, Vergie said, "He's *my* son, October — mine." She stormed out of the kitchen and went upstairs.

The whole house left her alone in the kitchen to boil the sweet potatoes and drink two cups of tea. It came like a new idea. David was *Vergie's* son, not October's son whom she had allowed Vergie to keep forever.

Later, when Vergie came down again to the kitchen, eyes red, she said, "I guess it doesn't have to be just one thing. I mean something else, like one of the little cars or something."

"Okay, Vergie — I'll think of something," October said quietly.

October settled on the shorty-pants suit that she would never see him wear. In the bedroom she laid it aside, imagining his determined face as he tried to pedal the miniature red fire engine Gene had gotten him — the one that, unlike a tricycle, was sturdy all around and would never tip over.

What you must know is that my last breath had indeed been a prayer — I would call it a special petition — for Lillian and Vergie. It seemed that perhaps this Christmas the bud of their joined lives became a blossom opening sweetly for one and swallowing the other. Whatever the case, I held for them.

CHAPTER 12

Just like always, every now and then they heard from October. Vergie was satisfied that the line had been drawn with a sharp stick, and that October would be wary of trying ever again to cross it. Aunt Frances, though, was the problem. After all her urging and fixing, dropping hints here and putting in a word there, Vergie would have thought Aunt Frances would be satisfied, too. The die being cast, and all that.

When it came to David, though, and the way Vergie and October had left things, Aunt Frances acted like she had an itch she couldn't reach. She never let Vergie get through the week without pushing her — "Talk to your sister, talk to your sister." Auntie mailed little cards to October, started calling her all the time, putting Vergie on the phone and making David say hi.

Just as Vergie had expected, October wasn't coming home for the summer. Said she was teaching summer school, saving money for a car and other things. She wrote many letters but addressed them only to Aunt Maude. Trying to say something, Vergie guessed. From time to time she sent little cards to the rest of them: How are you? I'm fine. Say hi to David. She sent him another pop-up card once. Signed it *Aunt Tee*.

According to Aunt Maude, October had met someone, a new man. "Going out with a nice man" was how Aunt Maude put it, and when Aunt Frances asked his name and what he did for a living, Aunt Maude didn't know. "She didn't tell me nothing else. Just said she's going out, that's all."

Aunt Maude told them, too, that October had gotten herself into a "little bit of trouble" with the school board in Missouri. Something about taking some little girl home with her without the mother knowing. The mother wanted her fired, but the school board didn't take any action. They did warn October.

Aunt Maude showed them the picture October sent of herself all dressed up. Supposedly she was in a fashion show and she had made the outfit. Letting them know she was doing just fine without them. Didn't bother Vergie. She didn't want anything bad to happen to her sister, but they were adults now. She suspected things would go along just fine with spaced-out visits, and none of this every-holiday and every-summer nonsense.

Vergie was no fool. She could see what October was doing. After a year of letters and cards and pictures, she said she was going to St. Louis to have Christmas with her friend Cora. Cora needed her, she said. Cora had a new baby. October wasn't coming for Christmas.

Aunt Frances and Aunt Maude had a fit. They had never had a Christmas with anybody missing. This wasn't about to be the first, and Aunt Frances laid on Aunt Maude to talk some sense into October's head. Laid on Vergie to write her a nice letter. "You-all are sisters. We're family."

But October didn't come. As far as Vergie was concerned, they did fine. They got David a tricycle — he was big enough now. They invited Mrs. Hopp and her nephew over for dinner. Gene's first cousin from Oklahoma was in Columbus and drove down to Chillicothe for Christmas dinner, so they had a fine table and a new way of celebrating.

Aunt Frances started her crusade then. Somebody needed to go out to Missouri to see about October. Families didn't do that — just drift apart like that. Everybody knew what the trouble was, but it was time to put it away. And Aunt Frances was taking charge. Once she drafted Gene, it was all over but the shouting. A Missouri vacation would do them all good.

Trouble was, Aunt Maude's hip gave her

more pain than two canes could relieve. How was she going to get around, and didn't October live on the third floor? By the time June rolled around, Aunt Maude hardly ever left the house anymore. Aunt Frances wasn't about to go without her. And so Vergie, Gene, and three-and-a-half-year-old David took the train to Oklahoma. To see Gene's first cousin, and since they were out that way, they might as well stop through Missouri and spend a weekend with October. What did she think of that? She sent a long letter to Aunt Maude, telling her to tell them to come for a week, two weeks, but a weekend was no time at all.

Dust bowl. And real Indians. That was Oklahoma. Down country, with David chasing grasshoppers and running from chickens. Gene's cousin had connections and got them into a real Indian ceremony. And then to Missouri.

October met their train at Union Station in downtown Kansas City, Missouri. Huge place, with taller buildings than they had in Columbus. October fed them the best barbecue Vergie could ever remember eating. Kansas City barbecue. She gave up her bedroom to the three of them and she took the sofa.

Their first morning waking up in October's little bitty place, Vergie saw that David had already gone out to the living room and heard him already begging breakfast. She stood in the crack of the open door and watched to see what she might see.

October lay on the sofa, looking into his face. Vergie realized October hadn't seen him since he could really talk. In fact, she hoped that David would talk to his auntie. He was something else, and Vergie didn't care if the whole world knew it.

David was asking for Post Toasties, and Vergie started to walk away from the half-opened door when she saw October take his hand in hers and run her hands all over his arms like she was feeling for lumps.

October sat up and said, "Give your auntie a hug," swept him right up. David was stiff at first; then, when she tickled him, he started giggling. She kissed him on the cheek, a little smack, the little smack Vergie could taste on her own lips. When October let go of him, he stood and looked at her like he was wondering if it was all right. And October smiled to herself. Vergie smiled to herself, too. October was her sister. She was glad they had come. Glad, too, that it was only for a weekend.

She went to the bathroom and heard David begging for cornflakes. Heard October tell him, "We'll let Vergie decide." And David tell her, "We have a whole bunch at home."

Vergie said sure, cornflakes was all right. David loved them. She and Gene could go for some more of that barbecue, but of course they had eggs and sausage and all the trimmings for breakfast.

Vergie had brought a little something she thought October might like. A little present, and after breakfast, she sent David to the bedroom for the surprise. Oh, he was quite the little man when he came back barely able to manage the box. And handed it to October.

"Mommie said this is for you," he said, just as clear as a judge. October took the box from his hands and opened it. Vergie had bought a crimson leather photograph album, spent large money on it, too. When she saw October's face looking at the first page, she knew she had done a good thing. On the first page, in an oval frame, Vergie had put the sepia-tone picture of a pretty, ginger-colored young woman with long hair, wearing a simple print dress, standing against a photographer's painted backdrop of a flower garden. It was Aunt Frances's old picture of their mother, Carrie, at sixteen, before she had run off with Franklin Brown. Vergie knew October had always liked that picture, and when Aunt Frances started divvying up old pictures, Vergie had saved it for her sister.

And other really good ones, too. The three

Cooper sisters — Frances, Maude, and Carrie, all young women then, posed in front of the same backdrop, looking like *gorgeous* was coined for them in their flapper-looking dresses and thick crimped hair, side-button pumps. Movie stars.

October got teary. "I thought you might like them," Vergie told her. "Aunt Frances finally let somebody go through her old pictures. All these are yours."

Vergie watched October see the pictures of the two of them as girls, and the group picture of the two of them with Aunt Frances and Aunt Maude and a bunch of orphans taken in front of the Children's Home. Who could forget?

"That's me when I was a baby," David said.

Vergie watched October take the picture all the way out of the paper brackets holding it, and held it up close to her face. She hoped October could accept it now without too much to-do. There was no reason for her not to have one.

October smiled and said to Vergie, "This is really something. Thank you, Vergie," and she put back the picture. Vergie had included one of her bathing David, Aunt Frances lighting candles on his birthday cake, Christmas with his first tree, one of October leaving in the snow on New Year's Day. Many, many pictures.

October didn't finish right then. She closed the album and hugged it. "I think you know what this means to me. Thank you for remembering." Vergie could see that she was happy. Maybe they were going to be all right.

About this Arthur man, Vergie had heard little. Only what Aunt Maude had told them. Nothing about who he was, how old he was, or what kind of job he had.

Once they were all dressed, October gave them the map for the day.

"I want my friends to know that I have a family," she told them. "And so I've planned a picnic where you can meet them. Little kids will be there, too. And Arthur."

"Arthur?" Vergie said. Like she had never heard of him.

October laughed a little. "I know Aunt Maude told you I've been seeing Arthur."

Vergie laughed too. "Well, she didn't give us anything to chew on. Just told us his name. I want to know if he's rich and handsome, and is he going to buy you a house?"

"Nothing like that," October said. "We're just going out, but I do like him. He's a teacher, too. At Lincoln Junior High. You'll meet him, but please don't tease him about getting married or anything."

Vergie couldn't wait. Finally October had met someone they could meet. And he might be nice. Her sister deserved that. A nice man who would take care of her.

Swope Park, October told them — the largest in the city, and it had one perfect spot for a picnic. As she drove her new, little-used Plymouth, she pointed out fir and pine, the zoo, the swinging bridge, and then the park's Area Number Five, with its stone picnic pavilions fitted with new pine tables and open hearths for barbecuing.

She introduced Vergie and Gene and David to her friend Donetta, who had brought her boys but not her husband. Another woman friend, Martha, had a teenage daughter, and her husband didn't come, either. Vergie had started to worry about company for Gene when still another woman friend arrived. Vergie had made deviled eggs, and was glad to help set out the food. Another couple arrived — the man, Alvin, young enough to be Gene's son, and they had a little boy, too. As Vergie watched the older children school the younger ones in the art of kickball, she noticed that David was shorter than Donetta's three-year-old.

She stirred lemonade and set out bowls and platters, and saw — along with the other women — that one of the white children from a shelter nearby had made his way over to the field to make friends. He stood near what would have been first base, swinging his arms, probably hoping to play. He looked to be five or six.

Then a man hollered out so loud everybody jumped, "Jeffrey! Get over here."

Even the wind stopped blowing. The ball stopped rolling. All the children stopped running, and Vergie held her breath. She looked around. None of the other pavilions had any black faces.

The children watched as little Jeffrey loped away. The women dug in to do what women-folk do. They took the rock salt of a day that had gone off course a little, sprinkled it over the cold, this-is-the-way-it-is reality of white folks packing up their picnics and moving farther away. And from the deep well of the women's shared hopes, they poured the sweetness of their children making friends and the age-old promise of good food to be had, and they became like the fingers of one hand, churning a summer day into magical whorls of memory.

They roasted hot dogs and loaded up plates in the first go-round at the table. David was a little wild man with so many other children around. He said whatever they said, stuck his hands in his pockets and tried to walk like the big boys, too. Vergie had never yet taken him to the zoo in Columbus, and so a trip to the Swope Park petting zoo came right on time.

As she and October and Gene and David and two other children made their way back toward the shelter, Vergie saw October's face light up and smile a little, before she looked away. She must have seen Arthur. Vergie strained her eyes and looked hard at the people around the shelter ahead. Yes, she saw a man squatting under a tree at the edge of the field, coat thrown across his shoulder, a big bouquet of red roses. Had to be Arthur.

As they went toward him, he stood up. Graying at the temples. Good. Tall enough, brown enough — he would do.

Vergie stopped and stood with her hands on her hips. "That must be Arthur," she said. "Looks like somebody can't stay away very long." She tickled herself.

October stopped, too. "I told you he would be here later. He's just somebody I'm seeing, so don't go making a big thing out of it." But Vergie saw how her sister skipped just a little.

"Hey," Arthur called to them. "Hurry up. I've been here all day." He had a nice ring to his voice.

October's friend Donetta yelled, "Girl, come get this man before he drives us crazy."

Gene chimed in under his breath, "Ain't

never been a Cooper woman that couldn't get a man to beg."

"Hush, man," Vergie told him, trying to find the degree of sober that an older sister should have.

October took Vergie's hand. "Arthur, these are my folks."

"Hi," he said to Vergie. "You must be Eugene," he said, and shook Gene's hand. "And this must be David." Vergie wondered what October might have said about David. She smiled as her smart little boy put out his hand, too. Then Arthur hugged October like she and Gene weren't even there. Vergie took David's hand and went on up to the shelter.

Under the shelter, the women herded the children into the cool, where a white tablecloth had been spread, and in the middle of it a sheet cake the size of a pillow case. Giant blue letters spelled out "SIX."

Nobody seemed to know why, until Arthur and October joined them. "I thought we ought to celebrate," Arthur said.

Vergie looked at October, who looked as blank as the stone they stood on.

"Don't tell me you forgot," Arthur said to her, brushing her cheek with his finger. Whatever it was, she still wasn't remembering.

"Six months," he said. "Our sixth-month anniversary — remember?"

The other women oooed and ahhhed. "We were afraid to ask, just in case it was something big and he had it wrong," Donetta said.

October was all grins, now.

"Momma, buy me one of those," Donetta said. "Arthur, you are a woman's dream — flowers and cake for six months. Please, man, talk to Kenneth."

Vergie thought it was nice — probably Arthur was showing off a little for the family, but that was okay. The roses had already brought him up a few levels in her book.

After the picnic, Arthur wanted to take them all out for the evening. A show at the outdoor Starlight Theater, where they could bring David, and where Vergie was sure to see at least one famous person. Vergie looked forward to spending the evening picking apart this Arthur man so that by the time they left, she would know what he was all about. When they got to October's place to change clothes, however, Aunt Maude phoned, sad and scared. Aunt Frances was in the hospital. She had had a stroke.

Vergie wouldn't be consoled. They never should have left her — they had to get back. Couldn't somebody drive them home? There was no way she could wait until the morning train. October got on the phone to Union Station.

Vergie held on to a single image for strength: Aunt Frances in her nurse whites, twisting her hair into a bun and reaching for her starched LPN cap. Every morning, predictable as day, Aunt Frances had planted that cap on the front of her head, and with that long pearled hatpin clenched between her teeth, had yelled, "You-all better hurry up — you're making me late." Every morning until they finished high school, Vergie and October had walked a few steps ahead of those two women, their aunts, to the corner where they caught the bus and the two girls turned for school. Nothing could change now.

October finished her calls. They were in luck. The four of them took the night train to Columbus.

CHAPTER 13

The doctor had already told them that it would be days before he could say one way or the other. To October this meant that he didn't want to tell them. And so she said that they should keep a vigil. Twenty-four hours every day, one of them should be right at Aunt Frances's side. Panic took hold of October every time she pictured Auntie wandering in the Valley of the Shadow. She looked at her — pale against the white sheets, slack and doughy — and prayed. Here it was now, Bible wisdom rolling off her own tongue and none of it went anywhere. *God is love.* If this was true, how could God let things like this happen? *Thy will be done.* Surely suffering wasn't it. *For everything there is a season, a time for every purpose under heaven.* Didn't October already have her season of grief, or was this just a continuation? But she prayed anyway.

Vigil it was. For three days they all took turns watching Aunt Frances breathe, talking to her absent eyes when they were open, cat-napping when she slept. Visitors couldn't stop coming — from the church, the paper mill, the hospital, the neighborhood. Some of Aunt Frances's bywords being proven. Reaping the kindnesses she had sown. And there were all the women from the Negro Ladies' League, too — a loosely gathered group that collected food and clothing for the poor. October recognized some of their faces.

The League had always left a sour taste in October's mouth, because her aunties had pushed it so hard. When she and Vergie were girls, the biggest notable event of the year had been the weeklong annual celebration for the Children's Home, and the Negro Ladies' League was always front and center. A season didn't end that hadn't seen those ladies — led by Frances, with Maude Cooper and their nieces — tramping around the Hopewell burial mounds or a Tecumseh site with a rag-tag flock of orphans.

Although Aunt Frances had never understood why, October had hated the orphans, and she suspected that Vergie had hated them, too. It made sense, when she thought about it. Vergie and October were orphans, too. But strange ones. Different. They knew it and the orphans knew it. Aunt Frances and Aunt Maude alone had had it in their heads that doing things with the orphans could somehow be good for their two girls. Auntie never let them forget that the two of them were better off because somebody wanted them. And as October sat watching Auntie breathe, she conceded that Auntie had been right.

Toward the end of October's shift on the third day, Aunt Frances opened her eyes again and made a humming noise. Nothing in particular. October took her hand and told her, "Try to rest, Auntie. The doctor says you need to have rest and quiet."

Again Auntie hummed, but this time with an edge to it. Gently, as if she were lifting a wilting flower, October lifted Auntie's head and held a glass of water to her lips. Not so good. Auntie moaned, "Um-umm," meaning no, tried to work her mouth, tried to form some impossible word. Her eyes fixed on the bowl of crushed ice on the nightstand.

"Oh," October said. She took a tiny chip of ice from the bowl and spooned it into Auntie's mouth. Then dabbed her lips with a tissue.

She sat in her chair, and Aunt Frances lay silent but with eyes trying to say it all.

"Remember the chickenpox?" October said. "How you rubbed my blisters with ice?"

With the slightest pressure, Aunt Frances pressed her fingers into October's hand. Yes, she did remember.

"You don't have to stay awake," October

said. "It's all right to go back to sleep. I'm not going anywhere."

She heard herself say it. Aunt Frances might not want to close her eyes for fear *she* was going somewhere.

But her eyes soon drooped closed again, her grip fell, and October found herself breathing with her aunt's shallow rhythm.

Tallies. Wins. Losses. Aunt Frances had been good to her, period. And she owed her. The bad things always come up at the worst times. October was bound to remember the worst storm that raged between them, when she was seventeen and hell-bent on changing her name. Those years before, and even right then in the hospital room, she believed it was one of the most important things she had ever done. But at seventeen she had been righteous with a capital R. Left no room for Auntie to bless or curse.

Auntie had challenged her, October had prevailed. But the arguments had left her with one regret. There at the bedside, looking down on the fading beacon of her early life, October remembered standing at their front doorway once, with her shorty coat over her arm, big as day. And Aunt Frances saying something final, like "Girl, if you go out that door, I'll make you sorry you were ever born." And October had spewed a perfect cruelty about spinsters — an easy target: something along the lines of Aunt Frances and Aunt Maude having no life until she and Vergie had come to live with them, and how they had not wanted *them* to have a life either.

What really bothered October that afternoon at the hospital was her remembrance of Aunt Frances's face when — with purest venom — October had proceeded to take away any hold Aunt Frances might have thought she had.

"You're not our mother," she had told her aunt. "You could never be *my* mother. You didn't sign anything legal to keep us, and I don't have to mind somebody who's just a relative."

And she had fairly pranced out the door.

And since that first incident of regret, she had done much worse — brought untold worries and hurts to her auntie's door.

That day at the hospital she thought back and saw her life as if it were a play that had started with one single event and then gotten blown every which way by the whims of God and men. That day at the hospital, she fully realized that life as she knew it had started with the death of Carrie. And wasn't that the way grief worked — throwing you back to what caused what, and who was to blame, and how much you had lost?

Over all the years that she had let the event begin to flood her mind and quickly evaporate, October had come up with a hundred ways to describe it. The word "murder" had never fit. The drama of "tragic death" took away the impact. "Father's crime" — too detached. "Family's shame" — too vague. "A man's insanity" — yes. "A woman's nightmare" — even closer. But nothing ever fit the way "The Killing" fit. It brought her down to the nitty-gritty, brought home just what their father had brought down on their heads.

October had been five years old — just five — a little girl with no idea that there were layers to what was happening. Over the years she had scribbled things, words on bits of paper, trying to get it right: a wall of water crashing against two new sapling trees. A gyre of wind sucking air into its spin and dipping down to touch the great and small thing that had been their lives. A natural disaster. How terrible it must have been for children — this was how she had always felt any emotion around it: as a secondhand sympathy for the children she and Vergie had been. Whenever she caught herself grieving, it had been for them as they had been then, two young girls.

It didn't seem logical, but for October the public *fact* of The Killing seemed to affect her life more than the private pain of losing her

two parents did. Having to be *his* daughter —
the daughter of a man who killed somebody.
Having to carry that name and that label
meant shame on you. Are you an evil person,
too? And she and Vergie had grown up without so much as a second cousin to show them
what a man was. Fascination comes from
that. Leads to all kinds of craziness.

Franklin Brown had been the source of everything that had been wrong in their lives.
But October couldn't say that she actually
hated him. Hate didn't touch all the things she
felt about him. Maybe disgust began to describe her feelings. And sadness, too, over the
terror that Carrie must have gone through.
Sadness over Carrie's heart that must have
been broken at the thought of dying. October's sympathy, though, always gave way to
the wish that Franklin Brown had somehow
come to realize to the nth degree what he had
done, and then that he had been forced to live
with it until his last breath.

Some of her vengeful wishes came from being tainted by someone else's crime. At nine,
and still named Lillian, she was a gangly little
girl with thick ropes of plaited hair. The white
freckle that was supposed to have turned into
a mole had become a dime-spot blemish on
her cheek.

Vergie, on the other hand, had become a

thirteen-year-old whose rounded heft refused to be disguised as ordinary ripening. For Vergie, the burden of child-witness to The Killing had worked itself out in pounds, or so they had all thought — she was older, she had suffered more deeply than her little sister, who had been too young to understand.

They *were* sisters, though. Where there are sisters, the flame of contention smolders, and difference is the very air it craves. They were way past the need for being baby-sat, way past the desire to nose around the landscape of their aunties' rooms. With the way she kept her closet and the files of papers in the cedar chest under that high bed of hers, Aunt Frances had already become the General, law-and-order.

They knew every piece of paper in the chest by heart. Early school drawings, birth certificates, baptism certificates, attendance certificates, bank papers — all that. And whenever they wanted, they could touch the small white Bible with the crumbly clipping, the *Herald* obituary that announced Carrie's death. Inside the back cover of the Bible, the black ink and backslanted scrawl of "Carrie Cooper" had faded to brown.

The closet, too, they knew: starched white uniforms hung like guards over the few other dresses Aunt Frances owned; paired white duty shoes toed a straight line. The bureau drawers gave up old-style white cotton stockings on one side and brown cotton stockings — hideous, October always thought — on the other. And, like a monument to an old dream, a solitary bottle of toilet water — precious in cut glass — on her bureau.

Aunt Maude's space had nothing like order. Lounging, rummaging seemed fine in her room. October remembered how Aunt Maude's clothes — drab to plain — had always been draped in layers over the chair in the corner and piled on her bedpost. She and Vergie always found a coffee cup sitting with the lotion and toilet water and combs and brushes on top of her bureau. Snips of newspaper and scribbled lists made a raggedy fringe around her mirror. And candy. Always a tin full of peppermint, butterscotch, lemon drops on her closet shelf, under her one black hat.

At nine and thirteen, October and Vergie had not outgrown their habit of after-school sweets. School-weary and famished, they had just finished helping Mrs. Hopp make rag rugs for the Children's Home one day and raced through the front door straight up to Aunt Maude's closet. They sat on Aunt Maude's bed, Vergie with the nice candy tin on her lap, and they raked through hard candy for best and next best.

October liked butterscotch, and there was one, but Vergie was faster. She popped it into her mouth before October could say *mine.* That gave them a way to spend the next hour. They could just bicker until October decided that nothing at all was better than settling for the sour lemon drops, which were all that was left.

Later, while they piddled with homework, Vergie went down to the kitchen and came back with a crisp green apple, cut supposedly in half, and a little pile of salt on a piece of waxed paper to sprinkle on the apple. She placed the smaller half — a peace offering nonetheless — on October's bed. "That's yours," she said.

October ignored it. Vergie was hungry, but she dipped-and-bit, dipped-and-bit slowly, until hers was all gone. She kept eyeing the half on October's bed, piddled and glared for a while.

"You know, apples start rotting as soon as the air hits them," Vergie said. "You'd better eat yours before it turns brown." To which October answered, "Let it rot — I don't want it." She didn't want apple, she wanted butterscotch.

Vergie wanted apple. "Okay, then," she said. "Starve if you want to." And she snatched up the other half and chomped off a huge bite.

What happened next had to do with the fact that each year, the Negro Ladies' League had sponsored an annual Children's Home trip, which *The Call* — the only national Negro newspaper — dubbed a "Noteworthy Excursion," to the zoo in Columbus. And each year until October and Vergie were too far into their teens, they were forced to "set an example" by sitting like bumps on a log with the orphans on the rented bus, eating shelled and salted peanuts.

There had been this boy, Clyde, a pipsqueak, but Vergie liked him, orphan or not. She had written his name on page 100 of all her books. And there had been this girl, Lila, fearless and feared. Lila was Vergie's age and had run away several times. "Seen the world" — undoubtedly all of downtown Chillicothe and the river. Wore makeup and smoked cigarettes, mostly butts.

During the zoo outing the year she was thirteen, Vergie had made eyes enough at the Clyde boy to convince him that she would walk over a hundred miles of broken glass barefooted if he would smile her way. With the rest of the orphans, Vergie and October had spent the day swatting flies, licking their shaved ice, looking at the same old animals, all of whom had silly names like Tiny the Elephant, and Gertie the Hippopotamus. On the bus back to the Home that afternoon, Clyde stuck a wad of gum to the back of Vergie's seat. On a piece of paper he scribbled "Gertie" and stuck the paper to the gum. Hearing all the giggles, Vergie turned around to see what else but Clyde, smiling at her. As the moment hung and trembled, Vergie smiled back. And then the moment hit and shattered. Vergie saw the paper. The orphan runaway Lila smacked Clyde with her fist. Too late.

Devastated didn't come close. For three days Aunt Frances and Aunt Maude had cooked and spread banquets for breakfast, lunch, and dinner, and Vergie had gagged and cried through them all. Aunt Frances had cursed the ground stupid Clyde walked on, telling Vergie that the boy was a heathen, an orphan with no home training. And Vergie cried into another day. They shook their heads, wrung their hands. Vergie cried into a second night. Over the third day, October had had the good idea that Vergie might be calmer if she had a new skirt to wear, a skirt like the ones Lila wore. October had just the right length of material, too; Aunt Frances had been saving it for a dress. That very day, Aunt Maude and Aunt Frances and October had pieced it together, and finally Vergie's tears dried up.

And so when Vergie gobbled up October's half of the apple that day a few months later, it was the strategic windfall that can bless all warring children. It would be years before October was able to understand how anger works. Why, in her meanest, cold-blooded fury, she had spat out "Gertie!" in Vergie's face.

Right away, though, October could see that she had hit her mark. Vergie's face began to break. But this time Vergie pulled herself together fast.

She arranged her face, lifted her chin ever so slightly, leveled her eyes at October, and said, "I'd rather be Gertie than a spotted *Lillian* any day."

The words weren't infected with any fatal poison. Some people had extra fingers, some had crossed eyes, some had had polio and would be crippled forever. October's white spot would turn brown again someday. She was fine — her feelings weren't hurt.

Oh, but Vergie had her. With lips all curled, now, Vergie had repeated, "I wouldn't be caught dead with that name." And when she saw that October still did not catch on, Vergie blurted, "Stupid. You're so stupid you don't even know where your sorry name came from."

October's face must have remained blank. She had never thought about it, really. Didn't get the point.

Hand-on-her-hip, Vergie had rained it down. "I'm named after Grandma Vergie Cooper," she said. And then the damning question: "Who do you think you're named after?"

Again, what did October know?

"Your *father's* people," Vergie said, quivering with the pleasure of having it out. "Poppa's sister who raised him. Her name was *Lillian*."

Dumbfounded, October called up reason to her defense. "You're a lie," she said. She threatened to tell Auntie. Any loose reference to Franklin Brown — his person or possible kin, his crime or punishment — any little remember-that-time about their early lives in Cleveland, their suspicions, old wishes, or nightmares had always brought a swift and unmitigated bawling-out from Auntie and Aunt Maude, too. October was sure that Vergie had made it up.

And then Vergie had spilled out unbelievable details. "His mother died and his big sister raised him and her name was Lillian. Ask Auntie. They used to live in Tennessee."

"Liar," October said, folding fast.

Vergie got louder. "Ask Auntie. She knows.

Everybody knows. That's where your spot came from. No-good crooks and slutty women — that's who you are."

Hands now covering her ears, October couldn't listen. How many times had her aunts told her that they were decent girls, that they had come from good people? How many times had they warned "their girls" away from "low-life" people who hung around the barbershop on Keane Street because "our girls" are better than that?

October threw back at Vergie, "We never even *knew* those people," trying to sound sure instead of whipped.

But Vergie was on. "Yes, we did," but there must have been some doubt because she went on with, "Even if we didn't, you still got their . . ." and she drawled, *"Lil-yan."*

"Shut up!"

"Lil-yan," Vergie slurred. "Lil-yan . . . Lil-yan . . ."

October swung at her, blindly, and her fist caught the corner of Vergie's mouth. Vergie's teeth cut the inside of her lip. She bled red blood.

Shocked them both for a split second. Then Vergie ran to the bathroom and, when she saw the blood, wailed like a trapped puppy dog. October went after her, but by then Vergie would have no apologizing.

"Get out!" she screamed and locked herself in the bathroom. October stood at the bathroom door, saying "I'm sorry" to the frame, but her words were way past lost.

Things might have gone better if Aunt Frances had been the first to arrive home to straighten out sister-squabbling quickly. But Frances had had the late shift at the hospital and wouldn't be in until midnight. And so as hours passed, the incident ballooned into a crime, like night swelling from a single shadow across the bedroom floor.

Aunt Maude got off from the mill at five, and Vergie burst out of the bathroom and stumbled down the stairs, greeting her with a garbled story, plenty of tears, and a swollen lip. Aunt Maude had calmed and soothed and whimpered with her and dressed her mouth with Mercurochrome. October had sat alone in their bedroom, waiting for whatever was to come next.

Aunt Maude, her face flat, opened the door and stood looking at October for a long time, and then her eyes welled up.

"What are we going to do?" she said, as if they were all lost. She looked into the air for an answer, then closed the door.

No one ate dinner.

Somewhere in what seemed the middle of

the night, October was shaken awake, to Aunt Frances's cast-iron "Get up, Lillian, and get dressed."

She had been expecting anything. Vergie had not slept in her bed. Aunt Maude's voice was an all-night murmur behind her door. Starkly awake, October had gotten herself up and dressed, shoes and all.

"Get your coat!" Aunt Frances yelled from downstairs and October did as she was told.

Frances Cooper — fully prepared in nurse whites and her navy-blue cape with the red lining — waited at the front door. Aunt Maude stood at the top of the stairs in her nightgown and watched as October and Aunt Frances went out into the night. October followed Auntie across the yard to the Hopps', where Mr. Hopp waited on his front porch. Cold night. Cold enough to see his breath huff.

"Okay, Miss Cooper," he said to Auntie. "If you're sure this is what you want to do, come on."

Mr. Hopp worked for the city, although his exact job was a question October could not have answered at the time. Whenever he left for work she had heard keys jangling at the hip of his coveralls. This night the keys jangled, too. Silence like the cemetery rode with her in Mr. Hopp's long, low Hudson to the downtown Chillicothe she had seldom seen at night. Corner lamps, cold and glaring, made sharp shadows against the still buildings, empty streets.

Mr. Hopp pulled up in front of city hall and sat still, looked at the building awhile, then went around the block, into the alley, and stopped behind the building. Fumbled with his keys. Where were they going? October couldn't imagine what punishment lay waiting — she knew only that Aunt Frances had thought it up, and it would be pretty bad.

"Okay, let's see what might be waitin in there for this one," Mr. Hopp said. Aunt Frances got out of the car and held the back door for October.

"Come on," she said.

Long hallways waited. And echoes. Two white policemen took Mr. Hopp aside to talk, then left. Aunt Frances followed close on Mr. Hopp's heels and October followed close on hers, down another long hallway that led to an iron door. Mr. Hopp unlocked the door and they entered.

When Aunt Frances pushed her forward, October saw the cells, eight or ten, side by side. In the half-dark she could make out lumps of bodies sleeping in some of the cells. And one cell door standing open. Mr. Hopp walked over to it, motioning for her to follow.

Aunt Frances nudged her.

"You want to sleep in here?" Mr. Hopp said.

October shook her head no. Up close, she could see the measly cot with no sheet, the stinky slop jar, the dirty stone floor. She wondered about the police — what would they care about a fight between her and Vergie? But she couldn't guess how far Mr. Hopp could go at the jail, and there was no way to know how far Aunt Frances's wrath would go.

A cold stone floor at night, being locked away, having to lie on that cot and use that slop jar — would Auntie do that to her? Was she finally just an orphan?

Aunt Frances had then opened the cell door farther and nudged her inside.

"This must be where you want to end up," she said. Then she said, "This is where your poppa ended up. He died in a place just like this. He started out just like you, fighting all the time."

She stepped out of the cell and clanged the door, leaving October inside the bars.

"Franklin may have given you his sister's name," Aunt Frances said, "— that's something you can't help. But you'll not have their ways and live with us, I promise you."

Dazzling. So her name really *did* come from

those people — people she knew only as too lowdown and dirty to be mentioned. And what else? Her father had been a character in a storybook, banished to never-never land. She had always thought of him as put away forever. The end. It had never occurred to her that he could die.

An aunt, someone named Lillian, the woman who had raised him? No one had ever bothered to mention this. The whole day had turned into a new life. Her blackberry skin was a given, but until that day the only other family resemblance October had ever taken into account had been the way she favored Carrie or Aunt Frances or Aunt Maude or Vergie. With one word, she had a life times two. She had hurt Vergie more than she had intended. Just happened. And then Vergie had opened a sewer with all kinds of gullies and gutters feeding it. Such a secret. All this time everybody had known.

October, even at the age of nine, had understood then that she was someone other than herself. That she was different from Aunt Frances and Aunt Maude. Different, too, from Vergie. Unwittingly, Aunt Frances had held a mirror in front of her, and even if she couldn't yet make out what she saw, she knew this: in more ways than one, the reflection coming into focus looked like a leper.

After that night, slowly at first, then whenever it wanted to happen, then with a vengeance, the name *Lillian* had become an accusation. Vergie's way of drawling out "Lilyan" could be an excruciating jab or a pinstick, depending on how raw October felt at the time.

Aunt Frances and Aunt Maude would step in a little with "All right, Vergie, that's enough."

But they, too, had got in the spirit of the curse. "Lillian" was the epithet when October's attitude became the stubborn cliff their reason couldn't climb. They tiptoed, never used the name unless they were put out with her. Otherwise they started calling her "Lily" or "Lily Ann."

But she called herself October to herself. October, for the month their mother had died. October, for the lack of any other name that she could put on to say how it felt to become another, stranger person.

Over time, though, she hardened. Turned her secret into a plan. When she got to seventeen, that was it. Old enough. She learned not to flinch so, and Vergie got tired of trying to use a dull weapon. Aunt Frances and Aunt Maude got tired, too, or guilty. However it happened, at some point they all dropped *Lillian* from the list of words they could use when they were mad, and replaced it with a permanent *Lily* for all occasions. Which sure enough proved that the name had kept some evil thing alive for too long. For a time anyway, October was Lillian to the world, Lily at home, and October to anyone who would go along.

It was always with a good feeling that she remembered the long swoon of puberty. A for-real new person, starting with her body and going on to the music of her own voice, every single nerve ending exposed in every single moment. Without telling anyone, she had fallen in love, first with the deciduous drama of autumn, the pungency of blade and leaf giving up the ghost. Fallen in love with poems, any poem, and with the sound of the flute, or a bird, or train whistle.

She had fallen in love with the boy who worked in Ford's grocery store, and because she never caught that boy's name, she had switched her love to the Reverend's son, home from Wilberforce College. Because he had never been around for long and had never noticed her, she ventured to speak to a boy in the twelfth grade who said hi to her once. He didn't need a name. They didn't need to talk.

Each night before bed, like the leper in *The Good Earth*, October had inspected every inch of her new body for white freckles. She was convinced that the brown would return, and since no other spots had appeared, she got it in her head that the sun had protected her, and spent more time outdoors.

When she had turned seventeen, old enough to give herself a new name, with two aunts who were only relatives, not parents, October found an accomplice. The Reverend's daughter, Dainty Bonner.

Dainty wore her hair twisted around a hair-rat, the way women did, in a crown hoop that she set off with jeweled combs. She smoked and had a boyfriend twenty years old. October had fed Dainty bits of the whole orphan story and the evil family she didn't want to be related to. Tortured friend. And Dainty had agreed that *Lillian* had never been a name that suited her, and that *October* stood out. And Dainty had known exactly where, in the courthouse, they had to go to do the thing right.

October had never done this before. She went to the courthouse unprepared. How could she have known about things like the proof of her birth or birth name, and how much money she would have to pay, and a fail-proof reason for a name change, and the six-week wait for it to be official. And so, on another not-so-brave day, she and her friend Dainty went back to the courthouse. This time she had rifled through Aunt Frances's cedar chest for papers and emptied her own secret stash for the notary's fifty cents. This time she had announced her intention to Aunt Frances, who had dared her to leave. This time, with her shorty slung across her shoulders, and her hand on the doorknob, she had disowned the only mother she had ever really known.

Under "Justification" on the form, October wrote a version of the truth. Instead of pointing to the bloodline, she wrote that Lillian was the name of the mother of the man who had killed October's own mother. No one would dare refuse her then.

Her mother had died on October 26, 1931. As she sat with Dainty on the bench outside the notary's office, a feeling came over her. She had finished something important, and something else had begun. Finally, she could hold on to autumn no matter what the season was, and have the perfect memorial to Carrie. She could have the perfect way to separate herself from her namesake forever — the perfectly unique name for a girl with a dramatic blight on the brown of her cheek, *October*.

On the fifth day after Aunt Frances had suffered the stroke, Gene brought Vergie to relieve October at the hospital. Reverend Carter had prayed his ardent prayer, and as they all stood around the bed, a nurse came in with a needle and syringe.

"We need to check her catheter," the nurse said. "You-all won't mind stepping out into the hall for a minute, would you?"

Out in the hall, October tried to sound like she knew what she was talking about and at the same time not scare Vergie.

"Vergie, I know that miracles can happen," she told her, "but remember, we have to be realistic, too."

It seemed to October that until she had entered Aunt Frances's hospital room that day, her own life had not been pinned down. As if at any moment she might be able to put her life in reverse and move into the life she wanted. Redeemable, she thought. But now she was beginning to see that Aunt Frances's death would nail things down. Up until then she had seemed to have a "real life" waiting somewhere, and one day she would wake up and be in her real life. One where Franklin Brown had not killed Carrie. Carrie was not in the cold ground. Franklin had not died in jail. She and Vergie had not been orphans. In a sense, up until then, Aunt Frances and Aunt Maude had been aunts, not parents. And in some part of her, October had always held out for the possibility of "real" parents. All of it, even the David chapter, could have been a dream, and there was time for it all to be corrected.

But now Aunt Frances would be the real mother who would be dead and buried, gone forever. Nothing could be changed. October's messed-up life would be the only one she would ever have.

Vergie said, "The doctor said that it may take a long time for her to pull through." October knew Vergie dared not think she might die.

October thought she ought to make it clear to Vergie. "And, Vergie," she told her, "it's possible that she might not be able to pull through — I mean, she might not make it. We don't know."

Fear blazed in Vergie's eyes. "How can you say that?" She stepped closer to Gene and grabbed his hand.

"I'm just saying *might*, Vergie. We have to be prepared for the worst. If there's anything you want to say to her, you shouldn't wait. That's all I'm saying."

"Darn it, October, you never look on the bright side. The doctor never said that, and he ought to know." She wiped a tear with her thumb. Gene put his arm around her, and they went back inside the room.

On October's watch the next morning, she had the sense to take her own advice. Say what needed to be said.

Auntie's eyes were closed, and October took her time forming the right words. Auntie's eyes opened and October gave her a chip of ice from a spoon. Auntie stared, and after a few minutes, October could see recognition in her eyes.

October went into how well she remembered the years, the sacrifices, the fevers soothed, the battles Auntie had mounted against the world for her and Vergie, whether they were wrong or right. As well as she could, she said how bad she felt about bringing a child into the world without a father, and giving him away, and fighting with Vergie. And still she couldn't find the words to say what needed to be said.

Auntie never relaxed her gaze.

October tried again. "There is one thing I want to tell you . . ."

Auntie's eyes burned.

". . . something I said to you once, a long time ago. And I never apologized, I never took it back. I know you know I didn't mean it, but I want to take it back now, anyway."

Auntie pressed her fingers lightly into October's palm. She could hear.

266

Looking into her mute face, October said, "I just want to thank you."

Auntie then made her little humming sound, but kept her eyes fixed on October's face.

"Thank you for being my mother." The tears came then, but October refused to lose the one chance to have it said. "You were a better mother than I ever gave you credit for — better than you ever knew," she said.

Auntie pressed her palm, and October knew a smile was in there.

October wasn't at the hospital that evening to see Vergie reading the Bible to Auntie, or to see the pain in her sister's eyes when Auntie had another stroke. She stood next to Vergie, though, all through the next day, as Auntie's heart marched weakly on.

It was then that I stood by and held for Frances, my sister. She never opened her eyes or pressed their palms again.

CHAPTER 14

On the weekend following the funeral, October made herself comfortable on the side of Aunt Maude's bed, wondering about her — what she would do without Aunt Frances. She remembered the photograph of the Cooper sisters and wondered what she and Vergie would look like in a few years.

Right now somebody would have to pick through Aunt Frances's things, and she didn't think Aunt Maude was up to it. At the funeral they had had to give her smelling salts. No more scares like that. Gene had taken David to watch the high school band practice and left the women to punctuate the sentence of mourning.

October heard Aunt Maude's cane-and-hobble above her, heard her hesitate at Aunt Frances's doorway, then hobble around up there in that forsaken space, stopping, probably shaking her head, probably weeping, shuffling on.

After a while, Aunt Maude called downstairs and October went up. Vergie, too, came to hug and soothe.

"What are you doing up here by yourself?"

Vergie asked her. October saw that Aunt Maude had pulled the chest and other boxes from beneath Aunt Frances's high-up bed.

"You-all might as well start going through her things," Aunt Maude said. "I can't do it by myself. Besides, she already gave me what I wanted most. I'll put away her quilts for the grands, or at least for David when he's grown. I'm keeping her brooch." She stood fumbling with the antique pin, shook her head too sadly, and left them to shake their heads, too.

October and Vergie dragged the wooden step over the floor and climbed into the high bed with one of the paper-stuffed boxes between them.

Vergie pulled out a few handfuls of paper. "What do you think we ought to do with all this stuff? She kept everything we ever did."

"I don't know," October said. She couldn't see herself hauling any of it back to Missouri.

Vergie began to make piles, sorting. "For instance, here's my old report card from eighth grade, and yours, too."

"You don't want them, do you?" October asked. Vergie didn't answer, meaning that maybe she did.

"I used to wonder why people kept this kind of junk," Vergie said. "Posterity, I guess."

Vergie was fingering a piece of dark blue

construction paper, aged to shreds. October watched her unfold the creases and reveal the dried and flaking white flour-paste print of a small hand.

It looked familiar. "Whose was that?" October asked her.

"Yours," Vergie said. "Don't you remember it?"

October took the piece of child artwork and spread it on her lap. She stretched her hand over it, trying to believe that this was how small her hand had once been and to remember how she must have dipped it in flour paste and pressed it against the paper.

"Imagine that," she said. "I was once this small." No big deal — just a fondness she felt for the little girl who had made the print.

Vergie said, "You should take it home with you, frame it." She was kidding.

"Yeah, but it seems like a shame to throw it away. In a way it's better than a photograph. It's proof that I was alive."

For whatever reason, that seemed to rub Vergie the wrong way. "I swear, October," she said. "Sometimes you can be so wrapped up in yourself. Aunt Frances died, not you."

October tried to explain. "You know what I mean — something tangible here that proves that this once was me."

"Prove it to who?"

"To anybody who's interested, I guess — to myself, mostly."

Vergie took the frail piece from October's lap.

"Um-hmm," she said. "I guess this is why people have children."

October didn't want to get on that road with Vergie, and she hoped Vergie would turn off soon.

But Vergie went on thinking out loud, figuring out life, a syllable at a time.

"Something like this makes no sense," she said, "unless you have a child who needs to see how one life leads to another."

"I know," October said. "This whole thing with Auntie dying has brought it home to me."

"If I didn't have David," Vergie said — didn't hesitate at all — "I couldn't have buried Aunt Frances."

That should have been enough. But no.

"At least I can feel good that when Gene and I are gone, David will carry on."

Vergie didn't seem the least bit aware that she might be barreling down a dangerous road, and she seemed to be ignoring all the signs.

"And his babies will take up after him," she said. "You know?"

With Aunt Frances's death and all, October

thought that Vergie had either had a lapse or that she now thought all uneasiness about David was behind them. Could it ever be behind them?

October answered Vergie's "You know?" with "Yes, I imagine so." The faintest suggestion of ashes filled her mouth. Maybe Vergie just needed someone to talk to.

"The Lord taketh away — I mean Aunt Frances. But the Lord giveth, too."

"Yes, right."

Vergie sat clenching more papers in both hands, looking off into the closet. "In that first year or two that we had him, I used to scare myself thinking it was all too good to be true. I thought something might change, and there we'd be — me and Gene — with nothing but a piece of paper to hold on to." Who did she think she was talking to?

"But then I started to understand it all different. And I wasn't scared anymore. I started seeing that David was really *our* son. I don't mean to step on you, October, but he was meant for us. And that's because *God* gave him to us. God didn't let me birth him, but God *gave* him to me and Gene. And once I understood that, I knew that God was never going to make us give him up."

October looked for any generosity and consideration that Vergie might be trying to give her. Vergie's words were so stripped of any thought about October and the way it had really happened that October had to wonder if Vergie had just forgotten whose decision it had been that she and Gene should have David.

October said, "Well, remember, Vergie, God works through *people,* and those people have to be willing." She owed it to herself to say that.

Vergie caught it. Didn't like it. She looked at October, smiled, shook her too-sure head. "God decides, honey."

October knew this would go nowhere, but she couldn't let it go. "Vergie, if things had been different, if I hadn't wanted you and Gene to —"

"You can just forget about all that, October. You and me will never see it the same way. We don't need to talk it out anymore. Not anymore."

She folded the paper print again and laid it carefully on top of the unearthed pile of papers between them, then slid off the edge of the bed to the floor.

Shook her head as if October was pitiful. "I wonder what it will take to get it into your head that David is really ours."

"Wait," October said. She sprung herself to the floor and tried to take hold of Vergie's arm.

"I'm just saying that it was my decision to make, and I made it — that's all."

The flare of Vergie's nostrils said it all. "You can think that if you want to, but we all know who saved who."

Too much. "Vergie," October said — she took Vergie by the shoulders, face to face, toe to toe. Vergie tried to look away, but October kept her face in her sister's face. "You act as if I had nothing to do with it."

"There you go." Vergie shook October off. "Always got to shine the light on yourself. What happened was meant to be." She started to leave the room.

October said to her back, "So I was meant to go through what I went through just so you and Gene could have a baby?"

And that made Vergie slow down long enough to say to her sister, "You did that to yourself, my dear sister. Don't go blaming it on the Lord."

"You just said that God decides. . . . I'm not blaming anybody — I'm just taking credit for the small part I played in giving you and Gene a life, is all. That is if you don't mind."

Where had she heard that before? The familiar ring of her own voice pointing out how her suffering had supplied someone else with a life.

Vergie turned, walking away. "You're so

selfish, October. Listen to yourself."

October spread her hands in front of her, pressing the air flat. Warm now, trying not to get hot. "You know what, Vergie? You were right — you and I are never going to see things alike, so we might as well stop trying."

The sound of Aunt Maude's cane on the stairs threatened them. She came to the door of Aunt Frances's room and looked in.

"I know one thing," she said. "The two of you better give up this nonsense before something gets said in front of the boy. Then what?"

Neither of them could say a word.

"Go ahead, now," Aunt Maude said. "Frances didn't have much, but she prized what she did have. If you don't want it, leave it be. I'll pack it up for the poor."

CHAPTER 15

Half of what October had learned at Emporia State Teachers' College had nothing to do with what she ended up doing in a classroom. But of all those poems she had read in all those English classes all those years, the one by the Persian poet had got it right. *The Moving Finger writes; and, having writ, / Moves on: nor all your Piety nor Wit / Shall lure it back to cancel half a Line, / Nor all your Tears wash out a Word of it.* If she could have lured it back, what half a line would she cancel? She was going on twenty-eight years old. Aunt Frances had been sixty-eight. In forty years, her life, too, might be over. Whose life would she have blessed so well that they would be holding her hand that last hour, saying thank you?

Arthur Terrell: he taught chemistry at Missouri State College, the used-to-be Normal School on Jericho Hill on the west side of Kansas City. Donetta, October's teacher friend, and Donetta's husband, Kenneth, had fixed them up. One thing for sure, Arthur liked her. He didn't mind saying so, and he didn't mind showing her. The other for-sure thing was that he was a good catch. Thirty-five and never been married. Had a Thunderbird and a two-bedroom place, and he bought roses for all the right times.

They were at a basketball game late in the fall — Mo State against A&T, big game. October sat with Donetta on the tier above the men; Arthur and Kenneth couldn't be bothered with explaining every play. Names had been called, and players from both sides had already come out. The boys were doing the little exercise they always did to warm up — lining up on either side of the basket and taking turns passing the ball and making layups, rebounding and all that.

The players cleared the floor and huddled. The band played "The Star-Spangled Banner," and the referee's whistle screamed. Tip-off. Mo State got the ball, made a fast break and two points in the first ten seconds of the game. The crowd stomped and yelled.

"Hope they pace it," Arthur yelled to Kenneth. "I'll bet we break a hundred."

Arthur liked basketball. October was learning something new at every game. "Cute outfits," Donetta said, looking at the cheerleaders. "I used to be a majorette, but you couldn't tell it by looking at me now."

A&T scored. Somebody fouled Mo State. Mo State made the free throw, and on the very next play they stole the ball and made a shot from midcourt. Arthur turned around — "Did you see that?" — face all out.

October smiled and nodded her head, clapping. He had a weak muscle in one eye that let the eye wander a little before focusing. He could laugh, though, and it took over his whole face.

Ever since she had come back from putting Aunt Frances in the ground, they had spent weekends together. Not hot and heavy, but nice. A whole lot of months, they had done the dating thing, minus sex. Up until she had left in the summer, he hadn't put his hands or anything else outside the safety zone. As far as she could tell, he was made that way. Respectful.

The night she had come home from Ohio, everything changed. For one thing, they finally slept together, and truth be told, October couldn't tell whether the heat came from being with Arthur or doing without.

Absence made fonder hearts. "You're getting your hooks into me, woman," he had told her. And look how well their lives fit together, he told her another time. Hint, maybe? Their lives did fit. She taught school, he taught school. Off and on she had a little part-time in Macy's alterations department, but mostly they both had weekends off. She liked sewing and he liked piddling with cars. They both liked ball games, though October could see baseball and basketball better than she could see oversize men knocking each other silly on a football field. Donetta and Kenneth were their friends. They had a few other friends in common, too.

First quarter and Mo State led by six. Donetta nudged her and whispered, "I know something you want to know, so ask me at the half."

October thought she had a clue already. Sometimes she caught herself in the daydream where she stood in a yard somewhere, grass cool, air warm, sun hot. Over in the shade a little boy squats on his haunches, digging in a patch of soft dirt with a toy shovel. He picks up handfuls, lets the dirt fall all over him, plump fingers smeared. When he looks up, the sight of her lights his eyes and he giggles. She sweeps him up, breathes in his smell, baby-cradles him into their little house with a porch, and on upstairs to douse him — slippery as a fish — in the bathtub. It's a feeling only blood can know. She hears a man — a father, a husband — driving up in his car. Who is he? He needs a face.

Arthur had made such a big deal about having Kenneth and Donetta with them this particular evening, October already figured out that Arthur had said something to Kenneth about making a move. So far, Arthur's face hadn't come up in October's dream picture, and she was hoping his would be the one. Surely, however, Arthur wouldn't do let's-get-married at a basketball game.

At halftime Arthur and Kenneth went outside to smoke, and October went with Donetta to the ladies' room. When they came out, the hallway swarmed with people going back into the gym. October glimpsed the back of a man walking with two other men and if — right at that minute — Donetta hadn't been itching to tell the big secret, October would have looked again.

"Don't say I said," Donetta said, "but Arthur is looking at rings. He told Kenneth he was waiting till Christmas. I'm supposed to be getting your ring size."

October's heart got real interested, but it didn't jump. "It's seven and a half, but he'd better ask me first," she told Donetta.

"I know," Donetta said. "You want the whole nine. I told Kenneth if Arthur is smart, he'll let you pick out your ring."

That wasn't it exactly. "You don't have to tell him that," October said. "It'll come up, and I'll tell him."

Back in the stands, October folded her coat, and just as she sat down, she saw him three rows down. He turned, talking to his friend, turned and locked eyes with her. James Wilson. Stunned.

A wave swept her mind blank, and she stood up and put on her coat without thinking a thing. And then she was looking at the back of him again.

"Who's that?" Donetta asked. "Where are you going?"

"Who?" October asked back. She sat down again and peeled off her coat. She wanted the ground to open and swallow her.

"That guy," Donetta said, smiling. "He caught you staring."

"I thought I knew him," October said. How could she explain leaving now?

And here came Arthur and Kenneth — hot dogs and root beer: let's get it on. They had talked. Kenneth motioned for Donetta to sit with him, and Arthur sat beside October. It helped. She felt better, being near him. What would she possibly say if James Wilson said anything to her? What was he thinking right then? What was he doing way over at the college? Maybe he lived over here.

The game started up again and she tried to focus on catching the finer points like traveling and goal-tending. Calm down. James Wilson didn't want to see her any more than she wanted to see him. She watched him talking and laughing with his friends. He looked short. Stocky. She would have done almost anything for him once. How could she have felt so close to him when he had been so far from her? How could she have felt so sure then and feel nothing but embarrassment now? What would he do if he knew he had a son in the world? Let this game be over soon.

You see, nobody had ever told my daughter that Shakespeare's was not the last word on love; that falling in love didn't always lead to forever, that sometimes love is meant to last for a season, and only for a season. Nobody had ever bothered to point that out to her, and how could she have guessed it? Probably if I had lived long enough, I would have been the one to tell her about love's open hand, about loving a man enough to let him go.

After the game they went to the barbecue place and sat in a booth. Arthur waited until they had eaten before he motioned to the waiter, who brought four glasses of Asti Spumante to the table a few minutes later.

"I just want to celebrate a little," Arthur said. "You're looking at a happy man." October hoped he wouldn't go any deeper.

"This is a special toast to two special people." He meant Donetta and Kenneth.

"You-all brought this woman to me," and tonight I want to make a toast to you. It's been the best thing that ever happened."

Too much, Arthur. October smiled and sipped with them. She was supposed to say something now, some heartfelt thing people say when they're in love. This was definitely Arthur's lead up to the ring.

"Here's to many more good times together," she said. Wrong note, but they all sipped. She had until Christmas to get it together.

Sometime before Christmas, on a Sunday morning that they spent in bed, while Arthur explained the hopscotch politics that could get him the department chair, James Wilson floated into October's mind again. When she was with James, she had been willing to bare her soul. She was beginning to understand that that hadn't been a thoroughly bad impulse, even if it had been unwise. Yet, with Arthur, she had kept her secrets to herself.

It took days, maybe weeks, but something about that riddle kept knocking against something else in her head, so that by the time she straightened up her thoughts again, she knew that she wouldn't be marrying Arthur Terrell.

She couldn't see herself ever saying to Arthur things that needed to be said: *I was once in love. I got pregnant. Well, actually he was*

married. Yes, I knew he was married. But re-
member, I was young and naive. I thought this
man was my life, and when he didn't want me I
thought that my life was over.

The baby? Another story. You see, I gave him
away. Yes, maybe I could have taken care of
him, but I didn't feel up to trying right then. I
would do anything to erase it, but I can't. I have
to live with it. You have to live with it, too. And
by the way, the little boy you met, David, Vergie
and Gene's son, that's him.

No way. Arthur was a careful man. She
couldn't see him ever being able to see her in
that light and say, *So what? I love you.* And she
couldn't see him sweeping David up into his
arms, either.

Up until that morning in bed with Arthur,
she had pretty much gone wherever the road
led her, and made enough messes to last ten
lifetimes. No more. She couldn't afford it.
From now on, she wouldn't set foot on any
road where she couldn't see around the
curves, and especially not on any road that
had a dead-end sign.

October might have just sat right there in
that taking-charge place if Vergie hadn't
called that very same morning. Five months
later, almost to the day, her aunt Maude followed Frances in that "innumerable cara-
van." Lay down and slipped away.

CHAPTER 16

The sound of shoveled clay breaking against Maude's lowered coffin was still echoing the morning in September when David opened the front door and began his climb to the top of the world. His first day of school hit so hard because both aunties were gone, taking a whole generation with them. October and Vergie, on the front line now, had no one to shield them. And here was David, marching on their heels.

Ohio schools opened before Labor Day, and not wanting to miss anything momentous to David's life, October arranged to start her school year in Missouri a day late. Of course, in her informed opinion, David was probably smart enough to have gone to school a year earlier, when he was months away from being five years old. Vergie and Gene had turned their heads the other way last year when the subject came up.

She was determined that there wouldn't be a fight. When you don't get the butterscotch you want, you eat the half apple held out to you, and you say thank you. October was glad to be there just to see it happen. Happy the night before just looking at his flat box of Crayolas, his little tin of watercolors, his blunt scissors and sweet-smelling paste, all laid out on the coffee table beside his new satchel. She wouldn't interfere. In fact, when she awoke to the sound of Vergie and Gene fussing over David's bath, she turned over and waited another half hour.

Doors were closing. He was five years old, going on six. At five, October had come to live with Frances and Maude. She could remember everything that happened from that day on. From this time on, David would remember everything, notice everything. If he were to somehow come live with her, he would remember how and why. Pretty soon, if the word *adoption* fell on his ears, he would understand it. And then the word *bastard* would make sense. The bottom line was that if he stumbled on the truth now, he would hate the mother who had given him away. Doors were closing.

Downstairs at the breakfast table, David had been brushed and shined like a new penny — long navy-blue pants, suspenders, plaid shirt. Just what she would have him wear. She had to hide her tears, pull herself together.

"Aren't you handsome?" she said to him, and saw his face cloud over.

"Momma said the children at your school wear high-tops," he said.

October looked under the table to see his new Buster Brown high-tops that he didn't like.

She wanted to reach over and touch his face. "They do," she said. "And they look nice. You'll see — everybody will have them on."

"Don't matter if they don't," Gene said. "They cost enough for you to wear till high school."

Vergie sat down to her toast and bacon. "Eat your oatmeal," she told David. "You won't get anything else until you come home at noon."

"I can't have a lunch bucket?" David asked, eyes so beautifully hurting in his brown round face.

Vergie shook her head. "I told you already, David, you come home for lunch. Every day. Next year you'll have to stay all day. Then you can take a lunch bucket."

October guessed this was as good an issue as any to work up jitters. David's eyes swam, and he sat with his arms folded, hands stuffed in his armpits.

"Don't you start," Vergie told him. "We've been through all this, David. Now eat your breakfast." October was undone, and she

287

could tell that Vergie was, too.

Vergie gave him a slice of her bacon. "Here, eat some protein. Noon is a long way off."

October asked him, "What's your teacher's name?" but he just hunched his shoulders.

"You know her name, Davy," Gene said.

It occurred to October that she might know her. "I know a lot of teachers," she said.

David munched his bacon. "I think it's Miss Borders," he said.

"Juanita Borders?" October asked, and Vergie nodded.

Her heart jumped. Some little something she could give him. Juanita Borders had gone to Emporia two years behind her; October remembered her as smart.

"I know her, David," she said. "I knew her when we were kids. I knew her when she was in college. She's very nice."

His eyes brightened. "Will she whip us?"

"No, no," October said.

Vergie said, "Nobody's going to whip you unless you act up, so just be good and you won't have anything to worry about."

"We'd better get to gettin," Gene said. "It's twenty till."

Vergie pinned David's name, address, and telephone number inside his pants pocket, with instructions that he not move an inch from the school door until she came to walk him home. And they prepared to leave.

School opened at nine o'clock. This first day, Gene had planned to go to the mill late, just so he could see David off. October had put off her trip to Kansas City by one day, just so she could see David off. Vergie had bought a new skirt and blouse for the walking-to-school look, just so she could see David off.

And where was school? Harrison Elementary. One of the newer schools, built like a rambler with wings off in a couple of directions, a front lawn, and the playground out back. The three of them walked David the three blocks in the warm September morning, Vergie and Gene holding his hands, October behind them, carrying his satchel. Anyone watching them would have thought David had some kind of handicap.

Too, too tiny, October thought. What did he know about the world? If anything happened, how would he know what to do? Look what happened to Emmett Till down in Mississippi. The picture of his mangled face with a bullet hole in his forehead leaped up in her mind. Fourteen. Tied to a cotton gin fan and dumped into the river, all because nobody in Chicago had thought to tell him about whistling at white women.

She couldn't think of a single minute that

David had been out of their sight. Someone — Frances, Maude, Vergie, Gene, October — had always given him what he needed before he knew that he needed it, figured out what scared him and kept it at bay. October hoped that Juanita Borders was as patient as she was smart.

Bare bulletin boards were surely not a way to welcome little children to school, even though they did make everything else seem orderly. In the doorway of the kindergarten classroom, Juanita Borders stood, directing traffic, and October rushed to say hello.

"October!" the teacher said. October still held David's satchel. "I didn't know you were back here," Juanita said. October turned to say that this little family of three was her reason. "Oh," Juanita said. "Is this your son?"

"This is my sister, Vergie, and her husband, Gene, and their son, David," October said.

Vergie stepped up. "I'm Mrs. Parker, and this is Mr. Parker," she said, correctly. "David is our son."

Juanita stooped to look into David's face. "You can go on in and sit wherever you like," she said. "Is that his?" She took David's satchel, ushered him into the classroom, and left the three of them standing without something to talk about.

When she returned she told them, "You-all

won't need to bring him to the room every day. Take a look at the playground. You can bring him there half an hour before school if you want to."

"Um-hmm, okay," Gene said.

No one had had time to feel how it felt for David to be out of their sight. They all hesitated to scout out the playground just yet. Finally, Gene stepped inside the classroom to wave good-bye to David. And since he did, Vergie did, too. And though October fought the impulse, she decided to see David one last time that morning, sitting at his square little table with three other children, among many other square little tables filled with other children, all with eyes wide, each wondering who those three people were, standing at the front of their classroom waving at that little boy in the suspenders.

Very little could compare with that First Day of School in Ohio, and so a dull beginning to the school year in Missouri came as no surprise. Teaching third-graders gave October a measuring rod for David. He couldn't yet print his name, but in three years, he would be learning cursive writing, long division, state capitals. Perhaps by then, things would have changed, and *she* would be the one to help him with his homework, introduce him to the world of history.

Sudden weeping, though, was a surprise. David seemed already lost to her. Vergie and Gene were not travelers, and now David was in school.

Maybe someday, somehow, she would have him as her own son again; maybe she wouldn't. In the meantime, if it meant spending only summers and holidays with her in Missouri — some holidays, anyway — she could see how everyone would benefit.

Vergie and Gene would just have to bring David to Missouri more. That was all. She rehearsed the words she would tell Vergie the next time they talked. Their family was too small to be out of touch, and October shouldn't always have to be the one to do the traveling. David should see some of *her* life, too.

On the heels of August in Ohio, October tagged along on a night out with Donetta and Kenneth. Since she and Arthur had parted ways, she had found that coupledom was a closed club, and that she used to fit in without knowing or caring how and where. Now, she was back to being the extra woman. And not a life-of-the-party type either.

On Kenneth's birthday, Donetta worked in a night at the Blue Room as a part of Kenneth's surprise. A jazz group that he supposedly liked were headlining, and Donetta wanted a party — everybody had to show up. And so she did.

October had this so-so winter white suit that she thought might do for the occasion. Winter white could always be dressed up or down; she wasn't trying to impress anybody. Before she left for the club, she checked the mirror and saw it could be better, but it would do.

Once or twice, as a big night out, Arthur had brought her to the Blue Room — enough times that if she wanted to, she could hold a conversation about this or that piano player, this or that jazz album. She read the papers. Charlie Parker's death was still a pall over the jazz world. She knew the big names — Miles Davis, Sonny Stitt, Dizzy Gillespie — and what instruments they played. She had swooned a time or two over Erroll Garner, and heard men talk enough about Bud Powell to know what it meant to "comp" on the piano. She still had her favorites — Dinah, Ella, Sarah, Count, and Duke.

Turns out they were a party of nine, and October felt right at home with Donetta's coterie of teachers-with-boyfriends. The Blue Room really was blue — walls, tables, chairs — with eerie, iridescent light that stepped the club up to surreal.

According to Kenneth, the leader of Jazz, Inc., had just won some kind of award. If October hadn't been just passing time, she would have been tuned in enough to make the connection. One man in the quartet that was Jazz, Inc., did get her attention, though, as he walked through the club and stepped up on the bandstand.

"That's Leon Haskins," she said. What a surprise that Leon had come this far already.

"Yeah," Kenneth said. "This is his group."

Cora's old lawyer friend, Alvin — whom October remembered from the Thanksgiving at Cora and Ed's — said, "That's right," and he pointed to October. "You were there, too, Thanksgiving. Now I remember. Lonny signed a contract with Blue Note right after that." He chuckled. "We knew him when."

To see Leon headlining at the Blue Room with his own combo was turning a nothing party into a night out. *He's made it,* October thought. Good for Leon.

As they played each number, she hummed the melody underneath. Eyes glued to the bandstand, the men at the table had a serious stake in every note. Fancy fingerings. They leaned in, heads bobbing with the rhythm, and October saw that if all else failed, she could take her cue from them.

Whenever Leon did some big thing like making a way-out barrage of notes just fall out of his horn, or when, from out of nowhere, the man on the piano made a sudden connection, the men yelled like they had gotten church-happy. Leon was good.

As the players left the bandstand after the first set — Donetta had said they were staying for two — Alvin yelled out to Leon and waved, trying to catch his attention.

"I'll bet he doesn't remember me," he said. "That was three or four years ago, wasn't it, October?"

"At least," she said. But she herself was watching Leon make his way through the tables and the crowd of awestruck people. Fans. He looked older, neater, polished. Some dark slacks with pleats, and a white shirt with his cuffs rolled up. The mustache and goatee were gone. His hair didn't have a part in it. Yes, his face had filled out, like he was eating regularly. His mouth smiled, but his eyes didn't. He was different.

"Hey, man," he called and waved to Alvin but didn't seem bent on coming over to their table.

"He doesn't remember me," Alvin said.

The first-show crowd began to thin, and second-show people began filling up the tables.

October and Donetta had to go to the ladies' room. When they got back to the table and got situated again, Leon just walked up from nowhere and leaned over to October. Put out his hand and joked.

"Hey, I'm Lonny Haskins, Ed's brother — remember me?"

She put her hand in his. "I remember something about a long ride to St. Louis."

She introduced him to Donetta and Kenneth, and Alvin finally had his chance.

"You don't remember me," Alvin said, "but we all met the same Thanksgiving Day. You had a gig in the Ozarks — remember? — and came up to Ed's for dinner."

"Right," Leon said. He looked at October. "If it wasn't for you and me, they wouldn't be married, right?" Leon sat down and looked at her, not soft, more like he was trying to remember if she was the same woman. Why did she wish she had worn something with the arms out?

Then Leon said, "Let me get the drinks," and motioned to the waitress.

Now Alvin and Kenneth and the rest could pull out their whole bag of jazz-ese about Leon's "axe-playing." They went through the ranks of players and tunes and who stole what from whom. Mostly, October listened.

Leon thanked them for noticing and then

turned to ask her if she heard from Cora these days.

"She's busy with a new baby," October told him, "but we still call each other every now and then."

"If you're here after the show, maybe you can catch me up," he said. Donetta touched her foot under the table.

"Um-hmm, sure," October said. Donetta didn't know it, but October and Leon went back a ways. Ed was the only person in the world who came anywhere near brotherly to October, and if Leon was anything to her, he was a long way down from Ed.

"I hope y'all dig the next set," he said, getting up and pushing the chair under the table.

"Nice talking to you, man," Alvin said, and Leon left.

One more thing. Right in the middle of a number during the second set, Leon worked in a few bars from Mendelssohn's wedding march. October smiled. And she had to clap.

At the end of the second set, Donetta had Kenneth's wallet out and was piling dollar bills on top of the check so fast, October thought she was teed off about something. But no, she just hurried everybody out of their chairs and into the crowd leaving the club. Everybody except for October.

"Call me tomorrow," she told her. "We need to talk."

Leon found her waiting. Judging from the way he was decked out, he had finally gotten the combination right: suave. Camel overcoat, fancy green alligator horn case swinging into the air saying hello. And there was an older man with him.

"This is my man Foots," Leon said. "He thinks he's my manager, so I let him hang around with me sometimes. . . ." And he turned to the older man. "Say hello to Miss October Brown," he said.

The older man looked like a has-been, with a rim of white hair around his bald crown, thick glasses, and a worn-out suit and shirt. He just nodded hello. October couldn't help noticing that knots of arthritis on his knuckles had stretched his black skin crisp, and she thought of Maude.

"You don't mind if we drop Foots off at the hotel, do you?" Leon asked.

When they got to the Akers Hotel and Leon let his manager friend out of the car, the old man reminded Leon, "We're supposed to leave at nine tomorrow. Don't let us have to come looking for you."

Little did he know, October had no plans for *that* kind of night, and she hoped Leon didn't either.

Leon drove off, talking about being hungry. "You can't come to Kansas City and not have some barbecue," he said, driving like it was his private road.

"I grew up on these streets," he went on, crossing over Brooklyn and going toward Twelfth Street. "Rexall's used to be right on that corner."

They turned into The Paseo, with its parkway trees and mowed grass. When they got to the corner of Eighteenth, he told her, "Once when I was a junior flip, I ran into Bird, right here, me and Ed. Bigger than life, that was Bird."

They saw the horde of people trying to get into Bryants at that hour and decided on take-away. Take away to October's place was what Leon meant. But it was fine. She knew that Leon didn't have family close around. Maybe she was the next best thing. He seemed excited enough.

At her apartment, she got out of her white suit and put on a pair of slacks and a blouse. Eating barbecue was a down-home kind of thing you did with your house clothes on, licking your fingers. She heard him in her kitchen rattling glasses and nosying in her cabinets and in her refrigerator for lemonade.

When she came out to the kitchen, he had

found his way to the bottle of rum, and no, he didn't want plates — whoever heard of using plates? What you do is you just spread out the butcher paper on the table. "You got napkins?" and "Boy, even these pickles look good," and he sat down and yanked off both of them a bone.

Fun, almost. October had the next best thing to kin in her house. At her kitchen table, they pried square slices of sandwich bread off slabs of ribs, cleaned the sweet meat off the bones with their teeth, licked their fingers, and found some decent "sounds" in her little-nothing collection.

"Tell me about Ed's baby," Leon said. She told him what she knew — when the boy was born and what he weighed. Cora had wanted to name him after her father, but Ed had won out. They called him Eddy Junior. Cora had said that Ed worshipped this baby and had gotten up for all the night feedings.

"That's Ed," Leon said.

Why did October sense that it had been a long time since Leon had talked to his brother? That until that night maybe Leon didn't even know they had had a son?

She found her picture of Eddy Junior at four months and handed it to Leon.

"He looks just like me," Leon said, handing back the picture.

She looked at it again. "A baby is a precious thing," she said.

"When he gets big enough to catch a ball, his uncle will come play with him."

"Think of all the things you're missing out on," she said.

"Yeah," Leon said. "I'll catch him later. Ed and Cora aren't going anywhere."

What did Leon know?

"Tell me," she said, changing the subject, "what it was like to win your big award."

"You mean the Newport thing?" he said. "It was sweet, real nice. I wish Ed could've been there."

"Tell me about it. Who gave it to you? What did you have to do to get it?"

"What did I have to do to get it?" He wiped his fingers on a paper napkin. "I had to play my horn at the Newport Jazz Festival. And I had to play it good, because all the critics were there. It's something you have to see." He swigged his lemonade rum and put down the glass.

"There's this casino, on this big lawn. Newport Casino. You stand at one end and you look out from this giant clamshell" — he waved his arms in the air — "you know, the stage where they rig the sound system. Here are all these people just like when we were in Europe, thousands of people."

He stopped and thought for a minute, grinned to himself, and shook his head. She could see his mind turning. He picked up the bottle and poured a little rum into her lemonade and his.

"Behind the stage, all of us, we're getting ready. We can hear Bird's music they're playing into the speakers. That was the way to start, you know, with Bird, 'cause he was gone. Dizzy headed up our all-star band. I was the only tenor sax," he said. "Only one." And he stopped again. October let him stay in his own world as long as he wanted.

"When our turn came, we did a tribute to one of my buddies who got killed the week before. Maybe you heard of Clifford Brown. After that we had the crowd in our hands. Dizz did 'Night in Tunisia' and the crowd ate that up, too. And then we did ours, our old standard — I mean, that's what you do. 'What Is This Thing Called Love?' It wasn't a tune I would have picked, but it was something that let me stretch out with some of my new ideas, until I got the framework I wanted."

She didn't know exactly what he meant, except that whenever it had happened, it had been a big moment for him, and he'd been really into it. She drank the rest of her drink.

Then he scooted back his chair and leaned

over toward her. The good part was coming.

"And then I stretched out," he said, stretching out his arms like he was blowing a horn. "I just riffed and the crowd broke out cheering, you know?" — really going at it, like it was happening all over again.

"I just did what I do, and the crowd went wild." He sat straight in his chair again. He poured more lemonade into both their glasses, and then a shot of rum in both. She knew she wouldn't drink it.

"Later on, Dizzy was pissed 'cause I took so long with my solo." He laughed, rocked his chair back on two legs. She laughed too.

"I just unwrapped my little bundle of goodies and laid it out. The crowd was with me. If I never cooked before, I cooked that day. Like I said, all the critics were there. *Downbeat* gave me the New Artist award."

October heard the old Leon telling his story, patting himself on the back. And rightly so. He had kept his promise to himself.

"And what have you been doing?" he said. "You tell me something."

What could she tell him? "I've been doing all the plain old things people do to make a life," she said. "Making mistakes, trying to fix them. Working hard, trying to get along with other people. No big awards yet."

"So are you with somebody now?"

"You are really nosy."

He chuckled. "I thought we were friends."

"We like two of the same people, and we stood up for them once, if that's what you mean by *friends*."

"So no go, Lonny?" he said, still smiling, like he thought he was expected to make a play, not even halfway serious.

"Um-ummm, no go," October told him. She was feeling relaxed but not *that* relaxed.

He looked at his wristwatch and she glanced at the clock above the stove. Three a.m.

"Then it's about time for me to find the hotel and get out of your kitchen, right?"

She stood and began folding up their mess. He did not need an answer, but she wasn't quite finished.

"Leon," she said, "I have to tell you, tonight was nice — just what I needed."

He got up and went to the sink, turned on the water, and soaped his hands. "Does that make me a chump or Sir Galahad?"

"Well, I hadn't expected to have a good time, and if it hadn't been for you, I don't think I would have."

"Sounds like one of those somebody's-been-doin-me-wrong songs, right?"

"Maybe a little bit of that."

"So that's the big mistake you're trying to fix?"

"No, no," she said. He had gotten the wrong idea.

She steered him back to the point. "Seeing you tonight was like having a little bitty piece of Cora here — you know, friends."

Leon's hands were dripping; he didn't see the towel. "Thanks, but no reward, huh?"

"I beg your pardon. *I* am the friend who stayed up with you all night and fed you Bryant's barbecue in her kitchen." She handed him the dish towel.

"Thanks for that," he said. "If you ever come to New York, I'll return the favor — take you to a real swanky place."

"A deal," she said.

As he went, he left her with regards for Ed and Cora and Eddy Junior, his new little nephew.

"Tell him his uncle Lonny is making a name for us in the city."

Good news. Ed hated St. Louis, and they were coming back! The letter from Cora said first of all that they had heard from Leon. Exclamation points and stars. He had sent a savings bond for Eddy Junior, thanks to seeing the picture that her sisterfriend October had shown him. Cora went on to say that she would come up to Kansas City to look for a house in three weeks but that she couldn't stay more than a few days. Look at the paper, she told October. And they didn't want anything in the new developments way out on Troost.

October clipped newspapers and made phone calls. Everybody knew Tim Crawford, the best black real estate man around, and she called him.

Cora got back to Kansas City one minute and got on the phone the next, worried about leaving Ed and Eddy Junior for four days.

Mornings, she and Cora ate breakfast together and October went off to school while Cora went off with Tim Crawford. He owned his own business, and so of course he pressed Cora about space for Eddy Junior and all the other children she and Ed might have, and a two-car garage, something up-and-coming blacks should have, attached to the kind of ranch-style house he happened to be building in the new Crawford Estates out on Troost. No, Cora didn't want that.

The houses that Cora did like were in neighborhoods where white flight didn't work so smoothly. One evening, when October joined Cora and the real estate man, she figured out how Tim Crawford did so well. He knew how to get around a bad situation. At first he showed Cora the possible houses only from the street. Once they narrowed it down to what she liked best, he found out which buyers were dead set against selling to blacks. He told her, "Unless you've got your sights set on a special place, we may as well save ourselves some trouble."

In the evening, October would get Cora to show her the picks for that day so that they could whittle down Cora's choices. If the houses were empty, all the better. October could walk around in those spacious living rooms. She could touch old bathtubs, trip up stairs into hallways. What a nice thing it was to have a sidewalk where a child could ride his tricycle. Later, October would remember that it was during that scouting-out with Cora that the seed had been planted for buying a place of her own.

After dinner, if she and Cora didn't go house-looking, they lazed around, catching up on the heart things that don't come unless there is time and lazing around. One of those times, Cora kicked off her shoes and fell on the sofa.

"I've been wanting to ask you — and don't try to duck me this time — what's going on for real with you and Vergie? Does what happened with David keep you upset?"

"No, I'm fine with it," October said. No choice — she had to be.

"This is me you're talking to, girl," Cora

said. "Don't you ever wish things were different? Don't you ever just want to go to Ohio and snatch him up?"

"It wouldn't work," October told her. She told Cora how she wished that Vergie would just wake up one day and give him back, and how in the world could that happen without David ever knowing that he had been given away in the first place? The rock — not having him with her; and the hard place — having him hate her. Even though Cora convinced her in that moment that it didn't have to be that way, that David could learn to love her like a mother, somebody was bound to be destroyed.

"Whatever happens," Cora said, "I guess I just want to know that you'll never resent me."

"Resent you for what?"

"Well, I always wonder what would have happened if I hadn't called your aunts. Maybe you wouldn't even have had him."

"The milk was already spilled," October said, "and you weren't the one to tip it over. I made that decision all by myself, and even with things the way they are, I'm not sorry. You should see him. He's a beautiful boy."

"I guess as long as this goes on, I'll always feel sad, too. The price I pay for letting you-all up under my skin."

How nice it was to have the sister without the things between the two of you that rubbed everybody the wrong way.

Another evening when Cora kicked off her shoes and fell on the sofa, she asked October, "What would you do if you had all the money in the world?"

October had turned to the news with John Cameron Swayze on her new television set. "Quit working, I guess," she said.

"I would buy me and Ed that house on The Paseo, and travel to California or somewhere till we got tired."

They were quiet. Cora added, "Instead of trying to teach shop to those knuckleheads at school, Ed could do carpentry till his arms fell off."

"He hates teaching, huh?"

And then Cora told what October knew had been eating at her. "It's partly my fault. I mean, I pushed him into it, and now I'm scared he'll quit. And if he does, we won't be able to pay the mortgage."

"If he's buying a house, he'll pay for it. You'll see."

Cora moved on. "You said you'd quit your job — are you telling me you would quit teaching if you could?"

October had never really thought about it. She switched to the most outrageous thing she could think of at the moment.

"If I were rich, I would go to Paris for a while, just to spend a little money."

"Remember I said you'd have all the money in the world."

"Then I'd buy me a house. And I'd buy Vergie and Gene a house right next door. And cars for everybody — clothes, all that."

"Then what?"

"Then I'd just sit around and look after David all day. I guess I'd sew, too, make all kinds of things."

"Like what?"

"Clothes. For people. I'd have me a little shop where I could sell them, too."

"You wouldn't make any money, you know."

"I wouldn't have to. I'd already have all the money in the world."

"You know," Cora said. She sat up. "Maybe that's what Ed should do. Have a little workshop in the basement. Goodness, I just gave myself a good idea. I'm so glad we're moving back."

CHAPTER 17

During the years when October and Vergie had put up with the orphans from the Children's Home, the Hopewell Burial Mounds was a mere field trip to them — a place where ancient spoons and forks were buried, where they hoped to see an arrowhead. Or, if they were lucky, they might find a four-leaf clover.

Around 1000 B.C., in what was now the Ohio part of North America, an ancient people had thought it was good to bury the dead on kames, the tops of the gravel left behind by melting glaciers. Later these prehistoric peoples simply piled earth on and around the bones of their dead, making the first mounds in the lowlands. No one had figured out what the other kind of mounds were about: scattered all over the same territory, they were strangely shaped and contained no bones. Ritualistic, maybe — ceremonial, archaeologists thought.

No one knew for sure who these people had been, though they called the mounds Hopewell for the first archaeologist who had dug in. These Mound Builders were around for a thousand years — then, apparently, they just vanished. Why, nobody knew. Anthropologists had conceded, however, that they bore a resemblance to the Choctaw Indians whom Europeans came upon centuries later. And, too, similar mounds from ancient times had been found all up and down the Mississippi Valley.

At night, crossing the Scioto River, October couldn't make out the mounds, though she knew they were out there, and knew that she would be hearing enough about them this trip. What little else there was to be seen — Tecumseh's memorial or the new restaurant and mall in the center of downtown Chillicothe — she'd have to see later.

Ten o'clock at night, and her new, used Impala had made it fine on two tanks of gas. On the way back to Missouri, she might venture to leave the air-conditioning on for longer than fifteen minutes at a time.

Six o'clock that morning, she had been standing at her kitchen counter in Kansas City, cutting boiled potatoes into cubes, making potato salad for the drive. Her mind had had trouble sleeping and the night had had trouble ending. Vergie was going to have the operation, put an end to her "female trouble," and October was going to run Vergie's house for a month, six weeks at the outside.

Help her sister recuperate.

Cora had come by to see her off, get the keys to water the plants, and, October knew, to sound her out a little. But Cora didn't rush it.

"Paper says it's going to be in the nineties," Cora said. "Not a good time for being on the road, especially by yourself."

October laid it to rest with the mention of the air-conditioning — which Cora and Ed didn't have in their Ford — and reminding Cora that the new interstate would get her there a lot faster than the old local roads.

It was then that Cora had ventured to ask about Vergie, how she was coping, and October had reminded her that Vergie always sounded like herself, always we'll-get-through-this. "She's probably scared to death."

"I would be, too," Cora said. "I guess there's a couple of bright sides to it, though," she added, "like you having David all to yourself for the rest of the summer." October nodded, putting a dollop of mayonnaise in the salad and tossing it with two spoons.

"Be careful," Cora said, "— you know you. Vergie will be in a rough place, and you'll be sorry if you start giving out ultimatums or make some kind of grand stand."

October had looked at her friend and told her straight that she was going to Ohio to take care of Vergie. Period. It was the truth. And Cora had said her usual " 'Nuff said," and made October promise to call from a pay phone when she got to the Indiana line.

Finally, at the end of that day, October made the familiar turn into the other part of her life. Most of the houses on Monroe Street had the steep, straight-sided gables of clapboard colonials, with peeling paint, sagging windows, missing screens, and balding lawns. Not like she had once seen it, or maybe just hoped it was. An occasional bedroom or dining room light showed her plenty of living deep inside, silhouettes of families keeping cool by keeping down the lights, families winding toward sleep. Her headlights caught a skein of children flying across a front yard. Outside was cooler than in.

Seven-fifty-two stood on its foundation of stone, with its wooden porch and posts, the wide picture window that you never could see too well because of the swing but that now was a 3-D picture of damask drapes swept back and tied to show off a porcelain lamp and fluted shade. Vergie had been busy. The front door, though, with its oval window, was the same door she had leaned against and slammed for years.

She started up the porch steps and *flip* went the porch light. There Vergie was, spitting image of Aunt Maude. Everything about her curved, arched, swayed, or bowed; the same round figure in a white blouse and gathered skirt ballooning over her hips, the same black hair with a few gray strands and thick braids across the crown held in place with a million Maude Cooper hairpins.

They hugged long. Vergie smelled like onions and Oxydol.

"That was quick," Vergie said to her. "You drove too fast. David's asleep, but I promised I'd wake him up when you came."

Gene came to the door, joked, "I saw that Cadillac drive up and said to myself, I'll bet that's October — anything that long and shiny is a Cadillac," he said. "I'll get your bags."

They went inside to see what Vergie had done with the house. At one time her aunts had been so proud of their worn wood floors, the wide front room with its comfortable divan and easy chairs and good light from the floor lamp and the console. Vergie had redone it with wall-to-wall carpeting, new sofa and chairs, and a small table where the hat tree used to be.

"Come see the side porch," she said. She had turned it into a den with a console TV and easy chairs for her and Gene.

Vergie went up to get David, and Gene

came in with Mrs. Hopp, step-stepping then resting. October could tell that Mrs. Hopp seldom made the effort to come across the yard anymore. Toothless and stooped, white hair in tiny plaits over her head, she looked up sideways and said she'd seen October drive up. "I said, I'll bet that's her."

October hugged her hello.

"It's good to see you girls together," she said. "You movin back?"

October said no, just for a while — a long while this time.

"Seems a shame, you living way out there in Missouri when everybody is here."

October heard David tripping down the stairs — had to be wide awake — and Vergie behind him.

"Hi, Auntie Oc," he said, face bright as the next morning.

"She's still Aunt October to you," Vergie said.

October loved it. "No," she said, "I like Auntie Oc. We woke you up, huh?" She touched his head — close haircut.

"Momma said you bought a new Impala," he said. "If you want me to, I can get your stuff."

"Bags," Vergie corrected, "and your father's already got them."

"Can I see your car?" he asked October.

For going on seven years, October had tried to hold his gaze whenever he looked straight at her. She would have thought that by now that piercing thing wouldn't get to her.

"You'll see it in the morning," Vergie said.

David whined that, shoot, he just wanted to look, and Vergie said all right.

October took him out to see it, let him get behind the wheel and turn on the interior lights. Come tomorrow or the day after, she would take him for a long ride. Her and him.

The next morning, the *Chillicothe Blade* was full of details. Front page. Archaeologists and historians had descended on them to figure out, once and for all, who the ancient Mound Builders had been, and why mounds.

Two miles south of Chillicothe, near the Hopewell heart, where thirty or forty mounds still stood — many on private property — excavation was about to begin for a new road. The archaeologists had to work fast or bulldozers would erase all traces of this particular piece of ancient Indian history. October thought it might be something for David to see.

Vergie shrugged her shoulders. Maybe, but she wanted him around today. And October understood how that could be true. And so Vergie made a project of ironing all of David's clothes. No matter that October was there, she wanted to be sure he had enough clean-and-ironed things for two weeks. And she paired up which pants went with which T-shirt, and none of his Sunday socks with his tennis shoes. And "Make him take a bath every night. Don't let him stay up after nine, either, 'cause he'll try, and Gene don't have no sense about David and going to bed."

Ironing board where the high-up bed had once been, ironed clothes stacked and strewn over the chairs, bureau now a catch-all for catalogues and old flowerpots — it felt like blasphemy to have that much clutter in Aunt Frances's old room.

"When he gets old enough," Vergie said, "I'm going to make this into an extra room for him. Put in shelves and all."

October took one of the T-shirts Vergie had just laid out, and started to fold it.

"No, no," Vergie said. "Hang it up or you'll have to iron it again."

Vergie went to the bureau and took a sheet of fine-grain stationery from the top drawer. Spoils from Aunt Maude's days at the mill.

"Write for me while I iron," Vergie said, and she began to try to capture her life on a piece of paper — the things she did every day and how she did them. Gene's timetable and his whims, David's habits — and the warnings he would need — as if once she had the operation she wouldn't be able to talk.

That evening, on the television news, they showed the mounds site — archaeologists with tools that looked like spatulas and toothbrushes, the pebbles and shards they had already found that, they said, dated back to A.D. 400. They showed ornaments and jewelry, copper things and pottery designs. Sculptured stone and clay pipes that had been carved with bird, bear, and geometric designs. The Mound Builders were artisans, they said. But there were also mollusk shells, remains of wild plants, husks of corn — things Mound Builders ate. They showed an aerial view of the Great Serpent Mound in southern Ohio — the biggest effigy mound in the Americas, they said.

As October sat watching with Vergie in the den, she looked out the window to see Gene's balding head; he was hosing down his old car out front. Cicadas had begun their dusk serenade, and David was somewhere up the street, playing. She could smell the ubiquitous honeysuckle, and see the fringe of violet, the wisteria dangling over the porch roof. What would *they* leave behind that people would find?

The camera focused in on the face of the newsman, microphone in his hand, spelling out the story of the Hopewell hierarchy that they had unearthed — the human bones, the luminary, his family, his friends. When a priest or chieftain died, they buried his whole life with him, including the voluntarily dead who followed. The newsman turned to a burial mound behind him: the skeletons of two wives, perhaps a sister, a medicine man with implements, a head servant, maybe, or a pipe bearer — all of them had accompanied the personage into death.

"Those poor people," October said. "Buried like that just because he died."

"It was their way," Vergie said. "I can understand it. It's like any other journey," she went on. "You want to see that they get there safe. Besides, they didn't want to go on in this life when they could be with him in the next."

"You believe in that?" October asked her.

"I'm saying I can understand it," Vergie said. She had a tea towel slung across her shoulder and a basin of green beans in her lap, snipping off the ends of bean pods, snapping them in two.

"Let me help," October said, reaching for a handful.

"This is it," Vergie said. "I'm just getting them ready, and that'll be that. Be sure to cook them long enough. Gene likes them cooked to pieces."

Already October wondered how she would watch a pot simmer and be at the hospital at the same time. Vergie had to be there at ten a.m. the next day. October and Gene would stay at the hospital while they ran the remaining tests. David would stay at Mrs. Hopp's until they got back later in the day. Early the following day, October would go with Gene, pray, and send Vergie off to what, October felt sure, would be a safe operation.

In the distance she heard the ice cream truck's organ grind and, closer, David's whine with Gene about Popsicle money.

"That truck comes around every night," Vergie said. "He doesn't need to buy it just because the truck comes. But I guess tonight is special."

October wanted to buy a Popsicle for him, and Vergie said, "Okay, but don't let him make a habit out of it while I'm gone."

October grabbed her purse. "Get me a Neapolitan ice cream sandwich," Vergie told her. "Get Gene one, too."

As October and David skipped down the porch steps to the sidewalk, she could smell the sweat and soap, and her hand swept his shoulder.

"They have soft-serve, too," he told her. She held out change and he cupped his two palms together, then ran ahead to the curb, bouncing and waving down the truck. October let him choose, change his money for loot, and dump the cold load of ice cream sandwiches into her hands without a "thank-you," then run his slurping way up the sidewalk. Parents — aunts included — were means to an end. And they were shields, too. For David's sake, Vergie's operation was to be just a little scar on her stomach. Why? So it wouldn't hurt anymore.

Once the sun was gone for good, and October could hear David sloshing around in the bathtub, she and Vergie caught the ends of the tight string of the coming ordeal.

Vergie started it. "The garbage man comes on Saturday. Gene forgets sometimes, so be sure the garbage is emptied."

An advertisement came on for *What's My Line?*, showing that Leslie Uggams would be on.

"Gene!" Vergie called. "Come look — they've got a colored girl on."

The glider on the front porch creaked, but Gene didn't come. Right in the middle of talking about how good Leslie Uggams looked, Vergie said, "David doesn't like Sunday school, so me and Gene usually let him go with us to the regular service."

Okay. October asked for details, and they went through the details of Vergie's hospital room, how was she going to call on a telephone with a three-party line, the problem of slim visiting hours, and, for the hundredth time, what to do with David.

"And I guess you don't have to stick to the menus if you don't want to," she said. October told her that she definitely would. After all, who but Vergie knew what Gene and David liked to eat?

And then, as Vergie began telling her how to fry the fish, October heard the tears that didn't want to come out.

She reached over and touched Vergie's hand. "It'll be all right, Verge." And she retold the thing about the two women teachers her own age who had had this same operation and how they had come back to teaching with a new lease on life. But Vergie had the "yeah-buts." Nothing October could say would turn the picture from doom to picnic.

The news went off, and Dinah Shore came on. Vergie got up to change the channel to *Perry Mason,* already in progress. She stood beside the console, wiping away invisible dust.

"Let me ask you something," she said.

"What?"

She faced October squarely and asked, "What would you do if anything happened to me?"

"What do you mean? Nothing's going to happen to you."

Vergie sat down again. "People can have operations and not come back, you know."

"Not many people, and not healthy people," October said.

"So what would you do?" she asked again.

"About what, Vergie? Are you talking about the house? Gene? David?"

"All that," Vergie said.

"I'd do whatever you wanted me to do," October said. She thought for sure that Vergie and Gene had gone over all this before she got there. This could be about a special something October alone could do. But probably it was about David.

"Well, then, here's what I want," Vergie said.

"Do I need to write it down?" October asked.

"No," Vergie said. "I just want your word. That's all."

"Tell me and I'll promise to do it," October said.

"I want you to promise that if I die, you will never tell David that I wasn't his mother. That I didn't birth him."

Blindsided her. "Vergie —"

"Promise," Vergie said.

It wasn't that October had big qualms

about not telling him. If he knew, he would hate her. But would he hate her forever? She couldn't promise.

"Nobody knows the future, Vergie," she said. "I can't say what I might think or say or do. . . ."

October couldn't fault Vergie for asking. In Vergie's place she would have done the same thing.

In the mean hinterlands, though, where she seldom let her mind wander, October caught a flash of perfect life — David looking up at her, cupping his hands for ice cream money, and Vergie did not exist.

October didn't promise. On the eve of life-or-death-maybe, they couldn't even stay in the same room. Vergie went to the kitchen and left October to watch the last few minutes of *Perry Mason*, where the prosecutor finished grilling the witness. When Perry Mason cross-examined, the truth came out, and the show was over.

Later on, Mrs. Hopp came over to wish Vergie well, and got October to walk her back over the dew-wet grass to her front door. Frail, her arm was a reed bent at October's elbow. When October got her to her door, she turned her head up sideways again, to meet October's eyes.

"You're a lot like Carrie, you know," she

told October. "She was green, but she had a lot of nerve. She went off with that man and never got over it." She unlinked her arm from October's and yanked open her screen door.

"She had a heart big as this house," she said, grabbing on to the doorjamb to help pull herself up into the dark of her house, then turned to hook the screen.

"You take good care of your sister," she said. "Your aunties would have wanted that."

In the night, October's mind wandered back to its usual haunts. Whom did she have in this world, if not Vergie? Vergie would be giving up her womb. And October? She had given away a son and at any moment could decide to have another.

The next day came and went with tests and decent manners at Ross County General.

At six on the morning of the operation, October and Gene left David — scared, but willing to be with Mrs. Hopp — and went to the hospital to wait out the day. They let Gene and October see Vergie for a few minutes before they "took her up." Sterile, decked out in green gown and bonnet, Vergie lounged on the bed like she was having her toenails clipped.

"I've left it in God's hands," she told them.

A nurse came and said that they had to cut it short. With Gene sitting right there beside

Vergie, holding her hand, October was going to have to get it out.

Maybe it was because she was afraid that Vergie might die, or because she was sure that she wouldn't, or because she was grateful that God had required so little of her lately, or guilty that her aunts were looking down. Whatever the reason, she gave it up.

"I'll let you two be alone," she said. "But, Vergie, what we talked about yesterday? You don't have to worry. If anything changes, I'll do just like you asked me to do."

She meant it. Maybe she just loved her sister.

The surgery went well. Two days later, Vergie was eating normal food and was strong enough to lean on somebody and walk to the bathroom. Every day at one, October left David with Mrs. Hopp and went to sit and talk with her sister. Yes, the garbage was out, yes, David was eating greens, yes, Gene liked the meatloaf. Every night when Gene left the house for the hospital, October knew he'd be grilled the same way about the same things. The telephone party lines were open for only four hours a day. But Vergie called David whenever she could — just about every day — even just a minute to say hi.

The last thing October wanted was for

Gene or David to want for anything that she could figure out and pull together. And it was a stretch. Up by six to make real breakfasts for Gene and any special thing she could think of for the lunch David would eat at Mrs. Hopp's. She made her own menus and baked something sweet each afternoon. Doing laundry sent her to the catalogue to price the new automatic washing machines. Vergie's sweeper ate the dust, but it was heavy on the stairs.

The first Saturday after Vergie's surgery, David came into the dining room while she was dusting, and he had a drawing in his hand.

"Here, this is for you," he said. "I drew it when I was in kindergarten."

October took her present from him — looked like an almost-square sun with rays out from all four sides. In brown crayon.

"This must be the sun," she said.

David looked at it to see why on earth she thought it was the sun. "It's a cage," he said. "Momma told me I should give you something I made."

"Yes," October said, excited now. This idea of a cage was far, far advanced even for a seven-year-old. This was abstract art. She looked at it again.

"Where was this cage?"

He hunched his shoulders. "It's like my old baby bed — you know, with the bars and everything."

"This is mine to keep?" she said.

He said um-hmmm, and told her he could draw her another picture if she wanted him to. But no. This one was precious to her.

That same Saturday, she put David in her car. Vergie was fine. Now that fate wouldn't be tempted, October decided it would be okay to visit Floral Hills.

David was none too happy. "I just went," he said. "I had to go on Decoration Day." But a ride in the Impala was worth the dull end.

The cemetery no longer sold plots — it had run out of space. In the section where Negroes had been buried, she couldn't tell path from gully or weeds from the shrubbery that lined the paths in the wintertime. Rust rotted the wrought-iron gate, and a few of the bars were missing.

Once they were out of the car, David knew the way and walked on ahead, showing her.

"Momma said my grandmother Carrie looked just like y'all do now, only she was light," he said over his shoulder. Lumbering along on stout legs, he swung his arms from side to side.

"That's what Aunt Frances said, too," October told him. They got to the little gravel path that led to the section where Auntie and Aunt Maude and Carrie were buried.

"Nobody knows where Grandpa Franklin was buried, right?"

"Right," October said.

"Momma said he used to play the piano." Then David turned around. "Why did he kill y'all's mother?"

"I guess he was mean. And he probably just went off."

"Momma hates it when I call him Grandpa Frank — you know, like Auntie Oc."

October explained how very little love had been lost between him and them.

"I know," David said. "That's why I said Grandpa Franklin. What do you call him?"

"Old Man Brown," October said, partly joking. She and David walked side by side, half on the path, half in the weeds.

"Where do they bury people when nobody comes to get the body? Momma said nobody came to get him when he died. What happened to him?"

How did Vergie know? "All I know is that he died in prison. We never knew when or where. Auntie told us."

In the welter of operations and death watches, it seemed a hard thing to her, too — somebody dying alone. Even if he deserved it.

"Was I born then?"

"It was a long time ago. Me and Vergie were probably still in high school."

David tramped down some weeds and walked across several graves. "I don't believe in bad luck," he said.

"I probably wouldn't like it if somebody was tramping all over Aunt Frances and Aunt Maude, would you?"

David side-stepped the next grave. "Unh-unh," he said.

The stone read, "Carrie Cooper Brown. Beloved sister and mother." A dried-out potted geranium leaned against the marble slab. October knelt and moved it, began pulling at the weeds. *Who were you? How much of you flows in my veins?* Already she had lived four years longer than Carrie. David stood back, watching.

"You-all's mother died a long time ago," he said.

"She was twenty-seven," October said.

"I hope I don't die till I'm a hundred," David said.

October told him he'd live to be somebody's grandpa, and he wandered away, looking at headstones.

October moved over two rows, to Frances and Maude, buried side by side, and when David saw her, he came, too, squatted and pulled weeds, watching her like he thought she might cry or something.

Just because she felt suddenly grateful, she put both her hands flat on her Aunt Frances's grave. A blessing. Grateful, too, that Vergie had made it. She and Vergie were fast becoming the older generation, and so far David was their only link to the imperfect dream of eternity. He would be the only one left to remember them. David reached over and touched the grass on top of the grave with his fingertips. He looked awkward trying to do what he saw her do and not knowing why. Eventually she took away her hands, and he did, too, and they walked silently back to the car.

She noticed that the day had heated up but stayed on the clear side. Why go back to Monroe Street, when they could ramble around a whole afternoon? David had never seen the greatest effigy mound in America, and neither had she. They could get to Adams County, as she had vaguely thought they might, and back by the time Gene got home. And so off they went, over the bridge and out to Route 32, across lazy farmland, through small towns and a cool stretch of forest.

When they got to the town of Peebles, October could see the forested hilltop they had talked about on TV. She pointed. "I'll bet it's right up there," she said to David.

"I don't see anything that looks like a snake," he said, and though she wasn't sure about this, she promised him he would see it when they got closer. And she began to tell him all she remembered about the Mound Builders and what she had heard on the news. He wanted to know what an effigy was, and she told him. He wanted to know how the ancient Indian people could have carried enough baskets full of dirt to build something that big. And how long it would have taken them. And of course October didn't know, either, but they both paused at the wonder of such a feat. Two centuries before Columbus waded in Caribbean waters, these people had thrived.

The Serpent Mound site was a park with other mounds too — conical ones — and with a ranger in a tiny pavilion, and an angled-metal tower where visitors could get a full view. Though there were no walls or roped-off areas along the narrow walkway around the whole thing, the signs all said "Do Not Walk Across the Mound."

"It just looks like a hill to me," David said.

"Let's go up in the tower and look from there," she said, and they climbed the wooden steps to the top.

"Look!" David said. "It's wound up like a rattlesnake. It's eating something, too."

Uncoiling across a forested hilltop, the giant earthen snake wound and stretched nearly as far as she could see. She read the legend posted in the tower. Quarter-mile long, four feet high, thirty feet wide. No human remains had been found there — it was not a burial mound. At the farthest end, she could make out its jaws stretched around an oval-shaped, earthen egg, which it appeared to be swallowing.

"How did they do that?" David asked.

"It had to take them a long, long time," she told him. "Generations."

"What was it for?" he wanted to know.

She guessed it had some sacred significance. Maybe it was a marker for the gods to see, should they look down. Or maybe all the mounds said to anyone who came looking, *Remember us, we were here.*

Once they were back down on the ground, David wanted to walk around the whole thing, and they started off toward the coiled tail, she following him on the path. They met a few other people, but the surrounding forest gave the place a cloistered feel. Sparrows powdered themselves in gravel dust, and an occasional breeze soughed through the trees. From the tower, the mound had been a serpent. On the ground, it looked like a long hill, yes, but smooth on top, and it ran for a quarter of a mile.

"Do Not Walk Across the Mound," the sign said.

October looked both ways and whispered loudly, "David . . ."

He turned around, and he must have seen the glee in her eyes, because he grinned. She grabbed his hand and like two scrappy rabbits, they scrambled up the hill — David mumbling about bad luck, and her laughing, telling him that it wasn't a grave — to the top, where a long, grassy plateau wound and stretched ahead of them. Holding his hand still, like a shot — just because she could — she took off running, laughing and pulling him along until she couldn't hold herself back anymore, and flew on off ahead of him, running a race with the girl she had been when she last ran for the sheer joy of running, arms akimbo, feet landing wherever they would, feeling her chest straining to keep up, running along the Greatest Mound in America with David laughing and whooping on her heels.

When she started seeing stars, she slowed down to a jog and stopped. David, too, laughing still, the two of them bent, holding their knees, huffing and puffing.

"You can *run*," he said, breathless.

"Yeah," she blew, "I *can*." She looked up. "I guess those people up in the tower can see us, but I'll bet we're not the first people to ever walk across a mound."

She scooted down the hill, ignoring the grass stains, laughing at herself. David followed. When they got to the car, she opened the door for him but then stopped and suddenly hugged him to her. "I love you, David," she said, "— do you know that?" into his hair.

"Um-hmmm," he said, hugging her back.

She released him and they got into the car and headed out of the park toward the highway and Chillicothe and Monroe Street.

As they cruised along toward the bridge David asked, "When is Momma coming home?"

It was the first time he had said anything about Vergie's being away. October told him maybe in a week. Was he worried?

And then, sliding out of his mouth as easily as a licked spoon, he asked, "Is it true that Momma can't ever have a baby again?"

"Who told you that?" October asked him. He was way too young to be hearing this.

"Brenda."

October got the details. Ronnie Whoever's sister up the street had told him.

When was this? One day. And what were they talking about? David didn't know. She just told him, and was it true?

October had her eyes glued to the road.

What do you tell a seven-year-old? Her third-graders were older, and she wouldn't have known what to tell them, either.

"I think that's something you have to ask your mother when she gets home," October said.

"How does a baby get in her stomach?" he wanted to know.

"You should ask Vergie," she said.

"When I was a baby, did God put me in her stomach?"

"In a way, I guess He did," October said. But then thought again. "Not exactly, though."

"You don't know?"

"When she gets home she'll tell you all about it."

"Can you have a baby?"

"Yes, I can."

"Why don't you have one?"

This was way out of the zone where October could hold a conversation with a seven-year-old, especially this seven-year-old. And since she didn't know what version of birds and bees he was supposed to know, she didn't answer right away. And wasn't that a Dairy Queen coming up right over there?

That evening, she sat and watched Gene and David devour her meatloaf and her peach cobbler, thinking that Gene probably didn't know any more than she did about handling birds and bees with David. Sitting with them at the kitchen table, listening up close to their lives, something was so right. Whatever it was, no amount of work or sacrifice could come close to tipping the balance against family.

With Gene at the hospital most evenings, October could sit with Mrs. Hopp and watch David go up and down the block on his bike. Meanwhile Mrs. Hopp would lean on her cane, happy to fill October in on who was pulling a creep with whom, how much money so-and-so paid for his car, whose children would turn out to be hoodlums.

October asked her one evening if she remembered that ticklish name-changing time at 752. Mrs. Hopp fingered the raisin mole on her chin, like the story started there.

"Well, you know you were headstrong, don't you? Frances and Maudie had a time with you. They never got over what happened to Carrie.

" 'Fore she died, Carrie wanted to come back here. You know that? I guess she thought her and him would do better if she was close to her folks. 'Course, he wasn't for it — he was a city boy. And your aunties — I guess they figured Carrie had made her own bed. No use encouraging her to give up — they wasn't pushin too hard for her to come back. Don't get me wrong, they wasn't nasty to her or nothin — just didn't push to get her back.

"Once he killed her, they had it bad. Had to deal with what they couldn't see before. Maybe she couldn'a took care of herself and two babies with a man like that. I reckon they both had plenty trouble gettin over the fact that if she hadda come back here to Monroe Street, she might be alive today.

"Then here you come along, chompin at the bit to be grown, and it scared 'em, givin yourself another name and all. You went off to the college and didn't pay them no mind 'bout comin back."

October had never known the details of her aunts' regrets. While Mrs. Hopp sat working her gums, October pictured Aunt Frances pushing like forty-going-north to get to the doorway of the Jacksons' pantry-bedroom that day, coming to save her girl and Carrie's. No wonder.

Mrs. Hopp crooked her finger in October's direction. "You find yourself a nice man 'fore it gets too late, you hear?" She said it the way she would tell a child about coming in before dark.

"Get a little love for yourself," she said. "Your aunties would have wanted it, you know."

After dinner one evening, October recruited David for kitchen duty, something that was not on Vergie's list.

"I'm washing — drying is the easy job," she told him.

"Momma does the dishes. I take out the trash."

"When me and Vergie were girls, we did them all by ourselves. I couldn't even reach the draining board, had to stand on a stool."

"That's for girls," David said, taking forks and spoons from the drainer.

"Suppose there aren't any girls — what then?"

"That's different."

"Well, if you were at my house, I'd have you doing them all by yourself."

David frowned.

"Maybe sometime you can come stay with me all summer. Your summer vacation. How would you like that?"

She hadn't meant to ask him — it just came out.

He grinned. "I would like it," he said. "I remember that time when we went to the zoo."

"You remember that? You were only four."

David stepped over to the kitchen table to start a stack of plates, talking about camels. October went on playing in the soapy water, thinking about possibilities.

"You remember the kids you played with at Swope Park?"

He remembered a little.

"Well, they all still live around where I live, and if you came for the summer, they would take you swimming."

He dried plates and stacked them, dropped spoons and forks into the drawer. October saved the glasses for herself.

David said that he didn't know how to swim, and October told him all she knew about easy lessons. She couldn't swim herself. They could learn together if he was there. Someday. Maybe. "If Vergie and Gene think it's okay."

Toward the end of the second week, the buzzing started. Vergie was coming home. October cleaned all over, Gene took his week's vacation, David pulled out his crayons and watercolors and made pictures for Vergie's wall.

The day Gene drove up with Vergie in the car, David went out to the porch and stood watching, like Vergie was a visitor. October told him to hold open the door for Vergie, but it took ages because Vergie had to take the steps so slowly. October wondered what he could be thinking, he had gotten so quiet. When, finally, Vergie got to the porch and let out a "whew," she looked at David and smiled.

All of a sudden he ran up to her, tears streaming, and buried his face in her stomach, holding on. October wanted to look away. All that time, he'd been riding his bike and taking his bath and eating his peas and waiting. October could see from Vergie's face that David was hugging her too tightly, but then Vergie was holding on to him, too. She was home.

And then she was really home. To her house, where she could see a speck of dust ten feet away and hear David whisper up the street. Not one to take it easy when anyone else was working, from day one she got up to make her own coffee. Then it was her own breakfast, and she'd throw in a couple more slices of bacon before she would sit down. After a week at home, there was no lying around for her. She'd stay up all day — in a chair, but up. Where she could supervise. It was her kitchen.

Vergie's kitchen. Whoever heard of baking biscuits in the cornbread pan? You don't cook beans in the little pot meant for rice. Seven eggs — not six — go into real pound cake, no matter what the recipe says; and nutmeg ruins the taste of sweet potatoes. Two women cannot run one kitchen.

Bleach in the white things, just the socks,

not the underclothes, dingy or not. Light starch for Gene's work clothes, heavy for his shirts. No rough-dried sheets on anybody's bed, and double rinse the towels to keep them fluffy. Two women spoil the laundry.

Until October had taken over, Vergie swore, David had never stayed outside after eight o'clock, watched television past nine-thirty, or slept past eight in the morning. He had never eaten lunch food for breakfast or talked back to Gene. What had gotten into him?

Once Vergie could wield a broom and walk backward up the stairs so she didn't strain herself, October knew that it was time for her to think about leaving. But first, the Mound Builders had put something on her mind.

Down on Bridge Street, the very bricks gave off heat waves, but the town had put new benches around some of the trees, and she noticed that white people sat around the trees, but black folks did, too. Just not to-gether. It had been years since she actually shopped along there, and now they had a mall — five stores and a cafeteria. She wanted something for David, and it shouldn't be a toy.

Inside Seider's, on a shelf against the mir-ror, she saw tiny figurines, crystal ballerinas, marble paperweights. And intricate, carved wooden things, a turtle with mother-of-pearl inlaid on the shell. And then *it* — a carved bicycle that could fit into her hand, with spoked wheels that actually moved and a tiny mother-of-pearl bicycle seat. A collector's item — had to be — and expensive. But this was the thing she wanted that would say to David, *I was here.*

Saturday she would be hitting the road. She thought she would give it to him Friday night. But Wednesday night, after dinner, David — happy that Vergie was herself and his again — volunteered to help with the dishes. Vergie had been sitting, drying, while October washed. Vergie laughed and handed him the dish towel.

"Let me see what you can do, boy," she said.

October handed him a plate and he wiped it dry, put it on the table. "See," he said. Then he said, "Auntie Oc said if I come to stay with her I have to do the dishes."

What did he want to say that for? October looked at Vergie and Vergie straightened her back.

"Who said anything about going to stay with your auntie?"

October started out, "I told him that if —"

And Vergie cut her off. "I'm asking David."

David said, "If you and Daddy wanted me

to, I could go see Aunt October by myself."

"Well, me and your daddy don't want you to. We *take* you to see Aunt October. That's how we do it."

"Vergie," October tried again, "I just thought —"

"That's okay," Vergie said. "David heard me. He knows now."

And she took the towel from David.

And then Thursday morning, before the sun got hot, the three of them sat on the front porch, October and Vergie jabbering about flowers, David listening in. Again, Mr. Master-of-the-House had a bright idea and went in to get them all a glass of lemonade. Very nice, David. Then a truck went by, and the kids in the back waved and hollered to David. He waved back.

He said to October, "That's Ronnie and Brenda."

Vergie said, "Ronald Stuart's kids — remember him?"

Then David told her, "Momma, Brenda said you had a operation so you can't have a baby anymore."

Vergie looked at October, and they both shook their heads. October took that moment to sip her lemonade.

Vergie told him, "If God wants me to have another baby, He'll put one in my stomach."

And David, clever boy, said to her, "Auntie didn't say God could put a baby in your stomach, did you, Auntie?"

If color could drain from Vergie's face, it did then.

"I said you should ask your mother," October said. "Remember, I said that she would tell you where babies come from?"

October saw the storm behind Vergie's eyes. Without a word, Vergie got up and moved so fast she knocked over the glass of lemonade next to her chair. She went inside and slammed the door.

David's face — and October was sure hers too — was a complete question mark. She chased Vergie inside. Vergie had gone on upstairs to her room, off limits, but October had to talk to her. And David had come halfway up the stairs, too.

The bedroom door was shut. October tapped lightly. "Vergie, can I come in?" Vergie didn't answer, just suddenly opened the door. She had wiped tears. And when she saw David coming behind October she yelled at him. "Boy, get back downstairs before I light up your hind parts!"

October stepped in, and Vergie closed the door and leaned against it.

"What did you tell him?" Vergie asked her.

October said, "Nothing." She hadn't told

him anything except that he should ask his mother how he got into her stomach.

"Why were you talking about it in the first place?" Vergie wanted to know.

"He wanted to know where he came from — somebody had said something to him, I guess."

Bad choice of words. "So you told him to ask *me* where he came from. You couldn't just say you didn't know? Why didn't you tell him what I told him? He's too young to understand about babies — you ought to know that. What were you trying to prove?"

"Nothing," October said. "Vergie, I swear, I just told him to ask you everything. I might have said that I didn't know about God and all that."

"You promised me you wouldn't tell him," Vergie said, and she started to cry. "You said you wouldn't."

"I didn't," October said, going to her, trying to touch her, calm her down. "It wasn't about us and David — it was just a question about where babies come from."

Vergie blew her nose. "You had no business talking about it to him. You knew what you were doing."

"I'm sorry, Vergie," October said. "You have to hear me when I tell you — David doesn't think anything. He's a boy, that's all."

"I'm sorry, too," Vergie said. "You gave me your word, and I thought I could trust you." She was calmer now, wouldn't look at October.

"This is the last time," Vergie said.

October didn't know what she meant. She didn't remind Vergie that the promise had been a little bit different from the way Vergie remembered it. But it didn't matter. She had said nothing. Neither one of them seemed to have anything else to say. Vergie stepped away from the door so that October could get out. When October opened the door, Vergie said, "If I ever leave you with David again, I hope God will strike me dead."

Vergie was like thin china right then. October knew that. They had taken her womb and David had spent too much time with October. She could understand that, too. She didn't want to fight, but she wasn't about to leave with that curse over her head. She didn't want to pull out the big guns, but she could if Vergie forced her.

The next morning, she waited until Gene was gone and David was on his bike before she found Vergie in the den, looking at *The Price Is Right*.

She didn't even sit down, had to stand up to say what she had to say. "Vergie," she said, waiting to get her attention. When Vergie's eyes didn't leave the TV, October went and stood in front of it. Bob Barker was loud in the background, but October was louder.

"You said I broke my promise. I didn't. But here's another promise."

"Shh!" Vergie said, looking around for David. October switched off the TV.

"I don't have anything else to say," Vergie said.

"I do," October said. She said it soft, but she was mad. "If you ever try to keep me from seeing David, I *will* tell him everything. That's my new promise, so don't go threatening me."

"When you tell him," Vergie said, "just be sure you get it right. I want to see you tell him you didn't want him. Tell him that and see what happens."

October retreated. "You heard what I said."

She left to go pack her things. If it took all she could muster, she wouldn't run. She would stay until Saturday, give David his little present Friday night. Vergie could like it or lump it.

Friday night she left the present on David's bed, wrapped in tissue paper in a little white box. He came to Aunt Maude's old room to tell her thank-you. Stiff. Worried.

She took that moment to hug him good-bye. "Don't worry," she said. "Everything is going to be all right. Me and Vergie get like this sometimes."

And then Saturday. Sour good-byes were the easiest. Nobody was supposed to care.

The car was all packed, and still, Vergie didn't come downstairs. Gene and David had helped, and Gene kept looking up at the bedroom windows, wondering if Vergie's face would be there. It wasn't.

October kept hoping, too. Suppose something happened to one of them. Watching David carry her hatbox to her car, knowing it would be months before she saw him again, though, hope turned into so much fluff. Down in her somewhere, even if they never spoke again, she wasn't about to let Vergie keep David away from her for good.

When it was finally clear that that was that, she hugged David and got into her loaded car. As she pulled off, Gene waved, and David did too. In her rearview mirror she watched them waving until the two of them were a snapshot that would last for a long, long time.

Part Two

Part Two

CHAPTER 18

Storm warning. Shaky ground.

When David was born, I did what was mine to do. I stood faithfully by and held for Lillian and him. And when she and Vergie started knotting up the thread between them, I held. When Frances was trying to make it back through the narrow passage, I stood and held for her, too. The same for Maude.

Lillian and Vergie were last and all to each other. When they made it their business to start tearing that apart, holding for them was mine to do, and I did it. But mothers and fathers owe their children; I always believed that. And Franklin and I ended up owing our girls more than most.

It was true that my last breath was a prayer and prayers get answered. Still, I did all I could to help them be open to whatever grace might come their way.

CHAPTER 19

Leon Haskins. Back in 1951, when he set his sights for Harlem, he didn't know beans about what he wanted.

All he knew was that Kansas City jazz days were over and the New York City scene was it. If he climbed out of his bed one day and found himself in Harlem, he thought he'd be set from then on. Coming from the Show Me state to the Apple, he would be one of the future kings.

After all, Coleman Hawkins had spent a whole lot of time in Kansas City, and he was Leon's first idol. Leon had other idols too: Lester Young, Ben Webster. Kansas City had grown them up and sent them like exotic seeds on the wind to swing-jazz fame.

And Charlie Parker. Bird. Leon knew the legend. How Bird had been to the woodshed behind his mother's house on Olive Street, taken off from there, and soared on flawless improvisation to his perch as the genius of modern jazz. And when Leon had gotten to Harlem, already Bird's imitators could be heard in every club that had a bandstand.

Late bloomer. That's how Leon saw himself. He was twenty-six then. Bird had been crowned king when he was twenty-two. Dizzy was older, but better longer. Miles Davis had just broken away and done something mellow, mournful, cool. Leon could list the players not much over thirty yet but at the top of the heap, recording with everybody.

Leon had two recordings to his name. Sideman recordings with nobodies. The trick, as Leon saw it, was to make something out of his Kansas City–ness. He gave himself a year to segue into his own style, the sound that would set him apart from all of them. Little did he know that this kind of determination was the very essence of what had lifted jazz to its lofty place.

And so, with his horn under his arm, Leon had stepped out of his furnished room on the third floor of an old Harlem tenement, skipped down the stairs and out the front door onto 119th Street, a valley that stretched across Harlem from Morningside to Kingdom Come.

That was September 1951. By September 1952, he had gotten his big break. An overseas tour with Lionel Hampton's band. And he had opened for Dizzy Gillespie at a nightclub in the Bronx. On his way. He had met his "family," as he called it, an old blues-player man with a common-law wife and a borrowed daughter.

If anybody had told him then that in six or seven years he would tuck tail and flee back to Kansas City, he would have laughed.

CHAPTER 20

If ever she was to have David sleeping under her roof in any form or fashion, October thought she would have to set Vergie's words aside and get busy. Step one, find a house, because her little apartment didn't offer anything but plain shelter for a child. Even for a visit, David would have to have his own room. And a place to play. And children to play with. All of that.

Tim Crawford, the real estate man, with his busy self, told her he would do what he could but not to get her hopes up for as good a deal as Cora and Ed had gotten. She told him she wanted to be in a house that had been around for a while, in a neighborhood near enough to school. Nothing less than two bedrooms and a real dining room. Aside from that, a basement and a backyard would be nice. Donetta and Kenneth also lived on the west side, where all the blacks were moving in. Between them, and Cora and Ed, October figured surely she would find something.

Meanwhile, eight-thirty to four found her doing what she was paid to do. For the moment the school was short-handed. With desegregation pressing, some of the best teachers were being sent to the front lines at white schools, leaving larger classes at the Negro schools to be handled by the unchosen few. October was one of them.

At school, the morning's second bell always sent the children skedaddling out of the hallway and into their classrooms before the teachers closed the doors. She and Donetta had classrooms across the hall from each other. She had third-graders; Donetta had sixth-graders, some of them just beginning to smell themselves, believing that that gave them permission to act ugly.

October had just begun to call the roll one morning when she heard somebody — a child? — talking way too loud in the hallway. She looked out the window in her door to see Donetta across the hall, talking to a boy who was as tall as she was. And the boy had his hat on inside. She saw Donetta closing the classroom door and the boy trying to open it again.

She opened her own door. "What's the problem?"

Donetta looked like she had swallowed fire. "Somebody is about to get his hand slammed in the door."

At that moment, the boy yanked the door open and tried to get in past Donetta.

"What do you think you're doing, little

boy?" she said. "Come on." And she took him by the arm, ushering him to the principal's office.

At recess, she and Donetta had playground duty, and October told Donetta her story of being falsely accused once for just such a scene.

"I wish his mother *would* come to school," Donetta said. "I have a thing or two I'd like to say to her."

Things had changed. Used to be parents were right there, lockstep with the teachers. Not anymore. The teachers were on their own. Which reminded Donetta — she wanted October to come to a club meeting next Sunday afternoon. Just a loose group of women, mostly teachers, who were thinking about ways to help children who seemed to be falling through the cracks.

"You know," she said, "tutoring or seeing to it that they eat lunch every day."

October thought of little Walter Jean Campbell. After the episode with the girl's mother, October had kept her distance. She considered all the other Walter Jean Campbells who needed help, and said she'd come.

The meeting at Donetta's — mostly familiar names and faces, mostly chitchat about piddly salaries and hardheaded children —

struck the familiar Du Bois chord. October needed to do more, get out more. This could be one way, a beginning. On the tail end of the meeting, when just about everybody was gone, Kenneth came home.

"I hear you're looking for a place," he said to her. "You ought to think about coming over here — there's a sign in every other yard."

He volunteered to drive around with her to see a few choice places whenever she wanted, and in fact, since she was over on this side of town, why didn't they all go right then? And that was fine.

Bungalow — that was the style she wanted and, even better, what she could probably afford. Donetta and Kenneth believed in pushing the point and took her where Tim Crawford had never been willing to go.

As they rode around, Kenneth told her he'd been meaning to get in touch with her anyway. Charlie Parker's mother still lived on Olive Street, and when Bird died, the college had started the Parker Fund. With money that musicians everywhere had donated in Bird's name, the college had created the Charlie Parker Visiting Professorship — a new position. Kenneth's job was to help find candidates, and they had to be from the Kansas City area. He mentioned venerable names like Coleman Hawkins and Lester Young. The college should be so lucky. Meanwhile, did she know how to get in touch with Leon Haskins?

"No," October told him. Why did he think she kept up with Leon? One night, and people make up stories. But something told her to be nice to Kenneth. She could ask Cora. "But I can probably get his address from his brother," she said.

"Good," Kenneth said. "We haven't been able to find him; thought he might be in Europe somewhere."

On Walrond Street, four or five blocks over from Cora and about a mile from Donetta, she found a place she liked — a remodeled bungalow with a screened-in porch and modern kitchen, unfinished basement, and small but fenced-in backyard.

"Told you," Kenneth said. "We've been all over these streets. You'll like living over here."

Step two. Once you choose a house, you have to get the bank to give you a mortgage loan. The house in Chillicothe had gone to Vergie and Gene, and October had gotten the nest egg. Frances and Maude didn't have much, but they left it for her. She had spent some of it for her car, and now she would wipe out the rest if they would just let her have a mortgage.

Easy. The man at the bank asked her for her life history, beginning with her first job washing dishes when she was sixteen. He asked her to name people who would vouch for her, and they needed to be people who *had* something, owned something. When and what she got paid and how she spent every penny. And then he told her not to bother calling. She'd get a letter saying yea or nay.

"You should have warned me," she told Cora on the phone. "I had to go back three times just to fill out all the information right."

"I had Ed," Cora said. "All I had to do was find the place. He took care of the rest. Don't worry, you'll get it. And when you do, remember I told you — it's more than a handful. You have to keep up with a house." She filled October in on her latest decorating woes, not to mention the new phase that had Eddy Junior saying no to her and biting.

Cora went on and October remembered to tell her about the Charlie Parker thing and ask her about Leon's address.

"Lonny will never do that," Cora said. "He's too big for us now. If he can't even send a Christmas card to his brother, he sure as hell won't move back here."

October thought aloud that it could be a

362

break for somebody like Leon — "You know, time off."

"A couple of years? Lonny wouldn't do that. He's been all over the world, girl. Every time you look up you see his name on some album. What would he want with a college job?"

"So you-all don't have an address?" October asked.

Cora told her that the last one they had was supposed to be some chichi place downtown or uptown or east side or west side in New York City. Anyway, the mail came back and she sent it in care of the musicians' union there. It was Lonny's birthday card. It never came back. She still had the address for the union.

Little Alonzo Phillips — a Walter Jean of sorts, only he was a boy, and not at all meek and mild — made it easy for October to imagine another whole career. She loved nothing better than to see a pair of little eyes light up with the right answer, when children finally learned how to put one idea together with another. Some days she thought that if she ever gave up teaching, it would be because of the mud she had to swim through to get them to sit still long enough for the ideas to osmose into their little brains.

Geography was not one of their best subjects, and the last hour of the day was not the best time to teach it, but if the lesson plans said do it, she did it. On the blackboard at the front of the room, she had drawn a sketchy map of the United States in colored chalk, with the Great Lakes and major rivers in blue. The children would be coming up to label all the bodies of water, including the oceans and the Gulf. And then they would label the major mountain chains and so forth.

Just as she drew the pointer lines for labeling, a chewed wad of bubble gum sailed past her, hitting the blackboard, but not hard enough to stick. And in one of those tricks of balance, she spun around, it fell, and she stepped right on it. Ropy mess between the sole of her high heels and the floor.

The class snickered.

She asked, "Who threw the gum?" knowing already.

"Alonzo!" the class was all too happy to say. Showdown. Alonzo and the teacher would entertain them away from the Erie Canal, wherever that was.

Before she knew it, October had slipped her feet out of her shoes and marched down the row to his desk. She saw herself grabbing him by the scruff of his shirt before she actually did anything, and thought better of it.

"No recess tomorrow," she told him. He grinned, like staying in was a lollipop.

"Go! Go sit in the coatroom!" she told him. "And don't let me hear a peep out of you."

Where would they be without coatrooms? The coatroom saved her from having to march him down to the office, or having to put up with him distracting other children from the side aisle. At the back of the class, the coatroom had a door, and she had half a mind to shut it, leave him in there where he couldn't see or hear anything. But she left it open and went on with the lesson.

After school, when all the children had collected their lunch pails from the coatroom and put on their coats and were gone, and after she had made notes on tomorrow's lesson plans and washed down the blackboards, Donetta came over. October got her purse from her desk and took her coat from the supply closet at the front of the room, and they walked together to their cars.

She had been home for about an hour when the telephone rang. The janitor had found Alonzo Phillips asleep with his coat on in the coatroom. Her principal was calling to find out what she had to say.

Later that night, after calling Cora, who was glad she no longer had to deal with that sort of thing, and Donetta, who said she should have just had him suspended, period, October would have calmed down enough to tell the story in a more plausible way, but at that moment on the telephone, all she could say was that she had forgotten him.

In the scheme of things, teachers were allowed mistakes, but not the kind that seemed to find their way into October's file at the Board of Education. There was a grievance procedure for parents to follow, and Alonzo's parents followed it to the letter. At the point when she received the written grievance against her, the bank had not yet decided whether to give her a mortgage loan. If a little bird told anyone at the bank anything about the situation with the board, she stood to lose a chance at a mortgage.

Alonzo's parents wanted her fired or at least suspended, or wanted at least to have her pay docked and have her put on probation. And so here she was again, asking all the people who had said she would be a good risk for a mortgage to say she would be a good risk in the classroom if the board would just allow her to stay. Docked pay and probation were punishment enough for an excellent, dedicated teacher who had made a mistake in judgment. Please don't mention the Walter Jean mistake. Or the long-ago trouble in Wyandotte County.

By the Christmas break, her fate had been decided. If she could keep her nose clean, probation would end in three years. Just when she could use money most, her pay would be docked, for half a year. Maybe if the money hadn't been taken away, or if she had gotten the house by December, she would have wagged it in Vergie's face. She just had to *see* David, see his face without all the fussing and fighting. As it was, she couldn't possibly demand any slack from Vergie. Not this Christmas. And so she didn't call or write. And she didn't go.

Something was holding her back, and it felt like she just didn't have the guts. What was she afraid of? Nothing. She sent a box addressed to David. A savings bond, a horn for his bicycle, and a dozen mincemeat cookies.

Winter wore itself out, melted away. What was spring, if it wasn't a promise? The sun lingers, wakes up the earth; the earth softens, invites plow and seed; seeds and buds sprout every shade of green; green cracks through rock and splits the air until a riot of pastel, pushing for full color, promises that every growing thing will be perfect. What was spring but a promise?

At school October walked on eggs, and strangely, the feeling kept her interested enough to ward off fear that the mortgage might not come through.

By the end of April, when Leon Haskins came to town for his interview at the college, she still hadn't heard from the bank. Kenneth and Donetta invited her to come to the dinner at Pucci's and then to the performance part — a set featuring the homeboy-made-good playing his horn with local musicians at the Reno Club. She would have to get over her embarrassment, the wondering who knew about her probation. Donetta and Cora urged her to let it go.

Missouri State's president and board would be there, looking to pick Leon apart. Kenneth and his group stacked the deck by inviting as many friends and fans as they could find. For October, the before-the-show dinner at Pucci's on the Plaza, where the chandeliers were as big around as the tables, was reason enough to say yes.

She went with Cora and Ed and met the others standing in the lobby of the restaurant, waiting for the reason they were there. Leon came with Missouri State administrators and their wives. She hadn't seen him for four years. He looked like a man in need of a good night's sleep — red eyes, almost-frown, and a nervous thumb that rubbed for stubble on his cheek. Nice suit, crisp shirt, no tie. He looked at her, but nothing seemed to register. The president had his ear, and as they approached, Leon seemed so determined to impress the man that they all had to stand there a minute too long.

He was saying something about teaching college students. Fingerings, tempo, harmonics. The president was uh-huh nodding, steering his wife by the arm, trying to follow the waiter.

Leon didn't seem to notice. "I've got recordings of the greats before they were great, and recordings from when they broke through," he said. "You can listen to all the records you want, but if you don't find your own thing, you'll end up being just a bad recording of somebody else. Youngsters need to know that."

Trying not to ignore Leon altogether, but wanting to get to the table with his wife, the president told him, "We can talk about this some more later."

"Sure," Leon said.

Leon seemed to be trying hard. October took it as a sign that he wasn't their man. She sat down beside Cora — six pieces of silverware, three crystal glasses, assorted plates and cups and saucers at each place setting, and fifteen place settings on a white-linened banquet table. Lavish.

Once the waiters began pouring water, she whispered, "How is it going?"

"Good," Cora said. "I think they like him. Ed's having a fit — I'll tell you about it later."

"What?"

"Later."

Family rumblings. Later Cora would tell her that Leon's possible homecoming might do wonders for Ed. Nobody ever wanted to see anybody fall on his face, but Leon had always been the one with perfect pitch and all. Ed used to play the trumpet, but each family gets only one genius. Ed had had to move on from music to something that would keep two nickels in his pocket while Leon became Mr. Big. Maybe Leon was coming down a peg or two.

Kenneth made a little speech to welcome everybody and told them to order anything they wanted from the menu. Most of the waiters were black, and they knew how to take care of their people.

Special cocktails first. Told them to stick to the shrimp and not bother with the escargots, and the filet mignon was better than the prime rib.

Small talk and good food. They talked about which restaurants had opened their doors, which ones still hung out the signs. Somebody asked Leon, Why now? Why would he interrupt his steady rise to teach at Mo State? October's ears stretched.

Leon shifted in his chair and crossed his legs. "It's all about Bird," he said. "I learned a lot from him. I didn't know him like I know my brother, but I saw enough to make me think about what might have happened if Bird could've stood still long enough to catch up with himself. Every now and then you have to stop and check yourself. That's a part of it. The rest? I'd like to try to go back to basics and the woodshed. You can't keep doing the same thing and call it jazz."

"Yeah, yeah, I hear you," Kenneth said.

Leon wasn't through. "The biggest thing, though," he said, "I'd like to try to reach back and get a few of the youngsters. Bring them along, you know — pull their coat. That's at the heart of jazz. One showing another one. You dig?" Jive talking a little, but Official went right on smiling and nodding, *Umm-hmm, all right.* Somebody asked Leon something about something Thelonious Monk had written. And Leon went into another long story about the first time that he had seen Monk.

From what October could tell, Leon had them in his hand. Wasn't he the real thing, the genuine article, and wasn't that enough?

At another lull, somebody asked Leon how

he had gotten started playing the saxophone. October thought she had heard that story before.

Leon looked at Ed before he answered. Ed kept his head in his plate.

"It's a long story," Leon said.

"Who's in a hurry?" More mileage for Kenneth.

"As a matter of fact," Leon said, "it started at the Reno Club." He looked again at Ed. "My brother took me to hear Bean play. I was a kid with a clarinet."

"Coleman 'Bean' Hawkins," Kenneth told everybody.

Leon continued. "We went and I never will forget, Bean played 'Body and Soul.' And man, when he brought out that boss sound he had and I saw what real saxophone was all about? Man, I had to have me some."

He put down his fork. "I didn't know what he was doing, but whatever it was, I wanted to do it, too. It was a week later I got myself a saxophone."

"A year," Ed said. "And Momma got it."

They all laughed.

Leon sat back in his chair and rocked a little, remembering. "That's the God's truth," he said. "Momma bought it, got it down at the pawnshop. Pete's. Man, I thought it was Christmas."

Dessert time. The waiters told them that none of the pies were any good but the Belgian chocolate cake passed for decent. And Leon went on answering questions. How well did he know Dizzy? What did he think of Sonny Rollins? Is Sonny Stitt the new Charlie Parker? Cool jazz, and West Coast jazz, and for-real jazz. More about the jazz world in two hours than October had heard in her life.

After dinner at Pucci's, they all went to the Reno Club for Leon's performance. At the Reno Club, October and Cora sandwiched Ed and let him interpret. He explained "pure" versus any other kind of jazz, how they had to improvise on the spot. No rehearsals. Hear the tune announced, a standard, then just launch into their own ideas, let them just flow, make it up as they go.

"Watch," Ed said.

" 'Honeysuckle Rose,' " Leon yelled out to the musicians behind him on the bandstand. October knew the song, hummed it as they played it through.

But then each one of them took a solo, improvising, while Ed explained "ride cymbals" and why "comping" was better than "stride piano."

And then, just when the music seemed to be settling down again, a spill of notes ripped the air, and Leon walked up to the front of the bandstand, sax in mouth, eyes closed. And blew that way, just a barrage of improbable combinations for a good ten minutes. October and everyone else in the club were either mesmerized to dumb, or yelling "Blow man! Tear it up, Lonny!"

Leon was their man. And October felt happy for Leon. Her part had been small, but who knew — it might not have happened without her.

Life is a water wheel. It turns. The trick is to hold your nose when you're under and not get dizzy when you're up. The day that October got the yes letter from the bank, she copied that James Baldwin quote onto a sheet of parchment paper in broad-tipped ink pen, to be framed and put on one of the many walls she would have in her new house.

CHAPTER 21

In the old neighborhood of two-story bunga-
lows that sloped down the long-hill part of
Walrond Street, dusk sharpened the geometry of A-shaped rooftops against the sky. Full
of humidity, the evening air would hold the
smell of roses all night. And first thing in the
morning, October would smell the dough-
nuts that Joe Shelley's son floated on sizzling
oil and doused with sugar. Two blocks down,
at the corner of Thirty-first, she could see the
bakery, watch the traffic light change from
red to green, and watch the silent cars trickle
by.

This was her screened-in porch. Her house.
All hers. Her neighbors with the trellis of
roses — the Baldwins next door. They had
brought over cold cuts the day she moved in.

Leon had said seven-thirty, and now it was
going on eight. She wondered if, instead of
the porch, she ought to wait in the house. For
the two weeks that he had been at Cora's, October had stopped by a few times to say hello
and to hold Cora's hand.

"It might be good for Ed," Cora had said,
"but I know one thing — I'll be glad when he

gets his own place. That horn drives me crazy first thing in the morning. Every day a new box full of his stuff comes from New York."

October had wondered aloud to Leon about the change. "After New York, it must feel strange to be out here," she had said.

"Like a fish out of water," Leon had told her. "I'll get used to it, though. It's not like I never lived here."

Cora had chimed in that she guessed he would just have to be a little cramped for a while. And Leon had jumped. "Don't get me wrong, um-umm. This is a sweet deal for me. And right on time."

A few days later he had phoned to tell October that he'd like to take her out for at least a drink. When she hesitated, he explained that he just wanted to say thanks.

"I was serious when I said this job was right on time," he told her.

"You're Lonny Haskins — you deserved the job," she told him.

"Kenneth Wallace said they would have moved on down the list if you hadn't given them my number."

"I got the union address from Cora. That was all."

"Well, I still owe you. The last time I tried to buy you dinner — a hundred years ago — all we could find was ribs. This time we ought to integrate Fred Harvey's Steak House. Say when."

"Okay, Friday, Saturday, but I don't think I want to get thrown out of Fred Harvey's."

"Friday."

School was out, and she had already started her little part-time in Macy's alterations. What she wanted most was to catch her breath and play with her house.

The very first thing she had done — even before the movers had set up her bed — was to hang the framed drawing of David's "cage" on the wall of the other little bedroom. From that point on, it would be the place in her house that he would know as his, whether he lived there for the summer or for the rest of his life or never.

Yet even as she fixed up his room, something kept at her, as if she were pushing against a tide that someday would wash her away. What was she afraid of?

Next, she had put her sewing machines — the new fold-down automatic and the old iron Singer — in the unfinished basement and put her old bureau down there, for all her patterns and fabric swatches and pins and zippers and tapes and buttons. Nice. Stood her dressed dress form in one corner. Someday she would ask Ed about turning the basement into a real sewing room. Meanwhile, it would be plenty room to sew.

She had bought a secondhand mahogany dining room set with six chairs and found an antique cocktail cart for Aunt Maude's antique pink pitcher and juice glasses. She hung curtains, bought a new sofa, and polished up all her old things. Wallpaper would come later.

Once she reached the point where the house began to look like somebody lived there, it was time. And it was the first of June, still time enough for something good to happen toward the end of the summer. Time to write to Vergie.

She wanted the letter to pull no punches and still say what she wanted to say in a way Vergie could hear. She needed to see David on her own terms now. They hadn't talked in almost a year, and she thought that by now it was a thing of who would hold out the longest. Vergie won hands down. After all, she had David. October had sent the package at Christmas. Vergie hadn't sent a card, hadn't called. That in itself was a sign. Vergie hadn't said she couldn't *see* David, but she had said that David could never come *alone* to see her, and that just wouldn't do. Why should she keep lying down and rolling over?

Some mornings she got up early just to walk around her house. She'd stand in the middle of David's room, with its skinny little bed, and make believe he was in the kitchen fixing himself a peanut-butter-and-jelly sandwich. She found a little bar of soap in the shape of a car for the sink in the bathroom; comic books got stacked on the closet shelf. A jar of marbles found a corner. Something had to give.

During that first week in June, one evening after Macy's had sweated the salt out of her, October sat on her front porch and wrote the letter.

Dear Vergie,
This letter will come as a surprise, I'm sure. I'm sorry that you and I haven't been able to work out our problems, but David is growing up now, and I feel that I shouldn't just sit and wait to see what will happen. We shouldn't sit and wait.

I'm not proud of the past. If I could have done better, I would have. I know that I gave David up, but, Vergie, he still feels like mine to me. Every time I see him, that's how it feels. I know I'm scaring you, but please try to hear what I'm saying. I don't want to take him away from you. I can't erase the years. But I love him, too. I want to be closer to him. I do think he has a right to know who brought him into the world. I bought a house, a big house. I want to see him here, in my house, and you can't always have the last say.

Please, Vergie, think about bringing David here in August to stay for a while, and yes, the house is big enough for you and Gene to stay, too, if that's the way it has to be this time. But when you come, please think about you and me sitting down with David and telling him the truth.

If I don't hear back, I'll just plan to come to Ohio again around the middle of August, and we can at least talk then.

Think about it, Vergie.

Love, October

First of July, waiting on the porch for Leon to pick her up, she was still waiting for an answer from Vergie.

Before she could put car and man together, she saw the dark green sports car roaring up the street and thought it was awfully loud. When it stopped in front of her house, she assumed it was somebody coming to see the neighbors.

It was Leon. She watched him getting out of the car, looking as tired as he had two weeks before, but neat and clean still.

"Ready?" he asked.

"In a minute." She went in to get her purse.

"Can we both fit into that?" she asked, laughing. She had long legs. Her dress was definitely going to get crushed.

"It's bigger than it looks, but we can put the top down."

"No, thanks," she said, laughing. "My hair flies all over my head without the wind."

They got in. An Austin Healy, he told her. He did sixty before they got to Thirty-seventh Street, and she had to yell above the engine noise.

"It must get hot in here!"

"Not too," he yelled back. "When I was driving across town this morning before nine, and the radio said ninety degrees, I thought about a nice Buick with air-conditioning. But I can't give her up." He patted the dash.

They went to the Brooklyn Café — not the greatest restaurant she had ever been in but it was nice enough.

While they waited to order, Leon told her he'd already been over to the college to "scope out" the situation and he wouldn't be at Cora's long. One or two well-paid gigs, and he'd be fixed. And what about her and her new house? Living high on the hog?

"It was a dream come true," she told him.

They ordered and food came.

"I know a little something about dreams," Leon said. She, for one, knew that about him.

"As long as you've got one, you know where you're going. Nothing to do but get there."

That was the Leon she remembered, bragging about the big time. He had gotten there, too, hadn't he?

He cut into his steak. "If we were in the city, I'd take you to Wells Famous Chicken and Waffles, the best restaurant in Harlem."

"Don't tell me you're missing New York already."

"Not really," he said.

"I've never seen New York."

"You've never been to the city? Nobody can tell you about it. No other place under the sun is like it, including Europe."

His horn had taken him all over the world, of course.

"Everybody everywhere understands jazz," he told her.

She thought about thousands of people adoring him in a foreign language.

"It has its downside, too," Leon said.

They skipped dessert, got more coffee.

Leon took a sip and slid into his storytelling voice. "When I was sixteen I wanted to be just like every jazz player I had ever heard of. I wanted to work those after-sundown hours while the world was sleeping. And while I was at it, I wanted to stay up and get in just *one* more little lick, you know? Follow that gypsy life. I wanted to be *it*, the hottest saxophone player who ever walked."

He sat back a little from the table, and she could see that he was nervous or worried or whatever made him keep up the jitters with his leg.

"Short of that," he said, "I wanted to be ace devotee to Bird, the guru, you know? I wanted to play boss horn and record with Blue Note for long bread, see my name in *Downbeat* on a regular basis. I'd get me a fox — you know what I mean — a real-hammer chick with a little bit of money to be my cheerleader."

October laughed.

He laughed too. "What can I say? I was sixteen. What did I know?"

It sounded like the faintest ring of regret to her. He was leaving something out. Something had happened to him, she could tell. He was thirty-nine, pushing forty. Was his dream over already?

For the fourth of July holiday, Cora and Ed invited October to come watch Ed do his first hickory-smoke thing in the pit he had built around back. They'd gotten fireworks, and

Leon had company in town. They wanted to make it into a party.

As it turned out, the day belonged to Leon and his musician friend, Kenny Clarke — Leon called him "Klook" — a jazz drummer. He smoked a pipe and looked to October like the father type. She found out that he did have children, in France. From what she could tell, he'd left Harlem right after Charlie Parker died.

They had all stuffed themselves and were sitting on Ed's handmade benches in the backyard. October sat on the steps to the back porch and listened. Wherever two musicians were gathered, Bird's name was bound to come up. Ed, though, opened the gates by reminding Leon of the first time they had seen Charlie Parker, wearing two overcoats, and how they had asked him if he was Bird, and he had just said, "Yeah, how you doin?" Bigger than life, Ed said.

And that led to Kenny Clarke's telling about the last time he had seen Bird, coming out of Birdland, the club named for him. How the midget emcee had held the door for Bird, and when Kenny Clarke had passed Bird on the steps to the club, he had seen tears streaming down Bird's face. His little girl had died.

And that story led to Leon's telling about

his last time seeing Bird alive, down at Birdland, too. And Bird was drunk.

"I did not want to see that," Leon said. "Bird drunk." He shook his bowed head, like somebody had just shined a cold light on his busted balloon. October could feel that side of him, the side that had had a very human hero.

Leon went on telling how Bird had cursed out the musicians like they had peed on the stage, and how he — Leon — wished he had gone up on that stage and got Bird before he just fell down in a chair and went to sleep. As October listened to Leon talk about the jones on Bird's back, she wondered about Leon — had he, too, had a jones on his back?

Cora had already clued her in on bits and pieces. Ed had told Cora that Leon had trampled all over some decent woman in New York. Treated her like dirt. Ed didn't give Cora the details, except to say that the wrath of God had come down on Leon's head. He hadn't been able to cut a single track on a single record in over a year, and all his big-time gigs started drying up.

"No wonder he wanted to come here," she had told October. "You know what they say about — pardon my language — shittin where you eat." And Cora had added that it was a good thing all the way around. Leon and Ed back together and all.

Storytellers. Leon and Kenny Clarke told about the funeral.

"Man, it was hard," Kenny Clarke said.

"I didn't go," Leon said.

"Stitt did 'My Buddy,' and everybody broke up."

October watched Leon shake his head again in that sad way. "Foots tried to get me to go with him, but I couldn't," Leon said. "Me and Foots went down to Abyssinian and saw the crowd, saw Dizzy passing out white gloves to everybody, I saw that long black hearse and saw that casket all polished and piled high with flowers and the women all bent and crying, and I couldn't go. Foots didn't even know I left. I just split. Went home and blew some coke and tried to forget it."

The jones thing she had wondered about. And the old man manager, too. October wondered what had happened to him.

"No matter how you live, or who you are, or what you've done," Kenny said, "someday you just up and die."

"Yeah," Leon said.

"Yeah," Ed said.

October wondered how — and *if* — Leon had gotten over his jones. He looked sober and sane enough to her.

More stories. Pieces of Leon's perfect-pitch-from-age-four story, and how Ed had to give up music lessons because Leon had *natural* talent. The two of them told it with plenty of laughs, but October knew what could be underneath all that ha-ha-ha.

She listened to Leon's funny stories about traveling with Lionel Hampton in Europe, and opening for Miles Davis and Dizzy Gillespie in the Bronx, and how awful he had been, then. And all the big gigs he and Klook had played with the Jazz Messengers.

All afternoon she listened. At one point, Kenny Clarke said, "I heard about what happened to Foots — his leg."

And Leon said, "Yeah, he was scared to go under the knife, but it didn't take him no time to be back out in the streets on that jack leg."

So the manager-man had lost a leg.

And at another point Kenny Clarke asked Leon, "Whatever happened to Ramona Jacobs?"

October listened closely for the rest of the story, but Leon wasn't saying much.

"She did okay, got a part in *Porgy and Bess*. I think she's in California now, married," Leon said.

Sounded to October like a happy ending. When she got to know Leon better, she thought she might get the whole story.

A week or two later, when Leon moved into his own apartment, October went over to help Cora help Ed and Leon christen the place. Two rooms, a table and four chairs, a bed, and a lamp. But hundreds of records, and turntables and amplifiers and speakers everywhere. And lots of bottles. A pretty collection of liquor bottles lined up on the kitchen counter.

Leon had bought rib sandwiches and coleslaw. Cora had provided the rest, including the paper plates and lemonade. As soon as everything was laid out, Leon pulled two of the chairs away from the table and sat October and Cora down in them, asked them to name a record they wanted to hear, to which they both said, "Anything."

Leon took out one of his LPs and put it on the turntable. "There's a cut on here that all the ladies like," he said. "Miles doing 'Someday My Prince Will Come.' " October recognized it was from the album called *Porgy and Bess* and wondered about the Ramona woman.

Leon wanted to fix them pink ladies. October didn't want one.

"Help me out," Leon said. "I'm trying to create a little atmosphere before the surprise."

"What surprise?" Cora and October asked at the same time.

He made the pink drinks, sat them on the floor beside their chairs and told them to enjoy Miles Davis. "Don't go nowhere," he said, and went to join Ed in the other room.

"What are they doing?" October asked Cora. Cora didn't know, but she said, "It better not be anything raunchy."

Both the men came out carrying horns. Leon had his saxophone, Ed had a trumpet. Cora's mouth flew open, but Ed hushed her up. "Don't say anything."

Leon turned off *Porgy and Bess* and turned on his huge reel-to-reel tape player. A piano began playing a slow, soft introduction to something. Then the drum came in with a nice rhythm.

Leon — sling around his neck, mouthpiece jammed between his lips — nodded to Ed, and they began blowing. "Body and Soul," it was. "Body and Soul" — they played it again, all the way through. "Body and Soul."

October sat back and watched the two brothers straining to make music, struggling to stay together, keep the same rhythm, even though Leon could have run away with it, each letting the other take his own kind of solo and then coming back to playing together, patching up whatever had been torn between them. She and Vergie didn't have the rhythm down pat. Their solos, even, were pitiful.

Misty-eyed, Cora kept her fingers up to her mouth the whole time, and when they finished, and slapped hands, Cora leaped up and ran to Ed. He hugged her.

"Don't cry, baby," he said. "We're just messin around."

"I know," Cora said.

October thought, *What a nice thing it is to be included.*

They ate and toasted Leon's new place and Cora broke out a deck of cards, threatening to make Ed learn to play bridge, once and for all. To which Ed said he'd rather play bid whist — same difference — to which Leon said he'd rather play chess. October sided with Cora. And so they tried bridge.

In the middle of Cora's play-by-play about bidding, Leon said he thought that bridge was harder than chess, and Ed said he really, really wanted to learn how to play chess.

"Say no more, brother man," Leon said. "You're looking at the master."

"Since when did you learn chess?" Ed asked him.

And Leon said it was a long story.

"You sure do have a lot of stories," Cora said. "Let's hear it."

Leon said, "Wait," and went to the closet,

brought out a box of carved chess pieces and a board, told them it used to belong to a friend of his, a master.

Ed picked up a carved-stone king. "Nice."

"I used to see a woman who liked chess," Leon said. *Get ready for a story.* "Like I said, this musician friend of mine could do two things better than anybody else — blow his horn and play chess. If he had lived, he would've been on top of all the trumpet players."

"Clifford Brown," he said to Ed.

Ed nodded — "Right."

October couldn't say she had heard him play, but the name had floated around her from time to time. Leon went on with his story about his woman who wanted the trumpet player to teach Leon how to play chess. But Leon hadn't wanted Clifford Brown to teach him anything.

"So how did you learn?" Cora asked.

"Clifford got killed," Leon said. He placed the rest of the pieces on the chess board.

Ed chimed in, "On the Jersey turnpike, right? Him and Richie Powell."

Leon nodded, and ended his story. "Right after he died, Mona sat me down and taught me how to play," he said.

"That was your girlfriend?" Cora asked, so October didn't have to.

"Yeah," Leon said. "I was late. Clifford had a lot of chess sets. His wife gave me this one."

"Your friend Clifford would be smiling right now," Cora said.

Leon said to Ed, "You can learn this in a couple of days. All you have to do is concentrate. Say when, and I'll bring it over."

October said, "I thought we were teaching you bridge."

Leon looked at her, and his whole face smiled, especially his eyes. It made her smile back.

"You can teach me," he said. "What say we do them both? Chess next time, then bridge the next, okay?"

"Okay," Cora said.

"I'll play whenever I'm around," October said. "Remember, I'm a working girl." That look from Leon had gotten her off track just a little.

The next time she saw him, they were both at Safeway. She saw the measly bread and bologna and bananas and soda pop in his basket and thought she ought to cook him something sometime.

They said *How're you doing* and *Fine,* and he said, "Remind me why I said I wanted to teach music to knuckleheads."

He had been giving master classes for the summer session at the college, and: "They think they know so much. When I was their age, I ate and slept with my horn. I'd practice sometimes ten, twelve hours a day. I never came up short."

She laughed. "Get ready. September is coming." She had heard from Donetta that Leon was doing well, that students were lining up to take his classes in the fall.

Leon told her, "My man Foots used to tell me that when you use hundred-dollar words, they hear, but when you play real music, they listen, eat it up."

"Then the lazybones will fall by the wayside, won't they?"

Leon said yeah, but he'd rather not have to bother with them. Said he hoped most of them would be serious.

And then he just opened his mouth, and "You can play cards with me — I won't bite, you know," just fell out.

Took her by surprise. So did her smile back at him. "Okay," she said. "But I'm still busy a lot."

"You can be busy," he said, "but you have to eat sometime, don't you? Sometimes when you feel like hanging loose, we'll play bridge or chess and drink pink ladies. Besides" — and he chuckled — "maybe you can introduce me to some of your girlfriends."

Was he trying to be funny?

So this was the way the Saturday night thing got started. Ed and Cora, October and Leon — usually at Cora and Ed's, because of Eddy Junior, but sometimes at October's, where Eddy could go to sleep on the cot in David's room. A little supper, any music anybody wanted to hear, a halfhearted start at bridge or chess, and a lot of shuckin-and-jivin fun.

And what else that July? Days at Macy's, basting and cutting and stitching and sneezing cloth dust. But, too, making cookies and hamburger patties and putting them in the freezer for August. Jotting down David-maybe sizes and marking the Sears catalogue.

Nothing from Vergie, though. At the end of July, the twenty-eighth, October had been antsy for days. Should she call? Would she have to do what she had told Vergie she would do — just go to Chillicothe? She could see herself showing up and Vergie having to let her in.

Then on the twenty-eighth, the mailman came, bringing the water bill and a letter. From Vergie.

Dear October,
It didn't surprise me to get a letter from you. I've been taking my time, thinking about all that you said.

394

Here's what is wrong. You had a baby once. You didn't want him, or you couldn't love him, I don't know which. But you gave him away. You gave him up. The problem was that you gave him to me and I'm your sister. If it'd been anybody else, there wouldn't be all this. I'm coming back to it later in the letter, but I have to tell you this first.

As long as I live, I will never tell David or let anybody else tell him. I am his mother. I decide. David's got me and Gene. It's all he knows and all he needs to know. Suppose our mother had just walked away and given us to Auntie and Aunt Maude. It would have felt a lot worse knowing she didn't want us.

I don't want that for David. I love him. I've raised him. He's all I've got. I hope someday you'll understand, but that's up to you. I can't do anything about that.

If David lived with anybody else, you would have forgotten all about him. But you see him all the time, and you can't let go. And so I'm telling you that I think it would be good for everybody if you just stay away for a while. Get married and have some babies of your own. David is ours. Maybe someday you'll understand.

We'll be gone in August anyway. Me

and Gene are taking him on a train trip.
Gene's cousin in Oklahoma invited us.
Yours truly, Vergie

My two daughters. Blood sisters. Both so strong. Neither of them making room for the other one. Trying their best to be through for good.

CHAPTER 22

Lonoke. From the train Vergie could see the kettle water tower lit in the night, announcing another tiny Arkansas town. L-o-n-o-k-e. She spelled it out to herself, just like she would have to David if he'd been awake. On into the countryside, black trees flew against a star-speckled sky. Two women in the rear of the train laughed and said something, but she couldn't make out their conversation. Across the aisle, Gene purred like a new car idling, dozing again. David — bless his heart — had given in and sprawled all over her, head in her lap, sound asleep, like most of the passengers.

The night train cut the time in two, and by sunup they would be halfway across Kentucky, almost home. Amos, Gene's cousin, and his wife, Helen, had put themselves out for her and Gene and David — fed them like prize pigs, let them have their bedroom with a high bed like the one Frances once had, took them fishing and to a real Indian corn dance and to honest-to-goodness church. One week was enough, though, especially since school was already bearing down on David again.

Vergie tried to stuff her handkerchief under David's sweaty head, and David opened his eyes, sat up. "Where are we?" he said.

"Lay on down, we're in Arkansas," she told him. He took the pillow she had brought for the ride, and leaned against the window, closing his eyes again. Vergie dug in her pocketbook for a Life Saver, and pulled out a chunk of peppermint cane in waxed paper.

She hadn't lied — not really. Amos *had* invited them, and it *was* August. They wouldn't be gone but a week, but October didn't have to know that. In her mind Vergie went over all the reasons she'd given herself if October should ever accuse her of not thinking about David: going-on-eight couldn't be too soon for a boy to ride on a train again. Gene's people were David's people, too. David needed a reward for passing third grade.

Deep down Vergie had it straight, but she went over it anyway. If October was determined to call herself David's mother, she would always be sprinkling hints here and there. She couldn't be trusted. Before Vergie knew it, all their lives would be ruined. David would know that his mother had given him away, and that could never be all right. It would hurt him too much. And even if, by some miracle, he got over it, he was bound to ask about his father — the man whom, luckily, October had forgotten. A married man running around on his wife couldn't be but so decent. David didn't need to live with that when he had her and Gene. And besides all of that, October had a way of making sure everybody knew she was Miss Big City, with her job and her big car, and now her new house. Vergie wouldn't put it past her to try to turn David's head. What would she and Gene do if October ever turned his head? If October couldn't see things her way, then she shouldn't be around David at all. Period.

Briscoe. A steel water tower. And there was the problem of his grades. She would never be able to explain to October about rewarding David just for passing third grade. B-r-i-s-c-o-e.

When she woke up again, Gene sat gnawing on a chicken wing. Something to do.

"You want something to drink?" she asked him, and he shook his head no.

Ubiquitous water towers, this one like a slatted wooden tub set on lattice stilts. "Shepp," it said.

"Tennessee," Gene said softly. On the trip out to Oklahoma, Vergie had listened to Gene telling David about Pap Singleton from Tennessee. How in the late 1870s the man had led thirty-some thousand Negroes — Exodusters — from the Deep South to Canaan land. Kansas, they hoped. It had never been a slave state. "That's probably how we all got to Ohio," Gene had told David.

Now something about the night, the darkness, the rumble of the train packed with sleeping people crowded on top of one another, she and Gene and David like a secret stealing through unheard-of places — it made her thoughts melt together, like she didn't have to sort them out right now. Like she couldn't keep them in any order. And she heard "Tennessee" repeated so clear it could have been her own voice.

Franklin Brown had been from Tennessee — probably his people, too. Exodusters. Men and women tramping with everything they owned on their backs, catching steamboats on the Mississippi.

And memories filter in: she sits on Poppa's knee. Tobacco and whiskey. The upright piano has curlicues carved into its face. A crimson fringe hangs around the top. Poppa shows her how to play with two hands, boogie-woogie, while he plays something else on the high keys.

One thing about secrets — once they'd been shook out and aired, there was no stuffing them back into that same little box. Once she had let the Lillian secret pop out of her thirteen-year-old mouth, anything was up for airing.

Sometimes it had been safe. Like the time at home once, when October had asked Auntie to tell her how Carrie talked, and what she used to say. And Aunt Frances had surprised them, smiling and saying, "She sounded like music when she called my name."

Mostly it wasn't so safe. "When did our mother get married?" Vergie had asked Aunt Maude once. Aunt Maude had looked at Aunt Frances like she was the living Bible.

Aunt Frances had answered with her own question: "What do you want to know *that* for?"

October had been shredding cabbage for coleslaw, and when she heard the subject opened so free, she chimed in on Vergie's side. "Dag," she said. "Why is it a secret?"

Frances had been rolling catfish in corn-meal and didn't answer right away. She stooped to get the iron skillet from under the sink.

"Nothing about your mother is a secret," she said. "We just don't talk about terrible things." She rattled around in the cupboard. "She's gone forever, and no amount of talk about dates and times can ever change that. It's something best let alone."

But Vergie remembered too much. She re-membered the time in the yard when her mother had leaned over the fence, talking to Mr. Bailey. Vergie had stood beside Poppa at the door and watched. It would have been all right if Momma had stopped when she turned and saw them — Vergie would have sworn she saw them standing at the screen door, her and Poppa — but Momma just laughed and kept on with Mr. Bailey. And Vergie never said what she knew was true. Poppa was mad. Another day, another night, and Momma was dead.

And there, in the kitchen that day, had been a chance to find out once and for all. Vergie had asked, "Did Poppa ever say why?"

Aunt Frances, still stooping, turned to give her the evil eye. Vergie pressed. "How did you find out that he died?"

Frances stood up. "I know you girls are growing up now, and you're curious. But believe me, you are better off not worrying about this. First thing you know, you'll be telling it to everybody and giving them something to hurt you with."

That was history. Frances was stalling.

Vergie watched her aunt go to the stove, pause, and let the heavy skillet dangle. Then she must have thought better of the question.

"The lady next door who kept you-all, she wrote and told me."

October said, "Did she know Poppa that well?"

"How did she know?" Vergie asked.

She could see Frances's jaw tightening.

"You weren't hardly past being a baby when she died," Frances said to October.

And to Vergie she said, "You were older, and that was too bad. You didn't have it so easy, but that's not reason enough for us to keep it going. Your poppa went to prison and he died there, a long time ago — I had my ways of finding out. Now, both of you just let it rest. It's the past, and believe me I would've changed it if I could've, but I couldn't. Now get out the applesauce and help me get dinner on the table."

Vergie, though, had felt like she had to make one thing clear. "We saw her on the bed, Aunt Frances."

And October said, "I wasn't that young."

"Hush up," Frances said. "You didn't do no such thing. Don't go makin up stories. You were at Cordelia Butler's house next door." Frances still held the skillet by its long handle, but now she waved it like a feather. "Your mama didn't die in that house — she died in Briar Memorial Hospital, Cleveland, Ohio."

"We did see her," Vergie said softly. "We both did."

Wham! Frances banged the iron skillet down so hard on the stovetop that the teakettle jumped off the burner.

"I've said it before," she said. "That's *enough!* He killed her, and he's dead. She should have *never* laid eyes on him. Right out of the gutter, him and his people. Didn't have sense enough to do something decent with his life, so he just messed up hers. You-all's too."

Her face had then relaxed a little. "Took her up there with him to the city, up there and . . . just took her life. Neither one of you should've ever had to look into his face, and you won't ever have to again."

Then Frances got a hold of herself and lit the gas jet. "It's a big enough burden to last a lifetime. Now let it alone."

They had let it alone.

Vergie peered out into the darkness of the Tennessee night. She thought she could make out white blossoms of magnanimous magnolia trees. Imagined a swamp, people tramping. Three generations of Coopers had come from North Carolina. Who were the Browns?

She had never given much thought to this other side — who they might have been. Worthless wanderers who mooched off other people. Yes, probably. But some of them had lived in that brave time. Some of them had waited at the docks for the steamboat to Canaan land; had ridden up the Mississippi, gotten off the boat at Illinois, and taken another boat up the Ohio. Those barely a generation after them would have scouted out the same territory, and left behind the woman who would someday give birth to Franklin Brown. And one day he would go searching for his kin in Cleveland, Ohio.

And even if things hadn't happened that way, any way she looked at it, some of the Browns must have wanted something decent, and some of them must have had guts enough to try to find it.

Burwood. B-u-r-w-o-o-d.

Sometime in the night, Vergie woke to the conductor calling, "Nashville! Next stop Nashville, Tennessee!" like a wake-up call, and Gene and David both jumped wide-eyed. Vergie looked at David yawning and stretching in the dim, city light. Dark, big-eyed, he looked enough like her to be hers. Short, but that would never come up, because Gene was short. There was a time he would have yawned and stretched and she would have tickled him under his arms. These days he didn't like her tickling him anymore; he thought he was too grown.

"Can we get off and get some pop?" David asked her. Gene had already stood up to stuff his shirt into his pants and put on his shoes again. Other people around them stirred.

"No," Vergie said. "There's lemonade in the thermos."

"The ice melted, and it's all water," David said.

Gene tied his shoes. "We'll be here at least a half hour. I'm going in to get a Hershey bar. You want anything?"

David buttoned his shirt and started going on about Hershey bars and Butterfingers and Nehi strawberry pop.

If it had been daylight, she might have let David off the train to buy soda pop or to use the restroom. Fisk University was there. Well-to-do Negroes lived in Nashville. Martin Luther King had just been through there organizing for more boycotts. Things were changing, that was true. Before she knew it, David would be going to school with white kids. But this was still the South, and though there was no sign posted, they were still in a Negroes-only car in that train. A year ago Ike had had to send troops to Little Rock. It was night, and they were in Tennessee. Hershey bars or no, David wasn't getting off that train.

"Nobody's getting off," Vergie said to Gene. He stopped tying his shoes.

"It's nighttime," she said. "We're in Tennessee. No need to go out looking for trouble."

Gene seemed to understand. He looked

past her to David. "We'll get off in the morning and get breakfast in Kentucky."

David slumped back down in his seat and popped the stopper on the thermos. "Can I drink out of the bottle?"

"No," Vergie said. "Somebody else might want some." She gave him a paper cup out of her basket.

Sometimes months would go by when she didn't have a single thought about losing him. And then something would happen, somebody would ask about October, or October would call wanting to speak to him, or she would see some strange expression on David's face, and a slow panic would start. What if? They had built a good life, she and Gene. They had done the best they could by David. The best they could. And still, sometimes the best wasn't enough.

When he was four, he could count to ten and recite A to Z. Right now, if she asked him, he could probably tell her how water towers worked. Gene had explained it to him once, and David could remember anything. At Amos and Helen's one morning, when Vergie had talked about how she got carsick, David had gone on and on about the new Interstate Highway System, which she didn't know he knew. "It's a cross between the kind of roads the Romans built for war a long time ago and

407

the new kind of highway the Germans have where you can speed all the time as fast as the car will go," he told them. "And guess how they're going to number it," he had said.

And when Gene had taken over, bragging that he knew all about the odd and the even numbers and all, David couldn't let Gene have the last word. He spelled out the how and the where and the why. And when Helen asked him, "How do you know, David?," David had smarted off, "I go to school," for which Vergie almost smacked him. He got himself straight and told them that a boy in his class had done a report on the civil defense. But David was a smart boy.

First grade had been tough, but wasn't the first year always hard? Second grade had been worse. *U* in reading. Unsatisfactory. *S+* in art, music, health, all that other stuff. *S-* in arithmetic, *S-* and *U* in spelling. And third grade, they had barely passed him, and passed him then only because Vergie had gone to school every week. Sat in the classroom all day and worked with the teacher after school. David just didn't try hard enough. No matter how she punished him, he didn't seem to want to do better.

His teacher would say, for instance, "What new meaning did you learn for the word 'through'?"

And David would whine to Vergie that the teacher always picked out the hardest words for him.

When Vergie asked him to pick out a certain word among similar words, he would gripe that if he got it right, she would make him do a harder one, and if he got it wrong, he'd have to read it a hundred times.

She would smack his bottom and make him choose. He would tune up to cry, and once the tears started, they were through.

One minute she was, "Boy, sit down and write those sentences out. Don't think you're too big for a switch." The next minute she was, "Just read one sentence and you can have another piece of cake." Bad, she knew.

And Gene. "Why don't you listen to your mother? Can't you see she's trying to help you?"

And then, "Why don't you leave the boy alone — can't you see he just don't know?"

Gene would tell Vergie, "He's been over that enough."

And Vergie would tell him, "You stay out of this. If it was left up to you, he'd still be learning how to count to ten."

Stayed on David about paying attention and doing his homework. She just couldn't figure it out. She and Gene spent every single night reading to him, making him spell and write so that he could get the connection, but nothing they did seemed to work.

As the train pulled out of the light of Nashville and into the dark again, David laid his pillow on her lap and laid his head on the pillow. "I'll be glad when we get to Kentucky," he said, yawning.

N-a-s-h-v-i-l-l-e. As far as Vergie could see, there was no water tower for Nashville. Even if there had been one, spelling it out wouldn't have made any difference. The fact was, David had never learned how to read.

CHAPTER 23

They made a deal. Leon would go to the record shop with her if she would go with him to Sears (kitchen stuff wasn't his thing). A little narrow record shop on Twenty-seventh Street had the best labels, so Leon said, and just by the looks they got, October knew this was the place jazz folks flocked to. They all recognized him; he ignored them.

"Women usually like this," he said, pushing a Modern Jazz Quartet LP under her nose. She had heard of the group, and they looked spiffy in their tuxedos around the shiny Steinway. But she waved him away and chose some others she liked — Ella Fitzgerald and Red Garland — while Leon stood back, smirking.

When he saw her choices, he said, "It's almost the sixties, and you're coming into the fifties with those," trying to be cute.

He hadn't seen the ace she held, but she gladly flashed it in his face — another LP she had chosen, *Lonny Haskins Plus Four*.

"Powerhouse," he said, grinning. "A woman will fool you every time." He told her a story about "my man Foots" and Foots's woman, Sylvia — how she never minded dotting Foots's *i*'s and crossing his *t*'s and was always one up on him. Listening to Leon's story, October thought she heard him yearning for something out of reach.

"I think I remember your friend Foots," she said. "Wasn't he with you when he came to the Blue Room that time?"

"He thought he was," Leon said.

"We took him to the hotel on The Paseo, remember?"

"Yeah," Leon said.

"You miss him?"

"Nah," Leon said, and he went on thumbing through "West Coast Jazz."

When they went to Sears, Leon refused to buy anything more than dishes for four, knives and forks and spoons for four, a pot and a skillet. She made him go with her to look at furniture she couldn't afford, and while they were downtown, she dragged him into the fabric shop, where he stood like a mannequin while she got material for her new suit. Later, in the Healy, pot trembling against skillet in the slot behind her seat, she got a chance to crow. "Speaking of the fifties," she said, "they have these things called toasters now, and steak knives, and can openers and egg beaters. You ought to think about trying them."

He smiled. "What I got was cool," he said. "I don't plan to get much beyond bacon and eggs."

The car hugged a corner too tightly and the tires made a little whine. Leon continued to tell her, "At *my* place . . ." and he stopped.

"You have a place in New York?"

"Had."

"I'll bet you never cooked."

"A little."

"Women there just to peel your grapes."

He laughed. "Something like that."

"Never married, either," she said.

He told her no, but that he did believe in shackin'. Why wasn't that news to her?

"Not me," she said.

"I know. Remember, I knew you when."

"Or you thought you knew me when."

"Tell me you weren't a nice lady."

"I was."

"Young and green."

"Maybe."

"Don't feel like the Lone Ranger," he said. "That time we stood up for Ed and Cora, I had a fire in me that wouldn't quit."

She wanted to ask, *Then what?*, but instead they pulled up to the curb and she started to gather her things and told him he could come in if he wanted to.

"You got anything good to eat?"

"Day-old chicken salad," she said.

"What are you doing later?"

She pulled her records from behind the seat and hugged them. "Listening to my new records — what else?"

"I guess I'll go on home," he said.

The breeze had picked up and the sun was almost gone. Leon held on to the steering wheel, already somewhere else.

"Why aren't you out getting up a combo or something?" she asked him.

"You know what it means to woodshed? It means you start all over again, make the shit happen all over again. That's what I'm doing. Woodsheddin'."

He dropped his arms and turned to her, and he started talking about jazz, how it was a wheel in the middle of a wheel, how everybody was hungry for something that they had to stretch for, something that defied everything they had ever heard. "That's me," he said. He tapped his chest with his fingers. "That's what I'm after. A new way to go, or I'm just another recording. Dig it? Put me on a turntable and spin me 'round."

He was wound up, talking about freedom and how "niggers are talking about being free, digging what we came from. That's me."

October nodded. She didn't know exactly, but she understood this personal quest was important to him. And then she watched his mouth open again with something left-field crazy about to fall out.

"Why didn't you ever get married?"

"Wrong men," she told him, not caring this time.

"Oh, so you did finally get with somebody?"

"What kind of question is that?"

"Well, when I knew you," he said, "I always thought nice was a coat of paint on a suit of armor."

"It's really chilly out here," she said. "Are you coming in or not?"

"Nah," he said. "Little Boy Blue is going to put on his mute and blow."

She told him she'd like to hear him sometime without the crowd. He told her okay. "When I know what it is, I'll play it for you."

The very evening after her shopping day, she turned on the radio in the basement and laid out her new piece of blue wool, pinned on the pattern, and began cutting. KCMO played jazz — for her, education more than anything else. And then she heard the DJ announce, "Coming up, Lonny Haskins and 'Footsloose.'"

She went upstairs to the telephone and dialed Cora. "It's all we listen to," Cora told her.

She called Leon. "They're playing one of your songs on KCMO."

"Yeah, okay," he said. No big deal to him, but she glued her ear to the radio upstairs. Really, for once, she wanted to be able to say something that was up to the minute, something about harmonics or ride cymbals — the right lingo. But all she could think was that he played so well, and how did he do that?

She called him back to see if he had heard himself.

"Nah, I know what I sound like," he said.

"I liked it," she told him. "You're really fast and you make a lot of little surprises."

He chuckled. "Pretty soon you'll be into chord progressions."

"So did you write 'Footsloose' for your friend?"

"Yep. I put it together. Foots liked it." Sad-sounding.

"You-all must have been pretty close."

"Foots was my main man — I mean, I always knew he had my back. He was always hip to what was happening."

"Did he play jazz?"

"Blues, jazz — it's like the same thing," Leon said. "Foots played the blues, but the blues runs right into jazz, so he knew it all. Mostly though, he ran numbers all over Harlem. Put him a shoeshine chair in the barbershop and shined shoes. Stepped on my heels, though, on every club date. Never did mind pulling my coat when he thought I was wrong."

Sad again. She thought maybe something had happened to the man recently. "Did he die?"

"Nah." He chuckled. "Foots is probably still hobbling around the streets on his jack leg."

"Well, I liked his song." And she did. And warmed to that thing in Leon that had made him write it.

This was in the fall, when Vergie's letter still stung, and when sitting and sewing had turned into a way to deal with her thoughts. More than a year since she had seen David. It was her own fault. She could have gone to Ohio, even for a weekend. But what to do about Vergie?

Sitting and sewing, she cooked up a plan. The Wednesday before Thanksgiving she would drive to Chillicothe, get there in the middle of the night and bang on the door. Gene would let her in and she would park her things in the bedroom and talk to David until Sunday. If Vergie didn't want to speak, so be it. Simple.

But when the time came, the best-laid plans

were only plans. For one thing, it snowed —
near blizzard with an ice storm on top of it —
the Tuesday before Thanksgiving. Quiet as it
was kept, October hadn't packed a single
stocking. The tide she had been pushing
against seemed to be washing away all the
starch in her, and washing away any hope of
having David even halfway.

And it wasn't Vergie's fault. October didn't
think she could claim David because when it
came right down to it, she didn't think she
could *tell* David. She had torn up Vergie's
letter, but she remembered every word. If
David knew that she threw him away, it
would crush him, hurt him too bad. She had
hurt him enough already. And besides that,
he would hate her. Change his name. She
would lose any chance to be anything to him.
And what made her think that she deserved
better?

Sitting and sewing, she began to think that
maybe Vergie had been right about staying
away and leaving them alone. It was impossible to see David and not wish, not want to be
closer. She couldn't get closer and not want to
tell him. She couldn't hurt him and lose him.

Sitting and sewing and wiping tears, she
thought maybe there was nothing to do but to
leave them alone and try to get on with her
life. It hit her for the second time since David

was born that she would have to start thinking of David as Vergie's son and not the son she had mistakenly given Vergie to keep for the rest of his life. Maybe the time had come for her to surrender, give David up for real.

Sitting and sewing and wiping tears, she wondered if every life has something a person has to face, some dream they hold on to, calling it hope. And then when the time comes, there is nothing to do but face the mistake, pay the price, and go on. She wondered if that was what balances things, grows people up.

Sitting and sewing night in, night out, how does somebody face giving away a child? The bad dream came only at night, and in it she always saw herself standing near a gurney along the wall of a large, empty room that she knew was a labor room, and she knew that she was supposed to give birth to a baby boy. Tile on the walls. Aunt Frances stood on the other side of the room, timing her. If she lay down on the gurney, the baby would try to come out. She tried to explain to Auntie that the nurse had to measure her first, to see whether or not the baby could get out, and that the nurse hadn't come yet. She went out of the room, wandered in hallways, looking everywhere for the nurse.

Then somehow she realized that time had run out ages ago. She was wandering still, and she knew that she wouldn't be able to birth the child now, because she had never been measured. She decided not to go back to explain, and she knew that the baby was left on the gurney near the wall — quiet, not crying — still waiting for her to birth him.

How does someone get on with a life?

Cora said that the new Ebony Fashion Fair was supposed to be coming to Kansas City in December. She ought to get herself together and go. Donetta and Cora both were already tripping all over themselves about it. And there was the harvest ball thing afterward. Think about it.

Sitting and sewing, she thought about Leon. Wondered if he would be okay with taking her to something like that. At the moment, he was the only man she knew well enough to ask. If she decided to go.

Leon said sure. He didn't mind going to some shindig with her. And he'd buy the tickets, even.

What she remembered most about the Fashion Fair was that it was all color. No little black dresses. And it beat anything she had ever seen before. Everything done to the hilt, with incredible models and incredible clothes, incredible music. So much so that if she had been in a better mood, she would have taken notes. Why hadn't she ever sewed anything for a fashion show? She knew about color. Why hadn't she ever thought about selling *her* dresses? It felt like a fashion show had always been going on, and she had never been invited.

She had pressed and twisted up her hair, and made herself a black cocktail dress with spaghetti straps that Leon thought was "outta sight," but she felt homemade and dull.

In the car, Leon had asked her what they were supposed to be — like lovers, or what.

"We're friends, Leon," she told him. "You know that. You're my escort. Don't worry. I'll even introduce you to some of my girl-friends." All of a sudden, he was getting on her nerves. "Besides," she said, "everybody knows there's nothing going on."

"Who's everybody?"

"This is Kansas City. You've been here al-most nine months. Everybody knows."

And all of a sudden he got serious on her. "Look," he said. "I know I said I wanted to meet some of your foxy friends, but I'm not trying to get next to anybody. My luck with women runs from bad to worse."

"Whose fault is that?"

He looked at her as if to say, *Watch it.* "Ev-ery woman I've ever been with wanted half the spotlight or my whole life."

"And what did you want?" Getting to be pretty good at his game.

"Somebody to hang with for a while. Not forever. At least not then. I never was too tough on that forever thing. Just chicken, I guess, or stupid. Guys can be knuckleheads when it comes to that."

"Look at Ed — he isn't," she said.

"Touché," he said back.

At the soiree after the fashion show, Leon was a hit — *Leon meet my sister, Leon I have all your records, Leon meet my cousin, Leon meet my friend Sonia, the piano teacher.*

And October watched him — pressing hands, holding eyes — eat it up. She wasn't up to the spotlight. At some point she slid her arm out of his and sat herself down with Cora and Donetta and their men. "Make room for Leon and me, and maybe one more. Cecelia is fixing him up with a music teacher."

"Good," Cora said. "He needs to be seeing somebody. The two of you are making me nervous."

Cora's attitude came as a surprise to October.

Ed jabbed Cora with his elbow lightly. "She already had two whiskey sours."

"Well, they are," Cora said. "You-all don't match," she said. And when Leon came over, Cora asked him about the music teacher.

"We didn't hit it off," he said. "She asked me if I ever played 'serious' music."

Fast music started up and Ed asked October to dance, but she was busy trying to get a little pep from her highball.

"Not this one," she said, "but ask me again."

Cora asked Leon, too, but Leon didn't want to, either. Said he couldn't dance, which October didn't believe.

"Goodnight My Love" came on. Once October got out there with him, she saw that Leon hadn't lied. A dancer he was not. Not even for the slow drag. For one thing, he nearly squeezed the life out of her, held her much too tight, and not tenderly, either. Bear-hug tight.

She told him in his ear, and he dropped his arms like a rag doll. She gave him a quick lesson — take her hand and put his arm around her waist close enough that she could follow him if he could lead, which he couldn't. Lesson two was that he should follow her. They moved a couple of steps.

He looked down at her. "I told you I don't dance." The uncool Leon, looking uncool.

"We're dancing," she said, but she wished for a little more.

Then of course, he opened his mouth in that way again. "You didn't have to disappear just because a woman smiled my way."

"Just giving you room," she said.

"I didn't need it."

Intermission came and went. Leon got bold and danced all the slow drags with a different woman each time. The women looked like they loved it because it was Lonny Haskins, and Leon looked like he loved it because he could keep up and talk jive at the same time. October didn't do badly with going through the motions. It wasn't a high night, but plenty of men were swarming around.

Then "Red Top" came on, a song she liked. Kenneth asked her to boogaloo with him, which she couldn't do, but why not try it? Easy. Just a little back action, a little bit of shaking it up, a few steps — she got into it. And when the music got louder, she and Kenneth let loose, laughing and outdoing each other. But as the song ended, and she discovered that she'd worked up a sweat, she thought she'd better sit herself right down and stay in her chair until the last dance.

And when the lights flickered and "For All We Know" started, Leon made a beeline over to her. At least he had his Emily Post down pat. On their way home, his thoughts were full of his name on other people's lips, and he ran off at the mouth about his albums and holding up Bird's name. So excited that when they got to her house, he asked to come in for an after-drink. May as well. She felt like she could use a little more cheer. Besides, he made good company.

In her kitchen he loosed his tie and she kicked off her shoes. She made sandwiches and he put bourbon in hot tea. When the last crumb was gone, he told her that he'd had a good time. "Thank you," he said. Silly face.

"I saw you shakin it, too," he teased, and told her, "I've never danced."

"I could tell." She smiled at him — nice, though. It had been pleasant enough.

Quiet time between them was all right, too. He was easy. Then he jumped out of his chair — "I'll be right back" — and went out into the cold with no coat on. When he came back in, he called her into the living room.

In the middle of the floor, he was putting a horn together. "It's my old horn, but it'll do."

She sat down on the sofa and curled her legs up. Pulled the throw around her shoulders. Leon tuned up a bit, and then got serious. "This is called 'Noel.' "

He closed his eyes and played. Ballad, she thought. Then, like he was in another world, he played the same thing, only faster, and threw in all kinds of little riffs and runs. October closed her eyes, too, and let it wash over her.

When he finished, he just knelt on the floor and took apart the horn. She could hear the wind creaking. The house had a hush on it. There was nothing to say but "Thank you."

He sat on the other end of the sofa and put his feet up. "I've been working on it for a while."

" 'Noel' — is that for Christmas?"

"Don't be too impressed with the title. I couldn't think of anything else. It's 'Leon' spelled backwards."

They talked. About his young life and hers. Ed and Vergie, Chillicothe and New York. Being an orphan and finding parents in aunts. In one of the silences in between, she heard his breathing, and saw that he was gone. She got a blanket to cover him, turned off the lamp, and went up to bed. She could hear the wind soughing through the cracks around her bedroom window. The sound caressed her, sent her slipping down the circular stairs of sleep.

CHAPTER 24

The next morning early, she heard the water running in the bathroom and waited until she smelled coffee to slide into her nice satin robe to see what Leon might be doing in her kitchen.

In white shirt and undershorts he looked too too naked for her, and she carried it off by making fun of his skinny legs.

He grinned. "I know you aren't crowing on my legs with *that* hair," he said, pointing a spoon in her direction.

"Just make my coffee strong," she said, and got right out of the kitchen. She came back downstairs with her quilted robe for him and a ribbon around her caught hair.

"Here," she said, laying the robe on his arm.

"I'm okay," Leon said. "What's the matter — haven't you ever seen a man's legs before?" His eyes were all over her face.

"Just put it on," she said.

He shoved in his arms. Too small. Poured two mugs of coffee and sipped one. Handed the other to her.

"I was teasing you about your hair," he

said. "It's wild" — he sipped again — "but I like it." He reached over and squeezed the tight wad of hair in the ribbon at the nape of her neck. "It's soft," he said and took back his hand.

In her kitchen, the two of them — hair wild, legs hairy — were suddenly a man and a woman.

October turned her back, went for the doorway. "You can make my eggs and bacon any time now. The apron is on the hook." Keeping it light.

"Okay," Leon said. "I can do that."

In the bathtub she could smell the bacon — and was that really French toast, and what was that feeling she didn't want to feel? Leon was a friend. *Right.*

Leon had gotten dressed, too, and they wolfed down his masterwork breakfast. He sopped up the last drop of syrup with his last bite of French toast, and let roll out, "So that joker broke your heart?"

"What joker?"

"The one who did you wrong. Four, five years ago you said he was your big mistake."

He remembered something she said four or five years ago? She knew she had never gone near anything about James when Leon was around. And then she remembered Arthur.

"Just the wrong man," she said.

428

"I asked you if you ever had your nose open for anyone and you dodged. Did you?"

"Why?"

"I'm trying to figure you out."

It felt all right. What was the big deal — she could talk to him.

"If you mean turning flips over somebody — yeah, I did that once."

"What happened?" Leon asked her.

"He went back to his wife."

"Ouch." Leon shook his hand like he'd just been burned. "One of those. A long time ago or lately?"

"Long time ago."

"And you never got past it. . . ."

October breathed in the air of the whole kitchen. As easily as an old song comes pouring out of a willing heart, she started talking.

She started out by saying, "I have a son . . . ," talking through the slow burn in her throat.

"Whoa," Leon said softly.

"Had — I *had* a son."

Leon was still as a pool of oil, letting her tell it as it came, and she didn't stop either, until Leon had all of it. The whole story.

She told him about James Wilson, how she had once thought being in love was always a two-way street that led to forever, once thought she knew all about it. How she hadn't understood the simple fact that she had loved a halfway decent man who wasn't free to love her back. Her fool-headed idea that he would leave his family. How, when she was pregnant and James didn't choose her, she had thought it was the end of the world. How at first she couldn't feel anything for the baby. He'd been like a consolation prize when she wanted James — the real-life teddy bear. How Gene and Vergie had stepped up, and how — without blinking — she had given him away. And a year later, when she screwed her head back on, it had been too late.

A stampede of secrets. How good it felt telling it all for the first time, and to somebody who didn't care about what happened or why.

October told him how she had quit trying to justify things, but that it had all come crumbling down on her head. And when she tried to explain her feelings for David, the tears started. She wiped them with a paper napkin and kept going.

Leon sat still. He had sprinkled salt from the shaker on the tabletop, and while he listened, he trailed a line through it with a toothpick. Roads every which way.

She cried and tried to tell him about being separated from Vergie. Because she was explaining the hurt she never wanted to heap on David's head, and how he deserved a normal life, she went on into the real reason that she and Vergie had been orphans — spat out the shame of having her father's sister's name, and how she changed it, and even told him what it was.

And then she was through. Relieved. Undone and done.

They sat at the table for a long time, not talking, her wondering what he was thinking. He made tracks in the salt. And every now and then he shook his head.

She got up and turned on the faucet, let the water run until it was cold, and filled up her glass. She unplugged her coffeepot and when she turned, Leon was right behind her. Like she was cotton, he put his arms all around her.

"So much for turning flips over somebody," she said into his shoulder.

"That explains a lot," he said softly to her hair.

She tilted her head to see what he meant.

"Just a lot," he said.

They stood like that. He rocked her a little. When she looked up at him again, he kissed her. Soft on the lips. And kissed her again. And she kissed him back.

She wanted to think about whether they ought to be kissing, and she started to say *Wait* or something, but before she could get it out, he had her face in his hands and kissed her deep. Right into her eyes he said, "You know I love you, don't you?"

She didn't know that fast, and he said, "I've *been* loving you."

She could see it. In his eyes were all the Leons she knew, and she got it real straight right then that she had gone further with him than she had gone with any man and it had all been by accident — just happened. And it had all been real good. And she didn't want to let go of that. Ever.

They kissed like that until she couldn't tell where she left off and he began and then they went upstairs. Later she would say she should have known he would be the best lover. He took the time. In the bedroom he didn't make everything perfect. No music. They were the music. No closed curtains. They needed to see each other. No bip-bam, thank you, ma'am. He began all over again, made her ache for him. Slowed her down, had her telling him yes or no while he searched and found. Took her hands and showed her how to touch him, make him feel good. "Like this," he said. And when he brought her, more than once, to the point where she couldn't hold cries in her throat, he would say *Like this? Deeper, or like this?* slowing down, until all the waves were caught and rode and spent.

They slept. When she woke and sat up to see his face, he opened his eyes and said, "Yes, this is me, too."

He told her that he hadn't planned to "move on his heart." He told her he had fallen in love too many times to do anything about it with her. But this was different. Wasn't no falling. He just loved her. It just happened to him when he wasn't looking.

And then it was October's turn to ask and Leon's time to tell.

"Did that woman break your heart, or did you break hers?"

"What woman?"

"Mona, the one you messed over."

"Did I mess over somebody?"

She looked at him. "I'm going to get us a drink of water. When I come back I want the lowdown."

She put on her robe, and when she came back, he took the glass from her hand. He looked serious.

"I didn't mess over Mona," he said. "We lived together for a while. She wanted the whole nine — I didn't." All matter-of-fact.

"Delores is the woman I messed over," he said in a new voice. And he tried to breathe in all the air in the bedroom. He sat up on the side of the bed with his back to her.

"She was twenty when I first met her. A

waitress at this restaurant where we used to eat — me and Foots."

"Twenty is young," October said, and she was sorry the minute it was out.

"That was years ago. She wasn't twenty when we got together. From the get-go, though, Foots was on my case about her, warned me to stay away from her, and I did. She was sweet, but she was a girl then. I already had a woman. She was everything to Foots — I mean, his heart. He cared about her. He and Sylvia took Delores in when she first came to the city. Dee didn't live with them, but they watched out for her, you know — young girl up north in the Big Apple."

He took a drink from his glass and set it on the bedside table. October wanted to rub his back, soothe him. She felt him being tight, having to get it all out. He looked cold with nothing on.

"If you want to talk about stabbing somebody in the back, I guess Foots is really the one I messed over."

"Where did you know him from?" October asked.

"Foots? I was roaming around Harlem that first couple of years and he was, too. Everybody knew him, but not everybody tolerated him. He ran numbers. Shined shoes up near Small's. He must have been sixty-something then, but he got around better than I did. He always wore that old visor on his bald head and his glasses. Every Friday he'd sit in the barber chair and get that little ring of nappy white hair cut. We just fell in together, I guess — right away we were partners."

Leon stopped and October sat still. She knew the sadness, felt it coming. She just didn't know any of the details.

"That old man loved the blues," Leon said. "He dug him some jazz, too, no matter what he said. He used to swear jazz was from the heart, but blues was from the soul, and he was a soul man. Swore he used to hang around with Blind Lemon Jefferson in Chicago. I know one thing — those crippled old hands could still hold a harmonica."

She remembered that Leon had told her once that the old man was never really a manager.

"He was a mess. Pissed me off so many times, trying to run my life, but he meant well, more good than bad. When I wasn't getting any action he'd tell me, 'You're the king, man.' And when I finally started making it, he would tell me I was tired. 'Anybody can play that,' he'd tell me." He chuckled a little and rubbed his hands on this thighs.

She wanted to know about Delores. He read her mind.

"A year or so before I came out here, Dee and I started playing house. I was set up pretty nice, a place out in Queens, I had my group, a couple of my albums on the charts, I'm cool, I'm a shiny silver dollar and she's broke — you know what I mean? When Foots got sick, Dee and Sylvia took care of him. Diabetes. He had to have his leg amputated. I helped with the bills. We were tight. Family.

"Anyway, after that, Dee moved in with me. She had a nothing little gig at this nothing little club. House singer, four nights for piddly change. She wanted to be another Ruth Brown, but she didn't have it.

"Don't get me wrong, I liked her, thought I loved her for a minute. Foots didn't like it, but she was a grown woman, damn near thirty. When it came to Dee, though, he would swoop down on me like a hawk on a mouse. He'd tell her not to listen to me. With me sitting right in his face, he'd tell her I was no good. Tell her, 'Ask him how many women he's messed over.'

"I think she wanted to break into the big life and maybe she thought I was the ticket. Anyway, I sweet-talked her away from under Foots and Sylvia. She kept my place when I was on the road — I mean, she could cook, and she liked things neat. Better than that, she didn't bitch about me getting high and staying up all night. Mona and me had fought all the time, 'cause she hated what I was into, you know. Dee, though, she tiptoed around and let me sleep all day. I'm making her out to be an angel and I sound like a dog. It wasn't that bad.

"Anyway, I shared the wealth with her — or, let me tell it like it was: I introduced her to coke. She never really liked doing it. Said it made her crazy.

"The cat I copped from turned her on to smack, which she said she didn't like either, but every now and then, she'd snort some. Everybody I ever knew who was strung out, shot up. Dee never shot up, just snorted sometimes. I'd pay for it. It wasn't much.

"We did fine for about a year. Then Walter at the club let her go, and she had to take what she could get — hole-in-the-wall joints. I couldn't take her being up under me every single minute — at the gigs, at the studio, at home. I started seeing another woman, this actress named Angela. She wasn't important. Just somebody to see. Maybe Dee knew about her, maybe she didn't.

"Foots and Sylvia caught me out in the streets with Angela one night. I was headlining at Spider Kelly's, and she was waiting for me. Foots and Sylvia were there and they read it.

"When the last set was over, Foots came up to the bandstand. He's on crutches, now — one good leg. He told me, he said, 'Lonny, go on home.' He said he knew that Angela was there at the club, and Dee was home waiting, so he told me 'Go on home.' I told him to kiss my ass.

"I went to step down off the bandstand, and that old man put out his crutch and made me fall. I tripped and fell, and my case and my horn flew every which way across the floor. I got myself up and picked up my horn. Foots was still yelling, 'Go home, nigger — take your sorry ass home.' The bouncer got riled at Foots cussing and swinging his crutches. I told him that he'd better be glad he had a jack leg because I would've whipped his ass. I was mad enough. Angela disappeared. Sylvia's crying about Dee, so I just went on home.

"That night I slipped in the door and slid between the sheets. I was tired, pissed, but I wasn't sleepy, and I didn't want to wake her up. Didn't want to touch her. I couldn't tell if she was really asleep, but I didn't care. She had won. I was home with her, shackled. I knew it was over. I didn't want to hurt her, but I knew I would. I was going to have to cut her loose, and I felt sorry for her because I knew she didn't want to go.

"It was quiet that night. I could hear my

own heartbeat in the bed, my own breath. I felt sorry for Dee. So I turned over, her back was facing me, and I touched her, rubbed her back. She didn't move and so I scooted closer and she didn't budge, so I turned on over and tried to sleep. I guess I sensed something because suddenly I tried to hear her breathing and I couldn't.

"I jumped up and turned on the light. I turned her over and shook her hard. She flopped without moving an eyelash. I ran and got cold water, threw it in her face. I couldn't tell if her heart was beating. When I reached for the phone, I saw the rubber tubing, the tourniquet, and I knew. I never saw a needle, but I knew.

"Anyway, I put her in the bathtub and got in with her, sprayed cold water until the ambulance came. They gave her oxygen, and I followed them to the hospital. They couldn't tell me right then if she would make it or not.

"I waited a whole day before I got up enough nerve to call Sylvia and Foots. I was at the hospital when they came, too. Foots wanted to kill me. For real. He wouldn't look me in the face. Just said, 'I'm through.' That was all. Took off his glasses and rubbed his eyes. 'I'm through.' He hasn't spoken to me since.

"Delores did make it. Many a time, even

now, I've thought about what would have happened if Foots hadn't acted a fool and sent me home that night. I haven't talked to Dee, either. I mean I wrote her a letter. Two. I don't know if she ever got them.

"They tell me God don't like ugly. I was heavy into coke. My new group fell apart. I let my house go. Played nothing but bullshit for a year, blowing all my money on lady, coasting. And then you gave somebody my address, and here I am."

He took a breath and let it all out. "This could be my one chance. I've got two more years here to get my shit together. I'm damn near forty. It might already be over."

Early that evening, when Leon had gone and October was left to marvel at what a day can bring, she got into her car and drove herself up to the bluff overlooking the river and the airport. Parked there, she watched the silver planes land and take off, watched the river change from earthen to sandy brown, watched clouds shift their animal shapes back to floes again. Then the western rim of sky caught fire and burned to varicolored embers. When dusk spread its neutral film over all the colors of the land and water, buildings and sky, she promised herself to hold on to this sudden slice of happiness. Easy, clear, and free, Leon was for her.

As the days went, October felt mostly humbled by her love with Leon. Lucky. And she thought maybe it was some kind of balance on the divine scale of what was fair. If her mind tried to wander too far in the if-only-David direction, she would tell it no. *Here is a chance. This is getting on with your life.* Leon called her his muse. Told her that finding her had been what got him to take his music seriously again.

The mostly wonderful weeks with Leon sped by, interrupted by only a rare evening that October spent alone, sewing and fending off David's face. And then it was Christmas. The second Christmas that she wouldn't be going to Ohio, wouldn't be seeing David. Or Vergie. Cora had invited her and Leon for the day, but since Cora had dripped acid when it came to the two of them as a couple, October said no — she and Leon would do something quiet together.

For the first time, she bought a tree. A real live blue spruce. And lights. And icicles and angel hair. And for herself, she pulled out all the stops. It seemed like a shame, now, that she had put away "flame red" as one of the too-bright boundaries that sophisticated dark women didn't cross.

Not anymore. She had designed a simple

sleeveless shift of red silk shantung with a mandarin collar. The matching brocade jacket was shot through with gold threads, and it hung loose with set-in sleeves. And she had attached a shawl that flowed in one sweep from the lapel to wrap around her neck, so that the entire outfit looked like scarlet-spun silk spilling out from a gold-threaded cocoon.

On Christmas Eve, she put it on. When she looked at herself in the mirror, nobody could tell her she wasn't gorgeous. Lines from Langston flitted through her head:

Jesus! . . . When Susanna Jones wears red
A queen from some time-dead Egyptian
  night
Walks once again.

When Leon knocked, she went calmly to the door and swung it open. "Merry Christmas," she said softly.

Leon closed his eyes and shook his head like she had washed away any resistance he might have had.

"Remind me to tell you something," he said, and came on in.

She lit candles. "We need 'Noel,' " she said. "Or something Christmasy." And boom, he had a whole collection of Christmas music from the stars, jazz and R&B. She put on music, tied an apron around her waist, and began to show Leon how to make popcorn in the iron skillet, the way she and Vergie used to do. He couldn't seem to get into popping corn, and she thought of all the Christmases he must have spent on the road with strangers.

They sat on the sofa with all the ornaments and icicles and the bowl of popcorn between them.

"I'm reminding you to tell me something," she said.

Leon played with her hand a little. "There's this piece Langston Hughes wrote where he talks about this woman, Susanna, in a red dress." And with his eyes fixed on the lines of her hand, he recited Langston's poem.

"He wrote that for you," he said, and kissed her.

They decorated the tree and munched goodies and listened to Leon's Christmas music.

Later in the evening, as they sat again on the sofa, he said, "I have something to show you," and reached into his jacket pocket.

It was a letter. Folded. "It's from Sylvia," he said, shaking it out for her to read.

"Foots is in the hospital again," he said.
"What for?"
"I don't know — she didn't say."

October looked at the letter — large-scrawled sentences that broke the news and gave Leon a telephone number to call.

"She doesn't say whose number that is, and nobody answers," he said.

October put two and two together. Sylvia was Foots's common-law wife or something like that. She would be at the hospital all the time, and not answering the telephone.

"Did you call early in the morning, or late at night?"

Leon hadn't, and he hadn't considered flying up to New York, either.

"You think I should just TWA out of here because Sylvia sent the news?"

October wouldn't do *should*s and *shouldn't*s with him, but she did point out that the old man had been family to Leon. Family was too important. He might want to find out if the trouble was operation big or toenail small.

"Doesn't he have diabetes?" she asked Leon.

And Leon did see the merit in being sure it wasn't serious.

"Foots wouldn't want Sylvia sending letters," he said. "I'm the last person he'd want to see."

"Just call, then," she told him. If Vergie fell sick, surely Gene would call. Wouldn't he?

She added, "Unless you think it's serious. I

444

mean, you don't think he might die or anything, do you?"

What did she want to say that for? He looked at her like she had been planning the old man's death. Then he started rubbing his hands together and got up off the floor. Went to the window to look out at the cold street.

"One time I was up on the Avenue, hungry, mouth ashy, shoes rusty, trying to stretch a quarter. Foots told me, 'Come on, son,' he said, 'you need to do something 'bout them shoes.' I went with him and got up in his shoeshine chair at the back of Grimes's place. And I let him do his thing.

"First he brushed my shoes off, getting rid of everything I'd picked up in the streets, you know. Then he took a little jar of soapy water and shook it up. Dipped into it with a toothbrush. He said stitching added class to the shoe, and that you had to keep it looking new. He worked up a lather along the stitched soles. Bleach would rot the thread, so he used soap and water, and rinsed with water and alcohol. Made them dry fast.

"He took his time, rubbed on a thin coat of tan wax, and told me that the leather was already what it was going to be. He said you're not covering it up, you're bringing out what is already there. And he smoked a cigarette and waited for it to set. And when he finished the cigarette, he went to zapping and slapping, flicking and snapping his rags and brushes. When he finished, and my shoes looked new, he told me that good leather would always shine. If you polish it right, the real thing shows through."

Yes, good lesson, and October understood it.

"I think that's why I always hung with him," Leon said. "Stuff like that."

She thought about her sister, and blinked back tears. She didn't know if Leon wanted to hear her advice, but she needed it said.

"I think if I were you, I wouldn't want to have him go without saying good-bye."

Leon half turned, looking shocked, and she went to him, got him to come away from the cold window. They drank their hot toddies. Played music and danced. Made love on the sofa. She missed her family.

Two days after Christmas she was sewing in the basement when Leon called to say that he had reached Sylvia, and that Foots had had his other leg amputated the day before. Leon had tried to get a straight answer about whether or not Foots would be okay, and whether or not Foots had asked for him. He told October she'd have to know Sylvia to understand why he didn't get an answer. But probably Foots hadn't asked for him. Probably he was going to be all right.

It occurred to October to ask, "What's his real name?"

And Leon said Foots Franklin was all he knew.

As the days passed, and Leon gave her dribbles and drabbles he got from Sylvia, October could tell he was worried. Every time they talked, Leon had something about Foots, like he was already writing the man's eulogy.

He told her tender things: Foots's arthritis and how sometimes, when Sylvia wasn't around, Leon had had to fasten Foots's shirt or tie his shoes. He talked about the times he had taken Foots with him on the road. The old man knew a lot about the jazz clubs in New York, knew owners and managers, jobs to be had. He knew which ones were cool and which ones were thin ice.

On the telephone one evening, he talked about how Foots had gotten him together with Gene "Jug" Ammons, the player who had made a hit out of "Red Top." How Foots had introduced them — had "pulled Jug's coat about me." It turned out that Gene Ammons had played the blues with Foots once upon a recent time at a club called the Zanzibar, and it was the first time Leon had ever heard of Foots playing anything anywhere.

"I must have known Foots three, four years by then. Back then, I knew he was crippled and couldn't play piano. He had never told me about the Zanzibar, though. So I just showed up there one night. Sure enough, he was the real thing.

"He's wailing on his harmonica, and singing the blues all about rotting in the pen, being in the joint. Now that was news to me. He had a hundred songs about it. That was the first I ever heard about him being sent up, too."

Sometimes her mind was like one of those combination locks. It would spin as far as it could go one way, then turn and stop at another place, spin and spin again until she heard the proverbial click. The name "Franklin" had been just an ordinary stop. So had the old piano-playing bluesman. The penitentiary thing got her serious.

"Where was Foots Franklin from?" she asked Leon. "Because my father's name was Franklin Brown, and he went to the pen, too. He was supposed to have died there."

Leon wasn't sure, but he thought "somewhere down south. To hear him tell it, he'd been everywhere, but I never did know where he was born."

"Was he ever in Cleveland?"

"I don't know. He never said. He talked a

lot about Chicago and Detroit."

"Where was he in jail? Leavenworth?"

"Joliet. He told me that. And he didn't have any kids."

"Did he tell you that, too?"

"No, but Sylvia told me once that Foots thought me and Dee were his children. In all the time I've known him, he's never said anything about any family, and nobody ever came around."

Leon told her, "Foots had one ace, Slick Moses — from the joint, too. Old guy. Slick had a son who was a doctor over in Brooklyn, and when Foots got out of the joint, the son got them a place to stay. I think that's how Foots got to the city."

He told her that anything was possible, but that he didn't think Foots could be her daddy. They didn't look anything alike. October tried to call up the old man she had run into on the one night Leon had been at the Blue Room, but she remembered nothing. Leon told her he was sure Foots would want to claim her if he knew there was a chance.

Suddenly October got all hot and jittery about trying to come up with the right questions about this man, trying to get at what Leon didn't know he knew. That night after they hung up, she dialed Leon right back.

"Why did he go to jail in the first place? —

that's the question."

Leon wasn't sure about that either. "I didn't care what he'd done. Like I said, anything is possible, but I can't see Foots killing a woman and forgetting about his children. Not Foots."

But Leon had never actually asked, and Foots had never said. Leon did say, though, that once when they were talking, he had said something to Foots about paying the price by doing the time, and Foots had told him that there were some things you could never pay for. Leon said that that had stuck with him, that maybe Foots had done something big.

How many years had Foots been in the pen? Leon thought he had been there during the war. Slick Moses and Foots used to talk about making boots at Joliet for the troops. And it was then that Leon put it together for himself.

"Damn," he said. "I bet that's where he got that name." He said he would ask Sylvia. October had got him going.

It wasn't New Year's yet when Leon called her, first thing one morning. It had started to snow and she had been daydreaming about being snowed in together with him.

"It's me," he said.

She said hi and what's up.

"Nothing much," he said. But from the sound of his voice she knew something had happened to the old man.

"You don't sound so good," she said. "What happened?"

"Foots is dying. Gangrene. They couldn't stop it."

"Don't tell me on the phone," she said. "Come over here. Please." She wanted to hold him. She wanted him to hold her. Too many questions swam around in her head.

"I think I have to go," he said. She could hear the regret.

"Okay," she said. "I guess you should fly. Now. Today if you can. How much longer does he have?"

"They're saying a few days, maybe."

"Who's with him?"

"Sylvia stays there day and night. All the guys from the barbershop come, but Foots can't see. He's pretty near blind now. She says I'd better come if I'm coming."

October needed time.

"You have to hear this," Leon said. "I told Sylvia about you — you know, about him maybe being your daddy and all. And I asked her if Foots's name could have been Franklin Brown. She was sure it was him. But to tell you the truth, I don't know what to believe. Sylvia said she always suspected he had kids.

She thinks I ought to bring you with me."

"Wait," October said. "I don't know that I want to go running off to New York based on what Sylvia is saying."

"Let me give you another reason to come," Leon said. And she listened, let him come to her. "I'm asking for me. I'm saying I don't want to do this by myself. Will you come?"

CHAPTER 25

For one brief second when Vergie heard October's voice say, "Hi, Vergie, it's me," on the phone, it felt like the sun popping out after years of rain. But then Vergie's mind came to attention and started scouting for clouds again.

"How are you?" from October got a "Fine, and you?" from her, and if she hadn't been so surprised she would have asked October right away, "What do you want?" But she waited.

"How's everybody?" probably meaning David.

"Everybody's fine. Merry Christmas, Happy New Year," Vergie said. "Did you get my card?"

October said she'd gotten it, and told her that she didn't send any out this year. Vergie didn't want her to explain. Cast die, and all that.

"I don't know how to put this," October said, "but I think I've found Franklin Brown. He's dying in a hospital in New York. I thought you ought to know."

It sounded like a joke. A trick. An excuse to call.

"Franklin Brown."

"Yes."

"*Our* Franklin Brown? Poppa?"

"Poppa," October said. "I think it's him, and he's in a hospital in New York. Dying, they say. I'm going up there."

"Who is *they?*"

Vergie listened to October go into this long story about her new man and some old man who was like a father to him, and finding out he'd been in the pen and all. How many Franklin Browns were there, and how many of them had been to jail? A whole lot, Vergie bet. Their Franklin Brown was dead and gone. It wasn't possible, but this was October.

"What do you want me to do?" Vergie asked her.

"Nothing," October said. "I just thought you'd want to know." October got quiet. Vergie didn't know what to say. She was still wondering what kind of man October had gotten mixed up with this time.

"I mean, you knew more than I ever did about him," October said. "You remembered more. If it *is* him, he would remember us, and you could . . . I don't know . . . ask him things."

Vergie thought about boogie-woogie. Mr. Bailey across the alley. This was October, and October believed it was Franklin Brown.

Even if it was possible, why would Vergie want to go watch him die?

"Why would you want to see him?" Vergie asked her.

"Because . . ." October said, like she was trying to say the right thing. "He was our father. I guess that's why. I mean, I never knew him really, but you did. . . ."

Vergie's thoughts tumbled. Why was it that Auntie had never said where or when?

October sounded like she had just found the real reason. "I feel like I owe it to myself, Vergie, to go see if it's really him. And if it is, I'll find out where he's been all this time, and why he never looked for us, I guess."

"You wanted him to look for us?" October could be such a child sometimes.

"I don't know," October said. "I just need to know, and I called to tell you that they think he's only got a few days. I'm leaving this afternoon with Leon. If you decide to come, Leon could get you a room where we're staying."

Vergie thought October ought to go, that maybe it would cure her. When October told her to write down the number for a Sylvia woman in New York, something told her to get a pencil and jot it down. Who knows — maybe later she would want to call to find out what happened.

They hung up. Vergie didn't even know that she was upset until she felt herself calming down. Probably the shock of hearing from October out of the blue. She couldn't drop everything and go anywhere. It was the holidays. She wouldn't dream of going anywhere without Gene, and what would they do with David? Franklin Brown had died in Leavenworth years ago. October could be so gullible. If he wasn't already dead, why would she want to go watch him die? Would he remember the piano? What did he think ever happened to them?

She sat by the telephone. Who could she call? Gene was still upstairs getting ready for work. David was still asleep. What if it was Franklin Brown? Mrs. Hopp was too old to handle David. None of them had ever been to New York. It was the holidays.

Hallelujah. They talked to each other. My life, with all its wonders and terrors, was long since over. Wonders and terrors were still unfolding for my daughters. I held for them — oh, I held for them.

CHAPTER 26

October's first time on an airplane didn't work out so well. Nobody told her not to eat much, and she was sick the whole time, couldn't wait to get off, and made Leon promise he would find some other way for them to get back to Kansas City.

Seeing what she saw on the trip from the airport to Holly House, though, made it worthwhile — a glimpse of the gush and noise and grandness that was Harlem. Everything. Everywhere. A corner of her brain sprang old Garvey parades and Father Divine blessings on her. Thirty years earlier, she would have seen the dicty-rich driving down from the very Sugar Hill that Leon pointed to. And VanDerZee would have been setting up his tripod to catch ladies in drape dresses with fur trim going into Madame C.J.'s. Men in chesterfields would have posed with one foot on the runningboard of the Duesenberg that business — with or against the law — had bought them.

From the taxi she heard slow noises. Soft blurs. Saw Chee-Chee's Bar and Grill. People inside, sitting along a counter, dumb backs in a row, hunched eating. Lin's Hand Laundry — a whiff of clean smell; fried-apple smell from Estelle's Kitchen. "The Flamingos at the Apollo" stamped on busy-print posters tacked to every flat place.

And fire escapes, iron vines of black and rust on the faces of brick buildings. The buildings too — sand, cream, umber, baroque and federal, austere and elegant, flat-topped and crowned.

And then the people. Couples. Singles. Swarming to and from lives. Going and coming like before-and-after advertisements at the beauty parlor. Like multitudes pushing their way to some great event. Yet these people were here every day, going home from work, and to work, and to and from a thousand other places. In their clothes they seemed to be giving every point of view from sporty-O to grace, wearing bomber jackets, capes, stingy brims and wing tips, French cuffs with work socks, police blues and old-style Garveyite caps, wide hoop skirts and spike heels, low-risers and tight gabardine. They all had style.

No wonder Leon had been so driven to come here.

Over one block from the famous part of Edgecombe and a short ride to Harlem Hospital, Holly House looked like a stump of a hotel compared to the high-rises all around it. Inside, Leon got them a room on the second floor.

Vergie had called October back that same morning to ask where they would stay if they came. She told October that she had asked Gene, and that he'd said it was up to her. If she wanted him to, he would drive to New York right then, pushing her to go. October had had to call Leon to get the name of the hotel. And when she had called Vergie back, and said that she and Leon would be going on Pan Am, and that it seemed worth it to get there soon, Vergie had gone back to saying that she shouldn't bother. But one more time, Vergie had called again, with a softer voice saying that she couldn't believe she was going to drop everything and spend that kind of money to come watch an old man die. Said they would be there sometime tomorrow. "I don't know why," she had said. Like the old Vergie.

October and Leon had been in the room no more than a few minutes when the telephone rang. Leon answered it. "It's for you," he said. October's heart fell into her stomach. She knew that it would be Vergie, and that she was probably not coming.

"Well, we're here," Vergie said. "What are we supposed to do now?"

God was still on the throne. Gene and Vergie were on the eighth floor, where they could see everything. She could hear David in the background chattering away. October had to just laugh.

Vergie chuckled a little, too. "We came on TWA," she said. "I got sick on the plane." October told her to wait in their room, and she and Leon would come up.

What two years of absence does, it freezes people in the frames where they once stood. It changes them to voices in the head, flashes of the real thing that can't be felt or heard or smelled unless it's in the flesh. Vergie looked older, and a little scared. Probably she, herself, did too. Vergie's hair was a mess. Probably hers was, too. Vergie had on a navy blue suit like one Aunt Maude used to wear, and she had lost a little weight. But she was Vergie, and October wanted to hug her.

They stood there in the door of the hotel room looking at each other, and Vergie looking at Leon. And then Vergie motioned for them to come in. "You-all may as well come in and sit down and tell us what's what."

Suddenly David. Standing between the beds. *Beloved* fit. He was beautiful in a different way this time, and she fought back immediate tears. He had changed already. Just from seeing him look and look away, she could feel him being more quiet, shy. Gene sat on the side of one bed and waved a little wave.

"Hi, Auntie Oc," David said. He took a few steps and held out his hand, awkward, like practicing his manners.

She wanted to hold him to her for a long time. "Hi, David," she said, and buried his hand in her hands. "You look so grown. So handsome."

He smiled at that, and looked down at himself, his suit and tie. "Momma said I should dress up."

"This is Leon Haskins," she said. Leon stepped up and shook Gene's hand and said "Hey man," to David.

David stared.

October felt Leon needing to hurry.

"We probably ought to get on over to the hospital right away," she said. And Leon told them, "We can get a cab out front, and later on I think I can borrow a car to get us around. Is anybody hungry?"

Vergie said no, not yet anyway, and October could see that David was taking his cue from her. He wouldn't say he wanted anything.

Above the front entrance, on the overhang of the roof, large brass letters spelled out

"Harlem Hospital." It was six o'clock. If they looked down the rows of brownstones, and up at the sky between, they could see strips of clouds and the last tip of sun bouncing flame glare off the windows.

David rushed up the steps to hold open the door.

"I remember when I was little and Aunt Frances was in the hospital," he said. "I had to wait downstairs with Daddy, and a lady gave us Tootsie Rolls."

As they went into the lobby, Vergie rested her hand on David's shoulder. "We're in New York now — you'll come with us," she told him.

They passed the information desk and the sign saying children under fourteen couldn't go on the wards. The woman at the desk looked David over but let him go.

October asked Leon about Franklin's floor. "I think Sylvia said fifth, 505-E."

On the elevator with a gurney carrying a blue-draped, sleeping patient, David squeezed himself between Vergie and the corner, avoiding any contact with the gurney. October wondered if he ought to be there.

David whispered to Vergie, "How will he know who we are?"

Gene told him, "He might not." Vergie and Gene exchanged looks. "Maybe you can wait in the hall," Vergie said.

David said "Okay" before she even got it all out.

When the elevator stopped, Leon took October's hand and Vergie and Gene fell in behind them, holding on to David. Marching on the granite floor, they sounded like a small army moving past open doors where October could see the rows of beds, patients and visitors sitting in chairs beside them, nurses smiling with trays of little cups. Medicine.

"I hate the smell," Leon said. She was remembering Auntie, and thinking what it was like for Leon. And she was thinking, too, *We are here. I hope we're not too late.*

"E Wing is down this way," he said, and held her hand tighter. "Did I tell you Sylvia said he asked for me?"

"This sure is a big hospital," David said.

Vergie said "Um-hmm. Remember, you'll wait right outside the room."

Walking. Walking.

"All this time," Leon said, "I've been thinking that the day would come when Foots would come bopping into a club, bragging about his protégé. But the time just went."

October touched his arm. "It's okay. He asked for you, and you're here."

If the man was past talking, how would she know for sure that he was their Franklin

Brown? And if he talked, how would they know that he was telling the truth? How — in front of a roomful of people they didn't know — would she and Vergie ask him anything, especially about Carrie?

Up ahead a clump of people stood outside a room, and then faces turned in their direction.

"Looka here," one old guy said. "If this ain't somethin." He came up to Leon and patted his shoulder.

"Boy, I'm glad to see you. I heard you might make it back. Foots asked for you."

"Is that you?" another man said. For a split second Leon studied the face, then slapped hands with the man. "Hey, how're you doing?"

And then a man in a porkpie hat, stub of unlit cigar stuck in his mouth, came out of the room. "Hey, Kansas City," he said. "I want you to know Foots's chair is gonna stay at the shop."

The man looked at October and the rest of them. "Is this your family?"

"This is Grimes," Leon said to October, slipping past the question. "October Brown and Vergie and Gene Parker, and David."

Everybody said hello to everybody.

"Wells just left," another man told Leon. "You think Foots'll wake up again?"

Leon didn't answer, just took October's hand and led them all into the room. David stepped back and Vergie turned around to tell him to stay right where he was, leaning against the wall, looking up into the faces of a generation of old men he'd never seen before.

The bed nearer the door was empty. Another old man stood with his back to the door, and the sight of him seemed to make Leon more nervous. An old-fashioned metal-frame screen had been placed between the two beds in just the right way to hide the upper half of the bed nearer the window — the bed with a still body on it.

Leon held tight to her hand. Beside the bed the woman who had to be Sylvia looked their way, and her face lit up. In a loud whisper she said, "They're here!"

Leon went to her, and as he did, he looked at the figure in the bed — the figure that, because of the screen, October couldn't see yet. All the blood went out of Leon's face. Sylvia stood up, and it looked like Leon lost his bones in her arms.

"Aw, sweetie," Sylvia said. "Don't cry. You're here now. He loved you, you know."

She was smallish, in a black straw cloche with a rolled brim, so that her tight gray curls were mostly hidden. When she stood up October saw the sleeveless blouse and taffeta skirt and soft ballet slippers with the elastic band across the instep.

The other old man there held out his hand. "I knew Kansas City would make it. How do, all y'all. Just call me Slick — Slick Moses."

Sylvia tried to smile at them. "Is this . . ."

Leon turned, no blood still, eyes wide but not crying. "Yes, this is October Brown and her sister, Vergie Parker, and Vergie's husband, Gene," Leon said.

Immediately Sylvia started to give up her chair. Leon waved her back. "No, no, that's okay — sit down."

He held out his hand and looked for October's eyes.

She had hesitated at the foot of the bed, feeling mostly like a death watch was a private thing, and that she and Vergie ought not to be there. It wasn't going to be easy with Leon sad and her sad for him, but mostly curious.

"Y'all come on in," Sylvia said, and stood up again.

Leon's hand was out, but October didn't go farther. And because he had seen her glimpse the body in the bed, he looked again, too.

Later he would tell her that the old man had gone down. Shrunk. With his eyes closed, his mouth open, struggling to take in each breath and forcing it out in whispers, he didn't look like the man Leon had known. The actual

Foots had "vacated the premises, gone to some hip city where he's hobbling around talking about the life he once lived."

From the end of the bed, October saw an old man sucking in breath. No connection to her, no resemblance to anyone she had ever seen. Black skin stretched across cheekbones, fuzzy rim of white hair, not her, not Vergie. His arms lay like long dark bones with hardly enough flesh to cover the knobs of his hands, and his hands were wing tips, fingers nearly on top of one another. Not a piano player's hands, not fleshy hands holding a fork, a knife.

Looking at this shell of a man, his legs gone, she felt no deep sadness and no relief. Even the edge of curiosity turned dull. She looked at Vergie, and Vergie dropped her head and shuffled around like she had spilled something on the floor. Gene stood holding the brim of his hat in both hands.

"He's been asleep since yesterday," Sylvia said. "Every now and again he might open his eyes, but he can't see much. Or he might say something, but he don't make no sense. I think he's been waiting for you to get here," she said to Leon.

Finally Leon joined October and Vergie at the foot of the bed and took October's hand again. Sylvia began to weep quietly and sat down.

Wiping her nose, she looked at October, then at Vergie, and nodded toward the bed. "That's you-all's father, you know."

"Probably is," Leon said.

To October it felt too much like an insult. "I don't think so," she whispered back to Leon. October felt Vergie shaking her head in agreement.

"Oh, he is, all right," Sylvia said. "He had children once. I've *been* knowing that. All he wanted was to see them before he died. And Lonny brought you here."

A whole lot of men die every day wanting to see the children they've given up or lost was October's first thought. She bit her tongue. Sylvia probably needed for everything to end right, have all his wishes come true before he took his last breath.

Sylvia wouldn't let go. "You're the ones he's been waiting for. When Lonny didn't come last month, I knew there was a good reason. God wouldn't let him stay away, knowing that Foots had to go under the knife, unless there was a mighty good reason."

She nodded at the bed. "This is the reason. He's your father, all right."

"No," Vergie said. "That's not him." Gene stepped up to Vergie's side and put his arm around her.

Slick Moses Mabry told them he was going

to get a cup of coffee. "Anybody else want one?"

They all said no. As he moved past October and Vergie, he hesitated. "You-all was good to come," he said.

Then the old man in the bed sighed a breath heavier than the others. Leon went to the bedside. As October watched, she saw the slits of his eyes open and close, then flutter. His breathing picked up. He moved a hand, and Sylvia rubbed his arm. His eyes fluttered open again, looked toward the side of the bed where Leon stood.

Leon bent over. "Hey Foots," he whispered, touching the hand.

"He can't see you, but he knows you're here," Sylvia said. Then louder she said, "We're here, Foots. It's Lonny."

Supposedly he was blind, but October watched his eyes roam slowly over the room, like he had come awake in a strange place. Even more slowly, his eyes focused where she and Vergie and Gene stood, at the foot of the bed. He peered like they were standing in fog.

He tried to lift his arm, reaching, and she wondered if he was trying to speak.

Then just above a whisper, he called, "Carrie?"

It stunned her, just stunned her. She grabbed Vergie and Vergie grabbed her, and they held on to each other.

"Carrie?" he called again. Then his arm fell limp, and he closed his eyes again.

All at once Leon was pulling chairs from somewhere and telling her and Vergie to sit down. Gene tried to get them to drink some water.

"Can he see?" Leon said.

"No, no honey," Sylvia said. "He's been doing that since yesterday. Ever so often he opens his eyes and he calls her name. He's started seeing her now. It won't be long."

Sitting now, October and Vergie held on to each other like they were afraid that they might suddenly wake up and find they'd been dreaming.

"Did he ever talk about Cleveland?" Vergie asked.

"I know he lived in Cleveland, long time ago," Sylvia said. "He didn't much like to talk about what happened, and this might not be the right time to say it, but I know he was sorry, and I know he went to hell for a long time. In the pen. He told me. He wanted me to know everything."

"What about David?" Gene whispered to Vergie.

She told him no, that it was too much for David. "I'll tell him tonight."

"S'pose he don't get another chance to see him?" Gene said.

"No," Vergie said.

"One of these days you might wish he had," Gene said. "He's old enough."

Slick Moses came in with a cup of coffee for Sylvia. "Delores is out there," he said. "She's lettin you-all have your time."

"Let me go talk to her," Sylvia said. "We're all family now," and Slick Moses helped her up and out of the room.

"I'll get David," Gene said. Vergie nodded okay.

Leon must have sensed his own time, because as October and Vergie sat letting it settle on them, Leon sat down and scooted the chair up against the bed.

The whole scene happened again, the old man trying to reach out, crying "Carrie."

October watched Leon making his peace with this shell of the black old man who had once been Franklin Brown.

"I guess she's coming for you," Leon said. He bent down closer to Foots's face. "I hope you can hear me when I tell you that I didn't know you ever had anything to show me. The whole time you were trying to set me straight, I thought it was only about my horn — you know, the music.

"I owe you a lot," Leon said. "You sent me

home one night. I wish somebody could've done that for you, saved you from yourself. Then maybe . . ." He stopped talking for a while and October knew he was trying not to cry.

Then finally he said, "I didn't know this thing between you and me was a two-way street. I thought it was all you. I know I'm late. I'm saying you're my ace, Foots. I hope you know it."

They stayed until nearly midnight, all of them. Leon said he'd sit watch with Sylvia. Could be all night. Finally, October went back to Holly House with Vergie, Gene, and David.

As they sat on the beds eating ham sandwiches and looking at the television screen, October had the truth in her heart and no answers.

"Are we staying until he, you know, dies?" David asked.

Earlier, when Gene had come back inside the hospital room with David, he had waited to let Leon have his time. And then Vergie had urged David forward.

"He was your grandfather," she had said. "You can say something to him if you want to."

David had stopped and looked and then

just went right over to the side of the bed and touched Franklin Brown's hand.

"I'm David," he said. Timid. Then himself. "You're my grandfather. Vergie Parker is my mother."

He looked at Leon who shook his head. "I don't think he can hear."

"Suppose he can?" David said. He turned back and touched the frail hand. "We thought you . . . we didn't know you lived in New York. I always wondered . . . I guess that's all."

He had backed away from the bed, keeping his eyes on Franklin Brown. When he reached the foot of the bed, Vergie hugged him.

"I wish he could say something," David had said for everybody.

And so sitting on the bed at Holly House, October listened to Vergie tell David that she didn't know yet if they would stay until he died. "We haven't had time to figure this all out," she said. "I was hoping he could talk. Or recognize us or something."

"It doesn't seem fair," October said.

Then television flags waved to "The Star-Spangled Banner," and it was time for her to go downstairs to sort by herself.

She dressed for bed, dozed off and on. Sometime in the night she heard Leon put his key in the door. She sat up and turned on the lamp, waiting just to see his face. He came in but didn't utter a word, just sat down and held his head in his hands and started to weep. Quiet. Foots Franklin Brown had died. She raised the covers. Without even taking off his shoes, Leon lay down beside her and she rocked him.

Over the three days that it took to get Franklin Brown into the ground, October hung suspended between her childhood and these incredible few days, between what she had thought was her real life and all the possibilities that had just died, between her life without David and this week of seeing him morning, noon, and night, again. She and Vergie said each other's thoughts aloud to themselves.

"I felt sad, but not like crying."

"Other people loved him. Isn't that something?"

"He turned into an old man who loved Leon."

"At least now we'll know for sure when he died, and where he's buried, but that's all."

Neither of them wanted any part of planning a funeral — just said that they would stay and pay their respects.

Leon spent hours helping Sylvia and Delores. When he came back to Holly House each time, he wrapped himself in October, sad and amazed at the same time. Delores was all right, he told her.

"She's singing with a gospel group, and they've cut a demo already. She told me she read my letters, but it takes time to let it all go. Some people hold out for a whole lifetime. I don't think Delores will just forget everything that happened, but at least she knows I tried to tell her I'm sorry."

With Franklin Brown found and gone, though October couldn't say that she had lost anything, she was beginning to feel lighter, like a weight had been lifted. A match had been struck in the dark. Not quite a candle burning, though.

On the day before the funeral, Leon came back late to Holly House with a pawnshop horn. Sylvia wanted him to play a song for Foots at the funeral, and he hadn't brought his horn with him to New York.

The small chapel of the Davis Funeral Home had room for only about fifty chairs, twenty-five on each side of the aisle. Once "the family" took their seats at the front, all the chairs were taken. Sylvia had insisted that October and Vergie and David and Gene sit in the front row, but that wasn't to be. The funeral director had placed only four chairs in front — room enough for Sylvia, Moses,

Leon, and Delores.

When Sylvia insisted that the chairs be re-arranged, October said no. She was happy to sit with her real family in the second row. The closed casket with a blanket of red carnations stood on a bier at the front. A preacher friend of Sylvia's conducted everything.

Simple. The organist played. The preacher read "I am the Resurrection . . ." from the Bible and said a prayer. Delores read out the names of everyone who had sent cards and made phone calls. Moses said he wouldn't apologize for what he wanted to say about his friend. Said they had met in the penitentiary. They had kept each other from going crazy. Vowed to stay friends on the outside, and had kept their word. *Honest,* he used. And *kindly. A tough old hide* and *a big heart.* The preacher read the obituary, which mentioned survivors: along with Sylvia, Leon, and Delores, two daughters and a grandson, but it did not mention their names.

As she sat listening, October tried not to fill in the part of the story she and Vergie knew — the part that nobody else could ever know. As far as she was concerned, nothing anybody said would change the fact that she and Vergie had lived a whole life with some dark things. How could the split of the two men who had been Franklin Brown be fixed?

Weren't funerals supposed to put every-thing to rest? She had finally come face to face with the man who had set the course of her life. There was justice in the fact that on his deathbed, he had been beyond seeing, and his last wish hadn't been granted.

When Moses sat down, Leon stood up. In-stead of facing them, he stood in front of the casket, back turned, and began to blow. Later he would tell her that the only part he had thought out was that he would begin with "Footsloose." A clear and simple melody, phrasing it like he was horn-talking to Foots. And did the melody again, as if to say, *You got it?* Then he broke into something that he knew Foots would understand, then swung into the hard and gutsy wail that must have been in the old man's ear for his whole life. The blues.

Leon told October later that he had done his best to be piano, harmonica, and the blues women and men who had kept it going. He played for an old man in a dark cell, his old man submitting to the knife one last time, his Foots, gone.

The scene at Sylvia's could only be de-scribed as a party. Fifty people at the funeral turned into a hundred people spilling out of Sylvia's one-bedroom apartment. Tons of food and drink and no space and October and Vergie pitching in with Delores to get things organized.

David. October watched him mix in with the people from Franklin Brown's life like he had always been a part of it, and asking for details, too. Listening to the stories, laughing like he caught on to the jokes even in pig Latin. What a difference a generation made.

October saw Leon looking around for her, and waved her fork in the air.

"I was wondering where you disappeared to," he said. "That looks good."

She told him that the song sounded different from the record, and he explained what he had tried to do.

"It was about him and me," he said. "I think he got it."

Vergie and Gene came and stood with them, all four lined up against the wall watching David.

Sylvia came up finally to talk to Leon.

"I guess you-all will be going back to Kansas City soon?"

October waited to hear his answer.

"I'll stay for a while if you want me to," he said.

"Dee's gonna move in with me now, so I'll be all right," Sylvia said. She looked at October. "Take care of him," she said.

"I'm glad I got the chance to meet you," October said.

And Vergie spoke up, too. "In a way," she said, "this closes a door that we didn't even know was open."

Sylvia lit a cigarette. "Foots appreciates you all coming and not making a commotion," she said. "I know he does. I just wish he could have seen you for real. But life is like that — full of things we'll never understand."

The five of them stood quietly, watching people come and go.

Then Vergie said, "Miss Sylvia —"

"Just call me Sylvia."

"I just need to ask you one thing. I hope you don't mind."

"Sure, honey," Sylvia said. "Come on back here where we can talk." She took Vergie by the hand, and Vergie motioned for October to follow, and she dragged Leon with her to a corner of the kitchen.

Sylvia turned to Vergie. "He's gone now. Anything I can tell you, I don't think he'll mind."

Vergie looked at October. "I want to know why," she said to her. "Don't you?"

October told her, "Um-hmm," and Vergie asked Sylvia if Franklin Brown ever said why he killed Carrie.

It was clear Leon didn't want to hear that

part. "I'll be out in the living room with Gene," he said.

Sylvia reached over and stubbed her cigarette in the sink. "You already know he had a quick temper," she said. "That was part of it." And she sighed.

"I think he thought he was going to be a big-time blues player someday. It was all he wanted. He did what men do — he ran around a lot. Drank. Gambled.

"Anyway, it was one of those things. She found out that he was going to leave her for another woman, and she burned up all his money. I don't know how much it was, but it was a lot to him. I think that would've been all right — he would've just left. But then he found out that she had set all his songs on fire, too. Burned up everything he ever wrote. They got to fussin and fightin and he just struck out at her with the first thing he laid his hands on.

"It just happened," Sylvia said, and took a breath. "He never meant to kill her."

Vergie had clamped her hand over her mouth, and tears ran down her cheeks.

"He was leaving us?" Vergie said. "*He* was leaving?"

"Some woman in Chicago," Sylvia said. "He knew he was wrong. They always know when they're wrong."

October had never known the story, but Franklin's part didn't surprise her. Nobody kills anybody in such a flash unless they've got a quick temper. And Auntie had always said he was no good, meaning that he ran around. But what struck October now was Franklin's decision to leave his family for the other woman. And Carrie's suffering, trying to make him stay. She flashed on James and shuddered.

"All this time," Vergie said, "I always thought Momma was leaving." And she went on to October about what she had always suspected of Carrie and why Carrie had died. How she had always believed she, herself, had had a part in it, too.

Vergie's secret guilt came as a surprise to October. And now here was the truth, springing Vergie free.

She watched Vergie cry all over again — "He was leaving!" — and begin to laugh a little. "Will wonders never cease?"

"Oh, that reminds me," Sylvia said. "I almost forgot. I've been waiting for today to divvy up Foots's things."

She told them to come on and pushed through the crowd, looking for Leon.

He and Gene stood together, looking lost.

"Come on, it ain't much. To tell the truth, he didn't leave but one box, and it's for you, mister," she said to Leon.

They followed Sylvia to the bedroom, just as crowded as any other part of the house.

Sylvia clapped her hands. "Okay, okay! Y'all have to clear out of here for a minute, I've got business."

The people sauntered out, eating and talking still.

Sylvia went to the closet. Leon said he remembered the tin box from years earlier. "One night before I left for a tour, Foots tried to give it to me."

"I remember," Sylvia said. She jerked on the chain and the light came on. October saw all the clothes and cartons, books and boxes jamming the closet.

"Tilt that down for me, will you?" Sylvia said to Leon, and he tipped the square tin box, caught it as it fell.

"I 'spect you know what's in here. It wasn't no secret. This was what he always wanted you to have from day one."

She handed it to Leon. October was curious, and Vergie, too, looked like she wanted to see.

"Open it," Sylvia said.

But before he could get the top off, Sylvia said, "Now I know this was between you and Foots — I mean, he sure wanted you to have it. But I know if he was here, he would tell you to let his blood relatives in on it too — you know what I mean?"

Leon had no problem with that — he smiled at October. "You want to open it? I think I've already seen a lot of what's in here."

She couldn't get over the fact that somebody could put a lifetime of anything into one tin box.

"No, that's all right," she said, "unless you do, Vergie."

"No," Vergie said. "You can go ahead."

Leon worked the top off and handed it to Sylvia. "Yes," he said, and he pulled out a wad of folded papers, handed them to October. "This is his handwriting," he said.

She took the little bundle of scrappy papers and gave Vergie half of them, then sat down on the bed. As she unfolded them, she saw scribblings of a crippled hand, pencil marks on yellowed paper, lines of songs. Blues songs.

"Look," Vergie said. She held up some of them.

One by one, they unfolded them and read out loud what they could of his thoughts set down in rhyme and rhythm.

After October had read several, she came upon a small envelope addressed in faded blue ink to Franklin Brown at a route number in Joliet, Illinois. The envelope had no return address, but the fading postmark seemed to be Cleveland, Ohio. Inside the envelope, a small pamphlet and a folded note. The pamphlet was a pocket version of the Twenty-third Psalm, "The Lord is my shepherd . . ." At the bottom, someone had written, "I still pray for you," and it was signed "Miss C. Butler."

The name meant nothing to October. She showed it to Vergie.

"That's Miss Cordelia," Vergie said. "The lady next door — remember?"

And then the briefest image of a face with a gold tooth and dimples flashed in October's mind.

"What's that note say?" Vergie asked.

October unfolded the note to see handwriting she would know anywhere. "Dear Cordelia," it said. "I know you mean well. I have appreciated getting your letters, but this is the last letter you will get from me. You can tell Franklin Brown that if you give him this address, we will move away. Tell him if he ever cared anything about the girls, just let them be. They have suffered enough. Sincerely, Frances Cooper."

She handed it to Vergie to read. For all those years, Aunt Frances had shielded them, kept them safe. To Frances and Maude Cooper, Franklin Brown had died the moment the knife had cut through Carrie Cooper's flesh. They had given October and Vergie a life without his cursed existence.

Then Leon fairly yelled, "I don't believe this, I don't believe it!"

"Isn't it something?" Sylvia said. "Show it to them."

"What?" October asked.

Leon held up a photograph and turned it over. "It says 1908," he said.

"That's really something, isn't it?" Sylvia said.

Leon sat down beside October on the bed and shoved it on top of all the bits of paper in her lap.

The half-torn, sepia-tone picture of the woman was crinkled and creased, but October could see that the woman was blackberry dark, with nappy hair parted in the middle and pulled back into little knots on the sides of her head. She looked the slightest bit like somebody October ought to know. The woman wore a long, long-sleeved, cottonish dress and a full apron. She sat on a chair in a yard. Behind her only half of a ramshackle little house was showing, because the rest of the picture was missing.

Part of a front porch and a window was still there. In the window on a hand-printed sign, October could make out the words

Lillian Brown, Dressmaker.

Just in that flash, she knew exactly how it had felt to be this woman. In some part of her, she *was* this woman, and this woman was her. And she could no more change that part of herself than she could change her breath. She was linked by blood to Lillian Brown just like leaves pop out on tree branches. And October knew that that was a *good* thing.

CHAPTER 27

October, Leon, Vergie, Gene, and David were all sitting in Wells Famous Chicken and Waffles Restaurant with enough food on the table to feed the whole place.

Since they were there, Leon thought they might as well see New York; he had taken them to the Empire State Building, the United Nations, Times Square, and the Statue of Liberty — all of that. He took them to the East Village and showed October his old apartment house, showed her Minton's and Monroe's, clubs where he'd played. He talked about how different they all looked to him, and not once did he want to venture across their thresholds at night. Not yet, anyway.

Marquees and showcases had announced musicians he might play with sooner or later, but none of it seemed to touch him. Making the rounds, David had caught on to who Leon was and had begun walking beside him on the street, hands in his pockets.

At Wells, Gene was working his way through a platter of pigs' feet and sauerkraut when he put down his fork.

He wiped his hands on his napkin, and said to Vergie, "We may as well get this out now — what do you say?"

She smiled like a girl and hunched her shoulders. "I guess so," she said.

Gene said to David, "How would you like to go to Kansas City with your Aunt October for a week or so?"

David had a mouth full of chicken, but he grinned. "On the plane?"

"Not now," Vergie said. "School starts next week. We're talking about in June."

"Yeah!" David said.

October's mouth dropped open on its own. She hadn't even wished for it yet.

"Alone?" she asked.

Vergie nodded. "Gene wants me and him to have a trip on our own. We'll bring David to stay with you for a week."

And so, by grace, my girls were getting there.

One thing I knew for sure then, and know for sure now: grace just is. Nobody can explain it, and it's not something you can deserve. Whether you recognize it or not, whether you feel grateful for it or not, it just is. Guilty or innocent, condemned or redeemed, when you think that you can't go on, and when you think that you've already gone on, grace is wider and deeper than you think, and it can change far more than you ever imagined.

There is no place where anything begins or ends, but by grace, everything comes in its time.

CHAPTER 28

October let them sleep — the three Parkers dead to the world from the twelve-hour drive. They had come the night before, with Vergie all of a sudden thinking they should have taken an airplane trip instead of suffering Gene's careless driving and a whole day of being carsick.

October plugged in the coffeepot and stood at her kitchen sink — too, too tickled. When it had percolated enough, she poured herself a cup and headed for the porch. At that hour, the sun had broken the horizon, but the air outside was still cool. She tied on her patience bonnet and sat her coffee on the floor beside the chaise on her screened-in porch. Time to give God what was God's.

Gratitude. She felt thankful, yes, even for the little detail of Ed bringing over two-by-fours for her basement. A dress shop should start small, and she had already applied for a loan.

A deeper sense of gratitude came, though, because Vergie was beginning to trust her again. They were here; by this time tomorrow morning, Vergie and Gene would be on their way to St. Louis, and David would be hers for a week. Vergie didn't have to worry; October would take him on any terms.

Added to that, since their days in New York, Leon had been making noises about spending the rest of their lives together, and then he had stopped making noises, but she had been still hoping.

It was a cloudy, cold Saturday when she had refused to believe that it could snow in April and was in the backyard, hanging out laundry on her new carousel clothesline. She had just stuck a clothespin on the fold of a towel across the line, when she heard the back door close and turned to see Leon. He had come through the house.

"What are you doing out here with no coat on?" he said. "It's freezing."

"No, it's not," she told him, fingers stinging cold. "It's spring. Look," and she pointed to the brush tips of green shooting out of the ground along the back of her house.

"Daffodils."

"And they'll be dead by tomorrow." He took off his overcoat and tried to put it around her shoulders. "Come on inside."

"In a minute," she said.

"October, I need to talk to you," he said. Too, too somber.

She dropped the wet pillowcase back into

the basket and pulled his coat around her. "What's the matter?"

He smiled a little, but not enough for her heart to slow down.

"Nothing. Just come on in the house."

She rushed ahead of him up the back steps and into the kitchen where it was warm, though now she was shivering. As soon he shut the door behind them and turned, she said, "Just tell me."

"Can we sit down?" he asked, pulling out a chair.

"No," she said. "Just tell me."

"I've been working this out in my head for a long time," he said. "I mean, I didn't want to make any promises I wasn't sure I could keep. . . ."

"Leon, just tell me," she said, trying to hold her mind still.

He grinned a little. "I wanted to do it right," he said, and he stuck his hand into the pocket of the overcoat she was still wearing. Her heart began switching gears but pumping just as fast.

When he brought out his hand, it wasn't holding anything she could have mistaken for a box. It was a piece of paper.

"What's that?"

"Will you let me tell you?" he said. And he was definitely grinning now.

"I've been writing something — this is the first page of it. I thought I wanted to surprise you with it." He opened the sheet out. A sheet of music. "October Suite," it said.

He went on, "But just a while ago, when I sat down with it again, I knew I could never put everything into a piece of music, and then I knew. I was sure, and so I had to come over here."

She held her breath.

His eyes were all over her face, telling and asking, and though she wanted desperately to wait for him to say the actual words, she leaped and threw her arms around him.

"Wait! Wait!" he said. He held her so that he could see her face. "You'll marry me, right? I mean, I haven't bought a ring yet. . . ."

She told him, "Yes, you crazy man, I love you! Of course I'll marry you."

And so as she sat on her porch being grateful for Leon, a sudden flood of the porch light made her jump and pull her robe together. Vergie opened the storm door and stepped onto the porch.

"Sure is nice out here," she said. "I'll take morning air over air-conditioning any day." Standing there with her back against the door and her arms folded, October could see Aunt Maude, and wondered what Carrie might have looked like if she had lived.

Vergie and company were sharing the one bedroom she thought of as David's. She had taken his picture down and put away the comic books: no need to set off bombs the first visit.

"I hope I didn't wake you-all up," October said.

"Not at all," Vergie said. "You know, I don't sleep too well away from home, but Gene and David don't have that problem. They'll be knocked out way after the sun is up."

"There's coffee on the sink if you want some."

"Might as well," Vergie said, and she went back inside. The porch light clicked off, and the paper man cruised up the block, tossing wadded papers at every porch. October went out to get hers and unfurled the headlines about more protests and boycotts and the National Guard. Below the fold, a picture of John F. Kennedy standing at the bow of a boat somewhere, looking away from the camera.

When Vergie came back to sit with October, she wanted to know what and where and when for David. October had mentioned the Paseo swimming pool, where Cora took Eddy Junior, and where Leon knew one of the lifeguards. Vergie was scared of polio, and though October had sworn to her that nobody got polio anymore, and checked to be sure David had had all his shots, Vergie was wary. She needed to see the pool, and October would have to take her there this morning. Of course Vergie remembered Swope Park, but it wasn't a pleasant memory, and with the protests and Emmett Till, and sit-ins and jailings, well, she wasn't sure David should be anywhere where he wasn't wanted.

"You've got a record player, don't you? And he can watch TV till the cows come home."

October promised her that if they did Swope Park, they'd only do Watermelon Hill.

"Leon wants you-all to come eat lunch with him at the college," October told her. "I think he wants to show off a little and test the waters with you about us getting married."

Vergie looked at her and half-rolled her eyes. "You'll never be able to tell me nothing about a man who does music for a living. But you're the one that has to live with him."

They sipped and talked until the sun exposed every detail of the houses across the street and turned the air sluggish. Inside again, October turned on the air and closed all the windows. In the kitchen, Gene sat with coffee, reading an old newspaper.

October said how-do and gave him the day's paper. "I hope you're starving," she said, "because I'm making everything you can think of for breakfast."

Gene grinned and nodded. To push him to chatting would be impossible, but he got enough across when he wanted to. October thought about the times — few — she had heard him and Vergie laughing together like girls. Love and old shoes by any name was a good fit.

"We're going to take a look at the swimming pool for David, and Leon wants us to eat lunch with him at his job," Vergie told him.

"Okay," Gene said, and murmured something about waking up David, then said, "Oh I'll let him sleep. . . ."

"Get him," Vergie said. "It'll take two or three shakings before he knows his name."

Between October and Vergie the feast grew: sausages, bacon, hash-browned potatoes, eggs, pancakes, fried apples, biscuits, orange juice, milk, and coffee — all the good stuff. They were laying it out when a blast of Ray Charles singing "I got a woman, way over town" came from the bedroom upstairs.

David must have been awake enough to find KPRS on the radio dial. He stumbled into the kitchen dressed and yawning, eyes lighting on the food like he had never eaten.

"Good morning," Vergie said.

"Hi, Momma, hi, Auntie," he said. "I woke up thinking I was at home."

Silence. Bombs already? Everybody let it pass.

October told him to sit on down, and Vergie told him, "We didn't fix all this food to let it get cold."

He fell into the chair and he was still gorgeous in nothing but a plain white short-sleeved shirt and khakis. Gene said grace and they dug in. As they ate, David tried to tell knock-knock-who's-there jokes and Gene stopped him. It seemed to October that telling jokes was David's way of getting past the fact that they were leaving. But she didn't dare say it.

Late morning, hunkered down on 180 acres of land in Jericho Park, the dozen or so brick buildings of Missouri State College were mostly one story high, sprawling on the manicured grounds.

"Right nice," Vergie said, looking at the huge urns choked with geraniums at the entranceway to every building. October had parked the car, and as they crossed the quad, she saw it through their eyes: white-trimmed buildings, benches around tree trunks, black-eyed Susans like a yellow pond on the green.

She thought of how Leon might see the four of them: a proud-looking woman in a pale blue shirtwaist dress, an older man studying the ground like the stones would roll out of their cement, a boy lumbering along on short legs, arms hanging too long at his sides, and bringing up the rear, a happy woman wearing a linen dress the color of smoke with a don't-you-know red patent-leather belt and red sandals.

October pointed out the buildings and steered them toward Fine Arts. Near the path across the quad, an art class sat sketching the buildings, and David stopped to watch them.

"I'll bet I can draw that," he called.

October and Vergie went on, and Gene stopped to wait for him.

"I wish he'd get that excited about his arithmetic," Vergie said. Just something to say. October didn't give it much thought.

"He's nine, and they get more interested in other things," she said. "As long as his grades don't suffer too much."

They walked farther, slowly, looking back, Vergie quiet. At any minute October expected Vergie to start finding reasons for David not to stay. Better to talk about school.

"How did he do for the year?"

"He did all right," Vergie said.

October looked back and saw David trying

to see over the shoulders of two students.

Gene called him, told him to come on. But David started waving for Gene to come back.

"Come on, David," Vergie called, and he listened.

Gene had caught up to them and they wandered through talk about school, October careful not to step on any toes. Grades were good.

"He could have done better," Vergie said. Real definite. "He's smart enough, if he'd just stay with it."

October thought she remembered something about average marks in reading once, and found herself wondering if Vergie had let his laziness in reading spoil his other grades.

She asked again, "He didn't do too badly in arithmetic, did he?"

"Well, he's not making A's," Vergie said.

Things were beginning to sound a little more like a problem. October wanted to know — exactly — what kind of grades David got. But tender toes and all, she wouldn't press.

They waited at the curb. Gene stood in the middle of the walk waiting for David. As they crossed the grass toward the street, Vergie said, "His grades were not that great."

This was new. Vergie had never let out this much about David. And October couldn't have been more pleased. And more curious.

"Did he fail anything?"

Watch it. She could feel the air getting tight. Tread softly. "Because if he did," she said, "he can catch up."

By the way Vergie placed one foot in front of the other and didn't look up, October knew not to say another word.

"Nothing like that," Vergie said. And then she softened it. "But you know he pretty much did real bad in reading, and didn't do a whole lot better in arithmetic. Music, gym, art, all that other stuff, he got S's, but that stuff doesn't count."

Should she say anything or not? Why was Vergie telling her so much and not enough?

"It's nothing me and Gene didn't already know," she said. "Me and Gene have been talking. I don't care about him going to college. I mean, Aunt Maude and Gene did fine at the mill. But he does have to get a diploma."

Hearing that, October had to breathe and think hard before she said anything.

"You know, Vergie, that doesn't have to be the case. Just because his grades are low one year doesn't mean that he's dumb."

"Oh, I know David is smart," Vergie said. "But I'm just telling you why I made him bring his books. We read to him a lot. He needs to study his arithmetic and read his reader every night . . ."

David and Gene had caught up, and they changed the subject.

"They were drawing," David said. "I draw things right out of my head. I never copy stuff, I just think it up."

Wrong time to be getting excited about drawing.

October had the bright idea that after lunch they should stop at the bookstore and she would buy David any book he wanted. Neither David nor Gene seemed to think that was a good idea, and Vergie was so-so.

"I guess it'll be all right, as long as it's not a comic book," Vergie said.

Right then October decided she would see for herself. She wondered what the school had been giving him. Wouldn't it be too good if, when Vergie and Gene came back, she had David interested in reading books? She could send him home with enough for the whole summer.

Just as they got to the door of Fine Arts, Leon came breezing out, looking too good. White shirt with rolled sleeves, and linen slacks that October had never seen before.

"Hey, everybody," he said. "I saw you-all coming. That's my office right up there," and he pointed to his window. "October tells me you-all are headed for St. Louis."

"Yes," Vergie said. She pasted on a smile. "We haven't seen you since New York."

"Right," Leon said. "I don't know what I would've done if you-all hadn't come."

Vergie smiled a real smile, remembering.

"Right now I'm just another teacher at the college, trying to put my program over on the young rebels."

Vergie thought that was funny, and she laughed. October thought Vergie must be starting to like him.

"Hi." He smiled at October, too, and shook Gene's hand, and, "Hey man," to David.

"I heard 'Mood Man' on the radio," David said.

Leon laughed. "You like it?"

October had never heard of what must have been one of Leon's songs.

Leon said to Vergie, "He sure knows how to make a man feel good. Naming my tunes."

"Oh, he's like that," Vergie said. "Real quick when it comes to facts and figures."

Leon took them by to say hi to Kenneth, gave them the tour, and had finagled a picnic lunch out behind his building, where shade kept them cool and private. A nice easy lunch.

It was not until they had gotten back to the house and had a good enough evening, not until Gene and David had settled down to snoozing in front of the TV and Vergie had begun repacking for St. Louis that October found the courage to mess with the peace.

"I know you're going to be worried about him," October said. Vergie was balling socks, and she tossed a pair onto the bed. She held up her hand as if to say, "Don't say it."

"All I want," Vergie said, "is that you keep him safe and make him read every day."

October heard the trembling. "I will," she said.

The next morning, Vergie and Gene left like they were going to the grocery store, not turning around to wave, not looking back.

October let the morning go by just listening to David talk about anything. On his own, David had bathed, brushed his hair, and put on shorts and his favorite high-top tennis shoes. They had had pancakes and stories about his friends at home. And after lunch she thought she could make a system and keep her word to Vergie.

According to the schedule she sketched out, each morning after breakfast she would sit at the dining room table, have a half-hour reading lesson, a short break, and half an hour of arithmetic. Then fun and lunch. And then, if he needed it, they could read another page or two in the afternoon or before bed. Otherwise, he was there to have fun. Eddy Junior was younger, but he knew the kids around the neighborhood. And there were Donetta and Kenneth's kids, too. And Leon and swimming and the movies at the Lincoln.

For the first day, thinking she'd be wise to start with something he could already do, she dusted off an old Heath reader. That would make him comfortable. Then she would push him. She pulled out tablets, pencils, dictionary, spellers, even old sets of flash cards with diphthongs and vowels. All kinds of tools.

After lunch, David took his seat at the dining room table and waited for her to sit down beside him. He was definitely more quiet. Scared, she thought. Okay. Open the venetian blinds, turn up the air conditioner, arrange the tablets, and she had the right mood. This was going to be serious school. But only for half an hour.

She told him that she just wanted to see what kind of problems he was having and she opened the blue-backed Heath reader. Told him to choose a page to read aloud.

He brought his hands from his lap to the book and said softly, "I haven't ever seen this book."

"Yes, I know," she said. "It's one of mine from years ago, but we can start with it. Then we'll do yours if you want to."

David opened the cover and saw the issue stamp. "Is this your school?" he asked, stalling.

"Why don't you find a story, any story, and read me a few pages," she said.

"I don't want to read any stories out of this book," he said, but softly, babyish almost. And never raising his eyes.

What to do? He needed to want to read, and she was making him unhappy. "You haven't even looked at it," she said.

"It's for little kids," he said. Now his jaw was tight. He ran his finger along the joint between the halves of her shiny mahogany table.

"It is for primary grades, but I thought we could start with something easy."

"I hate reading," he said. He hugged his waist and bit his fingernail.

She could hear his breathing. How could she get him to try? A few choice things buzzed through her mind, but she knew good and well that she wouldn't be able to force him to do anything.

"I'll tell you what," she said, taking the book from his hands. "We'll only do fifteen minutes today. Just fifteen minutes. This is supposed to be your vacation. We'll work on one story in this book to get an idea of where to go from here."

"I'd rather read from my own book," David said.

Compromise and you get success. "All right, then," she said, "choose something and read me a page."

David slipped his reader out of the stack and turned quickly to a story entitled "Ghost of the Lagoon."

The island of Bora Bora, where Mako lived, is far away in the South Pacific. It is not a large island — you can paddle around it in a single day — but the main body of it rises straight out of the sea, very high into the air, like a castle. Waterfalls trail down the faces of the cliffs. As you look upward, you see wild goats leaping from crag to crag.

Amazing. He read with expression. Knew what he was reading.

Mako had been born on the very edge of the sea and most of his working hours were spent in the waters of the lagoon, which was nearly enclosed by two outstretched arms of the island. He was very clever with his hands; he had made a harpoon that was as straight as an arrow, and tipped with five pointed iron spears. He had made a canoe, hollowing it out of a tree. It was not a very big canoe — only a little longer than his own height. It had an outrigger, a sort of balancing pole, fastened to one side to keep the boat from tipping over. The canoe was just large enough to hold Mako and his little dog, Afa. They were great companions, these two.

"Do you want me to go on?" David asked. October smiled, "Go on. You have a strong reading voice." She folded her hands in her lap and sat back to listen.

One evening Mako lay stretched on mats, listening to his grandfather's voice. Overhead, stars shone in the dark sky. From far off came the thunder of the surf on the reef. The old man was speaking of Tupa, the ghost of the lagoon . . .

And David went on with the grandfather's story of the white-finned monster that lived in the cave of the reef, and that tore into the fishermen's nets and ate all their fish, the same monster that had overturned Mako's father's fishing boat and caused him to perish. The boy in the story made a vow to avenge his father, kill the great white Tupa, and collect the king's reward for it.

After a while she told David to stop. "I guess you wouldn't like these other stories after all," she told him.

Then she asked, "Tell me why you didn't do so well in reading this year."

David hunched his shoulders and said he didn't know.

"Do you understand the pages you just read to me? Can you tell me what it said in your own words?"

Sure. He told her the meaning of the story, and she had sense enough to recognize that it was probably a review for him. She asked him about his biggest problem with arithmetic, and he hunched his shoulders like he wouldn't know why Vergie had said he did poorly.

"How about fractions? You should have started on them by now," October said.

"No, just plus and take-away and times tables," he said.

On a tablet, she jotted down several three-digit addition problems, some simple subtraction, and two-digit multiplication.

David made quick work of them and figured correct answers.

"Very good — are you sure you haven't been just goofing off at school?" She made a little chuckle. Again, he hunched his shoulders.

No real problems that she could see. She cleared the books and phoned Cora. Line up the neighborhood kids. David was waiting. Phoned Donetta and Kenneth, phoned Leon for the swimming pool. "David might as well get started on his Kansas City vacation."

She had a freezer full of hamburger patties she had seasoned herself, corn on the cob she had blanched herself, baked chocolate-chip cookies, and a jar full of quarters for popsicles. She had a week to figure out what else.

The next morning after coffee and newspaper on the porch, she went to wake David. The same brown study in white sheets that she remembered the first Christmas she knew him. This was her house. He could have an extra hour of sleep if he wanted it. Beside him on the bed, his arithmetic book lay facedown, pages splayed. And halfway under his pillow a sheet of paper. A pencil had fallen to the floor.

She closed the door. Why the book and studying late? He had spent the afternoon playing Ping-Pong with Eddy Junior in Cora's basement, had gobbled up October's macaroni and cheese. In the evening he had drawn on his pad of newsprint, and watched *Bonanza*.

About an hour later she heard the toilet flush and something bluesy on KPRS coming from David's room. She drained her cup. When he stepped out the front door, she said, like Vergie, "Good morning."

He returned it with no cheer. No meeting her eyes. And he had something in his hand.

"Anything wrong?"

"This is for you," he said, and he handed over a painting like he was surrendering stolen money.

The watercolor had a flower garden in the middle of a green quad. Instead of the yellow black-eyed Susans, he had painted in pastels.

"This is really good," she told him. "When did you do this? Where did you get the paint?"

Trying to smile, he told her that Cora had let him paint the day before. Why was he so sad? Missing Vergie and Gene already. And was he sorry he was there with her?

"We can call Vergie and Gene on the telephone this afternoon if you want," she said.

He said no — that was okay. And he brightened up when she thanked him for the painting and told him to fix anything he wanted for breakfast.

After breakfast she sat, excited, at the dining room table with David and flipped open the book she had bought at the bookstore. *Rip Van Winkle.*

"You'll like this." She put it in front of him.

David took the book in both hands and

looked at the pages the way he would look at hieroglyphics.

"I don't feel like reading," he said softly. He put the book down and slouched in his chair, looked away from her and fingered the joint of her table.

"This is the time for reading, David. It's a good story. Just read the first paragraph."

She began to read the first paragraph. Then told him, "Now you read starting right here."

He began with "the," but as he stumbled and stammered on, she could see that he skipped too many words.

"Go back," she said. "Begin again."

"I can't." Down went the book again, and he jammed his hands into his underarms, breathing hard.

"What is it? You can read this. Why won't you try? This isn't any harder than your reader. You did fine yesterday."

He shook his head. "I can't." He flashed a glance at her and his liquid eyes said it better.

She still didn't get it. She pulled out his own reader and turned to the ghost story from the day before, turned to the middle pages.

"Here, read this."

"I can't."

"Try."

He stuttered and stumbled, "Tupa . . . then

turn . . . yet . . . Mako . . . stand up . . . that . . ."

Then she understood. She took the book from him and flipped to the first page of the ghost story. "Read this, David."

Without even bothering to lift his head in the direction of the book, he began to recite the story. She watched as his eyes brimmed, but his voice held steady, reciting the story of the fearless boy who would slay a shark.

She wound her arms around him, kissed his head. "It's all right, David," she told him through her own tears. "Reading isn't everything."

If she had only known sooner. In the first grade. If only Vergie had told her something, or let her get close to him, she would have seen it. If Vergie hadn't been so scared all the time. But then who was she to blame Vergie? She herself was to blame. This was how things complete the circle. Vergie was too scared to ask for help, scared of her.

Still and all, October hadn't become a teacher for nothing. No time for pity. The least she could do was to try to pull something — anything — together. Even if it was for only a week. She had to.

And so on the second day of David's vacation she decided she would turn his life around, or die trying. Nobody ever got anywhere without being able to read.

She took only a couple of hours to get her arsenal together. After several hours of work with exercises, she thought she had pinned down the problem.

She made him read sentences to her. The sentence "We saw a boat in the water" came out of his mouth "We was a dot in the water."

She had him write. When she said, "Take the cat outside," he wrote "Tack the cat otsibe."

He wrote *confast* for *confess, remaber* for *remainder.*

Okay. Either he didn't know letters or he didn't know his phonics. *Every letter. Short* i *has the sound of* igloo. *Long vowels say their name. Words are made up of syllables.*

She began again, showed him the letter *b.*

"B," she said, its name. He said its name, "B."

"B, *b*uh."

"B, *b*uh."

Straight stick and round ball, she drew it. Straight stick and round ball, he drew it — sort of.

"B, *b*uh, *b*oy."

"B, *b*uh, *b*oy."

And all the way to "L" without a break. No swimming for a few days. They had work to do. Quick lunch, and while he ate, she sat on the porch and calmed herself by basting a seam in a baby-doll sleeve, got it wrong and tore it out. David had *word blindness.* She was sure of it.

After lunch she flashed the cards in alphabetical order. Right. Shuffle them. Mostly right. Words? All wrong. She saw him at the paper mill, pushing a broom. All that day, and day three and four, she didn't let up. Scrapped the outline and skipped forward to sight words. *Say them in one gulp.* Long list, but so what. After supper play time, but that was enough. Still, after four afternoons, he remembered only a dozen words.

Okay; every word, then, would be a sight word. The more he said them, the easier they would be to remember. When he could call words on sight, he could read. How long would that take — the rest of his life?

On day five, two days before Vergie and Gene would come carrying expectation's huge cup that she wouldn't be able to fill — she quit. This was the only visit David had had alone with her in her house. She fed him ribs and chicken and cookies. Watched his short frame zip through the deep end of the swimming pool, loud and happy to be zipping. She rented a bicycle so that he could ride with his new friends. She read to him, kissed him good night, watched him sleep, counted her blessings.

Patience and work. She needed time to work with him. As far as she could tell, David's memory was sharp. What he couldn't figure out he could learn by rote. The sight-word thing hadn't really failed. Slowly but surely, it could work. If only.

And then the last day came. Vergie and Gene came driving up with all kinds of hope. They had barely dropped their suitcases on the porch when Vergie asked, "How did it go?"

"We did all right," October told her. "You-all come on in and let me fix you something to drink."

They went inside and David — mute as a door now — went to the kitchen for the pitcher of iced tea. After drinks all around they came back to sit in the cool of the porch, David squeezing into a chair with Gene. Vergie picked him apart with her eyes.

"Just a week, and I swear you look taller," she said.

"I've been swimming almost every day," David said.

They tried chitter-chatter, but it didn't go anywhere.

"Vergie," October said, "I think we need to talk."

"May as well be now," Vergie said.

Vergie came into the house with her like she was being led to the electric chair.

They went into the dining room. October showed her the stacks of books. The pencils and tablets and flash cards and color-coded rules.

"David needs help," October said softly.

"I know," Vergie said. She stood staring at October's arsenal on the table.

"I think he needs a tutor," October said, "— somebody to go step by step with him."

"I know," Vergie said.

"He needs to slow down for a long while," October said. "Too bad he didn't start a long time ago."

"I know," Vergie repeated.

"It's going to take longer than a few weeks for him to catch up, Verge."

Vergie nodded. She knew that, too. Her lips pressed themselves together and her head bobbed: yes, she knew it all. "If I had only known," October said. Vergie's head bobbing yes.

"I would have helped him, Vergie." October felt the burn starting in her throat.

"You know now," Vergie said, and softly, she started to cry.

Then October understood. Vergie had brought David to her *knowing* this would happen. *Hoping* this would happen. She had given October a week to discover that David couldn't read.

"Why didn't you tell me, Vergie . . . ?" October started to cry, too.

"Help him if you can . . ." Vergie tried to say. "The whole summer. Whatever it takes."

Into each other's arms they flew. Sisters. The same height, same skin, same voice, same tears, for all the same reasons.

They wept, they knew and understood, for Frances and Maude and all that protection. They wept for the old man who had died, for the life they might have had with him. For Carrie, whose life he had erased.

They wept for Lillian Brown who — with who knew what-all in her way — had done an undoable thing at an undoable time, and for whoever came before her, and those before them, and on back to the ones they had forgotten.

They wept, they knew, for their own pitiful, wonderful selves, their stupidity and their courage. And for each other, fiercely loving and fearful sisters that they were. They wept because they were who they had in this world.

They wept because secrets did more damage than truth. Because sooner or later, one way or another, David would have to know the truth. And James Wilson would have to know the truth, with all the frightening possibilities that would bring.

And they wept for David, loving and trusting them all. For how shattered he would be, how betrayed. They wept because he would have so far to go — alone — before he would come upon the possibility of forgiveness.

They wept for the wonder of endings. Though they could never shape happy endings, they could go toward them, and marvel at how the pieces come together and fall apart to make new beginnings.

We stood and held for them.

Acknowledgments

To my family, my friends, the many writers whose works were my lessons, my advocates in the publishing world, all of my teachers in this vast classroom; and specifically to the Guggenheim Foundation and the Virginia Center for the Creative Arts for funding the time for writing; to my agent, Molly Friedrich, with her infallible instincts, ingenious wit, and complete commitment to the work; to Frances Jalet-Miller and Paul Cirone at Aaron Priest Literary Agency, who were indefatigable in their critique and belief in the early drafts; to Melody Guy and Daniel Menaker, my keenly insightful editors at Random House, who bestowed the gift of clarity on my vision for the book; to Bridey Allsbrook, whose "run-in" was a gem; to my spiritual family at Unity Center of Bowie, and especially "Butch" Mosby for the teachings; to my sisters Linda Smith and Joyce Smith, and my friends Sandra Carpenter and Bettye Wages for the shoring up whenever the waves were pounding; and especially to my children, whose love has a dailiness that will forever sustain me.

Bless you. Thank you.

The employees of Thorndike Press hope you have enjoyed this Large Print book. All our Large Print titles are designed for easy reading, and all our books are made to last. Other Thorndike Press Large Print books are available at your library, through selected bookstores, or directly from the publishers.

For more information about titles, please call:

(800) 223-1244
(800) 223-6121

To share your comments, please write:

Publisher
Thorndike Press
295 Kennedy Memorial Drive
Waterville, ME 04901